monsoonbooks

THE HILLS OF SINGAPORE

Dawn Farnham is the author of *The Red Thread*, *The Shallow Seas*, *The Hills of Singapore* and *The English Concubine* (which comprise The Straits Quartet, a bestselling series of historical romance set in 19th-century Singapore), *A Crowd of Twisted Things*, a novel set in 1950 Singapore, as well as numerous short stories, plays and children's books. A former longterm resident of Singapore, Dawn now calls Perth, Australia, home. Learn more about Dawn at *www.dawnfarnham.com*.

The Hills of Singapore is the third volume in The Straits Quartet.

Praise for *The Straits Quartet*

'Immaculately researched' *The Daily Telegraph*, UK

'Multiple protagonists and perspectives, both Eastern and Western, and elaborate description transport the reader to a fascinating time and place brimming with mystical and poetic flourishes' *Booklist*, USA

'Exceptionally well-written ... A beautiful story to relish on every page' *Review of the Historical Novels Society*

'Rollicking saga ... a brilliant evocation of the settlement in its early days, both in its physical details and socio-cultural nuances' *Expat Living*, Singapore

'Thoroughly enjoyable historical romance' *Lifestyle*, Singapore

Books by Dawn Farnham

A Crowd of Twisted Things

The Straits Quartet
The Red Thread (Vol.1)
The Shallow Seas (Vol.2)
The Hills of Singapore (Vol.3)
The English Concubine (Vol.4)

Anthologies featuring short stories by Dawn Farnham

Crime Scene Singapore
Crime Scene Asia (Vol.1)
Love and Lust in Singapore
The Best of Southeast Asian Erotica

The Hills of Singapore

A Landscape of Loss, Longing and Love

DAWN FARNHAM

monsoonbooks

First published in 2011
by Monsoon Books Pte Ltd
71 Ayer Rajah Crescent #01-01, Singapore 139951
www.monsoonbooks.com.sg

ISBN (print): 978-981-4423-61-8
ISBN (ebook): 978-981-4358-39-2
ISBN (box set): 978-981-4423-63-2

This second (updated) edition published in 2014

Copyright©Dawn Farnham, 2011

The moral right of the author has been asserted. All rights reserved. No part of this publication may be reproduced, stored in a retrieval system, or transmitted, in any form or by any means without the prior written permission of the publisher, nor be otherwise circulated in any form of binding or cover other than that in which it is published and without a similar condition being imposed on the subsequent purchaser.

Cover design by Cover Kitchen.
Map on pages 6&7 courtesy of the Singapore Land Authority and the National Archives of Singapore.

National Library Board, Singapore Cataloguing-in-Publication Data
Farnham, Dawn, 1949-
The hills of Singapore : a landscape of loss, longing and love / Dawn Farnham. – Second (updated) edition. – Singapore : Monsoon Books Pte Ltd, 2014.
pages cm. – (The Straits quartet ; vol. 3)
ISBN : 978-981-4423-61-8 (paperback)

1. Widows – Fiction. 2. Triads (Gangs) – Singapore – History – 19th century – Fiction. 3. Singapore – History – 19th century – Fiction. I. Title. II. Series: Straits quartet ; vol. 3.

PR6106
823.92 -- dc23   OCN859514432

Printed in Singapore
17 16 15 14   2 3 4 5 6 7 8 9

*For my children
Jennifer and Susannah*

*"You may house their bodies but not their souls.
For their souls dwell in the house of tomorrow,
which you cannot visit, not even in your dreams."*
Khalil Gibran, *The Prophet*

J.T. Thomson Map of Singapore Town, 1854. Plan of the town of Singapore and its environs. Surveyed in 1842 by Government Surveyor. Singapore, March 1854. (Courtesy of the Singapore Land Authority and the National Archives of Singapore)
Note: The original map indicates those properties holding 999 year leases and those holding 99 year leases.

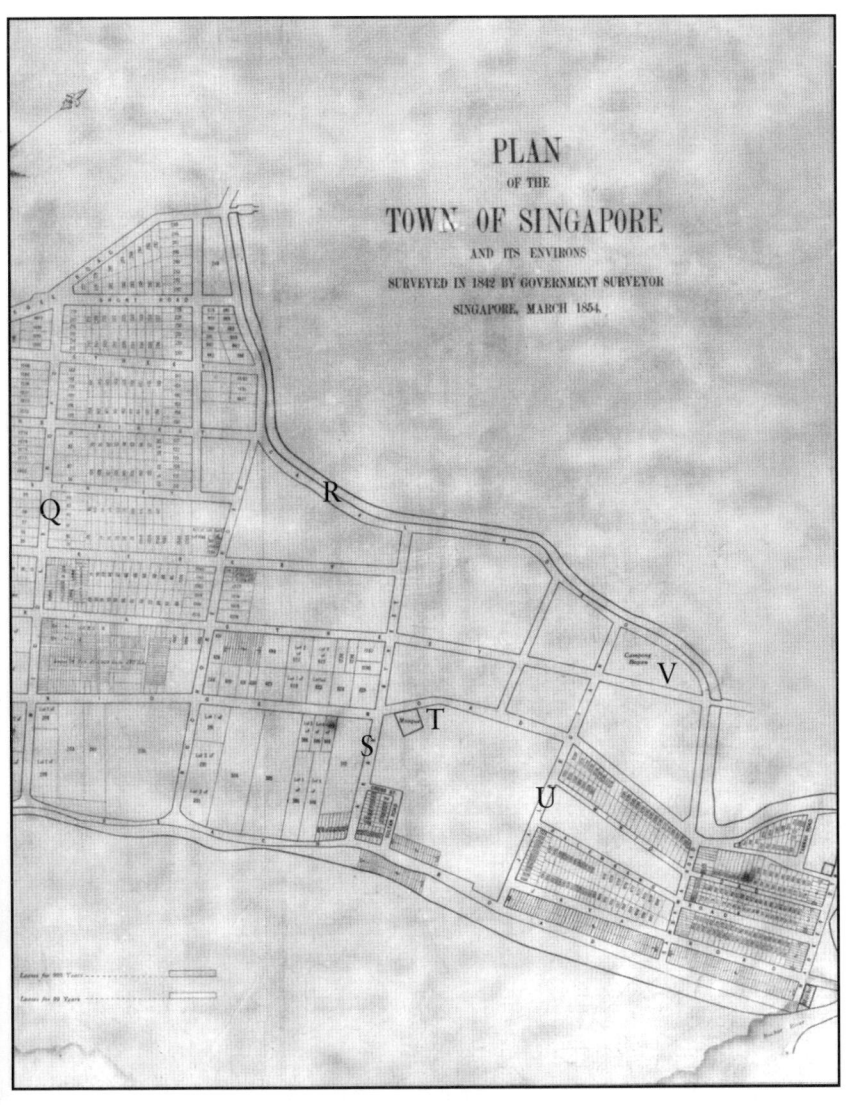

(A) Hongkong Street (B) Present-day Clarke Quay (C) Circular Road (D) Present-day Boat Quay (E) Government Hill [now Fort Canning] (F) Esplanade [now the Padang] (G) Protestant Burying Ground (H) Roman Catholic Burying Ground (I) Armenian Church (J) Coleman Street (K) Protestant Church [now St Andrew's Cathedral] (L) Orchard Road (M) Pauper Hospital (N) Convict Lines (O) North Bridge Road (P) Seleegee Road [now Selegie Road] (Q) Middle Road (R) Canal Road (S) Arab Street (T) Mosque [now Masjid Sultan] (U) Jalan Sultan (V) Campong Boyan [Kampung Boyan]

Glossary

Ang mo: A racial epithet that originates from Hokkien (Min Nan) and is used to refer to white people in Malaysia and Singapore. Literally meaning "red-haired", the term implies that the person referred to is a devil, a concept explicitly used in the Cantonese term *gweilo* (foreign devil).

Babu: A Javanese nursemaid.

Baju: A short, loose jacket worn in Malaysia.

Belanda: A Malay term meaning Hollander or Dutchman.

Bugis: The people of southern Sulawesi. They are still outstanding shipbuilders, sailors and navigators who have traded legitimately in the region for thousands of years. When the colonial powers displaced traditional trading relations of the region, the Bugis turned to piracy and slave trading.

Chunam: A fine stucco based on very pure or shell-lime, used for the highest quality finishes, often to external walls and roofs.

Kamcheng pot: A large covered porcelain pot usually decorated colourfully in pink and turquoise with phoenixes, peonies and other symbols of riches, honour and happy marriage. Such a pot would be presented to the bride at her wedding feast filled with glutinous rice balls and sweet syrup and be an honoured and treasured object to be passed down to future generations.

Kongsi: or "clan halls", are benevolent organisations of popular origin found among overseas Chinese communities. The system of *kongsi* was utilised by Chinese throughout the diaspora to overcome economic difficulty, social ostracism, and oppression. The word *kongsi* is used in modern Chinese to mean a commercial company.

Kris: The kris or *keris* is a distinctive, asymmetrical dagger indigenous to Indonesia, Malaysia, Brunei, Southern Thailand and the southern Philippines. Both a weapon and spiritual object, the kris is often considered to have an essence or presence, with some blades possessing good luck and others possessing bad.

Munshi: A degree in South Asia, that is given after passing a certain course of basic reading, writing and maths. The word munshi also became the name of a profession after munshies were hired as clerks in the government in British India.

Nyai: A native woman, consort, or concubine of a European man in the Dutch East Indies. The status and the fate of the *nyai* varied widely, depending entirely on the actions of the man. After Christian baptism, she could become his wife or he could legitimise her and her children as a secondary "wife". Once legitimised and recognised in law, she was entitled to upkeep by the man and to inherit part of the man's estate. In theory, and often in fact, a legitimised native *nyai* could quickly pass from being a slave to being a wealthy widow of a Dutch official or merchant. On the other hand, many *nyai* could simply be abandoned and, up to 1782, if they were still slaves at the death of the man, both the *nyai* and her offspring could be separated and sold to other owners. After 1782, this practice was prohibited.

Orang laut: The Malay term *orang laut* means sea people. Historically the *orang laut* were principally pirates.

Peranakan: Descendents of intermarriage between early Chinese male settlers in the Straits Settlements (Penang, Malacca and Singapore) and local Malay women. This Chinese sub-ethnic group adopted some cultural traits from the Malay community, as seen in their cuisine, dress and language, but also adopted many European customs thus elevating their social standing in relation to the singkeh or China-born immigrants. Also known as Straits Chinese. The men are known as Baba, the women as Nonya (or Nyonya).

Prahu: Literally, the Malay word meaning boat. There are many types of *prahu* throughout the islands of the archipelago.

Punkah: A large cloth fan on a frame suspended from the ceiling, moved backwards and forwards by pulling on a cord.

Qi: Also commonly spelled *ch'i*, this is a fundamental concept of traditional Chinese culture. *Qi* is believed to be part of every living thing that exists, as a kind of "life force" or "spiritual energy". It is frequently translated as "energy flow", or literally as "air" or "breath".

Sampan: A relatively flat-bottomed Chinese wooden boat. In Cantonese the term literally means "three planks".

Sireh: Malay word for betel. The leaves of the betel tree are used as a wrapping for the slices of the areca nut, lime paste and other ingredients and chewed as a stimulant.

Tao: Chinese character often translated as "way" or "path". It is based on the understanding that the only constant in the universe is change.

Tongkang: Bumboats, lighters or sea-going barges used in the Malay Archipelago for transporting goods from ship to shore and vice versa.
Towkay: A Chinese merchant.

Wei qi: Classical board game known in the West by its Japanese name, Go, and believed to have originated at least 5,000 years ago. Some say that the board, with ten points out from the centre in all directions, may have originally served as a forerunner to the abacus.

Others think it may have been a fortune-telling device, with black and white stones representing Yin and Yang. By the time of Confucius, *wei qi* had already become one of the "Four Accomplishments" (along with brush painting, poetry and music) that must be mastered by the Chinese gentleman.

Prologue

A sailing ship has a restless heart, never still, never silent.

At sea it is a dashing, driving symphony of roaring sail, clangorous iron and groaning timber. In port it is a soft concerto of chimes, rattles and creaks. From the flags of its main topgallant mast to the lowest regions of the bilge, it pulsates with sound. It brims with the music of its natural home: the consonant and thrilling harmonies of water and wind, the haunting cries of sea birds, the sublime anthems of the cobalt sea and the serenades of star-soft coves.

And the stirring, sinister and poignant plangency of men and their deeds.

Charlotte stood listening to the voices of the ship. Within the recesses of its wooden heart lay her memories of calm and storm, of freedom and capture, of brutal anger and loving joy. It was the repository of her marriage, filled with spectral shadows and sighs.

Tasty scampered up to her. When she did not move he gave a quizzical yelp. It roused Charlotte from her reverie, and she looked down at him and smiled.

James Elliott, Tasty's owner and captain of the *Queen of the South*, came forward extending his two hands. Charlotte took them and saw that James and Tasty, with their bushy grey eyebrows, grizzled cheek hair and deep brown eyes, had—seemingly through the mere fact of long acquaintance—come to resemble each other.

"My condolences, Mrs Manouk. I am so sorry that we should meet again under such tragic circumstances."

Charlotte pressed his hands. "Thank you, James," she said and moved to the rail.

Below, mounting from the cutter tucked against the ship's side, were her two children, Alexander and Adam, with their *babus*. Two young Javanese sailors slid down the ladder in a display of extravagant muscular virility and helped the women and children onto the deck. Both the *babus* were young and pretty, and Charlotte reflected briefly that she might have to keep an eye on them during the voyage.

The children would be settled in their cabin below deck. She left Captain Elliott knowing they would talk more at length when they were at sea. She knew James would want to talk about Tigran, her husband.

She stopped before the open door of the master's cabin.

Three years.

Three years since Tigran had died in a riding accident and left her mistress of this ship and of everything that his wealth had brought to her: the great estate in Batavia, the tea and coffee plantations and all his fortune spread far and wide in the East Indies.

Three years since she had set foot aboard this ship. She could see, before the mirror, his black and white scarf. She stepped tentatively into the room.

Their marriage, she supposed like any marriage, had been happy and, by moments, extremely unhappy. For those unhappy times she blamed herself. Tigran had come to Singapore and taken her to Batavia at the request of his sister, Charlotte's greatest friend. Though he was older than she by twenty years, it barely showed. He was handsome, strong, brave and clever. But these were qualities she had barely perceived when she married him. For she had wed him not for love but for the solidity and security his age and wealth offered.

He had known it, but he had married her nonetheless, knowing she was pregnant with another man's child, knowing she loved another man, knowing she was fleeing a scandalous relationship in Singapore. He had married her simply because he had loved her with all his heart. He had protected her when she was most vulnerable. She had learned, slowly, to love him back.

And then she had betrayed him with Zhen, the blood father of Alexander. Zhen, the man she seemed unable to shake from her mind and her heart. The man who was Chinese, married and living in Singapore.

She walked slowly into the cabin and gently touched the scarf.

She was grateful that through Tigran's generosity they had truly found joy and trust before he had gone forever. She had not expected to love him that way: a learned love which grew from such a poor seed. She had not expected it to bloom with such beauty.

She opened the silver and pearl locket which he had given her and gazed on his likeness. Three years of loneliness and loss, wandering the rooms of their life like a wraith.

She had made herself busy. Not God, not sympathetic utterances, no matter how well meant, could keep her from darkness. Only sensible industry and benevolent endeavour kept the shadows at bay. So she had busied herself, dividing the fortune between his children, learning the legalities and niceties of Dutch justice and the intricacies of liberal economics, putting the plantations in order, ensuring his widowed sisters were cared for—doing what she knew he would have wanted.

Now it was time to go back. Alexander and Adam required an English education, and this was to be found in Singapore.

She took up Tigran's scarf. The last skin it had touched was his, and now she tied it around her neck and looked in the mirror. Whilst she and his children lived, he would not die.

She went out on deck. The sails were flying up the masts; men were calling and clambering in the rigging. There was always a quivering excitement aboard a ship being made ready for sail, the anticipation of a leap into the unknown, for the sea could be a treacherous companion.

The *babus* came up on deck gripping the children, watching, half-terrified, for their feet had never before felt the unsteady movement of the sea, and they too were filled with excitement and trepidation at the strangeness of the ship and the voyage to a far land.

The men's voices raised the capstan chant, their sinewy muscles strained in unison and the ship lurched as the chain was pulled slowly aboard and began to inch forward. Orders flew about the ship from the foredeck to the poop. Aye, captain, aye, aye! The sailors were of ten tongues, but they all understood the language of the sea and its ports, a fertile and ever fluid blend of Malay, Portuguese, Hindustani, Arabic and English. Men moved in perfect harmony from deck to topmast, tying off, locking down, making fast, flying in the rigging with the litheness of dancers.

The wind suddenly grasped her hair like a hand as the sails began to roar. The flags, fluttering loosely in the breeze, snapped to attention, cracking like gunshot, as the ship, groaning, turned to the north. She moved to the carved rail at the stern and watched as the coastline of Java receded, her hair flying round her face, the check scarf fluttering violently in the wind, waving farewell. She put her hand to her neck and took up the locket. Then she turned and looked towards Singapore.

1

The ship was asleep. At least, those who had no night duties were sleeping. She liked this time, the night filled with stars, the moonshine like a silver trail, the soft splash of water swirling and sliding along the hull.

She looked around the cabin. It was surely the most luxurious accommodation to be found on these southern seas. A large bed with a kapok mattress and sheets of fine Indian cotton and satin stood under the four square ports. It was furnished with teak wood drawers, a table and soft chairs, a writing desk, lamps and books.

As she gazed at this room, her mind slipped to a time, a short time ago really, she thought, only nine years. How altered she had become, how extraordinary and unexpected the direction of her life.

When she had been just eighteen, her brother, Robert, had written to her to join him from Scotland, for though his new position as Singapore's chief of police gave him little remuneration, it came with a large house. Part of his small inheritance had paid her passage.

Charlotte and Robert loved each other as utterly as a sister and brother could. They had been born on the same day exactly one year apart. She knew he had saved her from marriage to some lecherous old squire and had willingly faced any hardship to be with him. They had grown up on Madagascar with the native children, barefoot and carefree. Her father had been a missionary with the London Missionary Society, her mother a beautiful French Creole.

The peace of this existence had been shattered by violence against all the whites, against the church and the orphanage, and she and Robert had been placed in the care of a young missionary and sent to live in Scotland with their grandmother and maiden aunt. Neither parent had ever been heard of again. The miseries of those years in Aberdeen had faded, for her Aunt Jeanne and her cousin Duncan had loved them both. She had grown very gradually to accept the strict tutoring under the steely eye of her grandmother, who made no bones of the fact that these half-breeds needed dragging into civilisation. She had not even minded the solitary existence: reading in the library of her long-dead grandfather, walking on the cliffs and sailing in the bay at Aberdeen with Duncan, waiting for Robert to come back from college.

She lay back on the bed and watched the moonlight roll along the floor with each motion of the ship. The wind blew in the open windows, ruffling her hair. How profoundly different from this, her voyage from England to Singapore.

She had voyaged on an East Indiaman, the *Madras*, a mighty thousand-tonne, three-masted, square-rigged, forty-gun merchant ship of the East India Company, which ran everything in the British East, including India and Singapore. The ship was designed and built for goods, not passengers, and the human cargo must squeeze itself in wherever space could be found.

The agent in London had found her the best place for a single woman travelling alone, at a cost which Charlotte knew took a good portion of Robert's money. This place was at the rear of the ship, beneath the poop deck, in a large space known as the roundhouse. The space was not round but a rectangle. No one could tell her why it was called thus. Because you could stand upright and walk round it, one said; because it cost a very round sum, said another. It was divided into cabins made of temporary partitions of canvas battened to the roof and deck, which could be quickly cleared away if the ship became involved in a battle.

Each cabin had a small window which gave light and fresh air, commodities, Charlotte had been quick to discover, which were beyond price on board a ship which would take upwards of seven months to arrive at its destination. High above the water, the windows, or "ports", as she was told to call them, seldom needed to be closed, even in rough weather. These cabins, though not spacious, were secluded and convenient. A few steps led from them all to the cuddy. There was no need to go out upon deck, or to go up or downstairs to meals.

"Thus, my dear, you will avoid many of the inconveniences of shipboard life," the agent explained solicitously.

He had seen that her youth and beauty would likely cause some havoc aboard a ship full of men at sea for months at a time. She was, perhaps, somewhat too slim but with skin like ivory, blue-black hair to her waist and long-lashed, violet eyes. He liked women's hands, his wife had lovely hands, and he saw that Charlotte too had slim fingered, graceful hands, the nails small and oval, perfectly shaped and delicate. He felt, suddenly, as protective of her as of his own daughters. He took out a large handkerchief and wiped his nose.

"I myself care not for such travel. No, assuredly I do not. I therefore have no personal knowledge of such matters, but may I urge your attention to the words of my friend, Mr Wilkins?" The agent took a paper from his drawer and began to read.

"The roundhouse rooms may be somewhat noisy from the boom and the sailors working on the poop deck, but the rolling of the vessel is circumvented by the shortness of the distance required to travel from cabin to table, a not inconsiderable advantage. More importantly, you may avoid, as far as may be possible, all the disagreeables attendant upon encountering persons engaged in the duties of a ship. It may seem fastidious to object to meeting sailors employed in getting up different stores from the hold, or to pass and repass other cabins, or the neighbourhood of the steward's pantry; nevertheless, if ladies have the opportunity of avoiding these things, they will do well to embrace it; for, however trivial they may be in a well-regulated ship, very offensive circumstances may arise from them."

He had put the letter on the table and looked up at Charlotte.

"You will forgive me for forwardness, my dear young lady, but your brother's letter was most insistent that I act somewhat *in loco parentis*. I feel constrained then to offer some advice."

Charlotte hid a smile. He was a little long-winded, but she could see he meant well. She had composed her face into a study of attentive and charming womanhood.

Yes, most lovely, the agent thought, and barely eighteen. The men will be sniffing around her from morning to night.

"Well, my dear child, there are several things I must urge you to treat most seriously. The first concerns items of your personal washing. Some women passengers have been known to hang washing out to dry from the roundhouse windows. This," the agent said, waggling his eyebrows and frowning fiercely, "is entirely unacceptable."

Charlotte was somewhat mystified but nodded solemnly.

"Nothing is so indelicate, indeed so indecent, as to see hanging from the windows of the ladies' cabins items of a delicate nature likely to inflame the ungentlemanly feelings of the common sailor."

Charlotte had lowered her eyes decorously, and the agent saw he had struck the mark. She was a good girl.

"Social decorum is of paramount importance, as I am certain you understand, in such a constrained environment. I have taken the liberty of proposing a fellow passenger, a respectable matron, Mrs Fortescue, as your chaperone. You are advised to drink no more than two glasses of wine at dinner and to vigorously decline invitations to play cards or backgammon. When walking on deck you may take the arm of a gentleman to steady yourself against the motion of the ship, naturally, but," the agent's eyebrows waggled again, "the conversation must be restricted to the weather and general matters."

The kindly agent had arranged to deliver to her cabin the furnishings she would need, for the price of the berth included nothing more than the space. The most important item was a swinging cot, suspended from the ceiling, allowing her to sleep through the constant rolling of the vessel, rather like a baby in a crib. In the day it was tied fast to the wooden side with hooks. A table and chair, bookcase and washstand were nailed securely to the floor. A small bathtub, her bedding and utensils, candles and candlesticks and the all-important chamber pot completed her belongings.

It had all been intensely exciting, the captain greeting them, a majestic figure, like a king to his court, the bustle and noise of Gravesend, the port seething with activity around this ship towering over her, its guns ranged along its bulwarks, grizzled sailors with gold rings in their ears swarming. Then came the hustle and bustle of setting up the cabin, meeting her companions on this long, long voyage, the departure from London, sailing down the Thames like Queen Elizabeth in this mighty ship, the lurch as they hit the open water of the Channel. The reality had hit very quickly in a storm in the Bay of Biscay.

The constant rolling of the ship, even on calm seas, had been comically ridiculous. Dressing and undressing became acts of supreme hardship: no sooner did one lift a leg or let go of the chair then one was flung to one side, only to slide back into the canvas walls at the next motion of the vessel. For the first two weeks she had been covered in bruises. She learned to dress speedily, either sitting in her swinging bunk or on the floor, one leg looped round the chair.

The noise in the roundhouse was a constant aggravation. The cabins were separated by a mere width of canvas. Every sneeze and yawn was heard, the snores like thunder, the sounds and smells of every bodily function magnified in the cramped environment. After a mere few days at sea however, and upon examination of the other accommodations, Charlotte had been eternally grateful to the agent and to Robert.

Beneath the roundhouse was the great cabin, where the single gentlemen travellers stayed. Because the great cabin was closer to the waves, in rough weather the windows were screened to prevent the sea coming in. These window screens were known as "dead lights" and didn't always fit very well, with the result that passengers, their bedding and other possessions became soaked.

But even this was better than where the less affluent men were accommodated. In this dark, fustian place amidships, reeking of human stenches, slung around the gun placements were quarters the other men shared, all sleeping slung from hammocks twelve inches from the ceiling, rolled into tubes like bats in a cave.

Robert, she knew, had travelled this way, and when she thought of this her heart became raw with love and pity for him, and tears welled and never once, not ever once, during the entire voyage did a complaint pass her lips. But for him she would have travelled in some cave-dark, stifling cabin or worse, in steerage, in the bowels of the ship, amongst the rats and the bilge water, cheek by jowl with the poorest passengers. Compared to the heat, noise and stench of below decks, her cabin had been a palace.

However, human nature decrees that despite our comparative good fortune we are not always happy with our lot, and time hung heavy for all on such a long journey. The ship grew salads and vegetables in boxes of earth on the upper deck, and Charlotte tended these, attempting to save them from the salt air, and occasionally took one or two of the goats on a tour of the deck for some exercise or played with the young steerage children who were permitted on deck for fresh air but corralled like the goats. She fed the poultry in the hencoop. She tried not to get attached to the sheep and lambs which would end up on the plate, but she allowed herself to care for the little goats which supplied milk for the children.

Everyone from the upper deck cabins ate in the cuddy by the cook's galley, under the poop. The food grew progressively worse the further they ventured from land. A breakfast at eight o'clock of boiled oats and sugar, corned beef and biscuit as hard as a stone, sometimes an egg if she felt like paying for it; at two, a hot lunch of chicken stew, cabbage and potatoes. Afternoon tea was at six o'clock, and at nine a cold supper of bread, cheese and whatever was left over. This was the menu from Monday to Sunday. When the vegetables ran out and after all the chickens had been slaughtered, there was nothing left but weevily oats, sugar, salt pork and biscuit.

Charlotte had been advised to bring her own supplies of tea, cheese and preserves, but by the time they dropped anchor at the Cape, whatever she had left was wormy and decayed. Rain water was only for drinking. Washing was in salt water, and she never felt clean, despite the quantities of soap she had brought. Without rain, after a week, the drinking water smelled and tasted foul and stale. When it rained she used her chamber pot and washing bowl to gather water to wash her hair so that for a brief period she might not feel covered in salt. She had a store of tobacco and brandy and bars of soap to bribe the sailors to get rain water for her and, in their leisure moments, to do odd repairs on the cabin. These came in handy also to encourage the steward—who had the service of thirty passengers—to supply hot water, bring tea, arrange laundry services or perform other duties above and beyond those he was engaged for, which were unspecified and negotiable.

Once or twice Charlotte was asked to attend at Captain Wentworth's table, especially after forming a flirtatious attachment to First Lieutenant Mallory, whom she was, however, careful to keep at arm's length. For this formal occasion everyone dressed in the most elegant clothes and was seated according to their social rank. Charlotte's own rank being rather humble, she was, naturally, not often asked to attend. She liked the old captain very much though, and he too, when he could, spent time with her, chatting about nautical matters and the Malay language which Charlotte spent much of her time, buried in Marsden's grammar and dictionary, endeavouring to learn.

The meal at the captain's table was well worth the eating and of quite a different order to her usual fare. The first time she sat down for lunch precisely at two o'clock, there were sixteen people, and the meal included pea soup, roast leg of mutton, hogs' puddings, two fowls, two hams, two ducks, corned round of beef, mutton pies, pork pies, mutton chops, stewed cabbages and potatoes. This was followed by an enormous plum pudding and washed down with porter, spruce beer, sherry, gin and rum.

After the meal the ladies withdrew, leaving the men to enjoy a glass of port. How the captain and the officers resumed their duties after this gargantuan meal rather baffled her, but this they did.

She had received the most pressing attentions from almost every unattached and many attached males aboard the ship. Charlotte's experience with men was limited to a few rather tepid fumblings with a friend of her cousin Duncan and a more lively exchange with Will, the good-looking son of a farmer, who had however, been whipped away into the navy before anything of consequence occurred. But she was not naive. Her life growing up on the island had been educational, her mother happy to explain the sexual nature of human beings, which she considered natural and which was on open display all around her. In Scotland, of course, the subject had been taboo, and she was glad she had acquired this knowledge and a certain down-to-earth attitude to it before arriving on those chilly shores.

There were few women on board. Of her roundhouse companions, three were travelling with their husbands and six were married women with children joining their men in India. The four who were single received almost overwhelming attention, even the devout and plain Miss Devenish, going out to India to save the young girls of Calcutta. Charlotte who was, by far, the most beautiful amongst them, was besieged with offers and attentions and often had to be rescued by Mrs Fortescue, the doyenne of the female passengers, who had set herself up as the chaperone of the young women on board. Charlotte had many occasions to be grateful to her despite her constant prattle, for the men's eyes, when walking on deck, at meals or at the musical evenings, stalked her.

The *Madras* might be designated female as tradition decreed, but men swarmed all over her, possessed her. There was a constant, palpable male potency everywhere on board, a seething current of barely repressed desires and dangers, from sailors and from passengers, whenever a woman appeared. All the women felt it and she knew for some it was irresistible. Far from the strictures of land society, on the swelling ocean, where danger, sickness, and watery death lurked at every squally, howling wind and darkening of clouds, they were pulled into a vortex of male passions. When she felt it whirl, particularly in the evening when liquor flowed, she kept to her cabin.

Lieutenant Mallory became her devoted guardian angel, his gentlemanly code unflinching, his courage unflagging under all dangers and other men avoided confronting him. When his duties kept him from his role as her protector, he did not object to her walking with one or two of the gentlemen, but it was understood that should Charlotte be in any way bothered, they would answer to him. Only when the ship was approaching Calcutta had she realised that, for him, the matter was a serious one. He had proposed marriage then, and she had been obliged to refuse him. For the first time in her life she had caused excruciating pain to another human being, and she did not like to think of it.

That these protections and her own good sense had been

invaluable she had discovered well before Calcutta. Three women had what was commonly known as the "French disease", the dreaded pox, and two of the single girls and four of the married women were pregnant including, unfortunately, Miss Devenish. Luckily, and apparently happily, Miss Devenish was agreeable to marriage to the father-to-be, a rather bemused young soldier travelling steerage, and relinquished a life of spinsterly devotion to the heathen rather easily.

What the married women were to tell their husbands she did not know, and nor did they. She spent hours in whispered and tearful discussions with them, a sisterhood of the sea, as they all made frantic calculations and exchanges of addresses of abortionists and pox doctors in Calcutta, before rushing off again to the arms of their lovers. There were no secrets and very little privacy aboard a ship, and Charlotte had often to turn away from the muffled groans in some dark corner or close her ears to noisy couplings a few cabins away. If this was going on continually on the upper decks, she could not imagine what was happening in the Stygian gloom of steerage.

It took eleven weeks to reach the Cape of Good Hope and ten days had been nothing but storms. Of their convoy of fourteen ships, two had foundered with all aboard perished and one was in a very poor state. Pirate attack from the African coast was a nagging undertone on all the sailors' lips, especially if the convoy got separated in a storm. The relief at arriving at the Cape had been overwhelming, and all the women and many men had cried with joy.

The land had a strange compactness under her feet. She kept being surprised when the wind blew, at not having to hang on like grim death to some spar or gangway, for their ship had never been still, and on the big waves had tossed them all like ants on a cork.

She had gone to a fleet-fingered Indian tailor for a dress, the cheapness and quality of which astounded her, and bound it carefully for her arrival in Singapore to preserve it from harm. She knew that every other garment she possessed would be a smelly rag by the time they arrived.

After the Cape, the ship called in for fresh water and supplies at Mauritius, then sailed for months without sight of land, across the vastness of the Indian Ocean. Sickness and death were daily companions. Scarlet fever ravaged the children in steerage. For a while they were called to sea burials every other day, until they all became callous and blasé. A sense of doom floated like a will-o'-the-wisp around the ship.

The soaring optimism of sighting Point de Galle in Ceylon and the fresh provisions carried out to them on a hundred little boats had buoyed their spirits. The mail was off-loaded and a quantity of fresh water allowed for washing. For two days there was merrymaking and a shipboard feast. They departed this little port with mixed emotions, glad to be gone, nearer to journey's end, but sorry to leave sight again of land. They were soon back to listlessness, everyone on board simply tired out.

No one, Charlotte thought, no one who has not spent more than half a year aboard a floating cattle barge with on every side and in immediate view the physical and spiritual degradation of humans thrown together for better or worse, besieged by urges, illness, fear and death—no one who has not heard and seen and smelled this can imagine the relief of its end.

Notwithstanding her feelings of hurting Lieutenant Mallory, she had quit the ship without a backward look. In Calcutta she spent a week in a boarding house, glad for a bath and fresh food—her first taste of Indian curry and its attendant inconveniences—selling her cabin furniture, waiting for the sleek schooner which would take her to Singapore, for the *Madras* stopped here. The sights, sounds and smells of Calcutta overwhelmed her, the heat too intense, the press of humanity too claustrophobic, and curiosity soon turned to impatience.

Captain Wentworth was retiring from the service of the East India Company. Lieutenant Mallory, promoted to captain, would take the *Madras* back to England. When Charlotte had discovered this fact, she was doubly glad her heart was not engaged, for the prospect of a return voyage or even of life in London or Calcutta awaiting a man who voyaged three quarters of a year was too grim to contemplate.

This had been Captain Wentworth's last long voyage. He was getting on, he said, and his family was in Calcutta. Seven-month voyages took their toll. He had rounded the Cape dozens of times, seen seas which made even him quail, been shipwrecked twice and carried the scars. In his youth it had been a life filled with adventure but now he had heeded the wishes of his heart and his family and bought a schooner. Henceforth he was his own master and commander, plying the seas between India and the Straits Settlements.

He had guaranteed Charlotte a cabin on his ship, and she had been delighted to wait and go on with him. This part of her journey had been light. The ten passengers shared the schooner with her cargo: iron goods, guns, English manufactures and Indian stuffs, bound for the Straits Settlements.

The months of strain, dread and grinding monotony on the deep ocean were over. As the ship entered the calm waters of the Straits of Malacca, Charlotte breathed the warm fragrance of the night air and felt the caress and promise of the East.

2

The day was grey as Zhen awoke, the rain falling softly. His wife, Noan, was lying, as always, turned into his body. He moved her hand from his chest and she murmured slightly in sleep.

He did not often sleep with her, but their third child was now one year old and it was time to make another, this time, hopefully, a son, for there were only daughters. So he spent most nights with her, making love to her, letting his essence flow, which normally, he would not. As a Taoist, the highest thought was to give joy to the woman through multiple orgasms which the man could absorb, retaining his own semen, building his strength. This "leaking", this "surrender", was alien to him. But when a child was needed, he had to obey Confucius and set his Taoist beliefs aside.

As he turned, Noan awoke and moved her body against his, silently asking. He had no real desire for her, but he let her caress him.

Noan was intensely in love with her husband. During her pregnancy he could not touch her; it was forbidden and she suffered his physical absence. After the birth, she was confined, unable to wash for fear of chills, her ears filled with garlic, her forehead plastered with *sireh* leaves. For almost two months she felt wretched, as custom decreed she must avoid any evil or ill wind entering her body.

There were only a few months when he gave himself to her willingly, and greedily, she wanted every minute of them. He took her full breasts in his hands, putting his lips to her nipples. Though there was a wet nurse, she continued to breast-feed not wanting her milk to dry up, for she knew it aroused him and she loved it when Zhen suckled her, feeling the motion of his mouth in the depths of her body, her breasts full and streaming, the milk running over his lips. She sighed, running her hands into his queue, grinding her body into his, this desperate longing for him more than she could contain.

Their marriage had been arranged and she thanked all the gods that had brought him to her. The moment she had seen him, she had fallen hopelessly in love with him. Nothing he did or did not do made any difference. She knew he did not love her like that and it was an agony that she had, every day, to bear. It was fearful to love like this, mutely. She was not allowed to tell him; she had no way to voice these emotions she felt for him.

He was a beautiful man. She had seen enough men now to know he was very beautiful, his face strong, his eyes deep and black, his lips full; his body was smooth perfection, broad shouldered, slim hipped, the long queue which hung below the curve of his back thick and lustrous. He was a man who knew women; she did not know how but he was always confident and imperative, his will only prevailed. Yet, in his own pleasure, he knew how to make her abandon herself, expected it from her, this fullness, this quivering enjoyment of their physical act.

Every intimation as she was growing up, every half-heard, half-understood idea was that women could not enjoy this act with their husbands. Short, messy and frustrating—let him do what he demands and be quiet. All these ideas had been banished by him. That all men could not do this she knew from talk with her cousins and particularly her sister, who was profoundly dissatisfied with her own husband. Now, as Zhen rose above her, she touched the tattoo of the Lord of War, the Lord Guan Di, on his hard, smooth chest. This image of martial virility filled her eyes, and she moaned and clutched him, losing herself in his deep knowledge of her body and this passion she felt for him.

Afterward, Zhen rose and washed at the basin. He threw open the shutters. Noan had returned to slumbering, content with their lovemaking, he saw. He had taught her how to be passionate and he knew she needed this contact. He wanted her to be content, wanted to make another child. She was a good wife; he knew she loved him. For him, however, the marriage was a contract, like all Chinese marriages. Love had nothing to do with it though he welcomed her affections. But he could not return them. His true love was unwavering. He loved Xia Lou.

Noan's pregnancy was long in coming. They had made three children easily and he could not understand what was taking so long this time. He was tired of it, this routine and for him, passionless exchange. At times he could hardly muster desire enough to become hard. Then he turned to her full, milky breasts, as he had this morning, which at least had the power still to arouse him. He longed for her to get pregnant. Pregnancy would relieve him of this onerous duty.

He felt depleted, wished for a return to his Taoist ways, which had become second nature. Noan's *qi* must be out of balance; the rashes she got occasionally were a sign. He would make up some herbs for her, bring the acupuncturist. When she was pregnant he would give up sex entirely, build his strength, return to the disciplines of austerity which calmed and centred him.

Noan watched him from the bed, the sight of his naked body, each hard line and curve kissed by light and shadow, the feel of his liquid dripping from her almost painfully pleasurable. Before each time with him, she was elated, almost light-headed. After came the fear, a bitter fear of the loss of this intimacy. She feared losing him to boredom of her, especially after several children more and as her looks, appealing she knew mostly in her youthful freshness, faded. She feared the loss to another wife perhaps, or the temptations of a child concubine.

Her own father had taken a fifteen-year-old girl as concubine only two years ago. She knew many wives were simply abandoned when their child-bearing had proved profitable and sons had been born. Then the man would honour his wife with splendid jewellery, fine clothes and golden *sireh* sets but bestow his sexual gifts elsewhere, and the wife would be destined to never make love again until she died.

This might be well enough for those who had unappealing husbands, but, for her, such thoughts made her anxious and needful.

Sometimes she broke out in a rash on her arms, which horrified her. She feared she would be repugnant to him and fretted, which made the rash worse. He had seen it and given her a salve; he could be kind, caring. He was a man of medicine, skills and knowledge learned from his father. When he was with her, like now, every night, the rash disappeared, but she felt it lying in wait.

Today, like every day, she would take the herbal drink and wash with the tincture she got from the Indian woman who knew how to stop a pregnancy. So far these had worked and she smiled: a nervous smile, for she felt a guilt, too, and a deep concern. How long she could keep this up she was not sure. She knew she must stop soon, for a lack of a pregnancy might, too, drive him away to another woman. She scratched her arm.

She secretly longed to share more of her life with him. These bedroom passions and the occasional pleasures of their children were their only contact and during them, though he hardly showed it, she sensed an absence. His *real* life was not with her or even in this house. The men ate their meals in the house but quite separately from the women. Their business was on the quay, in the godowns of the port. They took their pleasures, drinking, eating, whoring, and gambling outside. She had little idea what Zhen did all day away from the house or during the frequent times he did not come back at all, to eat or to sleep. He had a separate home above his medicine shop on Circular Road. When they had first married, she thought about this all the time but had come to realise that to continue to do so would drive her mad.

She knew he was a literary man. She had seen books once when she had gone to the shophouse to take some fresh linen. She knew this store was added to, from time to time, by a package from China when the junks came down once a year. The packages came from his brothers, though she did not know these brothers. She knew virtually nothing of his family in China. He never talked about them to her.

In fact the men in the house rarely talked to the women at all, for even had they been so inclined, they did not share a common language. Her sister's husband, Ah Teo, was Hokkien like Zhen, and while Noan's father could speak some Hokkien, the rest of them spoke only Baba Malay, the language of the Straits Chinese families, a complex mixture of Malay and Hokkien.

Noan had learned some English and some Chinese characters, for her father had indulged her, his first-born, a little. She was his favourite. The more so since marriage to Zhen, who had taken his name and would look after the rites for him when he was dead. Her father loved Zhen like the son he did not have, for her mother had borne four girls. The little bit of learning her father had given her had done her few favours, for she now felt its lack, felt like a silly, ignorant girl.

Sometimes she wished she could burst out of the house; she envied her sister her volatile and adventurous nature.

Lilin, the beauty of the family, was headstrong and within the bounds of the strictures of a Chinese family, did exactly what she liked. Noan prayed to Kuan Yin for those things which were important to her: the love and health of Zhen, a son for him, the long life of her father and mother, happiness for herself and her children. Since her marriage, Lilin rarely went to the temple. The marriage to Ah Teo was unhappy, Noan could see it, but in some ways it had liberated Lilin. As a married woman she was permitted to go abroad, in the town, visit friends or other family. The constrictions of maidenhood, which had confined them since they were twelve years old were gone.

Their father tried to avoid any confrontation with Lilin and in any case, now lived in the country at River Valley Road with their mother and his new concubine. Ah Teo had no control over Lilin either and the only person she was inclined to obey was Zhen. He was their father's adopted son, his heir, and head of this household in Market Street, which both couples shared. But Zhen was either absent or little inclined to discipline Lilin.

Noan could not know that Zhen avoided Lilin because he knew of this sister's feelings for him. Within days of his wedding to Noan, Lilin had found him in a robing room and lifted her sarong, putting his hand between her legs. She had been only fourteen. Since then, whenever she could, she touched his hair or rubbed against him.

He had tried to advise Ah Teo about sexual matters, given him a Taoist pillow book of sexual instruction but these subjects were difficult and embarrassing. Ah Teo was diffident, quiet and shy. He was a great asset to the Tan house in business, for he spoke good English, Malay and Mandarin, as well as Hokkien, Cantonese and Hakka. He had family in Manila, Cochin China and Bangkok who had been useful partners in commerce, for the Chinese commercial network was made up of marriages and relationships which enhanced the spread and wealth of the family. He was astute, shrewd and careful. He had been chosen, of course, for these qualities and not for his physical attributes.

A woman's wishes were completely unimportant. She was expected to obey. That was all. Unfortunately, Lilin, always headstrong, had grown less and less obedient, for Zhen knew that Ah Teo did not please her. There had been a child, a little boy who had died within a few months. This death had been a hammer blow to them all. Tan and his wife had taken it hard, and Lilin seemed to have simply thrown away all constraint.

Noan knew she should leave her husband alone but the sight of him washing, the cloth moving slowly over his torso, the ripple of the muscles of his back and buttocks, the hard beauty of him, tempted her too much. She rose from the bed and went to him, running her hands around his waist, over the muscles of his abdomen and down, pressing her body against his, her lips against the silk of his back. He felt exquisite, hard and coolly damp; her fingers tingled, touching his skin, hungry for him again. Zhen stopped her hand and turned.

"Noan! Enough." He spoke in Baba Malay and smiled to soften his words. "I will not come tonight."

He saw the effect on her face, an instant dulling of her eyes, her hands dropping loosely to her side, but he could not help it and said no more. He felt no need to explain himself to his wife. What he did was none of her business. He did his duty, which was becoming increasingly tedious and she must do hers: abiding in silence.

He needed a rest and wanted to spend the evening with Qian, his best friend, eating and drinking, talking about poetry and love and *her*, for only with Qian could he talk of this. He wanted to get drunk and be stupid and maudlin and laugh a lot, then roll home to his own bed to dark, dreamless sleep.

3

"Land ho" went up the cry from the crow's nest. Adam was asleep, but Charlotte heard Zan let out a whoop and the sound of his little feet drumming as he ran about on deck. She left her letter to Aunt Jeanne unfinished and went outside. Zan's *babu* was with him, of course; she never left his side. All in all, these Javanese girls had done very well. There had been a few squalls but no doldrums. The brig had made good time, five days. They had both been brave for they were, unlike her, not accustomed to sea travel. She knew there would be some time before land was sighted from the rail so she sat in the wicker chair outside the cabin and called the steward for some tea. She watched Alexander jumping and jigging along the rail and "helping" the sailors in their duties.

Seven years old and bigger than his nursemaid, he was the colour of pale coffee, darkened a little by the constant outdoor life he led. He was handsome, with dark, almond eyes, a mass of thick black hair which she left long, beading it sometimes like Tigran's. He had fretted for Tigran and had turned away from her at first. She hardly blamed him. She had all but neglected him for several years of his short life. But after six months of her constant attention, visits to Tigran's grave, the love of his aunt and the help of the Armenian priest, he had improved. He was tall, well made, strong and muscular, like his blood father. Charlotte was concerned, for she could see Zhen's build and his face in his son's. If they were ever to stand together, the resemblance might be remarked upon. But neither Alexander nor Zhen must ever know the truth. Her protective instincts were sharply honed. Alexander could not be known as a Chinaman's bastard son.

Whatever it took, she would make sure of it.

Alexander and Adam were close companions. Adam was five years old. He was of slighter build but had the same dark eyes and black hair. Where Alexander was headstrong and bold, Adam was quiet, serious and loving. She saw Tigran in him, the same kindness and good temper. Alexander could be rough at times, cruel, fearless, but since he had passed out of babyhood, with Adam he was always gentle and fiercely protective.

He turned suddenly and saw her and smiled. She drew a sharp breath. Zhen's boyhood face, she was certain, had looked like this. She smiled too, blowing a kiss. He ran over and threw himself into her arms.

"Mummy, tell me the story of the prince and the lion again."

Charlotte pulled him onto her lap. She had filled both boys with this story so that they might not regret their parting from the only home they had known, from Tigran's grave, from their memories of Batavia.

"Once upon a time," she began and Alexander smiled his gap-toothed smile, "there was a handsome and valiant prince of Sumatra. His name was Sang Nila Utama, and he was the son of the Rajah Chulan of India and the daughter of the God of the Sea. He was a mighty fighter and a mighty sailor. He wanted to build a new city and set out to search for the perfect place.

"He and his men went first to the islands of Rhio and were welcomed by the Queen. A few days later Prince Utama went to a nearby island to hunt. He spied a deer. While chasing it he came to a very large rock and climbed it to see where the deer had gone.

"At the top of the rock Prince Utama stopped and forgot all about the deer. Across the sea was another island with a lovely bay, white sands and green coconut palms. His men, breathless, came running behind.

"'What is this place?' he asked his minister. 'Temasek, my lord,' the man replied.

"He decided immediately to visit Temasek and ordered his ship be made ready. As they approached the island, a great storm blew up, and the ship was tossed about in the huge waves and began to take water. Desperately the sailors threw all the heavy things overboard to lighten the ship. But still water kept coming and Prince Utama finally threw his heavy crown into the waves. At once, to everyone's wonderment, the storm died down.

"He landed at the mouth of a fine river. The men needed food and they began to hunt. Suddenly, in the undergrowth, they heard a loud noise and his men, fearful, drew back. But Prince Utama went forward boldly, his bow at the ready. Quietly he moved, his hunter's instincts taking over, his eyes everywhere. His men followed behind, emboldened by their lord's bravery.

"Then, in the shadows," Charlotte paused for effect, "he glimpsed a great beast, a strange animal with a red body, a black head and a white breast. For a moment they stared, eye to eye. It was a magnificent animal. Then, suddenly, the beast turned and with great speed it disappeared into the jungle.

"'Did you see that?' he called to his men who were cowering behind the thick trunk of a tembusu tree."

Alexander laughed. He loved that part. Sometimes she changed the name of the tree to see if he was paying attention and he always cried out and scolded her. "A tembusu tree, Mummy, stop it!" Charlotte knew he saw himself as Prince Utama. He had a little bow and arrows and practiced shooting at the straw target which Captain Elliot had set up on deck for him.

"'What was that?' Prince Utama asked."

Alexander put his finger to her lips. "A lion!" he yelled, delighted, and Charlotte smiled.

"Yes, Zan, a lion! So Prince Utama scolded his men for their fear.

"The prince was very pleased. 'It is an omen of good fortune. I shall build my city here and henceforth, this island shall be named Singhapura, the Town of the Lion,' he decreed.

"And so it has been called down to this very day."

Zan wriggled off her lap, pleased with the story and rushed again to the rail, anxious for a sight of the Town of the Lion.

She rose and went to his side as he began to jump up and down and she saw, in the distance, like a small red flame on the horizon, the familiar cliffs of Singapore. Rust red, she had told Alexander, from the quantity of blood spilled on the shores. Another old name for Singapore was Tanah Mera, Red Land, and she had shown him on an old map of Singapore, so he believed her. It had been a pirates' lair for centuries, the beaches ringed with skulls rolling in the surf from the bodies thrown from pirate ships.

Alexander loved pirate stories, so she told him too of the Bugis men: the greatest seafarers of all the South Seas. Some lived now, peaceably, she reassured him, though she was not sure if that was true, in Kampong Bugis on the broad Kallang River. His eyes had nearly fallen out of their sockets, and he had jiggled with repressed excitement, and she had promised to take him there. Charlotte thought, with pleasure, of teaching him to sail, for both she and Robert were good sailors. They had learned first in Madagascar, then in the chilly waters of Scotland. To sail in the coral-strewn, limpid waters of Singapore was to partake in some small way in paradise.

The *Queen* drew closer to shore. Charlotte pointed out all the strange craft which were new to Alexander. He had seen the big East Indiamen in Batavia harbour, the square-rigged schooners and brigs of Western shipping, the long, dark hulls of the *prahus* and the opium smugglers of the Eastern archipelago. He had even seen a junk though not up close, but he had never seen the big men-of-war bristling with cannon, the yellow-sided Cochin Chinese ships bearing the merchandise of their king or the strange Siamese ships, Chinese bodies and European masts with huge carved sterns or the sailed steamships, with their white canvas, huge paddle wheels and long, sooty funnels. She gave him into the company of the first mate, who was happy to explain all this nauticalia to him and the meaning of the flags which fluttered from every vessel.

She contemplated the scene. She had never seen the harbour so busy. It was a constant movement of ships and boats, some in stately slowness, some darting, the whole like a nautical hive.

The only fixtures were the Chinese junks, fifty of them or so, huddled together, sails furled, yards housed and rudders unhung, standing almost motionless. In this state they resembled not so much ships as floating shops, offering, it seemed, from the articles hanging about them in every direction, all the manufactures of the Celestial Kingdom. She knew they would be here until the turn of the trade winds that would carry them home.

It was inevitable that the sight of the junks would take her mind to the night she had first arrived in the harbour, to the first sight of these strange and majestic masters of the ocean. And to *him*, of course. He was never far, always occupying a soft corner of her mind, not more than half a thought away. She shook her head and smiled, for she knew she would have to be dead before this desire would ever go away.

Finally Captain Elliott ordered the anchor to be dropped and Charlotte turned her eyes to the town. Little had changed: the big white mansions along the beach, the hill behind topped with the Governor's residence and the flagstaff. Fort Fullerton stood at the southern mouth of the river: a fort in name only, for its stone walls were low. Charlotte knew that a flurry of unexpected interest in Singapore had arisen in Calcutta and that funds had been allocated for its defence. This interest, however, had waned as fast as it had arrived and then funds had just as quickly dried up. In consequence, the wall was nothing more than a low embankment and the soldiers' barracks but a few rather straggling, hastily completed stone buildings.

The piers, like gapped teeth, projected from behind the godowns of Commercial Square. The Chinese town was hidden behind the octagonal red roof of the market.

Alexander appeared at her side, full of excitement, pointing to the stream of little skipping sampans and stately *tongkangs* emerging from the river mouth which lay concealed from view, rushing to do business with every new ship that dropped anchor. The decks of many ships would be crowded, she knew, from early morning to night with tailors, shoemakers, washerwomen and touts for every vice available, either on board or in the town. The *Queen* was almost instantly surrounded by them, the *tongkangs* bringing for sale fresh bread, eggs, milk, chickens, ducks, fish, fruit and vegetables, the sampans full of curiosities, all the men and women suing, in piteous voices, for permission to come aboard and making the most prodigious clatter.

Alexander, she could see, loved it.

She told the first mate to allow one of the curiosity sellers on board, for the amusement of the children. As the mate's head appeared over the side and he raised his hand, the clamour rose to deafening pitch. He pointed and, quick as a flash, the two chosen men had climbed aboard laden with cages of birds, parrots and birds of paradise, small monkeys, lizards, snakes, shells, corals, mats, wood carvings, trinkets and Malay daggers. She quickly ordered a basket of hideous shrunken heads to be removed. Adam was terrified, and the *babus* clung to him, but Alexander thought it a great joke and laughed. Finally Adam, watching his brother, began to calm down and went up to one of the monkeys. Charlotte sighed and told them there would be no monkeys and no daggers.

"We shall pay to free the birds and watch them fly away, eh?" she asked them, for she had a horror of such captive things. "And you may pick a pretty shell to keep."

Both boys looked pouty-lipped but reluctantly agreed, so long as they could open the cages. Charlotte gave some coins to the wrinkled old Malay, who looked utterly amazed as he watched the birds fly free.

Captain Elliott came up, waiting, and then told her they had permission to disembark. He ordered the decks cleared.

The sampan threaded its way skilfully through the anchored ships and turned into the crowded mouth of the river. The narrow entrance was fairly jammed with boats and the boatman gave the most ferocious yells and gesticulations. He was a copper-skinned Kling from the Coramandel Coast in India. He was clad only in a dhoti and chewed his betel, now and then spitting a red stream from his mouth into the river. Kajang-roofed sampans huddled on the low central bank of the river tied to stakes, the naked children frolicking in and out of the water. Adam was quiet, sucking his thumb, but Alexander was taking it all in eagerly.

From a distance she saw Robert and put up her hand. He waved. Charlotte pointed him out to Alexander and Adam, for they had never met this uncle. She felt on the verge of tears. To see Robert after so long. Four years—it was a lifetime. As she set foot on the steps of the landing stage, he swept her into his arms. His own eyes filled with tears and they held each other tight.

"Robbie, Robbie, I missed you."

Robert could not speak, merely nodded and held her tighter. Then he let her go as the boys came to her side.

"Ah, my young boys, Alex, Adam, my nephews. It is good to meet you."

Alex held out his hand, and Robert grinned and shook it, then bent and picked up Adam into his arms. Adam was a shy boy and looked terrified and set up a loud wail. Robert laughed and released him but instantly took up both boys' hands and set off along the quay, in front of the Court House, still easily the most elegant building in the town, to the carriage waiting for them where High Street met the river.

Before she followed him, Charlotte turned and gazed over the crowded little river to the Chinese town and the cavernous godown of Baba Tan, one of the richest merchants of Singapore and Zhen's father-in-law.

4

Zhen stepped up over the hewn log which barred the entrance to the Thien Hock Keng temple and out into the muddy street, walking along the bay towards the market. He had given thanks for this day at the altar of Guan Di, the God of War and of Good Fortune, the patron deity of the *kongsi*. The rain, which had been light, now began to fall heavily, and he took shelter in the crowded porch of the Fuk Tak Chi temple, watching the storm lash the bay to invisibility. He was in no hurry. He still had half an hour before a meeting with his father-in-law, Baba Tan, at the offices of McKendrick and Shaw, Law Agents, on Commercial Square. Today they would sign the purchase agreement for a new steamship, *his* steamship for his company, made in a country far away. He touched the chop seal in his pocket, the seal with which he would sign all documents. He gripped it tight.

Tan owned sailing ships, junks and hybrid Siamese vessels which flew the British flag in the China trade but Zhen wanted steam to power his ship. It was the future, he was sure of it, and his father-in-law had put faith in him and advanced him credit. This ship was like a dream, the first in a fleet which promised the great wealth he wanted. He had entered into this business with his brother-in-law, Ang Choon, a shipowner in Bangkok, who had taken Tan's fourth daughter as his second wife. Ang's first wife was a daughter of the richest baba in Siam who owned rice mills, and his ship would be added to Ang's for the voluminous and profitable rice trade in the region.

He had been invited to represent his father-in-law on the committee for the construction of the new building for the Chongwen

Ge, the first Chinese school in Singapore, which was being established on the grounds of the Thien Hock Keng temple. It was a great honour and revealed in what esteem he was beginning to be held in this town. To have come so far from so little—only Singapore could have done this.

The rain stopped abruptly, and to calm his mind and his excitement, he walked slowly along Telok Ayer Street, crossed Market Street into Malacca Street and emerged behind the godowns of the Square onto the piers.

The water of the bay, an intense blue, mirrored the sky. He never tired of this view, the ships dotting the bay, the constant movement of boats carrying goods to and fro, the hundreds of coolies in perpetual motion, loading and unloading. He thought briefly of Bukit Jagoh at Telok Belangah, the land for the house he would build one day, and of his own arrival in Singapore. Then he had been one of the lowliest of men, like those he saw before him now. His education, this precious ability to read and write, had separated him from thousands of others however, and he had been selected, as had his friend Qian, for marriage into the family of a rich Peranakan merchant house. This marriage to Baba Tan's daughter had changed everything and even now he could not always believe it.

He was not like many of the Chinese who came here, temporary, desperate to make money and return home as quickly as possible. He had noticed the real difference between the Teochew and the Hokkien. The Teochews always moaned on about home and going back, but the Hokkien, like him, were quick and adaptable. He loved Singapore. He called it that now, like the English, not Si Lat Po, the Chinese name. These white men were not "foreign devils". They were quick and clever and built amazing things, like steamships and machines that fixed your image. He admired this phenomenal capacity for invention. Everything wise and true and old was Chinese but everything new, everything useful for commerce, came from the West.

He had been in Singapore just one year when the East India Company's ship, *Nemesis*, had arrived into the harbour. When the flag was hoisted on the staff, almost every single person had left the town and crowded the seashore. The arrival had been awaited with incredible anticipation, for she was the first *iron* steamship to round the Cape: a ship made of iron, two-masted, with a paddle propeller amidships—a gunship bound for war in China. Zhen had disliked what the ship was doing, but he had never seen anything like her. He could not understand how she stayed afloat and even the Chinese merchants had talked about it for weeks. Since then she had been many times in Singapore, for she patrolled the waters of the Indian Ocean and every time he saw her, he watched her greedily.

He missed his family, especially his mother and younger brothers, but he did not miss China. Every now and then, when he sipped the red Fukien tea, he thought of his home there, of the mountains and the Taoist monastery where he had learned his disciplines, and of the fourth concubine of the local mandarin who had secretly and lengthily initiated him into the wonders of the flesh. Where was she now? But he did not miss the endless and grinding poverty which lay like a pall over the villages, the corruption of the officials or his father's opium addiction which had ruined them all.

The *kongsi* was all that had saved them from death and he had served it willingly as the *hong gun*: the red rod, the enforcer, and was loyal to it now. It had made him hard where he was soft from too much fourth concubine. He smiled. Taoism tempered it all and he was a Taoist to the bottom of his soul. And Taoism, the letting be, the unstriving Tao had brought him this fortune, no matter how strange it had been at the beginning entering a Straits Chinese family. They were a good family; his wife was a good wife; he had beautiful daughters and a fortune in prospect in a land where the officials, to his amazement, were not corrupt. In this too, he had learned to admire the British.

He had begun to understand a little about them as he had learned his English. They were, at least those who ruled here so far, incorruptible. This fact was almost unbelievable. Here, their word was a bond, their code one he admired though he could not quite understand it. He was not naïve; he knew about what the British were doing in China—invasion and forced trade. On one level he felt sorry but on another he could muster no emotion about it. China held no future for him like that which spread before him in Singapore, and he felt a strange and unanticipated loyalty to this place.

Then, in the midst of these reflections, he saw the ship. He intensified his gaze, uncertain of his own eyes but it was no mistake. Anchored in the bay was the black brig, its topgallant pennants flying in the wind, adorned with a Java panther, the emblem of the Mah Nuk merchant house. This was Xia Lou's ship, *Queen of the South*. She was here in Singapore! Blood rushed to his temples and he looked towards the European town.

He closed his eyes, remembering. He knew she was now a widow. The man she had married was dead. He could not count the number of times he had wished for this during their years of separation. Now that wish was tinged with a sadness not only for her but even for her husband, for he had met this man when Charlotte was in trouble, and had liked him despite their rivalry.

This musing was quickly overtaken by the thought of her in Singapore, close by, and of their last meeting. She had faced a choice: to stay with her husband and children or to come with him for her trouble had been opium, the dispeller of misery, and he, who hated it, had cured her of it. He remembered every moment spent with her, the hours of love and learning to talk to each other, the endless desire for her, the misery of separation. But, faced with the reality of his marriage, the sheer impossibility of a respectable life together, she had let him go.

"Then do not come to me again," he had said, "unless it is forever."

He turned away. He had been sure then but now he felt a tenderness, a quivering desire for her. He hardened his heart. They would meet; it was inevitable in such a small town as their social worlds touched. He loved her with all his being but it could not begin again: the hiding, the secrecy. He could not cross any further into her world. To be together, she must accept his way. He walked back to Commercial Square.

5

Charlotte had not been a fortnight in Singapore when the invitation from Government House arrived. There was to be a dinner and ball in honour of Sir James Brooke, the Rajah of Sarawak, and Captain Henry Keppel. Captain Keppel's book *The Expedition to Borneo of H.M.S. Dido for the Suppression of Piracy*, which contained extracts of the Rajah's personal diaries, had been published to feverish interest.

Charlotte knew that the exploits of the Rajah in these far-flung, pirate-infested seas were viewed in England as prodigious and thrilling, filling the chests of young men with pride and longing and the hearts of young ladies with quivering and romantic passions. The thirst for him had become insatiable. Captain Keppel's book was in its third printing. The Rajah had been the toast of London, been received by Queen Victoria who had seemingly also fallen under his swashbuckling spell, and been made a knight of her realm.

Charlotte responded with thanks. She would not miss this event for the world.

She had paid her respects to the Governor and his wife, as decorum decreed, and left her card. She had taken tea with many of her former acquaintances. Evangeline Barbie was still taking care of the priests at the Catholic Parochial House. The army of children of Jose da Silva were still the most populous in the white town. Robert's wife, Teresa, was a da Silva grandchild from his daughter by his third wife, a Chinese-Portuguese woman he had married in Macau. Da Silva was currently into his seventh marriage, the product of which were his twin daughters Isobel and Isabel, whom Charlotte knew well.

An invitation to dinner had arrived from Mrs Benjamin Peach Keaseberry, and this she now held in her hand. Benjamin's first wife had been a close friend. This marriage to Elizabeth had taken place, Charlotte thought, with indecent haste. His first wife was hardly in her grave before the banns had been posted. Benjamin, leader here of the London Missionary Society, was thirty-five and Elizabeth barely seventeen and Charlotte understood, pregnant.

She put the invitation down. She would go of course. She would not snub Elizabeth. Something had changed in Singapore in the last few years. An insidious and creeping respectability seemed to have taken over the town. Not perhaps a real respectability but the trappings of respectability. But then, she thought, perhaps all so-called respectability is mere sham.

In 1839 when she had first arrived, a mere twenty years after its establishment, Singapore was a town of men, had always been a town of men. There were few immigrant women of any sort, either white, Chinese or Indian. The Malay and Bugis villages were always filled with families and children for they were the natives of the island and the surrounding regions. It was then a frontier town, wild and not at all respectable. What women there were, were Indian convict women who became wives and companions to the Indian convict men or other Indian men of the transitory sort who came and went with the tide; boatmen, stall holders, buffalo farmers in Serangoon, guards in the godowns sleeping in the verandahs, milk vendors, water suppliers, barbers, tinkers, syces and peons.

The other Indians, the indispensable Chettiars, the moneylenders, rarely settled here. They came and set up their low desks in Change Alley or Market Street and their sole purpose was to get rich as quickly as possible and depart. The Indians who settled were the Chittys, who came from Kalinga, merchants and traders who married local women, dressed in Malay style and ate Malay food but were staunch Hindoos.

The local Chinese of the Straits, too, were settlers. They had long inhabited the port towns of the region. Towns like Batavia, Medan, Malacca, Penang and now the youngest, most ambitious of them all—Singapore. The first sailors and merchants had married local non-Mohammedan women, brought as slaves from Siam, Sumatra, Bali, the far Eastern provinces of the archipelago—for love perhaps, for companionship certainly. When they returned to China, they left these "number two wives" in charge of business until their return on the next monsoon. Their wives in China would have little inkling of this secondary home away from home. Gradually, as years passed, the Chinese men stayed and made families, marrying their daughters and sons amongst themselves. A hybrid culture had sprung up. The men may have forgotten how to speak Chinese; their sons never learned. The language became a mixture of Hokkien mostly, the language of the maritime south of China from where most of these men came, and Malay, the language of the women. They spoke Baba Malay and the men were called babas and the women nonyas.

These Peranakan families kept their women under tight control and their daughters locked up. They were merchants, clever and quick, who learned the language of the colonial masters and acted as the indispensable go-betweens for the whites and the natives of whatever town they found themselves in. No colonial city in the East could survive without these compradores. They married amongst themselves or, when they needed new blood—men for their daughters—they chose them from amongst the thousands of poor Chinese coolies who flooded into Singapore with every fleet from China.

No respectable Chinese women came from China to marry. It was forbidden. Women who came were smuggled out and sold to be prostitutes, enslaved by their own fathers who valued only sons, and had too many mouths to feed. Even though this trade was brisk, the number of Chinese girls and women in Singapore was always a tiny percentage of the male population. Life for the enslaved Chinese prostitute was usually short and brutish. She had to serve the thousands of Chinese and Indian coolies, the soldiers of the army stationed in Singapore and the constant stream of sailors who washed up onshore. Death was often preferable, opium suicide common.

The white men might talk of home, of going home for years, but most stayed. Life was easy and free in the East. As for white women in Singapore, there had been a few wives of the officers, officials and missionaries, the many young girls of the da Silva family and the occasional arrival, like Charlotte herself. Men who did not care to risk the dangers of disease in the brothels or the dispiriting anonymity of loveless encounters took native girls as "wives", *nyais* as they were called. Robert, himself, had had his *nyai*, Shilah, for many years before his marriage to Teresa. She had not yet had enough time to talk to him on this subject.

Nothing had changed for the local communities. It was in the European community that the change had come. The previous governor, Samuel Bonham, had been a bachelor; he paid no heed to how the young men spent their time, content to invite them into his bungalow for convivial evenings and otherwise leave them to their devices. He was old school, a man raised in ruder times when liaisons with native women were considered normal and because they kept one from whores and the attendant diseases, even healthy.

The arrival of Colonel William Butterworth, Companion of the Order of the Bath, had brought an insidious change in attitudes. He was a decorated soldier, where almost all governors before him had been civilians. He was newly come to the Straits, where most had spent all their lives here. He was married and his English wife brought a certain social expectation to the settlement. He was, in addition, a prig. His attitudes were those, she supposed, of a Great Britain which had never been in so close contact with its Eastern settlements as now. The sailing ships of the previous centuries were slow. Mail, orders, attitudes, were a year away from Singapore if they came at all. Men did as they pleased, made decisions and acted on them without thought of "back home".

Now, steamships could travel at unheard-of speeds, and the new Egyptian Overland Route carried mail and passengers from Southampton via Gibraltar and Malta to Alexandria, up the Nile to Cairo, eighty miles by camel overland to Suez, down the Red Sea to Bombay and on to Singapore. A newspaper printed in London could now be read only forty days later in Singapore. It was unimaginable. The connection to "back home", so long severed, was quickly being reestablished and with it, the feelings and attitudes of the mother country.

Charlotte felt almost like "old school" herself. She had been only nine years in the East, but her experiences had made her wary of this newfound "respectable" Singapore. She did not like so much the changing attitudes to the mixed marriages which had been so common only a few short years ago. Then a white officer or official would have sought a wife, with pleasure, amongst the mixed-race girls—the children made as a result of married liaisons between white men and native women.

Now that was not always the case. Isabel da Silva, a plain young woman, had had the great misfortune to turn down marriage to a lieutenant in the Madras Regiment in the hope, as she told Charlotte, of a more handsome prospect. She now found herself in a position of less good circumstances for, within the space of two years, an officer of the regiment who had hopes of promotion would find such a union an insurmountable obstacle to advancement.

Her dark brothers and sisters, the offspring of Jose da Silva's six previous marriages, counted against them. Isabel was now engaged, at her mother's urging, to the son of a Spanish merchant and his native wife from Manila. She did not care a fig for this man, she had told Charlotte, and despaired of her life with him. She envied her sister Isobel, who had caught an Englishman, a merchant from Prince of Wales Island.

Perhaps, mused Charlotte, I am sensitive to these changes because of my own life: a child born of the love of a Scottish man and a Creole woman, I love a Chinese man and am the widow of an Armenian Dutchman whose mother was the child of a Dutch–Indian marriage. She shook her head. It all seemed so pointless. Her own children were half this and that. All this blood nonsense gave her a headache and she disliked these insidious attitudes which she felt creeping like a shadow over the town.

Doubtless if Butterworth had the slightest inkling of any of this, he would have ripped up the invitation in a trice. This thought gave her a small moment of pleasure, and she stopped her musings and returned to the tasks of the next few days, one of which was enrolling her beloved little half-Chinese boy in the best school in Singapore.

Charlotte picked up her parasol and set out through her gardens.

It was early and the air held a comparative coolness that only the dawn and the dusk can bring in a tropical climate. She was going to the blessing of the Church of the Good Shepherd.

Charlotte greeted Evangeline and sat amidst the considerable congregation, both European and Chinese, gathered for the event. The activity and vitality of this Catholic community stood in stark contrast to the benign indifference of the Protestants.

She had been to St. Andrews many times over the years and always remarked on the general absence of the population, the sleepy and indifferent attitudes of the few who were there. One rainy Sunday, long ago, when Tigran was alive, she, Robert and John Thomson, the Surveyor of the Straits Settlements, had gone to a morning service.

"If the English be the true church, it is evident the East India Company do not think so," John Thomson had murmured.

St. Andrew's seated perhaps four hundred people, but around them there had been but twenty worshippers. Three emaciated young ladies had occupied one pew, an old man with his dark wife behind them. A corpulent bald gentleman fanned himself, a pretty blonde sat with her old mother. Men from the garrison had occupied other pews. Above them the punkahs waved like the wings of birds in flight.

In the dusty silence, suddenly the organ had pealed forth. The Reverend White and his clerk entered. The service was read, the responses made by the clerk flippant and indifferent. The congregation played no part. Psalms were given out, the organ boomed, a pagan native boy exerting himself mightily pumping air, but neither the clerk nor the worshippers had sung. The sermon had been tedious platitudes. No charity was asked, and the congregation roused itself and departed.

As they had walked through the extensive gardens which commanded the finest sea view in Singapore, Charlotte was moved to ask John his opinion on this.

"It is a mystery," he had said. "The Company pays its chaplains magnificently but what for, it is difficult to discern. The curate does not visit his people, good heavens no, he plants nutmegs. For the Company forbids him, under the heaviest penalties, to be an apostle to the heathen, and John Company is more powerful here than his heavenly Master. He is the *burra padre*, you know, the great man's priest, not the *coolie padre*, ministering to the poor."

"So why build such churches John? Look at this place, magnificent, on the finest piece of land in the whole town."

John had shrugged. "Not for religion certainly. Perhaps some abstruse point of East India Company policy lost to reason. The Europeans do not attend church and the natives are all pagans or Mohammedans. Patronage, doubtless then, to the political bench of the bishops in parliament. Who can say? The visible and familiar sign of England, even in a dusty landscape? All I know is that the chaplain is here because he is well paid, and his only thoughts are how to make money and go home."

She thought of this now and looked around her. No wonder then that the Catholic Church found such fertile ground. It was all but abandoned to them. Good for them then, she thought, if they do some good. She took Evangeline's arm in hers and smiled at her friend.

6

Zhen tossed his head back and swallowed the small cup of rice wine. It tasted good and a feeling of mellowness crept over him. He lay back on the thick cushions on the floor and looked up at the ceiling. He loved to be in this room. This was Qian's inner sanctum. This had been Qian's dead father-in-law's bedroom and strongroom, he knew. When the old miser had been alive, he kept his treasure chests in here and never let anyone enter. Sang had been the most miserly man in Singapore but immensely rich and powerful. He had been head of the *kongsi*, the society which ran everything Chinese here in Singapore, the temples, the coolies, the farms, everything. When he died, ten thousand men had been ordered to his funeral. The British authorities could not believe their eyes. Despite the vast numbers of Chinese pouring, with each monsoon season, into Singapore, the administration never increased. Zhen smiled, nothing had changed much. The *kongsi* still ran almost everything.

Still, Sang had lacked the one thing he craved. He had no son to carry out the rites for him. Two daughters had been born to two wives, but no son had ever survived. So Qian, like Zhen, educated and poor, had been selected to marry the second daughter and despite his personal leanings towards the "pleasures of the bitten peach", had managed to sire two healthy sons on his young wife, Swan Neo.

Husbands were often selected from the pool of poor coolies that turned up on these shores in their thousands each year: fresh new Chinese blood for the local merchant's daughters, men who spoke the language and understood the ancient rites. Swan Neo spoke Hokkien, a somewhat old-fashioned type of Hokkien, but at least she and Qian could talk. Zhen had been forced to learn Baba Malay to talk to his own wife, for she had been born and raised in a Peranakan family

Qian could not have known his luck. Everyone knew Sang was rich, but how rich he discovered on the second day of his marriage, when he had found the chests of silver and jewels in this room. Qian had taken Sang's name, and now he ran the company and his own sons were the heirs to this vast fortune.

Zhen poured himself another cup of rice wine and drank it down quickly, gazing upwards. The ceiling was decorated with wooden beams painted in gold and black with writhing dragons. Carved folding doors stood back, showing the open inner courtyard into which late golden sunlight was pouring onto a pond filled with flitting gold and red carp and touching the leaves of great pots of bamboo. The floor was made of gleaming, cool, green and white Malacca tiles. It was secluded, opulent and expensive. Here Zhen knew, Qian made love to his young catamite, a half-Chinese half-Malay boy called Salim whom he had rescued from a brothel.

Here Qian and Zhen could be alone in their close friendship, alone to talk and get drunk. Here in this place, Zhen could truly relax. In his own home, the top floor of the shophouse on Circular Road, he could find peace but there was always a servant or someone to bother him. In the house in Market Street he shared with his wife and sister-in-law, there was absolutely no peace. Only here could he truly do as he pleased, for Qian, despite his humble beginnings, now lived like a Mandarin.

He looked up as the subject of his ruminations came and sat down next to him. Zhen punched him lightly on the arm and poured him a drink.

"She is here," Zhen said.

Qian knew exactly who Zhen was talking about. He contemplated his friend lolling, loose-limbed, half-undressed, beautiful, on the cushions. He recalled the day in the coolie house when they had stripped off their clothing and washed in the streaming rain in the air well courtyard. His first sight of Zhen's body had been his first inkling of his own desires. Now though, he could relax in his friend's company.

"I see. What do you intend to do about it?"

Zhen poured more wine.

"Nothing." He shook his head. "Just look at her."

Qian fell back on the cushions and began to laugh.

"She is here and you will do nothing. Just look at her. This is delightful talk, for I know you are a man of small passions and a soul filled with poetry. Perhaps you will write some for me. I believe it is commonplace to begin by being in the misty mountains, contemplating the moon ..."

Zhen smiled.

"Well, nothing for the moment. What can I do? Of course I want to ... want her ... But you know the situation. Unless she is willing to be my ..."

He looked at Qian, whose smile had widened. This subject, Zhen knew, always amused Qian. The mere idea of a white English woman becoming the concubine of a Chinese man in Singapore always put him in high good humour. But it had once terrified him. Zhen had pursued the lovely Xia Lou Mah Crow with a single-mindedness which made Qian fear for his friend's future and her mind. He knew the depth of Zhen's feelings and his resolve. That their love affair had not been detected, that Zhen had married Noan and Miss Mah Crow had gone away, had been a source of the greatest relief.

Now she was back, a widow. Free, he thought. Free and very rich. As rich as himself perhaps. The thought was fascinating. Much richer than Zhen.

"Well, thunderhead, if you ever want to meet her quietly and talk to her—not just look at her and think of the misty mountains—then let me know. I would like to see her again. She is a lady." His voice softened, and he realised that really he did like her and would like to see her again.

Zhen heard it and stopped being fierce. Yes she was a lady. His lady and yet not his.

He sighed and dropped back on the cushions. Qian poured them both some wine. Zhen changed the subject; this one just went round and round. Qian knew he would come back to it when he was suitably drunk and filled with longing.

Zhen tossed back the cup of rice wine and took up the chopsticks to pick at the food which was spread out on a low table.

Qian turned the subject to business.

"The gambier farmers are moving to Johor. The land survey by this Thomson man has meant that for the first time, there are rents to be paid. The new roads to Kranji and Changi mean the government men can move out and see for themselves. Many of the farmers are getting out. The prices are picking up for the Europeans are becoming interested in gambier also."

Zhen nodded.

"Well, well" he said. "This will sort itself out. I am part of a syndicate which is presently in an interesting position with the Temenggong. He has recognised that the Chinese are now his staircase to wealth and power, not the piratical bunch of *orang laut* he has been controlling. He needs a land base. He is shrewd, the cleverest Malay I've ever met and he knows where his fortunes lie. He is opening up land in Johor for development."

Qian poured rice wine and nodded.

"My influence in our *kongsi* is useful, for we need to quickly establish ourselves in Johor before the Teochews get involved. The Dutch are kicking them out of Rhio and they are landing up here in Singapore. There will be trouble."

Qian looked at his friend. They both understood how things stood here in Singapore. The Europeans had no way of controlling the profitable agriculture of the island. Their attempts at spice and sugar plantations had failed for the poor soil. The nutmeg trees had survived for a while but a disease had wiped them out. They were left with no alternative but to cooperate with the Chinese merchants who provided money for the gambier and pepper farmers and vitally, all the Chinese labourers.

The entire source of income for the town of Singapore came from the revenue farms and the taxes on the houses and properties of the town, in particular the opium farm, which supplied over fifty percent of government revenue and depended on the addictions of the labourers themselves. These farms were profitable undertakings, but there was a great rivalry for this profit between the Hokkien and the Teochew which could spill into violence.

"I'm bringing Min back to Singapore. Old Khoo is exchanging two of his brothels for the idiot son's debts. I need you to make it good with the *kongsi*."

Qian poured more rice wine, and Zhen raised his glass and drank. They trusted each other absolutely and preferred to do business together wherever possible. They had first met on the road to Amoy, on the road to the port and the junk which would take them to Singapore. Qian, physically weak, had found a protector and friend in Zhen, and Zhen had liked Qian for his resemblance to his youngest brother. Zhen's second daughter, Lian, was already promised to Ah Soon, Qian's first son. United, they would have one of the greatest merchant houses in all the South Seas and share grandchildren. These networks of marriages and alliances formed the basis of the Chinese business empires.

"Min still loves you, you know," Qian said.

Zhen shrugged. "What can I answer? Whores love anyone who is kind to them." He poured more wine.

Qian frowned. Zhen was being unkind. He did not think of Min like that. She had been sold into prostitution as a child. Zhen had been her patron in his early days in Singapore. When she had been beaten and left for dead by an English sailor, Zhen had saved her life, seen her cared for and placed in the care of Qian when he had become a wealthy man overnight. Qian had bought her out of the whorehouse in Singapore and set her up in business in Malacca.

In a hard world, she had been lucky; she knew it and so did they. They had fallen together and now she was able, at least, to live a life over which she had some control. Zhen's words had been thoughtless. He did not want anyone to love him but Xia Lou Mah Crow, that was the truth. Not his own wife, not Min. Qian knew that Zhen would like all these other women to leave him alone.

And now she was here in Singapore, this woman he loved to desperation, wanting the impossible. Wanting, in effect, for her to agree to be his concubine. Qian despaired for his friend. He no longer felt like laughing. They both drank, and Qian brought out the *wei qi* board and began to talk of home.

7

Government House had not changed. It stood square and solid on Bukit Larangan, looking down benevolently on the town, as it always had. The original building had been made of rough planks, Venetian shutters and an attap roof. Over the years it had been rebuilt in hardier materials, brick and tile, and this was the building before whose portals her phaeton now drew to a halt. Charlotte thought this house reflected in every way the unpretentious and simple origins of the town itself. It seemed to grow as the town grew, improving in construction and size to reflect the energy of the spreading streets around its feet.

The hill itself was wreathed in myth. She knew that the first Resident, William Farquhar, had taken a party of men and cut a path to its top against all the terrified and tremulous agitation and advice of the Malay inhabitants. Haunted, they said, that was certain: haunted by the ghosts of past kings and no one should set foot on it. The remains had been revealed of the foundations of a large palace and there was a grave. The holy *keramat* of Iskandar Shah, last Malay king of Temasek, or so it was told, lay on its flanks. A spring that flowed from the southwest corner of the hill, now on River Valley Road, served to supply water for the ships in the harbour but was said to have once been the bathing place of Malayan princesses.

It had a mysterious, antique quality. To Charlotte it had the most personal attachments. Beloved friends lay in the Christian cemetery on its lower eastern flanks and further round, hidden perhaps by growth and time, was an ancient nutmeg orchard where she had kissed Zhen for the first time. She had never been back. She tried not to allow her mind to run away, to think constantly of Zhen, but now, on this hill, she did. Love for him was still as powerful as ever, flesh speaking to flesh, but that was hidden deep. She could not pretend they were primeval creatures running barefoot in the forest, driven by their urges and instincts. They were this, perhaps, but they were also creatures of society. He had been clear: if she would not accept his terms, which were, in effect, to be his mistress, his English concubine ... She stopped thinking about him.

The reception and dinner were in honour of the Rajah of Sarawak, Sir James Brooke, and his appointment as Governor of Labuan, a barren, coal-rich island off Northern Borneo. Charlotte had met James Brooke briefly once or twice before in Singapore and looked forward to renewing the acquaintance. He was an easy man, an adventurer who had turned fortune his way, it seemed, but there was nothing pretentious about him. He had donated over one hundred volumes to the Singapore library and she was thankful to him that many of the tomes had been novels, for she remembered, he was an admirer, like her, of Miss Austen. It was he too, to whom all Singapore was indebted for the title awarded to the Governor. He had named Colonel Butterworth, *Butterpot the Great*, to general hilarity and the term, unbeknownst to the Governor, had stuck.

She had read *The Free Press* yesterday.

This appointment, besides the advantages we may expect to derive from the experience and abilities of Sir James Brooke, is satisfactory as marking that the British Government are not disposed to give way to the extravagant and unjust pretensions of the Dutch; but that on the contrary, it is intended to maintain our rights to an equal footing in the Archipelago.

She had smiled. Nothing had happened to diminish the constant rivalry and dislike of the Dutch and English in this part of the world. Singapore stood constantly she knew, as a thorn in the side of the Dutch East Indies, taking away trade and influence—just as Raffles had intended.

The Colonel and Mrs Butterworth welcomed their guests inside the main hall. What little she knew of the Colonel was not promising. The kindest comment she'd heard was that he was not liked. The manner of his rise to the Governorship though he knew nothing of the Straits, his patronage by Lord Ellenborough, the Indian Governor-General, his nepotism, his superior attitude, his utter disdain for the old merchants and officials who had brought Singapore to her place in the world. These were dire indeed, but his worst indictment was his obsession in matters of dress. He had ordered black dress, not white, should be worn at official functions and had set out minute regulations. In Government House these dress codes were obeyed, but elsewhere white was worn in petulant disobedience.

When Charlotte appeared, Butterpot moved forward to welcome her. Everyone knew of her widowhood and the fortune she had inherited. She was easily the wealthiest woman in Singapore, even perhaps in the whole of the East Indies. Doubtless the Governor expected, one day, that a woman of her wealth and beauty would attract the eye of a Baronet, perhaps a Duke, on some voyage back to England. He could not have guessed that Charlotte had not the slightest intention of marrying anyone under English laws, which would immediately deprive her of her fortune and pass it into the hands of her husband to do with what he wished. Were a prince of the realm himself to seek her hand she would refuse him. If she married again it would be in Batavia, under Dutch law, where Tigran's fortune and his children's rights were protected.

Her thoughts flew to Batavia, to her home, the grandest estate in the city, but not for long. Charlotte was happy, in so many ways, to be back here, to be surrounded by her native language, to *understand* her acquaintance. She embraced Jeanette Butterworth warmly. The Colonel had been fortunate, Charlotte thought, in his choice of wife for where he was pettifogging and pretentious, Jeanette was broadminded and down-to-earth. How the conversations ran in the privacy of their sitting room Charlotte could not imagine.

Standing at Jeanette's side were her sister and her brother-in-law, Captain and Mrs Charles Faber. Captain Faber was the object of the accusations of nepotism since his appointment as Superintending Engineer of Singapore, a task for which, the entire town agreed, he was entirely unsuited. He was a thin and faded man but with the same supercilious air of self-aggrandisement that so marked his illustrious brother-in-law. His wife was simply mousy and quiet. He fawned over Charlotte's hand and Charlotte disliked him immediately.

As drinks were served, she was joined by Robert and introduced to a variety of men and women whose names she immediately forgot, all but Captain Charles Maitland, who she was surprised to find, made a strong first impression.

Captain Maitland was of medium height, powerfully built, with shoulder-length chestnut hair and brown eyes. She knew he was an engineer but he looked like a fighter. It was an intriguing combination, and she found herself observing him in conversation with Colonel Butterworth. He spoke very little though this was, of course, the normal state of affairs with the Colonel, who would rather hear his own voice than any other. Butterworth's interest in Captain Maitland was aided doubtless by the fact that he was the younger brother of Sir Henry Maitland, the Foreign Secretary to the Government of India.

He was neither interested in nor perturbed by the Colonel and stood politely, simply waiting, she thought, for the right moment to move away. Self-contained, she thought. He was a self-contained man; his thoughts elsewhere. And this elsewhere, Charlotte thought, was the most interesting thing about a man who looked built for audacious and soldierly deeds of derring-do, for it was amongst the glass containers, dials, charts, logs and needles of the Magnetic Observatory at Kallang that his mind dwelt.

They had been introduced briefly and Charlotte recognised that her gaze had been drawn to him because, beyond the usual *politesse*, he had paid not the slightest bit of attention to her. It was a rare occurrence as the press of young officers and midshipmen around her confirmed. She fanned herself and smiled at them and continued to covertly assess Captain Maitland.

He was not handsome of face particularly, his nose rather broad and his chin too square. Despite the attitude of ease he adopted, standing, his hands clasped behind his back, she felt he had enormous constrained vitality. Then some couples moved between them, blocking her view, and she joined Robert and his wife, Teresa, standing with Charles and Eliza Dyce.

Robert patted Charles lightly on the arm. "It is the most terrific thing. Can you believe Charles has been made Sheriff of the Straits Settlements?"

"Sheriff?" Charlotte smiled at Charles. "Is that something like the Sheriff of Nottingham, Charles? Will you prevent the rich from being robbed to help the poor?"

Charles smiled. "Indeed, madam, I shall, though our local Chinese Robin Hoods are more inclined to keep their ill-gotten gains to themselves."

"Not so romantic, Kitt," Robert said. "More like the local magistrate."

He turned to Charles. "But not unworthy for all that, eh? Considering what a lazy devil he was in college, dreaming and sketching, totally lacking ambition—the despair of his good father."

Charles laughed, and they talked of their days at Marischal College in Aberdeen, which both acknowledged had not been onerous. Charlotte smiled and linked arms with her brother. He and Charles Dyce were great friends and shared a love for amateur theatricals.

"The most important subject was 'regular attendance', although I occasionally enjoyed Virgil," Robert said.

Charles laughed. "I spent most of my time drawing. It is fortunate indeed that the same examination questions appeared year after year else neither of us should ever have graduated."

Robert grinned and turned to Charlotte. "You must send Alex and Adam when they are old enough. What it lacks in rigour it makes up for in social enjoyment and useful introductions."

Alexander and Adam? To Scotland? Charlotte had not thought about this. It was commonplace enough to send one's children home for their later schooling. She supposed that was the right thing to do.

Charlotte suddenly and deeply missed Tigran standing by her side, so solid and loving, supporting her in everything, adoring their children. She could have consulted him. He would have known what to do. She felt a great loneliness descend on her and pleading the heat, walked quickly out onto the verandah and looked down to the town.

From Government House atop the hill, at night the European town was all but invisible. Lights traced the long, dark curve of the river in the Chinese town; brightness came from the lanterns of the boats huddled together in the middle of the river. From here it was easy to see why the Chinese called this part "the belly of the carp", for it swelled plumply. On the harbour, the lamps of the night watch, like glinting sparks, bobbed on the ships at anchor. She took her handkerchief and pinched it into her eyes, breathing deeply, the effort not to sob taking all her will. It took her like this, in the most unexpected moments.

In the distance, on the edge of the world, a sheet of blue lightning burst silently across the sky, illuminating briefly the forest of masts on the water. She stopped crying. Was it a sign? Charlotte knew she was becoming obsessed with signs but she could not quite help herself. Every natural manifestation seemed a signal from him sent to comfort her: a swift breeze on a windless day, the end of a rainstorm, a bird's passage. She smiled, knowing he would have laughed at her. She wanted to feel his arms around her, lean her head back against his chest, holding her secure. Oh, Tigran, she thought, why?

"Mrs Manouk?" A voice spoke from the darkness of the verandah, and she started and turned.

"It is John Thomson. I am sorry to have startled you."

Charlotte shook her head.

"No, Mr Thomson, not at all. I was taking some air, waiting for our illustrious guests to arrive."

Thomson came up next to her.

"May I ...? Would it be all right to say how sorry I am about ...?"

Charlotte put her hand on his arm, stopping him. John Thomson was an architect and the Government Surveyor of the Straits Settlements, and Charlotte liked him very much. He was slim and pale, with short, dark, wavy hair, a long face, a long nose and soulful eyes. He was young, she knew, twenty-two, yet he had a grave earnestness which made him seem older.

John thought that Charlotte Manouk was the loveliest woman he had ever met. She was dressed in sombre half mourning, a deep purple dress with black trim and a black shawl. Her only jewellery was a silver and pearl locket and pearl earrings. He could see she was still grieving. He was very sensitive to such matters and thought women the most spiritual of creatures. These widow's weeds could not disguise her beauty though—the lustre of her black hair, the depth of her violet eyes, her grace. John had had experiences in the jungles of Malaya when he was a mere lad in his teens, surveying plantations in Penang and on the mainland. He had been offered young girls, the custom shocking but commonplace. He was not tempted. When the time was right he would marry, and the native women held no charms for him at all.

He gazed at Charlotte with feelings of profound respect for her widowhood, but stirrings also of something else. She had taken a mirror from her purse and was wiping the corners of her eyes. She had been crying, he saw, and his heart went to her. The stirrings turned into a tiny trickle.

"Mrs Manouk," he began and she smiled.

"John, call me Charlotte, or Kitt, everyone does who knows me. We are almost the same age and cannot be so formal, surely."

He bowed, disarmed. "Thank you. Charlotte, er ... Kitt, would it interest you to accompany me on some of my outings? I sketch a great deal and move about the island continually. I have a sailboat. If one day ..."

Charlotte turned to face him.

"Yes, John, I would like that. Thank you."

She smiled at him and he felt enveloped in radiance. The mere trickle of a moment before turned into a stream, and he felt a rush of warm happiness enfold him.

The band suddenly struck up, announcing the arrival of the guest of honour and John offered Charlotte his arm to return to the ballroom.

8

Zhen rose in frustration. Noan was asleep and the night was hot. He went to the window to catch a breath of air from the air well. This irksome presence every night made him short-tempered. He longed for his freedom. The arrival of Noan's period yet again had given him some relief though it was a deep disappointment. He had stayed away for eight days. Eight precious days, spent with Qian. Now, again, he had made love to his wife. He strove to please her, making a link between joy and fruitfulness. The rashes she had sometimes had disappeared, and she seemed fresh and happy; her balance had returned. But his seemed increasingly out of alignment.

He leaned his arms against the sides of the window and stared down into the well. The moon was full, he had just realised, and was reflected like a silver orb in the water which lay on the stone floor. He looked up, and it was overhead, and the moonshine was so bright it illuminated everything around him. A faint smell of sandalwood floated on the air. Its odour kept off mosquitos and the servants burnt it in the courtyard.

His thoughts turned as always to her, to Xia Lou. He wanted to see her, to talk to her, though it was impossible. He had bitten back these desires for months and now the heat and this frustration and his annoyance with Noan put him in a black temper. He decided to leave, to go to his home on Circular Road.

He dressed quickly and went out into the corridor. As he went down the stairs he heard a noise, a door opening somewhere. He stopped briefly then went on. A candle was burning in the courtyard and the moon was so bright it was like a dusky evening. Then he saw Lilin entering the courtyard from the kitchen and stopped. She looked up and started, giving a small cry, seeing his shape standing there in the moonlight. She had not been sure if he would be here tonight, for Noan's period had just finished. Her heart gave a painful leap. The sight of him—just this—made her pulse race. She could not help it. She had wanted him since the first moment she had seen him at her sister's wedding. In the moonlight, in silhouette, his physical presence made her weak.

All but stunned that she was here, at this hour, Zhen went up to her and without a word took her by the arm and half dragged her through the courtyard. The noise, small though it was, roused a servant from the kitchen and Zhen waved him away. Damn it, there would be servant gossip tomorrow. Taking up a night lamp from a table, he pulled Lilin into a small room near the side of the building which was used for stores and shut the door.

"It is two o'clock in the morning. What are you doing, where have you been?"

Zhen was seething. The words escaped from his lips in a half-whispered fury of Baba Malay. This was too much. He was in charge of this household and here was this woman, against everything decent, coming and going as she pleased. If Tan were to find out ... Zhen felt keenly Tan's censure, his own loss of dignity. He almost flushed with shame.

Lilin was silent. His physical proximity had made her weak at the knees. His grip on her arm was painful, yet it filled her with excruciating pleasure. She put out her hand and touched his cheek and he sprang away, dropping her arm, as if he had been stung. He had never hit a woman in his life, but his hand trembled with fury, and he controlled himself with difficulty.

She stopped moving and looked at him in the flicker of the candlelight. "I do what I want." She made to move past him and he barred her way with his arm.

"I do what I want, as you do." She whispered it, looking up into his face. "As you do with your white whore."

Zhen could not believe her boldness; she had no shame. That she should compare her actions, a woman, with his. To call Xia Lou a whore! Momentarily he could find no words.

Lilin looked into his eyes and her gaze held them. Her tone changed, her face softened.

"But I will stop. I will stop if you will be my lover. I will obey you, worship you." She sank to her knees and wrapped her arms around his legs.

"Please, Zhen."

Zhen felt such a confusion in his brain that he could not think how to respond, what to do. This woman, this sister-in-law, this wife of Ah Teo, was proposing that, in return for her obedience, he should sleep with her. She must be deranged. He was still at a loss, his mind racing, when suddenly her hands moved between his legs and she put her mouth against him. He jerked backwards quickly, away from her.

"Get up Lilin and stop this. You bring shame on your parents, your husband and your sister."

He went to the door but before he could open it, she said very quietly, "You think your dear wife, my dear sister, is so pure, eh?"

Zhen rounded on her. "What?" he hissed.

"Before you demand obedience from your sister-in-law, you should perhaps first see if your wife is so very obedient and compliant."

Zhen could not fully grasp what she was saying. His Baba Malay was much improved, but some things he did not follow. However, he understood she was accusing Noan of something.

He gripped her arms and shook her. Then he saw the look of sexual longing in the droop of her eyes and let her go. Lilin picked up her embroidered bag from the floor and straightened up.

"Ask Noan why she is not pregnant after three months. Ask her what the herbs are in the old *kamcheng* pot in the kitchen," she said as she pushed past him.

He let her go. He would have to deal with her tomorrow. And he would speak to Ah Teo, this man who could not control his wife. He felt a leaden resentment towards Ah Teo for putting him in this position. Zhen had no desire to be the ruler of this house, though he knew it was his duty. What bad luck had struck him, to have such a fiend under his roof.

And now Noan. Could it be true, that she was deceiving him? He felt a small pain in his mind. He would have sworn on all the gods that Noan was incapable of deception, of such a dereliction of her duty to bear children, to give him a son, to give her father posterity. These months in her bed, his own wishes put to one side. His bad temper became worse as he thought of it, and he left the room and took the stairs two at a time, back to their bedroom.

She was still sleeping quietly when he entered the room. He lit a candle and went to the bed. She was curled up towards the wooden wall of the back of the bed and he could not see her face. He knelt next to her and shook her, and she woke suddenly, alarmed and frightened, and looked about her. When she saw him, she laughed in uncomprehending, nervous relief. He could see she was trembling. He had scared her. Zhen felt a cold calmness descend on him.

"Noan, three months and still no pregnancy. Tell me about the herbs in the *kamcheng* pot."

Noan looked at him, her eyes wide and filled with fear. Her lip began to tremble. "How ...?" she stuttered and began to cry.

"It's true, eh, you have been deceiving me. Not just me but your father and mother too, to whom you owe everything, every duty." He put the candle on a small table.

"I ..." she began. He waited. She wanted to tell him of her love for him, this endless desire for his presence, for the passion she had for him. She wanted to tell him that there would be a son, many sons, if only she could have him for a bit longer for herself. She wanted to tell him how she longed to share his life, his secrets, his pain, his desires. She wanted to be his wife in every way. But there were no words. She hung her head.

He looked down at her. "I will go now. You will destroy these herbs, stop taking them. I will come back in one week, for three nights. If you are not pregnant by the end of this month I will not come again. I will suppose you barren and must think of taking a second wife. Do you understand?"

Zhen did not wait for her reply. He turned and left, anxious to be gone, away from this house. He felt a moment of sorrow at treating Noan in such a way. She was a sweet, timid woman and he liked her, but he could not put up with this deception. It was impossible.

He guessed her reasons. He was well aware of her passion for him. He could not return it nor had he any need to. These were not the requirements of his marriage. He forgave her but he had to scare her. His threat to take a second wife was hollow, for the last thing he wanted was another woman, but he hoped it would shock her.

Noan turned and buried her face into the bolster. She began to cry. To lose him? The thought was unbearable. He had been so severe. How had he found out? Then she forgot this question as her body shook with sobs. She was guilty—what did it matter how he knew? He was right. She would destroy the herbs. He would come back; he would come back, but only for three nights. She began to tremble. A second wife! Her greatest fear. She must have a son. She turned on her side and pulled her knees to her chest and scratched her arms, which felt suddenly as if they were on fire.

9

Lilin looked at her sister over the kitchen table. She could see that Noan was quite miserable this morning. Usually, after a night and morning with Zhen, she was radiant. When she knew Zhen was in the bedroom Lilin listened in the robing room, heard them talking, heard Noan's moans. It made her half-crazed with desire. She had grown to hate Noan. Lilin could not understand how this plain little toad had got Zhen. Lilin was the beauty; he should always have been hers.

She rose and went to her sister, patting her on the arm. "What is the matter big sister? You look unwell."

Noan did not raise her head. She had, after furious thought and bouts of crying, come to the conclusion that only Lilin could have told Zhen. Only she would dare address Zhen in such a straightforward and bold way. Lilin was out of control; everyone knew it. Noan had been told that Zhen was coming to dinner tonight expressly to speak to Ah Teo.

Noan was pounding lemongrass, shallots and chillies in a large stone pestle and mortar, and the smell of bruised and pungent spices filled the air. She was making a favourite of Zhen's: *belachan* clams. She would add galangal, blue ginger and much less *belachan* shrimp paste than for her father, for Zhen liked it less sour. Both sisters should be enjoying this time together, cooking for their husbands. Lilin was supposed to make a favourite dish of Ah Teo's, but she had not bothered with any of this for years. Occasionally Lilin supervised the maids as they cooked dishes she liked, but other than that she rarely set foot in the kitchen. She liked to be out of the house and would disappear for hours to the market. The maid often came home with the shopping alone, though, and Noan had long since stopped thinking about what her sister could be up to. But now Lilin had interfered in Noan's business, in her husband's.

"Leave me alone," she said and continued pounding. This morning she had burnt the herbs in the *kamcheng* pot.

Lilin sat down again. "What is the matter, what have I done?"

Noan looked up from her task, stopped pounding and gripped the pestle. She threw a look of such dislike at Lilin that Lilin was taken aback and rose quickly and left the kitchen. Noan returned to pounding, taking her anger out on the chillies.

Lilin went through the central courtyard and glanced into the pond where goldfish were flitting. The mid-morning sun was slanting into the open-air well. She loved this place, with its cool tiles and great pots of bamboo and plum. She had been born in this house, her father's, confined here at twelve to prepare herself for a husband. She had studied the cooking, the beading and embroidery just like Noan. Everyone had remarked on her sewing skills. Everyone had said how lovely she was. She had made herself ready and then she had seen Zhen go not to her but to her drab sister. And she had been served up with Ah Teo, clever and thin. His legs were like spindles, his shoulders bony, his chin sharp and pointy. He had terrible skin and was useless in bed. Every day Zhen was before her eyes, tall, muscled and handsome, prodigious, she knew, sexually prodigious.

Ah Teo had produced a pillow book. Even now she could find delight in the ridiculous sight of him in his nightgown with his stick legs emerging, clutching a book of sexual positions which, she supposed, she was meant to assume. Unfortunately, his member was not up to the task and she had laughed until tears streamed down her face. He had not returned for many weeks. Eventually, she knew, they must do it, and she had let him plant his disgusting seed inside her. She had become pregnant. For months she had found a great and unexpected happiness. And she had given birth to a son, the first grandson of the Tan family. She had outdone her sister, who had only been able to manage two girls. This boy, this son and grandson, what happiness had this event caused. She had been feted, praised and adored. She had even found a momentary affection for Ah Teo.

And then, at three months, he had fallen ill, this tiny boy, and died. The world of the household came crashing down. A pall had lain over the family for a long time. In the wake of her grief, Lilin had simply thrown caution to the wind.

Ah Teo had ceased to come to her and soon she had met the English trader in the market place. One day she had sent the maid home with the shopping and gone with him to his house. She couldn't speak a word of English nor he a word of Chinese, but he was big, well-built and knew what he was doing—speech was unnecessary. He treated her like a whore, and she liked it, couldn't wait for the feel of his rough hands on her skin, holding her, making her do things she hardly knew she liked. Threats and money had kept her maid silent, and she had met him on and off until he left Singapore. She had had one abortion and had got a disease from him, *lin bing*, a yellow pus disease. She had been terrified, but her maid had got herbs from the medicine shop, and it had gone away eventually. She knew she was probably scarred inside and there would never be any children.

Through the trader and others after him, she had learned English. This knowledge she kept secret, but she could easily understand when Zhen and Ah Teo spoke together in English which they sometimes did.

The lack of sons had been a subject of enormous discussion. Noan seemed to have difficulty conceiving and Lilin knew the reason. Her father had recently proposed adoption of a boy for both Zhen and Ah Teo, so anxious was he for the matter of posterity to be settled. That or take on new wives. There was no need for Noan to be so annoyed. She was breaking all the rules. She well knew her only job was to bring forth sons. As for Ah Teo, if he wanted a second wife, good luck to him.

Lilin looked at herself in the mirror. She was just twenty-one years old but she felt, sometimes, like an old woman. She was still lovely, her skin fine and fair as a candle, for which she had been nicknamed. She applied the faintest touch of rouge. Last night she had been with the Frenchman who was, she could see, rather in love with her. He was a romantic, this Gaston, old and wealthy. When

73

she was available, she sent a note with her maid and they walked to Commercial Square, where he had a covered carriage waiting to take her over into the European town, to his hotel, The London Hotel, which stood on the corner of High Street and the Plain.

Mrs Gaston and his children were in France for a year at least, if they returned at all. Lilin knew that some European women could not stand the sun and heat and left. At the hotel she had her own room furnished in French style. Gaston gave her European gowns, make-up and jewellery, and she was his jewel. She could speak English and nobody in the Chinese town, least of all her father, suspected her of being there. Gaston had no inkling whose daughter she was. Her father and mother were far away on River Valley road. Usually, Ah Teo and Zhen came to the house in Market Street only to eat.

She had quickly discovered the separation of the two towns. Chinese merchants might meet up occasionally with English merchants at balls and dinners but otherwise never came to this side of the river. All Gaston's staff were Indian or Malay, even the cooks. If Gaston expected Mr Whampoa or a party of Chinese, she simply did not come. She knew everyone there thought she was a common whore, like the other Chinese girls who came to the men at the hotel, but she did not mind in the least. After all, in most senses she was. But Gaston knew she was not like them, attached to an *ah ku* house. He knew she was different, but he asked no questions and protected her.

With Gaston she was free. She learned to drink French wine and smoke a cigarette. She could do what she wanted. His body on hers later was a small price to pay, for she liked him. He was a tender man. He had been an actor, sang French songs and made her laugh.

Now she was idle. She was slightly anxious at Zhen's discovery of her last night. But, after all, what could Zhen and Ah Teo do? What possible course of action was open to them? She speculated that they would try to bully and intimidate her, but what did she care? Ah Teo was never at home to watch what she did. It would be horribly inconvenient for him when he'd rather be with his whore. Zhen too could not watch her every moment. Would they lock her up? The idea was ludicrous. Lilin knew that her father and mother would not want her in the house at River Valley Road, where there would be bad feeling and arguments. Her father was busy with his new concubine and second family. No, they would do better just to leave her alone. She rather wished now that she had not told Zhen. What did she care if Noan never got pregnant? It had been impulsive—but she had done it to get revenge on him, to shock him. And she had. She shook her head and smiled. No, there was nothing they could do.

She heard a child cry. It was Lian—Lotus Flower—Zhen's second daughter, her niece. She was five years old and the prettiest little girl. She reminded Lilin of herself, and she had a soft spot for this child. She still thought of her little son, such a lovely boy, though she knew she should not. A dead son was like a curse on a house, forgotten instantly, disposed of quickly and without ceremony. But in her heart she still held him dear and though she knew she should not, she sometimes went to the temple and lit incense and said a prayer for him.

She went along the landing and saw Lian being rocked by the maid. She had fallen and bumped her head. Lilin went up and took Lian into her arms. Her mouth was a little pink bud and her hair a long, black shining tail. Lian hugged her aunt. She rocked Lian and kissed her gently on the cheek.

Noan had come when she heard the cry and now contemplated her sister and her daughter. She was still angry but the sight of Lilin with Lian softened her heart. Lilin had lost her only child, a son. Though the house could not mourn, the women did. Noan, as a mother, had felt the dreadful importance of this loss. Now, she suddenly felt ashamed. She should have been pregnant now with Zhen's son. He was right; she had a duty to her father, to her husband. Only a son could bring posterity and eternity to the family. Only a son could honour Zhen. Her selfishness was unforgiveable. She went up to Lilin and touched her daughter's head. She could see Lilin's love for this particular child.

"Younger sister. Will you not try to have another child? I know you do not care for your husband but perhaps ..."

Without answering or even looking at Noan, Lilin passed Lian into her sister's arms and walked quickly from the room.

10

Charlotte sat in the new public library of Singapore in the west wing of the Institution. She was waiting for Alexander's class to finish. She rose and went to the window and looked down over the gardens. The breeze moved the tender leaves of the trees in the garden, flickering sunlight on the ground. She glanced through the book in her hand. *Oliver Twist*, by Mr Dickens, a man she approved of wholeheartedly in his recently reported support for the abolition of slavery.

She heard her name called and turned her head to see a face she cared for very much. It was the Munshi Abdullah and he was grinning from ear to ear. She had been his most enthusiastic pupil, enjoyed learning Malay and talking about poetry. Now she rose, and he took her hand and shook it enthusiastically. She curtsied very low. She was delighted to see him.

He was unchanged: the same coppery skin with the very white teeth. The same kindly eyes with the squint. The same melodious tones. He spoke superb English, was a devout Muslim but worked tirelessly with Benjamin Keaseberry, improving his Malay skills, assisting him at his school by the Rochor River and at the Malay School in Telok Belangah, which his own sons attended. He translated biblical texts and the gospels for Benjamin's Mission Press on Commercial Square. He had been Raffles's scribe and knew everything about the establishment and growth of Singapore.

When she told him she was waiting for her son, he laughed and said he would wait with her. He would like to meet her boy. His own children, four boys, were well, the eldest ones good students.

Charlotte knew he had lost his daughter when she was merely eight and his wife, in childbirth, a few years later. He was Malacca born and bred. After the death of his wife and daughter he could not bear to stay in the house, which had too many memories. He had sold up everything and now made his life in Singapore, where he was esteemed and sought after as a teacher and a scholar.

Together he and Charlotte wandered slowly towards the opposite end of the Institution where the boys had their classes. The centre of the building was occupied by a small girls' school. "I have been busy," he told Charlotte, "on Benjamin's encouragement and John Thomson's, writing my memoirs. I have chosen to write them in the Malay vernacular. Benjamin agrees that is the most lively and I have a certain pretension to be the first such author."

Charlotte smiled. "How wonderful, Munshi. You have such a lot to tell. The years of Malacca, the life of Raffles and Olivia, the birth of Singapore." Charlotte could see the pride he had from talking of this work. The Munshi was the most unusual Malay she had ever met. His mind was wide and receptive; he sought the knowledge of the Enlightenment with a thirst that distinguished him utterly from many of his compatriots, at least any that she had ever met. She knew of his critical analysis of the Malay ruling class and its despotic and feudal concept of *kerajaan*, which squashed initiative and concentrated power into the hands of the Rajah. This is what the British called Malay laziness, this keeping down of the people, their lack of schools, which kept the people ignorant and fearful. This the Munshi could not abide.

These were ideas her own mind had grappled with in Java. The Munshi admired the English for their organisation and their liberalism. Not for their power, but for the way they administered power. His admiration stemmed from what he perceived as their rational thinking, purged of religious superstition. He sought for his own people those fruits, but she was certain he was a man ahead of his age. To speak to her, a woman, of these things: this alone set him apart.

As they talked, a bell rang, and within a few minutes Charlotte saw Alexander, wandering along the corridor, chattering gaily to a very slight Chinese boy. Alex was so well built and tall for his age that the Chinese child looked tiny. When Alex saw her, he smiled, a light in his eyes, and her heart constricted. She loved him so much. He came up to her and put his hand in hers. Then, with all the dignity of his seven years, he bowed to the man his mother was talking to and introduced his small friend, Sang Ah Soon, asking to be introduced to the Munshi. Abdullah was delighted and smiled at the boy. When he found the Munshi was a Malay gentleman and an English scholar, he composed himself very tightly and said,

"*Selamat tengahari, nama saya Iskandar.*"

Abdullah beamed and Charlotte laughed. Zan had Malay and Hokkien classes and he was learning very quickly.

"Iskandar," the Munshi turned to Charlotte. "A noble name and one well suited to our world. In a few years I will be his tutor, if you agree."

Charlotte looked at him. To have such a man tutor her son as he had herself! To have him spend the pleasant hours discussing language and literature with Zan, opening Zan's mind, this fatherless boy, now Tigran was gone, expanding his world view, his whole being. She felt, she knew absurdly, that he was as Aristotle to the ancient Alexander, and she felt a tear come to her eye.

The Munshi saw her face and was touched. He very quickly said, "Will you join me soon to visit Kampong Glam and the Sultan's Palace? There are stories I can tell and a tiger to see."

He looked at Zan and saw the boy's eyes gleam, and felt the same attraction and liking he had for his mother. He turned his gaze to the small Chinese boy. "And Ah Soon too, if his father agrees. You know the boy's father very well, Charlotte," he said, smiling conspiratorially.

Ah Soon looked down shyly and said nothing, and Charlotte looked quizzically at the Munshi. Zan tugged at her hand and she could see a friendship had formed. But who was the child's mysterious father that she knew so well? Not Zhen—he had girls.

The Munshi smiled even wider. "This is your pupil, Qian's, first-born son."

Qian's son! She looked at him intently and now saw a certain likeness in the pointy ears and the shape of his jaw.

The Munshi departed with promises as yet uncertain to be fulfilled and Ah Soon joined his amah, who was waiting with the carriage to take him home to High Street.

They went outside into the afternoon sunshine. The day was hot but the wind from the sea cooled them, and Charlotte had chosen to walk home. They wandered through the shady gardens of the Institution slowly, Charlotte asking Zan questions about his day, Zan filled with the excitement of school and learning and friends.

Then there was a small squeal behind them, a girlish squeal, and they stopped and turned. A pretty little girl, brown-eyed with dark ringlets shining and jumping round her face, came running down the path, followed by a young woman. Charlotte's eyes were taking in the girl, pretty now of course, but whom she could see would be a great beauty, so it was some moments before she looked up and with a certain shock, recognised the face of Shilah, Robert's *nyai*.

Shilah too, was in a state of some confusion. The children had quickly joined hands and gone to chase some squirrels which were racing around the big trees. It was obvious that they knew each other. Charlotte remembered that there was a girl's school in the central part of the building. There were only eleven students, six boarders and five day students. This girl was a day student, obviously.

Charlotte had not seen Shilah for years. A silence developed, unbidden, as they watched the children. "Her name is Amber," Shilah said finally.

Charlotte opened her eyes very wide. Amber! It was an unusual name, so very unusual, yet it was the English way of saying the name of her own mother, Ambre, the Mauritian Creole woman who had married her Scottish father. Amber! How could she be called Amber ... unless ... She looked intently at Shilah and Shilah nodded.

"Yes, Robert's daughter. He did not tell you." She smiled ruefully. "They are cousins."

Charlotte was astounded, absolutely. A daughter! Robbie had a child, and he had not told her. She could not believe it. Since his marriage Robert had not talked of Shilah. But not to reveal this! It was incredible.

Charlotte looked again at Shilah. She was unchanged, still a very lovely woman, but something different about her eyes. Charlotte knew she had seen sadness. Robert's marriage, of course, it must have caused profound pain. She felt her heart go to this woman but Shilah was guarded and showed no emotion.

"I ..." Charlotte faltered, feeling the injustice of this relationship which Robbie had begun, feeling the guilt of a sister. Shilah said nothing, watching her, watching with one eye the children playing.

"I am sorry," Charlotte said finally. "Sorry for this trouble Robert has caused you."

Shilah did not move. It was some minutes until she spoke, "I would like the children to be friends, cousins, to know each other. Robert has recognised her legally, you know." Shilah looked up, into Charlotte's eyes. "He has recognised her as his daughter. She has his name and he supports us. He is a good man. His wife will soon have her baby but she too knows about Amber. Do not blame him. My life is of my making, I wanted your brother."

Charlotte looked down at her shoes. Shilah took a step forward and put her hand onto Charlotte's. "Do not blame him please," Shilah said. "He loves Amber, remembers your mother in her name. It pleases him I think; he does what he can. This is the world we live in. I would ask only that Amber, Alexander and Adam can be friends, cousins. Is that possible?"

Charlotte looked at Shilah's hand on hers. She remembered everything Robbie had told her of this woman. Shilah had been the illegitimate and unwanted result of a momentary encounter between an English soldier and an Indian convict woman, both gone or dead before she was six months old. George Coleman had taken her into his house and given her an education, taught her English and to read and write, but she had known no true mother or father. He had sought a husband for her, but she had fallen in love with Robert, and that had been that. She had been Robbie's *nyai* for years, until he had contracted to marry Teresa. Charlotte had met her only once before, years ago, and her abiding memory of Shilah had been her quiet assurance and her confidence in Robert.

Shilah had not changed though her life had obviously been

turned upside down. And she still loved Robert, Charlotte could see that. It was something that always shook Charlotte's heart, a love for her brother, for she too loved Robert unconditionally, unreservedly, utterly. Their life since they had been no more than ten and eleven had been together: parentless, alone, transported by strife from the warmth of climate and family in Madagascar to Scotland and the chilly embrace of their widowed grandmother. Their Aunt Jeanne and their cousin Duncan had loved them, though, and this—and more than this, their own closeness and devotion—had got them through childhood and beyond. Charlotte must love anyone who loved Robert; she covered Shilah's hand with hers.

"Yes, that is right. They are cousins, she is Robbie's daughter. They must be friends. And we must be friends." She looked into Shilah's eyes and smiled. Shilah too, smiled, and they recognised something within the other: a love unacknowledged perhaps, by any but themselves. Emotionally, how was she different to Shilah? Silently, secretly and hopelessly loving one man. Charlotte looked over at these two children who could never know their fathers properly and felt a deep sadness.

Shilah could not know any of this, of course, but Charlotte admired as she had years before, this woman's smart and deep resourcefulness. She would abide and deal with her life as it came. It was an admirable quality. Charlotte would only learn later the price Shilah had paid for this calm and accepting nature.

"Tomorrow, after school, let us take the children to my home on North Bridge Road. They can play in the garden and we can talk," she offered. Charlotte thought at first Shilah was going to refuse but the other woman's body suddenly lost its tension and she smiled and nodded, withdrawing her hand.

"Thank you, yes."

Now Shilah called to Amber and the girl came running, flushed and pretty. Zan followed her, his long hair flowing around his face, sweating, and Charlotte bent and kissed his damp, salty cheek. Tomorrow she would make sure he knew that Amber was his blood and he should love her as she loved Robbie. And Amber too, would know Charlotte was her aunt. Charlotte smiled suddenly, happy to have this niece, to be as kind and loving to her as Aunt Jeanne had been to Robert and herself.

But she would like to have a few words with this brother of hers.

11

Boat Quay was teeming with its usual crowded and noisy bustle. John Thomson's bridge felt sturdy underfoot. It had replaced the Monkey Bridge built over twenty years before, which had become so shaky, worm-ridden and unsafe that it had been demolished, leaving Coleman's seven-arched brick span as the only means to go, by foot or carriage, from one side of the river to the other. The walk was longer and since most people went on foot, there was a great brouhaha. Butterworth had gotten into a tussle with the merchants; it was not the government's business to replace the bridge and they might as well get used to it for he would not change his mind. *The Free Press* had been full of the business and the matter was resolved, ultimately, when someone had searched the records and found that indeed, the government had engaged to maintain a bridge at this place. With a great deal of annoyed mutterings, Butterworth had been forced to find funds and Thomson had been engaged.

The bridge was a simple wooden construction joining North and South Bridge Roads. A footbridge on one side allowed a view down over the town and river. Charlotte stopped and gazed on the town. Adam, at her side, knelt, holding the railings and peering down at the mass of kajang-roofed boats lying below. A young native boy looked up at him curiously. Adam smiled and waved but the little boy remained expressionless.

He looked up at his mother and she shrugged. He was little and loving and wanted everyone to be his friend, even the little boy on the boat, so far removed from him in everything. His *babu* trailed behind them, and when she saw Adam pout a little she came up quickly and took him into her arms, hugging him. Charlotte shook her head—such a spoilt child he would be if she let him. But she let it go, and they continued over the bridge and down onto the quayside.

Alexander was in school. She had arranged to lunch with Teresa on Commercial Square and to view the extraordinary new invention from America, the Howe's Automatic Sewing Machine, which was being demonstrated at Little, Cursetjee & Company.

She deliberately chose to direct her steps in front of Baba Tan's godown. She would greet him if he was there. Why not? She knew him well. And if Zhen happened to be there too, well ... The little rush of blood to her face she brought under control immediately and fanned herself.

Whampoa greeted her. He was outside his vast godown, which serviced the British Navy. They knew each other well. Whampoa's English was formidable. He spoke it as well as any Englishman and better sometimes. Charlotte knew now, that his real name was Hoo Ah Kay, Whampoa being the island of his birth and the name taken by his father for his business. They chatted a little while, Adam, shy, hiding his face in the *babu's* sarong.

Whampoa whispered a word to a boy and he ran off, returning within a few minutes with the old sweet maker, his daughter and his cart. Charlotte smiled. She had seen the sweet maker at work before but Adam had not.

He was making dragon's beard, a Chinese sweet. The man took a pliable yellow disc of palm sugar. He began to knead and stretch the disc until it had a large hole in the middle. He wrapped the disc around his hands, dipped it quickly in rice flour to prevent sticking and began to pass it through his fingers, like a skein of wool, stretching and folding. As if by magic the one strand became two, then four. He dipped again, the rice flour flying and floating as the strands doubled and redoubled. Again and again, that's eighty, now two hundred and twenty, more rice flour, now six hundred and forty. Whampoa smiled at Adam's face, watching entranced as the sugar became more and more strands, finer and finer, the rice powder filling the air like snow. Finally the man stopped; the yellow orb was transformed into the finest silk-like threads, ten thousand of them, shimmering like a snow maiden's hair, as the powder drifted down to the ground, surrounding the sweet maker in a field of white.

The man laid the delicate bundle of threads on a tray. He cut them quickly into short lengths. His young daughter sprinkled roasted peanuts, sesame seeds and shredded coconut into each of the beards and folded them into a cocoon. The whole entertainment had taken no more than a few minutes. Adam's mouth was standing open.

Whampoa took one of the sweets and offered it to him. All shyness fled. He took the dragon's beard candy and put it into his mouth, then smiled. Whampoa gave some coins to the sweet maker, who quickly wrapped the remaining sweets in a banana leaf cone, handed the cone to Adam's *babu* and with a toothless grin, moved off.

Charlotte turned then to see what Whampoa was looking at. It was the top-hatted figure of Baba Tan, who had come up to her. She curtsied very deeply to him and made Adam bow. She knew very well Baba Tan was utterly charmed by these English gestures.

"Mrs Mah Nuk, how sad to see you in this way, but how nice you have returned to Singapore."

She nodded at Baba Tan and introduced him to Adam. As he shook hands cheerfully with the little boy, he took her in. She was even more beautiful than before.

Children had not affected her figure, still willowy and graceful. She was dressed in that tight fashion, the bodice revealing curves the way the English women did so immodestly for one's delectation but yet so modest, he supposed they thought. The bodice was high for daytime dress but Tan had attended enough English dinner parties to know that the neckline ebbed a good six inches after sunset, revealing the white European bosom, sometimes to excellent effect depending on the wearer. Charlotte's skirt was full and flowed gracefully around her. The colour was very becoming, a dark blue muslin, trimmed in white, her hat the same. She was in half-widow's clothes. He prided himself on knowing a great deal about the customs of these quaint people. He was also curious as to what would happen when she saw Zhen whom he knew was working in the godown today with Ah Teo, his other son-in-law, on the accounts.

Tan knew a thing or two about Zhen and Charlotte, the main one being that they had been lovers: before she married and after. The other was that it was over, he had been assured. But then she had been away; now she was back. He hoped he would not have to be severe with Zhen. He could see her appeal though. Most English women he found appallingly unattractive but her ... jet-black hair, beautiful, exotic eyes, like a princess from a far land. An ebbing neckline would, he knew, look very well on her. She was the sort of woman, he imagined, that if you were rich enough you sought as a foreign concubine. He dismissed these thoughts as a little unworthy but was plagued still with curiosity.

Tan invited Charlotte into the shade of the verandah, for the day was getting hot but she declined charmingly and with just the barest glance into the cool, dark shadows of the godown, she opened her parasol. The *babu* swept Adam into her arms and they quickly walked down the quay to Tavern Street and turned, disappearing from view.

Zhen turned back into the godown. He had watched from the darkness as she talked to Tan and had looked at the little boy by her side. He could see a resemblance to the father. He had made love to her as she carried this child, caressed the swelling belly, felt its movements under her skin. It was as if it was his own, as if he had nurtured the seed inside her, given her the strength of his very essence.

He had known his resolution would be difficult, but until now, he had not realised how difficult. Every emotion was the same as the day he had seen her on this very spot years ago. She was like light, surrounded by light. He loved her. It was irresistible, this feeling for her, like a mighty bore on a river, swamping the banks of his heart. He clenched his fist and stayed his mind from running down these uncontrolled ways. But he was filled with gladness that she was here on this island.

He heard Tan come in from the street and moved quickly to the back. He could not bear to talk of her to anyone just now.

Charlotte swallowed her disappointment. She should not long to see him as she did but her thoughts would not always obey her. Then she smiled and took a deep breath. Meeting was inevitable, and how she would smile at him and wish him happy. She took Adam's hand and he began skipping by her side.

12

Charlotte put down her cup and gazed around her. This was a room she knew very well. It was the drawing room of the Mission House on the corner of Bras Basah and Victoria Streets, where she had so often sat with Benjamin Keaseberry's first wife. The second Mrs Keaseberry was Elizabeth Scott, niece of the harbour master.

When first they met, Elizabeth had been a flame-haired, buxom thirteen-year-old. Now she was twenty-two, still buxom and flame-haired, with very white skin which she took pains to protect from the sun. She was also very pregnant.

Elizabeth was irate and Charlotte suspected that she was often irate or at least irritated. Benjamin, she had told Charlotte, was as scandalised as herself. They were discussing the actions of Butterworth in relation to her uncle. Under the pretext of the man having entered his illustrious presence dressed incorrectly—that is, as he always dressed— Butterworth had dismissed him and replaced him with a favourite of his own. After so many years of service. It had taken him down, yes. Certainly he was very low. "Poor Uncle," she wailed and Charlotte waited for her to regain her composure.

Her grievance was justified. William Scott had been harbour master for twenty years. To be summarily dismissed on such a flimsy accusation! It was a sign of things to come, she was certain. Soon the new people coming from England would be at home as much in this wonderful exotic island as they were in Watford! The thought was shudderingly awful. The two other women present sighed in sympathy.

Maryanne Norris was the wife of the Assistant to the Resident Councillor. She had just finished bemoaning the terrible situation for civil servants. The officials were in a pitiable way. The East India Company ran Singapore on a shoestring. Government salaries had remained the same for more than fifteen years despite the steep rise in the cost of living, the quadrupling of the population and a threefold increase in trade. It was a disgrace.

The government in Calcutta was obsessed with reports and statistics and with no literate clerical class, it fell to all the civil servants to spend pointless hours in their compilation. The schemes which had formerly existed to pay tuition fees and bonuses to officials who attained proficiency in Malay, Siamese or Chinese had been abolished years before. Charlotte had read about this in *The Straits Times*.

There is no government anywhere in the world so inadequate at addressing its people as that of the Straits, the editor had written. *Chinese translations of new laws must be made in Hong Kong. Judicial work falls to the Governor and the Resident Councillor almost entirely without help. Cases go unheard for months and the jail is packed with men awaiting trial.*

Charlotte found a great deal of sympathy with Mrs Norris, for Robert too, worked so very hard with too few ill-paid policemen. A force of 130 men was left to deal with a population which, she read in the paper, had grown in ten years or so from 17,000 to 50,000.

Keeping his policemen from the corruption of bribery was a great headache and Robert could not even blame them, their salary was so poor. He was forced, through a lack of senior officials, to double up as Magistrate and Officer of the Court. It was not his salary which had made him comparatively rich. Like all the government officials, they sustained their existence by property development or plantations in the countryside. It was Robert's properties in the town and his coconut plantation at Katong which provided the bulk of his income.

Isabel da Silva, who had fidgeted during this conversation, sighed with relief at its end and now found a degree of animation. Isabel's engagement to the man from Manila had fallen through. He had got some other woman pregnant and been forced to marry her. She had not wanted the man from Manila, but now that he was no longer available Isabel bemoaned her fate and found that she had been almost in love with him.

Charlotte was sure that Maryanne, Isabel and Elizabeth spent many hours together discussing these and other injustices at length. Currently, Isabel's mother was seeking a new husband for her daughter. Appeals had gone out to Isobel, her twin, to find a husband like her own, an English merchant. Unfortunately, Charlotte could see, the strain told somewhat on Isabel. Her face was bloated and red, and she had gained weight. She had never been a pretty girl and now ... well, she was well over twenty, with looks waning.

"Actually, I am rather glad the Manila gorilla fell through. I would much rather have Captain Maitland."

Charlotte looked up from her tea. Isabel had designs on Charles Maitland? Why not, she supposed, but thought Isabel must surely be disappointed. She was certain Sir Henry, Foreign Secretary to the Indian Government would balk, no matter how unfairly, at the prospect of a mixed-blood merchant's daughter marrying his brother. Also, Captain Maitland hardly struck her as a man in search of a wife, or even remotely interested in women.

"Have you met him, Charlotte?" Isabel asked, picking up another piece of cake.

"Yes, briefly. He seems a rather introspective sort of man."

"Oh, no! Not at all. He is not the least like that. Serious perhaps but I admire a man of science. But he comes often to our house for musical evenings. He sings very well and he is part of the players at the Theatre Royal in the Hill Street Assembly Rooms."

Charlotte was astonished. The seemingly taciturn Mr Maitland, a player?

"Why, there is a performance next Saturday night of *The Merry Monarch*. He plays Mary Tree."

"He plays females uncommonly well," Elizabeth added and Isabel nodded, cramming cake into her mouth.

The prospect of the dour Mr Maitland in female apparel was too good to be missed, and Charlotte agreed to attend. Isabel said that she would go immediately to Little & Cursetjee to pick up the tickets.

The talk turned to the popular subject of Rajah Brooke. Isabel was entirely in love with James Brooke, she avowed. He must be so lonely, there in Sarawak without a woman by his side. So handsome, so dashing. Every woman's dream. Yet he was alone. She could not understand it, she confessed.

Charlotte agreed that she too found the Rajah charming. She had been invited to visit him. "I do not intend to go but it is charming of him to ask."

Isabel let out a loud cry, a small explosion of cake crumbs escaping her mouth. "Oh Charlotte, you must go. Will you not take me? I should so love to see his house! And the head hunters. It is all so thrilling and romantic."

She began to pout and Elizabeth too, joined the chorus of protestation. "Yes indeed, Charlotte, you must go and take Isabel. Such a pity I am so near my time."

Elizabeth looked slyly at Charlotte. "Perhaps he means to marry you, Charlotte. A rich widow might be just the thing for a new king. I hear he is in need of funds. Would you not like to be the Ranee of Sarawak?"

Isabel looked at her friend with shock and her jaw dropped.

Charlotte laughed, not least to allay Isabel's rather bizarre fears.

"I have no intention of marrying Rajah Brooke, I assure you both."

Charlotte shook her head slightly. The whole town had become crazed with the Rajah.

An idea suddenly entered her head. Her thoughts turned too much to Zhen lately. A change of scene might be just the thing. And Rajah Brooke was a charming man. She was suddenly curious about his life in this strange place called Sarawak. Perhaps she would go after all.

13

Charlotte went to kiss the children. Adam was sleeping in his small bed, his face in sweet repose. He was every inch Tigran's son. Adam's *babu* was eating in the servants' kitchen, but later she would sleep at his side together with Alexander's *babu*. She touched his cheek. She moved over to Alex. He too was asleep, his arms flung round his head. She stood and looked down at him. When he was asleep, his face unanimated, she could see Zhen in his lips and the turn of his jaw. He was so handsome, like his father. She bent and kissed his cheek.

Alex was eight years old. It was time to allow him greater freedom. She had given this a great deal of thought. No father, no man could truly guide Alex or Adam. Robert was a good uncle but too busy. She had decided to get a syce for Alex, a young man who would go about with him, protect him, be his friend but also an example to him. The choice was not easy.

She left the room and went downstairs. She was looking forward to a visit to the Assembly Rooms on Hill Street, and the presentation *The Merry Monarch* at the Theatre Royale. She knew a little about this play from the playbill which she had received with her tickets.

When his mistress, Lady Clara (Charles Dyce), accuses the Earl of Rochester (Captain James Scott) of being "the chief cause of the king's irregularities", the Earl agrees to help reform Charles II (William Napier). He takes the King to a seaman's tavern run by old Captain Copp (Robert Macleod). There he deserts the King, leaving him to fend for himself without any money. Copp threatens to have the King arrested, but the King escapes through a window. Realising the Earl and the lady have had his best interests at heart, the King is forgiving and promises to mend his ways. He pays his debt to Copp and gives him a fine watch as well. The role of Mary, Captain Copp's niece, is played by Captain Charles Maitland, and that of Edward, a page, by Thomas Keane.

She took up her bag from the hall table, went outside under the porte-cochere and took a seat in her carriage. Her syce, Ravi, led the horse and began to trot down the driveway. Charlotte still could not quite get used to this manner of conveyance, with the Indian man, a flaming torch held aloft, guiding the horses to their destination. It was somewhat irksome in that the horses proceeded only as fast as the syce could run, which, to be fair, was often very fast indeed. It was peculiar to Singapore, she was sure.

The Assembly Rooms was an unprepossessing building nestled into the base of Bukit Larangan on the corner of Hill Street and River Valley Road. It had little to recommend itself, Charlotte thought, as the carriage drew up. No elegance at all. In fact it was downright ugly. It was constructed not of brick and marble but of lath and plaster, with an attap roof—no more, really, than a large hut. To the left of the main lobby was a ballroom and, to the right the theatre, with a well for the orchestra. The musicians from the regiment were playing and the music at least, was good.

Charlotte saw Teresa in conversation with her mother and Eliza Dyce and went up to them. Teresa greeted her sister-in-law warmly. Teresa's baby was due in a month and the heat was a trial, she said. Fortunately tonight was cool, a breeze blowing in from the doors and the punkahs waving above them. Acquaintances came up to the group to pay their compliments. The hall filled up, and Charlotte could see that the evening was not confined as one might have imagined, to simply the Europeans of the town.

A great many Chinese and Indians were present. The two richest Arab merchants in the town were also there. Perhaps, they all wanted to see the amusing spectacle of the white people making fools of themselves, Charlotte thought. Why not? She did. A bell sounded and the gathered throng moved slowly to their seats. There was not one free place, Charlotte noted. Theatricals, amateur or otherwise, were rare in Singapore and when they were staged, very well attended. She took out her fan and waited, eager now for the play to begin.

Nothing was quite like the experience of amateur theatricals in a community so small as that of the Europeans in Singapore. Everyone knew everyone and the suspense of waiting for neighbours and friends to step out of their lives and onto a stage was one quite peculiar to such a place. The sense of pleasurable anticipation, the willingness to be entertained, to enjoy the evening, was heightened. She could hardly wait to see Robert as the corpulent and bibulous Captain Copp or Charles Maitland as a woman! As she gazed around the room, Isabel da Silva waved to her, and Charlotte smiled and waved her fan. The orchestra began to play softly and the curtains swished apart.

The play advanced, the appearance of each actor greeted with loud applause. The sight of Billy Napier bouncing on stage, bewigged and powdered, as the dissolute King Charles, brought the house to its feet. He took several bows but when the audience had settled again, the sound of his broad Scottish accent emitting from the King's mouth, caused such hilarity that it took many minutes for the play to continue. When Robert appeared, almost unrecognisable as the fat Captain Copp, Charlotte and Teresa looked at each other and laughed. Then Charles Maitland entered, mincing, his body cinched into a corset, his face made up heavily, on his head a wig of long black hair. The audience raised a shout of hilarity, and Charles bowed slightly and turned to Robert, waiting.

"What Mary, my little blossom, what cheer? What cheer?" Captain Copp went up to his niece, who was the same height as himself.

Charlotte and Teresa, the whole house, burst out laughing. Anything looking less like a little blossom could not be imagined.

"Who are they, uncle, those people who make such a noise?" Charles said in a voice of feminine sweetness and looked pointedly at the audience. The house came down, tears were streaming down half the faces in the room.

The scene continued, with each reference to Mary's feminine gentleness greeted with laughter. Then Robert, as Captain Copp, raised his voice in song. The audience waited. This song, repeated many times throughout the play, was always cut short. Robert turned to the audience.

"In the time of the Rump
As old Admiral Trump
With his broom swept the chops of the Channel
And his crew of ten breechers
Those Dutch sons of ..."

Mary put her hand to his mouth hurriedly.
"Oh, oh, Uncle, don't sing that horrible rough song."
Charles threw a look of painful maidenly embarrassment at the audience and the whole house burst into laughter.

When the play was finished, the audience rose in prolonged and hearty applause. Afterward, Charlotte went to the dressing room. Robert turned as she entered and waved a hand lazily. He was still covered in make-up and she laughed again at his comical appearance.

Robert looked over her shoulder and she turned. There stood Charles Maitland, still bewigged and made up, the slightest sign of a shadow on his chin. Somehow, in this ridiculous feminine apparel, with a wig and make-up thick on his face, he still contrived to be utterly masculine. He turned his dark eyes onto her.

"Mary, my sweet child," Robert said, laughing, addressing Charles as his stage character, "you know Charlotte I think."

Charlotte turned her gaze to Charles. He bowed.

"Congratulations Captain, on your excellent and comical portrayal," Charlotte said smiling.

"Mrs Manouk, thank you."

He addressed Robert and mincing said a line from the play, "Ah, my good uncle, you are always so careful of me."

Robert laughed and took Charlotte's hand.

"Be careful Kitt, 'the first glimpse of a petticoat—whew!—up boarding pikes and grappling irons. No child, mustn't venture in those latitudes.'"

Charlotte laughed again and Charles smiled and bowed. "Forgive me, I must now quit these heavenly garments."

Charlotte watched him move away.

The Dramatic Society had laid on a late supper. Charlotte and Isabel returned to the supper room. Within fifteen minutes Robert came up and took a glass of champagne. A few minutes later, Charles Maitland, restored to his masculine garb, joined them. Isabel da Silva immediately left her mother and slipped her arm through Charlotte's.

"Oh, Captain, you were so very wonderful tonight. Had I not known, I should have thought you a woman, certainly."

Charles smiled and bowed over Isabel's hand. She giggled and fanned herself.

Charlotte could think of nothing to say. She found herself suddenly tongue-tied and could not imagine why.

Charles picked up a glass of champagne and tossed it back quickly, then bowed to the company. "I must depart, forgive me. My journey back to Kallang is quite long." He put out his hand to Robert who shook it.

"Goodbye, dearest Uncle. Until Friday evening." Charles grinned at Robert as he spoke, then held out his hand to Isabel and took hers, bowing over it. He then turned to Charlotte. She curtsied and held out her hand. He took it and she suddenly felt a shock, as if a little fizz of lightning had passed through her. She had not felt this sensation since she had touched Zhen.

Charles drew her hand to his mouth, not touching it with his lips though, and she drew in her breath sharply, trying to control these unexpected reactions. He dropped her hand and looked into her eyes. She read there too, an extraordinary surprise.

"Perhaps," he said and paused, "perhaps you would care to visit the Magnetic Observatory on the Kallang River." He gazed at Charlotte, then suddenly seemed to shake himself. "Miss Isabel too, of course." He looked at Isabel and she simpered and giggled. Then, without waiting for a reply, he bowed, turned and left the room.

14

Charlotte's carriage stopped in front of the doors of Qian's compound on the corner of High Street and Hill Street. The high roof curved delicately upward, adorned by ornate porcelain tiling. The doors were a faded red with brass studs. Two huge paper lanterns covered in Chinese script hung to either side of the doors. The entire compound was surrounded by high walls. It ran from High Street to the edge of the river where the godowns lay. She was here to take Ah Soon with them to join the Munshi on a visit to the Sultan's compound at Kampong Glam.

She stepped down from the carriage with Alex and hand in hand, they went up to the door. As she approached, as if secret eyes were watching, one door swung open and a servant bowed low. She stepped up over the threshold and entered the inner room. This, she now knew, was the first court, the visitors' court, separated from the rest of the house by an ornate carved wooden screen that ran from ceiling to floor. A marble-topped table stood in the middle of the tiled floor and the walls were lined with heavy black carved wooden chairs. She stopped and waited. Alex looked around. Though Ah Soon had come frequently to his own house on North Bridge Road, this was the first time he had set foot in Ah Soon's house.

He loved it, the high-pitched roof and curving tiles, the beams painted with golden dragons and swirling blue and white clouds. Charlotte too took a long look around. Everything was solid and restrained and yet exuberant at the same time. From Zhen she had learned an appreciation of the heavy symbolism which lay all around them in this room, the motifs of harmony, good fortune, longevity.

The symbolism was so rich, it was difficult to remember.

A squeak of pleasure came from behind, and they turned. Ah Soon had arrived and behind him, his father, Qian. They both bowed solemnly and then smiled broadly. Qian held out his hand to Charlotte, and Ah Soon took Alex's in his and waited.

"Welcome, Miss Charlotte," Qian said, shaking her hand.

Charlotte smiled too. Qian, dear Qian, Zhen's loyal friend.

"Miss no longer, Qian. I am Mrs Manouk as you know very well."

"Always Miss Charlotte to me."

Charlotte turned towards her son. "And this is Alex, my eldest boy, Ah Soon's friend."

Qian looked at Charlotte. She was still so lovely, this woman Zhen loved. He could see how difficult it must be for Zhen to give her up. Her figure was unchanged. She was still a willow, still exuded a kind and charming nature. She had a radiant beauty and a keen and tolerant mind. He could see it was a meeting of body and mind, an almost perfect union of Yin and Yang, she dark to his light, soft to his hard. Society, with all its laws and strictures stood in the way, but he could see that in a natural world they were meant to be together.

He nodded at her and turned his gaze to her son. He took Alex's hand and shook it in the English way, and Alex bowed slightly. Qian looked at him and saw it immediately: this was Zhen's son. Qian was absolutely sure of it. He recognised the Chinese tilt of his eyes, though they were not so dark, nor so narrow. But more than this, it was in the bones, the jaw and the cheek, that he read Zhen's blood. Ah Soon was so much his own son, every skinny bit of him, his face the image of his own, that Qian could see Zhen everywhere in Alex. He made no sign however, and smiled at Alex.

"Come inside. Perhaps you would take some tea before you go off on your excursions."

Charlotte could not believe how well Qian spoke English. Ah Soon said something quickly to Alex in Hokkien and Qian smiled.

"Alex speaks our language very well, Miss Charlotte. Did you know?"

Charlotte looked at her son. She knew, of course, that he spent time in the town with his syce. She wanted him to learn the Chinese language but this was the first she had heard of how well he was doing.

"No, Qian. Does he?"

"Yes indeed. Almost as well as my own son. Certainly better than Ah Soon speaks English."

Qian looked at his son. "Ah Soon, more study I think."

Charlotte laughed as Ah Soon bowed.

"Today he will practise, for we shall speak English all day."

Charlotte too, turned to Ah Soon. "Eh, Ah Soon, English today."

Ah Soon looked up at his father and Alex's mother. "Yes, of course. It is a pleasure," he said in very good English.

They all burst out laughing and Qian nodded permission for Ah Soon to take Alex to explore the house.

Qian led the way around the screen and into the first open courtyard. The sun was slanting in, for it was early, casting flickering glints on the ponds of goldfish and the pots of white lotus, some in bud, some in bloom. Such a lovely flower, Charlotte thought fleetingly. She remembered it was the symbol of the Boodha, representing the possibilities of the human spirit, its feet in the mire of earthly mud but its pristine beauty facing the sky. She had thought this a powerful and touching sentiment. The sounds of the street had completely died away. The peace and silence of this inner court, filled with glinting sunlight, had a unique charm. On either side of the court were rooms and Ah Soon pulled Alex into one of them.

"These are sleeping quarters, rooms for eating."

As if they were in a temple, a sudden odour of incense wafted on the air.

"Offerings," Qian said looking at Charlotte's face. He could see her curiosity. They walked through this court and into the inner apartments. The odour of incense became very strong and Charlotte could see that the smoke rose in heavy whorls from the two altar tables. One was adorned with porcelain gods, pictures and Chinese writing. She knew that the very high black wood table was the ancestral altar. It was covered with silver goods, an ornate incense burner filled with smoking joss sticks, high candlesticks, dishes and cups. The spirit house stood in the middle of the altar and Charlotte knew that here reposed the ancestral tablets of the Sang household. A portrait of Sang hung over the altar. He had died only a few years ago and it was his spirit, and those of his predecessors, which were propitiated here.

Zhen had told her something of these beliefs in the spirits of the ancestors. At death the soul of the departed cleaved into three manifestations, one remained here in the spirit house, one reposed in the grave and a third, after a passage through the hellish regions—helped on by offerings from the living—eventually ascended to heaven to act on the family's behalf, bringing good fortune and longevity to the men and perpetuity to the family. The Chinese world was inhabited by wandering souls and ghosts needing endless attention.

How tiring, Charlotte thought, when Zhen had told her that it was not the men but the women who were charged with this constant care. Care for the living, care for the dead, Charlotte mused. A Chinese woman's lot was not to be envied. Unappreciated during her life, forgotten after her death unless she were a matriarch of importance with many sons. Zhen had explained this to her though he did not care about this sort of thing. He followed the Tao and for him the afterlife did not exist.

To either side of this room stood double doors. Qian ushered Charlotte to the right to a corridor which led to a small courtyard, where, in the centre, a gnarled tree cast its deep shade. Here, at a table made entirely of green and white porcelain, Qian invited her to sit. A servant appeared with tea.

Charlotte knew, in a moment, that this house, this kind of house— its sun-glinting courtyards, its separated spaces, its cool and green silences—was somehow, part of the Chinese soul. The outer walls defended the inner apartments from noise and the uncontrollable outer world. Here everything was ordered, contained and peaceful. She remembered Zhen moving gracefully in the Tai Ji, the dance of the Tao, as he had called it. Graceful, contained, the inner part balanced and peaceful, separated from the shocks of the world for a moment. She sipped the fragrant tea and thought that finally she glimpsed something of Zhen's deep soul that she had not seen before. The longing for him came in a powerful wave. It was as if he were here, surrounding her. She put down her cup and rose, thanking Qian, and moved out of the courtyard.

Qian waved to the carriage, then turned and walked back to his own apartments deep in thought. He was almost certain that Ah Rex was Zhen's son but what he should do with this suspicion he had no idea.

15

Munshi Abdullah was waiting outside the mosque at Kampong Glam. When Charlotte's carriage pulled up, he came forward from the shade, his umbrella raised. His youngest son, Ibrahim, was with him. He was just a little older than Alexander and Ah Soon. The boys ran forward, greeting the Munshi politely, Malay style as they had learned, and Abdullah smiled broadly. Charlotte too curtsied to him.

"Thank you, Munshi, for taking the trouble."

The Munshi put up his hand. "No trouble, no trouble. My pleasure."

They turned to face the mosque and Charlotte put up her parasol. The mosque had not changed aspect in all the years Charlotte had been in Singapore. It was a large, square, low building, with a high pyramid-style roof of four layers. Each level of the roof was finished with curving finials, like the curved beak of the hornbill. She had seen this style in Java; it was quite common. The building had originally been of wood and attap, but it had been rebuilt, and now it was of brick and red tiles. Adjoining it was a square, double-roofed antechamber, where shoes were removed and ablutions performed. Her sojourn in Java, her reading of Raffles and Crawfurd had taught her something of the religion of the Mohammedans.

Charlotte looked at Abdullah standing with the boys. They had removed their shoes and entered. Abdullah was pointing out the pulpit, explaining the call to prayer. Charlotte, like Zhen, did not believe in these religions of gods and prophets. In this, as in many things, they were instinctively in tune. But Abdullah was of the faith and nothing could have recommended it more. It did not seem narrow, like the Christian church. Her experiences of the Scottish Kirk had chased her as far as possible from these moralising pulpits. Perhaps this faith had its zealots too but Abdullah was not one. His intellect was wide. He could translate the gospels without the slightest loss of his own faith, content to leave to others their own beliefs. In Java too, the drowsy drone of the Madrasah boys reciting the Koran was peaceful, the call to prayer musical and beautiful.

Abdullah joined her. He knew the boys could only take a little of looking at buildings. They had really come to see the tiger which the Sultan kept. The group turned, therefore, and walked along to the gates of the compound. When Charlotte had first visited this place it had been nothing more than the poorest-looking bungalow surrounded by ramshackle walls and two watchtowers, the Sultan's followers sprawled around in huts. She had never seen the Sultan, who had already fled from Singapore before she arrived, but Abdullah had told her about him.

Tungku Hussein had been the eldest son and heir-apparent of the last Sultan of the intact Johor empire, which had included Pahang, the Rhio islands and Singapore. The Johor sultans claimed descent from Parameswara, the first Sultan of Malacca. They had fled before the Portuguese invasion. They counted themselves, Abdullah had stressed, the first amongst all the royal families of the Malays because of this ancient lineage.

When Tungku Hussein's father had died, Hussein had not acted to claim the throne and had been usurped by his younger brother, who had the support of both the Bugis powers and the Dutch. Hussein had been living penniless in Rhio when Colonel Farquhar, well aware of the situation, spoke to Raffles. In order to thwart the Dutch, they offered the throne to Hussein with the backing of Temmengong Abdul Rahman, the father of the present Temmengong, who had then been living as ruler of Singapore island. He had fled from Rhio, having fallen foul of Hussein's brother. Thus were the treaties made which ceded to the East India Company certain rights to the island, and thus was made the rival Sultan of Johor.

Hussein had acquired in one swoop wealth, prestige and land. Kampong Glam was given to him and an allowance of $1,000 a month. His entourage, his followers, his harem followed him to Singapore.

Of course the money was all too soon not enough. His expenses increased and so had his demands. Raffles had been frustrated and annoyed, but it took Crawfurd to deal with him. In 1824 things came to a head. Crawfurd had withheld the funds, forcing the Sultan into submission and had quickly negotiated the complete transfer of power over Singapore and her surrounding islands for the sum of $30,000 and a lifetime allowance of $1,300 a month.

From that moment Hussein's prestige had plummeted. Crawfurd did everything in his power to force him to leave. When the ladies of his harem ran away because of mistreatment and sought British protection, Crawfurd, against the most vociferous arguments of the Sultan, granted it. Crawfurd also forced a road across the Sultan's compound despite a show of defiance. The humiliation of the Sultan had been complete. But he stayed on in Singapore and from that time he had been quiet. For ten years at least.

Abdullah had stopped before the gates of the Sultan's compound and drawn the children around him in the shade. He began to tell them about the first Sultan. Charlotte smiled, for his recollection of this man was vivid. Whilst she listened she took in the new walls, neat with *chunam*, and the Istana which George Coleman had built in the style of a grand colonial house for Hussein's son and heir, Tungku Ali.

"Now listen, oh my little ones. At the time that he came from Rhio to Singapore this man was of average proportions. However, when he became Sultan his body grew plumper and plumper as time went on. His obesity became so exaggerated that he looked square in shape, for he was very short. He became no longer recognisable, with his small head and neck buried under so much fat that it looked as if he had no neck; his round face, squinting eyes, button nose, wide mouth, spreading chest, paunch distended by layers of flesh, thighs which met in the middle, spindly legs without any flesh, splay feet and a raucous voice which jarred on the ears."

The children were agog, mouths open.

"When he spoke he snapped and snarled, scaring everyone. His body was sallow. He was so fat he had not the power to support his own legs and had to be carried everywhere."

The boys stared. "What happened to him?" Alex said finally, curiosity burning.

"He grew so lazy he could not run the affairs of his own household. He grew to depend on a young man, a commoner called Abdul Kadir. Whatever this man said, good or bad, the Sultan agreed. The Sultan lost all sense of his responsibilities to the world. Of course all sorts of tales were told about this Abdul Kadir and became common knowledge amongst the people of all races in Singapore and Malacca. Plots were hatched among the Sultan's followers to murder Abdul Kadir."

The boys gasped and looked at each other. This was the most thrilling tale they had ever heard. Charlotte knew he was not telling them everything of course. For the accusations and tales were of adultery by the Sultan's wife.

"Some of the Sultan's followers took the matter to the governor of Singapore and told him not to blame them if they were to try to put him to death. The governor tried to reason with the Sultan but he just said that they were all against him. He could only trust Abdul Kadir. Now the followers were very, very angry and Abdul Kadir did not dare leave the palace, he was so afraid. Finally the Sultan grew so worried that he sought some means to bring about Abdul Kadir's escape, for he was convinced he would be murdered that very night."

Abdullah paused and the boys jiggled impatiently, not daring to speak. The Munshi smiled and looked at Charlotte.

"They dressed Abdul Kadir in a woman's dress and a veil and got him into the Sultan's carriage and through the milling crowds because the people were scared of the Sultan. They smuggled him out of the palace, through this very gate."

In perfect unison, the boys looked up and around them. This place had been the scene of such exciting events!

"He went into hiding in the town and everyone was searching for him. Finally at dead of night he got aboard a boat, still dressed as a woman, and went to Malacca. From that moment, the Sultan was like a hen that has lost her young. He was moody and angry and hated all his followers and sat about as if he were heartbroken."

Ah Soon let out a long "phew" of amazement. A man crying for another man like a girl. He looked at Alex and they both shook their heads.

"Sir, what was wrong with that Sultan?" Alex asked very politely.

"Why, everything, Iskandar," Abdullah said looking at Alex. Alex nodded.

"Eventually, the Sultan could stand it no more. He took his wife, his two sons and his four daughters and left Singapore in a boat. After many dangers they arrived in Malacca. From that moment Abdul Kadir became as the ruler himself, for the Sultan agreed with everything he said. The Sultan's monthly allowance from the English went into the hands of Abdul Kadir. Immense sums ran like water through his hands. The Sultan's possessions went to the pawn shop in their thousands; things made of gold by the sack load, diamonds in handfuls, fine silks, all pledged away for paltry sums. Anyone wishing to see Abdul Kadir was granted an audience as if he was the Sultan himself. He never walked but went about by carriage and horse day and night. Many wanted to take his life."

The boys nodded vehemently. Charlotte could see they were indignant. Ah Soon had made a little fist. She wondered if she should stop this story but the boys were utterly wrapped up in it, and Charlotte did not quite dare to stop the Munshi.

"Nobody dared do anything, for they still feared the Sultan. To Abdul Kadir's face they feigned respect and when they saw him they did obeisance. But they plotted and plotted. Finally, their moment came."

Ah Soon shot up, too excited to sit. Charlotte threw a glance at Abdullah, and he nodded.

"Abdul Kadir was stabbed with a kris, but not hurt badly. An English doctor saved him. The Sultan turned all his Malay followers out of his house and married his daughter to Abdul Kadir, although Abdul Kadir was already married with six or seven children. And he was given the title *Tengku Muda*, the young prince. Everyone in Malacca was amazed.

"But mark well, my little ones, how great is the wisdom of Allah in working his purpose among men." Ah Soon sat down, calmed now, and the other boys nodded sagely.

"When the poor, foolish Sultan died, it was the end of Abdul Kadir, and he died, too, not long after.

"Here is a lesson, my young boys. Take care of your body and your mind. Remember that Allah sets his face against foolish tyrants and brings to ruin the greedy, the boastful and the stupid."

Abdullah stood up and the boys thanked him, delighted with this tale of woe, of mighty fallen and divine justice.

"And now, a tiger!"

The children squealed and ran into the compound. Charlotte followed with Abdullah.

"An exciting tale and you tell it so well. What about the present Sultan?"

"Tengku Ali. He is as weak-minded as his father. He is not recognised as Sultan of Singapore by the English. Hussein's disgraceful behaviour set an irrevocable stamp on this family. Ali is permitted to live here with his followers. It is he who commissioned this palace. The English pay him a pension. However, at present, they favour the Temmengong, who is much smarter than Tengku Ali and on excellent terms with Governor Butterworth. Ibrahim has been useful in putting down piracy, or so it is perceived."

They had turned around the palace and entered a garden. The boys ran ahead. Two guards with krisses came forward, and the boys stopped abruptly and looked back at the Munshi. He spoke to the guards, and they turned and led the way to a clearing which contained a large cage of bamboo. The guards began poking a stick at the tiger, who looked lethargic and underfed.

Charlotte could not watch. She lacked the stomach for this kind of thing. The boys would be thrilled by it but it had no appeal for her. She spoke to Abdullah, who nodded, and she went back, through the garden and the gate of the compound. Her carriage was waiting and she mounted it, sheltering from the sun under her parasol.

"Mrs Manouk, what a pleasant surprise."

Charlotte turned and was astonished to see Captain Maitland approaching on horseback. He swung down and came up to her, leading his horse to a stone water trough.

"Captain, what brings you here?"

"I come this way sometimes when I am going into town." He shifted slightly. "However, I must confess I saw your carriage and came to investigate."

Charlotte smiled and opened her fan. "My son is visiting a tiger but I have not the heart for it."

"Yes, I know, poor thing. Better to be shot."

Their sentiments were in tune and Charlotte warmed to him.

"Would you visit the observatory, Mrs Manouk? I should like it."

Charlotte sensed a teneseness in him. He had blurted the invitation out. Small talk was obviously not his strong suit. She looked into his eyes. He tilted his head to one side, waiting. It was a charming gesture, boyish.

"Yes, Captain, I should like that."

He smiled. "Tomorrow. Tomorrow morning. At ten o'clock. I shall have finished my observations."

She smiled and he stopped. He took a breath, realising perhaps his brusqueness. "Sorry. Would ten o'clock be suitable?"

"Yes, Captain, entirely suitable."

He bowed, the look of pleasure on his face making her smile.

She could hear the boys coming back and put out her hand to take her leave, then suddenly remembered. But it was too late. He had moved forward and taken it, putting it to his lips this time. She felt the pressure of his mouth on her hand and sat very still. He too remained motionless for a fraction too long. She gently pulled her hand away.

The boys, all three, came rushing out, excited about the tiger, which had been goaded into action and had roared. They were chattering excitedly. Charles had remounted his horse and quickly cantered away. Charlotte smiled and thanked Abdullah, offering a seat to him and his son. It was all agreed. They would return together. The boys squashed up together, giggling and chattering in an alarming mix of bad Malay and bad English.

As the carriage departed, she opened her fan and cooled her face.

16

Charlotte dressed with particular care. She had chosen a frock of pale green and white cotton, the sleeves of cotton lace falling fetchingly along her arm. Her hat was fine straw weave with a wide, soft ribbon of green falling down the back. It was a spring gown, a young woman's gown, she knew, and she did not care. This attraction she felt for Charles Maitland was entirely unexpected but somewhat undeniable.

The day seemed suddenly rather lovely. The wind was brisk and cooling. The sky was blue with wisps of small clouds. It was a perfect day for a ride. Today, she decided, she would drive herself. The small gharry trap was brought round. Ravi held the reins and handed them to her with a look of such utter disapproval that Charlotte could not help but smile. Her thoughts flew momentarily to Tigran, who had taught her to drive a carriage. Thank you, she thought, my darling. Can you hear me? These inner dialogues with Tigran had stopped somewhat but occasionally they just bubbled to the surface.

Ravi mounted behind her and she clucked the horses into movement, turned out of the gate and set the carriage towards Kallang. The going was firm for the most part along North Bridge Road. She proceeded along Jalan Chondong and Jalan Trang, where the road was muddy and potholed. To his evident pleasure, Ravi jumped down and guided the horse, turning by the police station onto Jalan Rochor. Here the road went over the Rochor River and turned onto Kallang Road, which was in reasonable repair. It was a short distance to the iron bridge which Coleman had built over the Kallang River. As they approached it, she could see Charles Maitland's house on the banks of the river.

Charles was waiting by the bridge. He was dressed in fine black cotton breeches and a snow-white shirt, both of which showed his figure to some advantage. He was powerfully built; his shoulders filled the shirt, which was open at the neck, revealing a little of the dark hair on his chest. She knew he had dressed this way for her, as she had for him. He came forward immediately as she pulled to a halt and without a word put out his hands to lift her from the carriage. It was so unexpected that she had no time to protest. Her waist was in his hands and he held her firmly, lowering her slowly to the ground. His grip was so strong he moved her as if she were a mere feather. When her feet met the ground he did not release her. His hands stayed on her waist, almost encompassing it, and she felt that, one moment more and he would have taken her against him and kissed her. She looked down, embarrassed at her own feelings. Ravi had moved forward to take the reins and grunted slightly.

Charles dropped his hands, somewhat shame-faced at his boldness. There was an awkward moment. Then Charles indicated to Ravi where he could tie up the horse and turned. "Welcome to my humble abode, Mrs Manouk."

"Kitt, please, Charles, if you don't mind. Everyone calls me Kitt."

"Kitt, yes, thank you." He laughed suddenly. "Sorry, I am not much good at small talk. You may have noticed. I am a man of science. We are not very good at that sort of thing. Forgive me."

Charlotte looked at Charles and opened her fan. A man of science who had the build of a warrior, played women on the stage, and held her in his hands like a feather. He was dangerously intriguing.

"A tour—I was promised a tour, was I not?"

"Yes, of course." Charles turned now and led her down the path towards his house. It was a simple building, made of brick with an attap roof surrounded by coconut trees. A large verandah encircled it and to the front, brick pillars stood partly in the river, overlooking the expanse of water. Though the day was hot, it was cool, a breeze blowing off the river. Small blue kingfishers flew in and out of the jungle opposite, hovering and plummeting into the river, seeking fish. Tall grey and purple herons picked their way delicately along the far bank.

"My feathered friends," Charles said. "I also have a family of otters for neighbours, to beguile my working hours. The work of the observatory is rather painstaking and tedious, and they are enjoyable companions."

Charles led Charlotte off the verandah and through a small grove of trees to the observatory. It was a simple but commodious shed containing a variety of brass instruments. To one side stood a tower, some thirty feet high.

"The tower is for observing the direction and velocity of the wind. The rain gauge is there also. I have been taking measurements since I arrived in 1840, so there is a nice amount of information now."

Charlotte realised that Charles must have arrived just before she had departed for Batavia.

They turned away from the tower and entered the observatory. Charles told her, "The aim of the observatory is magnetic observations. You see, I am but a humble spoke in a vast wheel of observatories stretching around the world. Fifty-three. Major Sabine is the leader in this research and convinced the Royal Society that there was no greater undertaking for maritime people than the measurement and understanding of the magnetism of the earth. Fortunately, the fluctuating and unreliable movements of the maritime compass, and its dangers to ocean navigation convinced the Admiralty that this was so."

"I'm not sure I understand."

Charles smiled. "Well, you see, the magnetic north pole, which the compass detects, seems to be in a constant state of movement. It alters in place and intensity. This has deep consequences on navigation of course, hence the Admiralty's interest. Some scholars suggest that it is perhaps the earth's own core which is responsible for this instability. The job of the magnetic observatories is to furnish measurements from all corners of the world to see if this is true. We do not know whether this magnetic variance causes changes in the weather. This would also be very useful to know."

Charles stopped and turned to Charlotte. She had been looking at his books and charts. "It is complicated," he said.

"No, no," Charlotte protested. She did not understand its detail or begin to make sense of his notations, but she could see it was important. He had explained it well. "I understand that it is a great work. It will make the seas safer. It is a laudable aim."

Charles smiled and they turned back towards the house. "It is rather tedious work sometimes of course, but one must always bear in mind the larger goal. What I record here, what others record all over the world using the same instruments and the same formulae is gathered together, and gradually we begin to understand. What we do today will benefit all future generations. In our humble way we carry on the work of such great men as Halley and Faraday. Already some of the first up-to-date world magnetic charts have been drawn up. It is, for me, a very exciting time."

Charlotte nodded. His enthusiasm was infectious.

They walked back to the verandah. A canoe suddenly appeared on the water, filled to the brim with Bugis boys. Curious, they had come to see the white man and the woman. Charles called out to them and waved, and they all began laughing. Several jumped out of the boat and began swimming for the far shore and the others paddled madly behind them.

Charles grinned and called for tea. "These boys are the most curious of creatures. Their kampong is just around the turn in the river as you know and they never tire of coming to see me. They bring me fish and shells and all manner of things they think I am interested in. In return I give them tea and sweets and try to explain what I'm doing, which they do not understand in the least. One told me they thought I was trying to catch the moon in my tower and what a fool I must be, for I would most probably need a net."

The two chatted in the friendliest of manners for some time. She asked Charles about his family and told him of her own life on Madagascar; the years that she and Robert were orphans in Scotland, how she had learned to sail. Charles too could sail well. Necessary, he added, for any man living in the conditions he had chosen, always in proximity to the sea. Charlotte enjoyed this verandah, with its diving and wading birds. The otter family appeared for their amusement, floating on their backs, clutching fish in their paws like small children playing.

As their conversation progressed she told him of her life in Batavia. Charles had made observations there, and she realised that at one time they had both been in that city together, yet their lives had never crossed. His intensity had floated away, and he told her amusing tales of his time with the Dutch, whose own scientific interests were barely visible.

Suddenly the Malay houseboy appeared with another young man.

"Tuan, I am sorry. Fifteen minutes."

Charles looked up at the clock on the table opposite. "Oh dear, I am sorry, Kitt. I have to go soon. Duty calls. The time has gone so fast. And I am a man ruled by time."

He hesitated. "You know, James Brooke is a friend, a great friend. He has asked me to come to Sarawak, to make observations. I wish very much to go."

Charles looked at Charlotte, who was toying with her teacup, adding sugar. Really the tea was terrible, she thought. The man lived too much alone, it was obvious. No one but a Malay servant to care for him. She had not been paying attention.

"An assistant has finally arrived to continue the work here until my return. I am planning to leave in the next week."

Charlotte looked up now. Leave, next week? she thought. When I have just met you?

"Oh, really? I see. How long will you be away?" she asked. She put the cup to her lips distractedly, then remembered and put it down on the saucer.

"Several months. There is a great deal to observe."

"Yes, of course. Pulled thither by magnetic attraction." Charlotte laughed lightly though she felt a constriction in her throat.

Charles looked up and smiled. He had a lovely smile, the more so because he used it so little and obviously only on those he cared for. Charlotte rose quickly. She had wanted to reach out to him, touch his hand. No. More than this, she had wanted to walk into his arms, feel them around her. Now such thoughts felt foolish.

She moved towards the door, reaching for her hat. "Thank you, Charles, for a delightful and informative visit."

Charles bowed, suddenly distant. Charlotte turned, frowning. His attitude, so warm, even passionate, on her arrival, had cooled. She did not understand. She made her way to the carriage and climbed up, picking up the reins. Ravi, who had been half slumbering in the shade of a tree, jumped up and scrambled onto the carriage.

"Goodbye, Captain, and bon voyage."

"Kitt," said Charles, but she had jigged the horses into movement and before he could say anything more she set off down the road.

Charles turned and went to the verandah where her cup lay. When the Malay boy came to clean the table, Charles waved him away. What are you doing, Charles Maitland? he thought. In his mind he saw her lips on the cup and he rested his head against the back of the chair. Not again. He had been quite wrong to be so forward. What on earth did he intend by it? And now he had hurt her.

"Damn," he said loudly and got up. He had let his heart rule him once before. It was so easy to be swept away. And what did he have to offer a woman of such beauty and wealth? He rose and walked towards the observatory.

17

Alexander ran over Thomson Bridge. This was his favourite part of the day. He was accompanied by Tarun, his syce. Tarun was an Indian-Malay man of about twenty years of age. Tarun's job was to watch him, take him places, keep him safe and bring him home. Luckily, Alexander thought, Tarun had many friends among the boatmen on the river and in Serangoon, also in Telok Ayer, around Boat Quay and seemingly everywhere. Tarun had been born in Singapore to a former Indian convict turned boatman and his Malay wife. His mother had died of fever when Tarun was the same age as Alexander, and he had been raised by his father on the river and in Kampong Kerbau, where his father's new woman lived, raising buffalo. His mother tongue was Tamil but he spoke fluent Malay.

Charlotte had engaged him to improve Zan's Malay, for with the *babu* Zan only spoke Javanese—and not even good Javanese, but baby Javanese. It would not do here. Tarun took him to school, picked him up and together Charlotte let them wander around Singapore from two until five in the afternoon. Tarun knew that he and Alex must return home to North Bridge Road by five o'clock. That was the rule.

Charlotte had investigated Tarun carefully. He was a pleasant young man. He had married at sixteen and already had two children of his own. His father had crushed an arm in a boating accident, for the river was a dangerous place, with *tongkangs* and sampans constantly smashing against each other in the crush of the boats. Tarun's father could no longer work; the woman in Kampong Kerbau had deserted him and this, the accident and the hardship, had made him old before his time. Tarun had been a boatman for a time but was very grateful that Charlotte had taken them all into her compound.

Tarun's wife cared for his father, who could sit under the mango tree with their children, and she helped in the laundry of the house. Tarun's own duties were not onerous, and he was paid quite generously, and his shelter and food were supplied. He had arrived in a kind of heaven and he liked Alexander very much. He took care of him as he would his own sons. When they were older, they would all roam around Singapore. This roaming was a source of hilarity in his family. The idea of paying someone to wander about was at first a source of wonder and then amusement. Of course he must also take care of the horses and the carriages and carry out gardening duties in the morning. Alex and Adam played with his sons under the mango tree and Adam too, could chatter in Malay with these boys.

Charlotte knew that Tarun did not fully understand. Charlotte wanted a man to be around Zan. His true father could not show him how to be a man, and Tigran, who would have been wonderful, was gone. She needed a man who was already a father, had fatherly instincts but was young enough to be his friend too. Zan's Malay had become very fluent, and he had become strong and smart and independent, qualities she desired for him. She wanted him in the company of men.

When he was in the town too, he spoke to the Chinese and his Hokkien had become very good, the natural chattering abilities of a child, for he translated for Tarun who spoke no Chinese. Tarun did not trust the Chinese workers and shopkeepers in the narrow streets of the town. He knew the Indian boatmen well but even as a young child had stayed away from the Chinese.

But his orders were clear. Alexander must go everywhere in the town. One day to the Chinese quarter, one day to the Indians in Serangoon, one day to Kampong Glam and one day to Kampong Bugis by the Kallang river. On the fifth day Charlotte took both her sons out on Robert's boat, teaching them to sail on the quiet waters around Pulau Brani.

Alexander jumped round a post and onto Boat Quay. He loved the river, loved the day spent here. Tarun would josh with the Indian boatmen. He knew them all and Alexander was deeply impressed. To know every man on the river! Such a thing. Tarun showed him how to steer the sampan, and the other boatmen encouraged him and laughed, slapping him on the shoulder till he hurt. Alexander shared their food, this spicy stuff of southern India, and chattered to them in terrible Tamil.

When he first came here he had wanted to be a boatman, to take the big *tongkangs* out to the ships on the harbour. Of course when he was in Serangoon, he wanted to raise buffalo, and in Kampong Glam he yearned to make boats.

But eventually it became clear to him that it was Kampong Bugis on the Kallang River that he loved most. There he wanted to *be* Bugis, a Rajah Laut, the king of the sea, a pirate if need be, a man who ruled the waves. Yes his favourite was the Bugis village. The men were hard and copper skinned. They handled boats like no one; they owned the sea. He loved them and strangely, they took him in and even his Indian guard.

Tarun was even more wary of the Bugis than of the Chinese, for they were warriors. But they liked this English boy who came and sailed their boats with their own boys, who was brave and willing. And Tarun, too, was clever with boats. They had not seen this before. And the boy understood them. The Bugis language was a mix of Malay and Javanese, and here in Singapore more Malay than Javanese, and he found he could talk to them. This ability, above all, had amazed and endeared him to them. The women gave him *lepat loi*, glutinous rice cooked in coconut milk and wrapped in banana leaves. The men gave him a small kris which he kept concealed from his mother but which he loved like life itself.

Today Tarun had stopped to talk to a boatman, and Zan ran off to the Malay boys and their cockle-shell boats. For two doits they carried passengers across the river, and they shouted to him as he arrived, pulling him into the boat and showing him how to steer what was really nothing more than a large basket. All he could do was make it go round and round in circles, and they laughed and joshed him. Finally some customers arrived, and the boys loaded up and moved their boats swiftly away from shore.

Alex began to wander along the quay. He loved the godowns and shops here. He wished Ah Soon was here, but today his friend could not come. Each shop was a wonderland of stuffs from everywhere in the whole world. He knew geography now, knew about Scotland and Armenia and Java. And Singapore stood in the centre of his world, on the trade routes of the English ships, standing on the lip of the Straits of Malacca, of travel from India and the West, from China to the East and guardian of English trade in Southeast Asia. This town was important and he was proud to live here. He knew he had a home in Batavia but he never gave that place a thought. He had vague memories of speaking Dutch with his father but they had mostly faded.

He knew very well Mr Whampoa's godown, an emporium of everything naval. He turned briefly to seek Tarun and saw him still talking. He knew he must not lose sight of Tarun in the busy Chinese town. Not because he was fearful but because he knew Tarun would be anxious and his mother would be angry.

Alexander knew his way home but he knew too, despite his young years, that if he was lost Tarun would suffer, and Alex would not be permitted to roam any more. So he lingered longer than usual in front of Whampoa's emporium, looking at the shipping tackle, the infinite variety and sizes of cords and rope; the tools, the axes and chisels, lanterns, nails, spikes and hooks. A family of kittens had made a home in an old basket, future mousers for the godown, and he played with them for a little while. It was a boy's dream, a ship's chandler, and he inhaled the musty and pungent odours of turpentine, tar, pitch, linseed oil, tallow, lard and varnish.

In the back were a vast variety of livestock: poultry, pigs and sheep in pens, parrots and cockatoos in cages, ducks and geese below them on pools of water. There were ovens for baking bread, and aromas of fresh bread mingled with the dirt and smell of the animals. The noise of cackling, bellowing, braying and bleating simply added to the appeal, and Mr Whampoa's godown was Alex's idea of paradise. He never tired of exploring it.

Two Chinese boys he knew from the town came up, and they all chattered. Then one of the boys took out a woven rattan ball, and they began a game of *sepak raga*, moving swiftly to keep the ball in the air. Two old men yelled at them. Alex could play *sepak raga* well, for it was a schoolyard game, but the two boys were much better, and they laughed as he fell over, lunging for the ball. Alex laughed too and let out a string of swear words in Hokkien, which provoked sudden uproarious laughter from the shopkeepers and coolies. The sight of this young white boy, dressed in European clothes, swearing like a Hokkien sailor, could only cause merriment. And Alex played to his audience, pleased with himself, knowing it was unusual.

He felt rather than saw the presence of a large Chinese man approaching him and looked up. The two other boys ran off. Alex had not seen this man before. He would have noticed, for the man was tall and strong, unlike most of the Chinese men in the town who looked skinny. He was a towkay, Zan knew, from his dress.

His eyes met Zhen's. Alex bowed as Chinese manners required. The man stood stock still, saying nothing and Zan frowned a little. His hair had fallen around his face, and he was hot and brushed it back around his ears. Actually he thought the Chinese bare head must be cool and sometimes wanted to lose all his hair entirely. Of course his mother was horrified but, Zan had begun to discover, mothers had most peculiar ideas.

The man, finally, spoke up in Chinese. "Hello," he said. "What is your name?"

"My name is Ah Rex," Alexander said, enunciating his name in the Chinese manner.

Zhen was bewildered. He tried again in English. "Are you an English boy?"

Zan smiled, surprised the man spoke such good English. "I am half- English and half-Dutch, sir. I am Alexander."

Before he could continue, Tarun rushed to Zan's side and, throwing a glance of deep suspicion at the big Chinese man, he took Zan's hand and pulled him away. Today they were supposed to visit the Indian temple in South Bridge Road, where devotees were preparing for the festival of *Thimithi*, the fire walking ceremony.

Zan bowed briefly to the man. Zhen watched as the Indian guard walked quickly away with the boy and disappeared. He could not quite organise his thinking. This boy, this English boy, looked like Xia Lou's dead husband, the way his hair was braided, long, to his shoulders, with jet beads. Yet something in his size, the shape of his jaw, in the tilt of his eyes, was different to the second son he had seen. He could not put his finger on it. But that this was Xia Lou's first son, Zhen was almost certain.

Within him awoke a fervent desire, a desire he had not thought about before this moment. He wanted a son. He was still annoyed at Noan. Tomorrow he must return to her and this time, he wanted a child. He would not be cold and quick as he knew she feared. Nothing would change. He wanted a child conceived in the joy of passion, of her desire and his. His thoughts, thus diverted, turned to Xia Lou. This was her son. He smiled inside his mind. Such a good-looking boy, strong and tall, clever and polite.

Can I meet you? he thought, Can I talk to you? About children, about life. He missed her, suddenly, in a completely unexpected way. He wanted to talk to her, to a woman full of intelligence that he loved and trusted. He wanted to share something of his life with her, his thoughts and dreams. The way it had been before they had ever made love, getting to understand each other in the old orchard on the hill. Yet it was so hard. There was this ultimatum standing between them. He wished, at that moment, that he had never voiced it.

18

The Temenggong's village was a surprise. His house, the Istana Lama, was not the large, straw-roofed ramshackle wooden hut which she had heard about but a whitewashed European villa with green shutters and roof tiles. Similar buildings and pavilions stood all around the main palace. It was unexpected though she could not now think why. Singapore was full of surprises of the architectural kind.

Telok Belangah meant "cooking pot bay", some said from the *belangah* or clay cooking pots used by the southern Indians, which were made there from the local red clay, others said from the shape of the land itself, which resembled such pots. Charlotte had sailed many times around the stilt houses of Pulau Brani but had not ventured into the area where the Temenggong and his followers lived between the north side of Pulau Brani and the mainland, nestling into the foot of what was now, incongruously known officially as Mount Faber, though no one ever called it that. The waters, she had been told, were dangerous; the Temenggong's men were all pirates and cut-throats. The sight, therefore of a neat village surrounding a small mansion was unexpected to say the least.

Prahus and boats of many kinds lay idly in the bay or drawn up on shore. The number and variety of native craft was astounding, and many visitors here remarked upon it and sketched the boats. The bay itself was large and serene, the waters a limpid blue. A series of attap houses on stilts marked the residences and fishing stakes of the *orang laut*, the sea people who were the Temenggong's men.

The day was exceptionally fine, the sky filled with small white clouds like powder puffs. Occasionally they would pass across the sun, casting black shadows on the water, allowing one to perceive the crowds of bright fish flitting just beneath the surface.

On a high promontory stood a fine mansion. This was Mr Kerr's residence on Bukit Chermin. William Kerr, Charlotte had discovered, was a close friend and confidant of the Temenggong. He had purchased this land from the Malay leader and was a principal business colleague in the increasingly profitable gutta-percha trade.

Behind the village rose the wooded slopes of the newly named Mount Faber, covered in pineapple trees. A rough track was just visible, running around the hill. John Thomson, who was sailing the boat and who was generally a mild-mannered and polite young man, was fulsome in his criticisms of the engineering abilities of Edward Faber.

"Look at the pathetic thing. It is stupidly narrow, so narrow that two persons meeting can barely pass each other. When it rains it is washed away. The flagstaff has been repaired a dozen times but still persists in marching down the slope. And for this marvelous feat of engineering, the entire area has been named for Faber. Such are the advantages of being the Governor's brother-in-law."

Charlotte smiled. She knew of the ridiculously low bridge over the river, so low the boats could not pass under it at high tide. Faber had suggested a remedy in the permanent dredging of the river bed—a suggestion received with scorn. His reputation had been established at a stroke. She knew that the roof of the new Ellenborough Market building at Kampong Malacca had proved too heavy for its sides, and great cracks had appeared. Also, the remodelled landing stage on the bank of the river had collapsed. Faber was currently commissioned with building the new gaol and bets were being taken on how long it would remain standing. Faber was the butt of every joke, and John Thomson, as an architect and engineer, found his patience tested at the mere mention of the man's name.

Soon their craft came to rest against the small jetty, and a handsome young boy with a small entourage came forward. He was perhaps thirteen years old. Tucked in his belt was a kris in its scabbard; the large, ornate handle protruded from the belt. Charlotte knew well the importance of the kris to a Malay man. It represented authority and virility. From the heavy silver gilding and the size of the kris, Charlotte deduced that this was either a son or nephew of the Temenggong. The boy raised his hands charmingly to John and Charlotte and said, in good English, "Welcome to my father's house. You are most welcome indeed. Welcome, welcome. How do you do?"

Charlotte realised that this boy was Abu Bakar, Ibrahim's son. She knew he attended Benjamin Keaseberry's Malay School at River Valley Road, where the Munshi gave instruction. He had spoken to her of this boy, of whom he had high hopes. The Temenggong sent two of his sons there. She knew that Butterworth had encouraged him but still, it was such an unusual and enlightened action that Charlotte was predisposed to like him. She had seen the Temenggong only once before, and he had appeared haughty and unapproachable, surrounded by hard-eyed men with weapons.

The boy suddenly took up Charlotte's hand and began pumping it up and down and laughing with delight, until John stepped between them and directed a hard stare at the boy, who, seemingly unaware, now jumped and skipped ahead of them towards the white villa which lay nestled into the slope of the hill. Other than the Temmengong's guardsmen, there seemed to be no men in the village but the women and children all came crowding out down to the beach to see this white woman who was here to visit their chieftain. They watched silently as Charlotte and John passed between them, not unfriendly but curious and unsmiling. Charlotte was glad to reach the smooth terrain before the house and see emerge from it two men.

One was European, small, mouse-like, with slightly buck teeth and a very pale complexion. The other she recognised immediately as the Temenggong. She remembered his slimness and his height but had not recalled his extreme good looks. His face was well-shaped, with high cheek bones, an aquiline nose, shapely lips and piercing, dark, intelligent eyes. He looked almost Roman in his features. His dark hair was short and slightly wavy, and over it he wore the elaborate and elegant *tengkolok*, the rakish silk turban of the Malays. His tight-fitting long coat of green silk was threaded with silver and fell over loose silk trousers; his undershirt was pure white, setting off his fine brown skin. His kris, silver and studded with diamonds, was tucked into his fringed black waist sash. He looked every inch the powerful leader of warring and piratical men, and Charlotte was struck.

She curtsied very low to him and he smiled at her, a smile of brilliance and she could not help smiling back. He was utterly unexpected.

The Temenggong too seemed to find Charlotte's looks appealing, leisurely examining her and smiling until she blushed slightly. John glared and frowned at William. He understood why Charlotte seduced every man she met, but for goodness sakes, the man was a chieftain and a Mohammedan. He should be more circumspect.

William stepped forward and introduced Daeng Ibrahim to Charlotte formally in Malay, and Charlotte made the usual *politesses*. Then the Temmengong unexpectedly held out his arm to Charlotte to accompany her into the house.

Charlotte hesitated. She knew that Mohammedans were very careful around women. Certainly their own were kept well out of the way, in harems, she had heard. Of course this harem business was very intriguing. She had glimpsed it only once in Java. Apparently, however, the Temenggong did as he pleased, and she smiled her thanks and took his arm.

"Do not be alarmed," he said to her in Malay in a low voice. "I have learned something around the English for so long and understand how to be the English gentleman when it suits me."

They entered the house and she found it to be the epitome of a grand English country manor, complete with Queen Anne chairs. The Temenggong's place was usually, evidently, a raised dais covered in green velvet cushions. This he did not use, however, and, motioning everyone to sit, he took up a chair next to Charlotte's and murmured to a servant at his elbow.

An elaborate ritual followed. Porcelain teacups arrived with an English silver teapot and English tea. Plates of macaroons, seed biscuits and gingerbread were laid out on the table. However, with the arrival of the magnificent silver and lacquer *tempat sireh*, the table departed from England and arrived on Asian shores. Since her previous encounter with the chewing of the betel, Charlotte had learned the proper etiquette for refusal. When offered, she smiled and put out her fingers to touch the betel box, recognising the hospitality of her host.

She noticed that the Temenggong took nothing, and she remembered, suddenly, that it was Ramadan, the fasting time for Mohammedans. He would take nothing until after sunset.

A great deal of small talk followed, the Temenggong asking about her family, her late husband and her children. They discussed Robert and his difficult job policing the settlement. He asked John about his surveying work and the prospects for a lighthouse at Pedra Branca. They talked of the Dutch at Batavia and, with William, his plans to settle a new town at Johor, over the straits. The Temenggong was easy to speak to, and she enjoyed re-using her Malay which had grown a little rusty. The announcement of further guests interrupted them. It was probably just as well as John appeared to be becoming red faced.

The Temenggong went to greet his guests, and William and John approached Charlotte, who said, "What a fascinating man. Tell me something of him, William, please."

"With pleasure Mrs Manouk. Daeng Ibrahim is a most delightful and clever individual. In business he is shrewd; in personal dealings, charming."

John snorted slightly, and William threw him a sharp look.

"Well, well, John. Do you not agree?" Charlotte said.

"He is charming of course and shrewd. He is also head of a piratical band of fiends."

William put up his hand in protest. "That is over. The Temenggong has but recently received the highest award from Queen Victoria for his help in eradicating piracy in these waters."

"Such nonsense. It suits him now, but for years he has had the blood of many good men on his hands."

"Times change, John, and the wise man changes with them."

Charlotte was mystified at this debate and she listened carefully, trying not to be distracted by the muffled sounds of greetings from an outside hall somewhere. William looked annoyed.

"Allow me to explain, Mrs Manouk. What John will not understand is that it is we Europeans who have interfered for centuries with the legitimate trading of the Malay chieftains. Since before recorded time, the Malays traded with each other and with China. When the Portuguese came, they disrupted this trade and organised monopolies. The Spanish followed, then the Dutch, now the English. What were these people to do? Down the years, the taking of plunder, the controlling of the seaways, became a legitimate means of business. Not a worthy one by our more enlightened times, I grant you."

William put out his hands and shrugged his shoulders, and John snorted his disdain.

"William is in business with the Temenggong, you understand—the gutta-percha business. His interests are entwined with Ibrahim's. He is bound to defend him. And Ibrahim is not Malay anyway, he is Bugis. He calls himself Daeng, which is a Bugis title, and they are the most fearsome cut-throats who ever roamed the seas."

This was getting interesting. Gutta-percha had been discovered in Singapore, and Charlotte knew it was a kind of malleable resin which the Malays had used for centuries as handles for their *parangs* and for whips. It had been introduced to the English world by Dr Montgomerie, the settlement's chief surgeon. It was used to mould decorative and household items and tubes, but she had not realised it had become such a valuable commodity.

"Gutta-percha has recently been used as insulation for telegraph cables under the Hudson River in New York and across the English Channel with great success. Its protective properties in water are second to none. With the inevitable spread of the telegraph, its potential seems limitless," William said and smiled. "And the Temenggong has lots of it."

"And William is his agent and adviser," said John.

John claimed that the Temenggong's new-found respectability relied on this trade, which had rapidly made him extremely rich. His lands in Johor were filled with gutta-percha, and he controlled, by fair means or foul, the trade and the prices of this article. This was an example of his shrewdness, for few Malay chieftains would demean themselves to the business of trade.

"Since, however," John added, "the gutta-percha usually arrived in the Temenggong's hands through robbing ships and stealing cargoes, perhaps he finds it fits very well with his former way of life."

William made a *moue* and frowned. "Ibrahim is a quite remarkable individual. When his father died he was but fifteen years of age and his resources were slight. The pension his father had negotiated with Raffles and this kampong here at Telok Belangah were all the family had. He was cut off from the traditional Johor court at Rhio and so had no title. He was not recognised officially as Temenggong until 1841, when he was thirty years old. To survive as ruler he had two unappetising alternatives: he could be a puppet or a pirate."

Charlotte listened raptly. William had a way of telling this story which was gripping.

"For many years in his youth, times were very hard. Personal power and prestige are what keep seafaring people loyal to a leader. He had none. Sultan Hussein of Singapore, the ostensible leader of the Singapore Malays, was disgraced and fled to Malacca, where he died. Hussein's son was unrecognised and weak. Ibrahim's followers drifted into piracy."

It was all so fascinating. John however, was annoyed; he put down his glass and said contemptuously, "Drifted indeed."

Charlotte looked sharply at him. She wanted to hear this story and John, who sensed her interest, looked annoyed but said nothing more.

"It was Samuel Bonham, the governor in 1835, when Ibrahim was in his twenties, who realised that without a strong Malay leader in Singapore, the piratical hordes which roamed the Straits would never be brought under control. No Temenggong, no Sultan—these bands of men held allegiance to no one. They marauded south of the Straits of Singapore, fleeing to Dutch waters whenever chased by the British."

William tilted his head towards John. "Doubtless unsavoury acts took place ..."

John pursed his lips.

"However," William continued, "once he realised where his best alliances could be made, he acted swiftly and decisively. And ..."

William now turned to John, "Bonham was forced to find a means to fight piracy which cost the Singapore government nothing, the East India Company refusing to pay anything and the merchants refusing to pay taxes."

John nodded. "That is true. The merchants would put up with anything, even piracy and murder, to avoid paying taxes."

"Ibrahim withdrew support for piracy amongst his followers and used his growing influence with other leaders in the peninsula," William explained. "Naturally the open backing of the colonial authorities, and several successful raids on pirate strongholds, increased his personal reputation. Many people sought refuge with him in Telok Belangah. He became the intermediary between the government and the Malay chiefs."

William took a drink of tea. He had a rather feminine way of holding his cup with his little finger crooked, Charlotte noticed. Then he went on: "That was when I became involved with him. It has been a struggle for him. He was rewarded only a few years ago by being officially recognised as Temenggong Sri Maharaja of Johor, not only by the British but importantly, by the other Sultans of the archipelago. In the absence of a legitimate Sultan of Singapore, he has become the most important Malay leader here. Governor Butterworth has full confidence in him."

John snorted and William ignored him. "Now he has seen the commercial potential of the land he controls in Johor. He has had the wisdom to cooperate widely with the Chinese community, granting land leases to develop pepper and gambier plantations. However he is also astute enough to make sure he retains control of these *kangchu*, or headmen, with scrupulous documentation and close supervision. No one who knows the organisational ineptitude of other unruly Malay sultans can fail to be impressed by Daeng Ibrahim's foresight and vision. He will make of Johor a mighty state.

John looked at William sharply and remarked, "And those who go with him will make their fortunes and the devil take their morals."

William shrugged and smiled.

Their conversation was interrupted by the entrance of a group of Malay men, several Europeans and three Chinese merchants. To her absolute astonishment, Charlotte saw that one of the three was Zhen.

He stopped abruptly at the sight of her and she too, was transfixed. Then the Temenggong entered and the moment passed. Her heart, which for that moment had been normal, suddenly began to beat hard, and she felt very hot. She waved her fan quickly and turned to John.

"I fear we are intruding," she said, desperate to leave. "We have taken up enough of the Temenggong's time. He is a busy man."

She rose and took John's arm. Ibrahim had glanced up as she moved and now came to her side.

"I am sorry our party has been interrupted. Some unexpected business has come up. Forgive me."

She could hardly concentrate on what the Temenggong was saying. Zhen had moved away from the group and was making his way towards her, but he hesitated to approach her whilst the Temenggong was speaking. She wished he would not. Charlotte did not trust herself or her emotions.

"May I invite you to the Istana again, Mrs Manouk?" The Temenggong smiled and she curtsied, hardly aware of what he had asked.

"It is for Hari Raya, the festival which marks the end of the fasting of Ramadan." Ibrahim turned to John. "Of course, you are also invited, Mr Thomson. I always have a large party. With fireworks."

John bowed and the matter was settled. Ibrahim nodded to Charlotte and spoke to his minister, who was at his elbow. She was immediately surrounded by a small group of guards and realised that Ibrahim was paying her a great honour. For better or worse, Zhen was unable to reach her, and her last view of him was as she turned on the jetty and saw him outside, staring down to the landing place. She wanted to raise her hand, but suddenly John took her arm and helped her into the boat. By the time she had twisted out of his grasp and looked again at the hill, he had disappeared.

19

Charlotte was in the garden, directing the planting of a grove of pretty yellow flowering cassod trees. It was early, the day still fresh, when a servant came racing towards her. A policeman tuan was here with a message, the servant said.

She went back to the house and found Edmond Hale, one of Robert's European sergeants in a state of agitation. Before she could speak he said, "Robert. It's Robert. He has been injured down at Rochor. Attacked, there's been an attack."

Charlotte's hand flew to her mouth. Robbie injured, my God! She stared at Edmond, unwilling to believe it.

"I've just had word. I thought you should know. Stay here Charlotte. I will go and send back news," he said firmly.

But Charlotte put up her hand. "'I will not stay, Edmond. I must come with you." She called Malik, her major domo. A man of grace and efficiency, he would take charge of the house immediately. She considered herself lucky to have him. He was something of a snob but she did not mind. He had served Governor Bonham until the Governor's departure. Butterworth had no need of him, for he had brought his own butler and staff from India.

She and Edmond took to the carriage and set out for Rochor Road. Though he moved quite fast down North Bridge Road, Edmond was forced to slow constantly for the state of the roads was dreadful with great potholes here and there, especially as they approached Kampong Glam.

"Damnable roads, makes our job twice as difficult. No one wants to pay for the upkeep, though God knows, the convict labour is free," he grumbled.

Charlotte could hardly take any of this in. Why was he talking about roads when Robert might be in mortal danger?

The carriage crossed the intersection by the Sultan's mosque very slowly, for here the ground was muddy and churned. The track, for it was merely this, was all but impassible at Jalan Trang, and by now they could hear the sounds of men shouting. Edmond got down and, with Charlotte following, they advanced down the track. A great number of Malays were gathered, mingled with some policemen. The noise grew tumultuous, but none of the Malays was making a sound. The din came from around the corner on Jalan Rochor, where the police station was situated. Heavy noise, voices raised, sticks beating tin, a roar. Then she saw a man being carried on a stretcher, covered in blood. She let out a cry and ran forward, but she quickly saw it was not Robert. The poor man was Chinese and was horribly beaten.

Edmond spoke to the two peons carrying him. "The Chinese interpreter, beaten by the mob. I've told them to take our carriage, get him to the hospital." Edmond had to yell over the din.

Charlotte's robe was now heavy with mud. She was having difficulty walking, and Edmond, anxious for her, told her to wait. But she was too afraid now to wait alone. The press of men was all around, and two policemen, seeing the Europeans and recognising Edmond, came to their aid.

As they turned the corner, Charlotte saw, to her horror, the full import of the situation. The noise came from the angry, distorted faces of thousands of Chinese men. The number was incredible; they formed a great mass so closely melded together that they swayed like black foam on a river. Above them rose a sea of flags and banners. It was, Charlotte knew, the massed members of the *kongsi*, the Chinese society which regulated affairs in the settlement. Their lodge and temple were on Rochor Road.

A line of policemen formed a thick cordon at the Rochor bridge, guns raised. Only this bridge separated the furious mass from the other side of the river. The lane and banks on the far side were thick with men, banners lifted, voices raised in a chant. *Pah, pah, pah*, it sounded like. Strangely, through the din came the sound of a Chinese band, its high tones a countermelody to the chant. Charlotte stood transfixed by this powerful, violent symphony of sound and music which ebbed and flowed, until Edmond took her arm and pulled her into the police station.

Robert was seated on a chair inside, his face bloody. His arm was hurt in some way, she could see, hanging limply at his side.

"Kitt, Kitt, oh dear. Why are you here? It has all got out of hand so very quickly," he cried.

Charlotte shook her head and called to one of the men for some water. Taking up her petticoat, she tore a great strip and began to wipe Robert's bloody face. She could see he had received blows.

Robert smiled wanly at his sister and turned to Edmond. "You should not have brought her here, really Edmond."

"Not Edmond's fault. I would not stay away. We had news you were injured."

Robert winced as the water stung his wound. "Captain Cuppage is still out there, guarding the bridge. He has sent for the army. We cannot control this number of men. Why there must be five or six thousand of them."

"What has happened, Robert?"

"All this because of a funeral. The head of the *kongsi* died two weeks ago, and an application was made to me to bury the body with due form, which for the Chinese means a very public procession. You know what it is like, Charlotte, lots of show and so on."

Charlotte nodded. She was worried about Robbie. She had cleaned the wound as best she could, but it needed a surgeon. She tore another strip and wound it round Robert's head. Then she made a sling for his arm. He was in pain; it showed on his face though he made not a sound as she tied the sling around his neck.

"I consented to the procession so long as the number of followers did not exceed one hundred. Fine chance! The procession was to proceed directly through the town to the burial ground at Mount Palmer and be carried out in an orderly fashion. Other mourners were permitted to gather there, at the burial site. All this was agreed to by the leaders of the *kongsi*, and now you see the result. Why, they lie as they breathe."

Edmond had gone out to check the bridge. Now he came back with Captain Cuppage in tow. "Adam," said Robert, "what news?"

"Still, for the moment. I think there has been a bit of shock at your wounding, and they are deciding what to do. Most of the noise is for show. That was a foolish brave thing to do, Robert."

Adam smiled at Robert and bowed to Charlotte. He had never seen this sister of his friend, and he was, despite all the fracas, glad to see that reports of her looks had not been exaggerated.

Charlotte nodded at Adam Cuppage.

"What happened, Captain Cuppage?"

"Your brother saved that poor Chinese man from certain death."

Robert was drinking water, some colour returning to his face. Adam Cuppage continued. "We got reports of this huge mob gathering at the river, and the whole force was mustered. When we got here, I took up guard at the bridge and Robert went to talk to the leaders, for this appearance of six thousand men was too much. Of course they said they had no control over what the men did. What nonsense. These men are here only by their bidding! Well, as Robert was about to come back to me, a scuffle broke out, and the men began attacking the Chinese interpreter with iron bars. Robert went back and used his rifle butt to get the men off the poor fellow and brought him out. Not without the knocks and bruises you see upon his person."

A policeman, breathing heavily, interrupted them. A heavy drumming had begun. "The procession is on the move. We cannot hold them."

Robert looked at Adam. "Good God. The whole town will be pillaged." He rose, shakily.

"Edmond, you must stay here with Charlotte. We must contain it, cut off the side streets. They don't want to stay here. When it has passed by, take my sister home."

Robert looked severely at Charlotte. "Do as I say, Kitt."

Charlotte nodded.

"Come on, Adam. Get the men organised, keep the procession moving down North Bridge Road. Don't let any strays off on the cross streets."

The two men left, and Charlotte and Edmond waited inside the police station with a cordon of men before the door. The sound of drumming had increased, and the music of the band had suddenly risen to a fever pitch. Robert's men moved back slowly from the bridge before the procession's leaders who were carrying the large banners, until they blocked Jalan Rochor, forcing the procession to turn on Jalan Trang. It was the first test and it was successful. The men turned; the band passed; the mob came on and then the huge catafalque, carried by sixty men, passed before their eyes, its purple embroidered covering shimmering with gold thread. The men, a seething, chattering mob, went by. It seemed to take a long time, but finally the music faded, the drumming dimmed and the last stragglers moved on.

The policemen guarding the street dispersed and Charlotte knew they would run to join their companions, down the parallel lanes, leapfrogging the procession.

Edmond and Charlotte made their way out into the now quiet street. Her carriage had gone. The streets were a muddy morass and they began, slowly, to pick their way out, down Jalan Rochor to the beachside bazaar, turning onto Jalan Bugis towards home. The streets had emptied, everyone returning to their usual pursuits and the wind had picked up. The boatmen were hammering boats on the sand; some fishermen were repairing nets. A group of children followed them, chattering for a while, until Edmond shooed them away. Everything was normal. Charlotte could hardly believe the events of a mere fifteen minutes ago had actually happened, were still happening in the town.

That night she went to Robert's house on Beach Road. He was freshly bandaged and Teresa was fussing over him, pouring tea. She looked tired. The pregnancy and the strain, of course, of Robert's injuries—the anxiety—were wearing on her. How he had managed with his arm, she did not know, for Dr Oxley had declared a fracture and it was now constrained inside his splint of gutta-percha.

It was the second time in a very short while she had discovered the useful properties of this material. Dr Oxley had perfected the use of it for broken and fractured bones. When pressed sheets of it were immersed in hot water, they became so pliable they could be applied to the patient and moulded to form a perfect splint. When they were cold they became as hard as plaster. After the patient was healed, a little warm water would return the sheet to its original malleable form, so it could be removed easily. It was marvellous and Charlotte examined Robert's arm in admiration. He was not in pain. He had been prescribed a little opium and she could see he was at ease.

Her mind, very briefly, strayed to opium. She had been an addict for a time, cured now. It was old history. Still, the thoughts of the pleasures of opium were like the pleasures of love: they lingered in the mind, never far away.

Today, however, she dispelled them quickly. Her attention turned to the news of the day. The procession, she learned, had been contained. The troops had arrived in number and the mob was prevented from entering the town, corralled away from Hill Street to turn down Coleman Street and cross the bridge at South Bridge Road. From there the going was straight to the Chinese burial ground, every crossroad sealed off.

"It is not over yet. Stay close to home, Kitt. I have discovered there is a trouble between two rival *kongsi*. I had thought there was but one, but it is not so. The Teochew and Hokkien *kongsi* are rivals. The Straits merchants here in Singapore are trying to break the Teochew monopoly of the gambier agriculture both in Rhio and here in Singapore."

Robert put his hand to his head. His voice was vibrant, excited. He could see everything clearly. Charlotte knew this was the first stage of the effect of opium. All pain dulled, but the mind as clear as a bell. "I have been a dupe and this wound serves me right," he said. "Chew Tock, my voluntary interpreter, turns out to be no other than the head of this Hokkien *kongsi*. When the other side saw him at my side, they imagined the worst and I have also discovered that there were many of his men in the crowd itching for a fight. Tan Tock Seng has told the Resident Councillor that bitter and hostile feelings exist between these two parties. I fear things will get much worse in the coming weeks. There is a battle going on which we barely begin to understand."

Robert sighed and suddenly seemed to wilt. "For the love of the Lord, Teresa, take away this tea and bring me a whisky."

Teresa started to speak but Robert put up his hand. "Please," he said and smiled wanly. Teresa left the room.

"Kitt, I have to speak to you."

Charlotte frowned slightly. Robert's tone was anxious, but she detected the opium underneath, loosening his tongue. This usually preceded the last stage, the dulling of the senses entirely.

"Yes Robbie, of course. What is it?"

"I have ... done something." His voice was becoming very low and slow. He was very tired, she could see. The opium was taking effect. He needed to sleep.

Charlotte rose and went to him, taking his hand. "What, Robbie? What is it?"

"I have ... Shilah."

Robert's head began to loll. The opium was taking him to the land of pleasant dreams. Charlotte frowned. "What, Robert? What about Shilah?"

He raised his head and smiled a dreamy smile. She recognised it. Dangerous dreams. "Shilah ... I ... Shilah." His head fell back onto the cushion of the chair, and she knew he was far away.

20

Zhen looked at the women in the kitchen. The family was gathered at the mansion on River Valley Road. Noan's mother, aunts and cousins and her father's third concubine were making glutinous rice dumplings for the Dragon Boat Festival in two days.

Noan was pregnant and happy at her family's pleasure. She could see that her father and mother were refreshed at the thought of this birth. But it was tempered by anxiety. So much trouble with Lilin. Her continued absences from the family home, her stubborn nature, these were causes of anxiety for everyone. Noan's third sister had been married away, to the son of the Kapitan at Batavia. They would not meet again until Chinese New Year. Her fourth sister was married to a wealthy merchant in the rice trade in Cochin China. He was, she had heard, not a young man. Two sisters gone and one so lost. She felt a terrible, love for Lilin, who seemed so very far away.

Noan hoped this child would be a son. Zhen had spoken of his wish for a son, and she desperately wanted to give him this gift. Things had improved between them. His anger had died away at the announcement of the pregnancy. He came more often to the house at Market Street. She had been quite sick with this pregnancy. A boy, all her aunts told her. Sickness means it will be a boy.

The rashes had gone. Zhen had brought a salve, and his presence at the family home and in her bed reassured her. The problem with Lilin would not go away, however. She knew Zhen had talked with her father, but he did not want to deal with Lilin. Her father had been unwell recently. He had passed much of the business to Zhen and Ah Teo. He went every day to the godown or the sago factories, but he seemed happy to pass the decisions to his sons-in-law.

Noan prayed often for her father. Her mother was very healthy and enjoyed her social round of cards and lunches, chewing the *sireh*, gossiping. The third concubine waited on her hand and foot. Sometimes Noan felt sorry for this girl. She was still only eighteen. She had been married to Noan's father at thirteen, had three children, three boys, in quick succession and now, as her father had grown unwell, she was abandoned to servitude. Despite the sons, she occupied a low place in the household, especially as her father paid less attention to her.

Lilin's presence at the family gathering was obligatory but she did not join the other women. Ah Teo, Zhen, her father, her uncles and cousins, all the men, were sitting on the verandah watching the maids with the children in the garden and chatting. Lilin watched them from the living room. Ah Teo had taken to smoking cigarettes, and she smiled. Gaston gave her cigarettes, and she smoked from time to time. She had entirely given up chewing the betel. Gaston disliked it. Actually all the Western men disliked it. It was a custom of her aged relatives, and she had come to hate it, too, almost as much as she disliked wearing this shapeless *baju* and sarong. She looked down. Her figure was entirely concealed.

Noan came out onto the verandah with the maid, bringing tea to the men. Her belly was big and the men said something to Zhen and they all laughed. Noan blushed slightly and served the tea. Zhen smiled too, but tenderly, Lilin could see, at his wife. She felt a coldness and a desperate wish for them all to be dead. Especially Ah Teo. He had taken up with the whorehouse keeper in Amoy Street. She had found out through one of the girls who worked there. This woman, Min, was disfigured and low, but Ah Teo had rented a house for her in Hong Kong Street. A whore for god's sake! Zhen knew of it, she was sure, for this Min was a crony of his and the loathsome Qian. What filth they all were. She turned away.

The men ate lunch together in the formal dining room, the women separately from them in the room off the kitchen. After lunch the men napped or talked. Her old aunts and uncles went home. Her mother and father too, were napping. Lilin was sitting in the garden in the deep shade of a mango tree. Noan went up to her and sat down. Lilin did not look at her. She looks pale, Noan thought.

"Lilin, we see you so little. The children miss you. Lian particularly."

Noan stopped. She had no idea what Lilin did all day and most of the nights. There had been a time when Lilin was kept in the house. She had had a guard, was not permitted to go out. It was horrible. Lilin was crazed, screamed and ranted all day, upset the children. She had been sent briefly to her aunt and uncle in Malacca, but within weeks they had sent her back. Ah Teo was told off, told to deal with his wife, but he could do nothing. Nobody could. So they had let her be. Zhen and Ah Teo had spoken to her. No scandal, and she could come and go as she wished. And an allowance, she had said to Ah Teo, smiling. He had agreed. Now Zhen said nothing, Ah Teo said nothing, her father had given up.

Noan took a deep breath and said boldly, "Lilin, what do you do every day? What do you do at night when you do not come home?"

Lilin looked at her sister. "Are you sure you want to know?"

Noan hesitated. She was a little afraid of what Lilin might say, but she nodded nevertheless.

"I fuck a white man. I drink wine and smoke cigarettes. I am free."

Noan's hand went to her mouth. Her sister had spoken like a man, in the language of a man. Her voice was empty, hollow.

"Shocked, big sister? Ah Teo has his whore and I have mine. No one knows. I am very careful. The aunties and uncles, the cousins, they know nothing. They live in Malacca, in any case." Having said as much as she seemed to want to reveal in this place, Lilin looked at her hands, took up her bag, rose and beckoned to her sister. "Come, walk with me to the big pond."

Noan fell into a slow step with her sister. When the house disappeared from view, Lilin took out a pouch of tobacco and paper and deftly rolled a cigarette and lit it with a lucifer, inhaling deeply. Noan was fascinated. She had seen Ah Teo smoke. How did it not burn the mouth? she wondered, but she did not ask.

Lilin looked at Noan and the bulge at her waist. "You know, if you do not obey, they can do nothing. It has taken me a long time to learn it. Maybe in China they can send you somewhere, but here in Singapore, if you do not obey, they can do nothing. We live in our father's house, we are given possessions. When I married Ah Teo I received jewellery and furniture. It is mine. I have sold some, you know, but now they give me money to shut me up."

Noan was silent. She had never heard such scandalous talk but somehow it made a kind of sense. "Does my husband know?" she asked quietly.

Lilin laughed. "Know? Of course he knows. Well, not exactly what I do, but about the money." She stopped and turned to her sister. "He expects obedience from you but he has a woman, you know it. I've told you. A white woman."

Noan turned away. She wanted to hear no more. She began to walk back to the house. Lilin stood, smoking, watching her sister retreat. Noan could not face the truth, she thought, but perhaps it was better that way. She had a child to bear; what did the truth matter?

Lilin wandered towards the pond. The wind had risen suddenly and was moving quietly around the trees. She dropped her cigarette underfoot. Then, on the breeze she heard voices and turned. There was a pavilion by the pond, a Chinese pavilion with a green tiled roof and upturned eaves: her father's conceit, a touch of old China in his garden, a China he had never even seen, a country he knew nothing about, with a language he could not speak. How despicable they all were with their ridiculous pretensions!

She moved slowly between the trees and listened carefully. It was Zhen and Qian. Lilin was surprised. Qian here? She had not seen him come. That was not surprising, though. It was possible easily to come to the gate at the garden.

She moved very close. The back of the pavilion was screened with lattice against the rain and anyone could approach without being seen, for the view was of the pond. They were speaking, she realised very quickly, in English. In Hokkien she would have understood nothing, but in English she did.

" ... see her." Zhen was speaking. Lilin crept forward. She

was intrigued. Why were they talking in English when both were Hokkien?

"Are you sure?" This was Qian. "To start again, Zhen Ah."

"It is too hard to be without her."

Lilin stayed very still.

"I love her." Zhen hung his head.

Zhen was hurt. He was talking about the white woman, she realised. Lilin's eyes narrowed. She hated her, this woman with power over Zhen, the man she wanted more than anything.

"I must meet her. Qian, will she agree?"

Qian looked at his friend and put his hand on his arm. Years before he had helped Zhen to meet Xia Lou, had taken her to the orchard of nutmeg trees behind Bukit Larangan, where they had their first kiss. Their love had truly begun from that moment, and that it was enduring was no longer in doubt. When she had left Singapore, Zhen had mourned her like a dead wife. Qian had helped Zhen write to her in Batavia. She had never answered but Zhen never stopped writing. Zhen knew now that she had not received his letters, but that was not what mattered. For all the years before they met again, he had never stopped writing.

"Yes, Zhen Ah, she will agree. I will ask her. She will remember."

Zhen looked at Qian gratefully. Yes, if Qian asked, she would agree. This memory, the moment in the orchard, with the leaves falling slowly around them as they had tried to speak to her; this they all shared. It seemed strange now that he could speak English so well, strange that he had not been able to talk to her. He remembered that first kiss as if it were a moment ago: the feel of her in his arms, like a soaring ascent to heaven, the rush of his blood as he put his lips to hers; lifting her tight against him, her arms entwining his neck, their bodies locked together, the world blotted out.

Zhen smiled at Qian, patted his friend's shoulder and they both rose and left the pavilion. Lilin watched them go, her heart filled with bile. Zhen would never be hers. The realisation came like a lightning bolt. She had been waiting; she understood it now. The English merchants, Gaston—they had been ways to spend her time until Zhen saw her, wanted her. She had convinced herself it was only a matter of time. Her beauty would capture him. Suddenly he would see her, notice her and everything would be instantly wonderful.

But she understood it now, with a hideous clarity: he would never want her. Years of absence from this English woman had done nothing to dim Zhen's feelings. He wanted her more now than he ever had. Lilin sank to the ground and tears of frustration and anger poured out silently, staining the leaves. Anger at this longing she had nurtured for so long, anger at him for loving another, anger at her blind stupidity. When she could cry no more, she crawled to a tree and sat against it.

She opened her bag, took out the pouch and slowly made a cigarette. Gaston had showed her how to do it, supplied her with tobacco. She had smoked opium, but she did not like the deep drowsiness it caused. Tobacco was different, relaxing without the stupefaction. She lit the cigarette and inhaled deeply. It calmed her and she contemplated the information she had just acquired. The time for stupidity was over. She knew, in her deepest part, that she would never stop wanting Zhen, but she would no longer long for him, build dreams around him. Now different objectives began to surface in her mind and the most satisfying was revenge. Revenge on Zhen and revenge on the white whore.

She crushed the cigarette into the ground, grinding it into the earth. Then she rose and walked back to the house.

21

The night was particularly warm, and all the efforts of the punkah wallahs to create coolness were of little use. The men gathered at the house in Armenian Street were waiting, sweating gently, for their leader to arrive for a meeting of Lodge Zetland of the East, the gathering of Freemasons in Singapore.

On the agenda tonight was fundraising for the Chinese Paupers' Hospital and the Seamen's Hospital which Mr Thomson had built on Pearl's Hill. Also to be addressed was the progress of the proposed building of the Horsburgh Lighthouse on Pedra Branca. But most of what would be dealt with was the most pressing of problems at present, the Chinese secret societies.

The Worshipful Master of the lodge was late. Robert was chafing slightly at this delay. He enjoyed the lodge meetings, the conviviality of the company of old friends, but tonight his arm was hurting. Robert Woods, *The Straits Times* new owner, was talking vehemently with Catchick Moses. Catchick had recently sold the newspaper to Woods, a man who liked crusades. Probably he was still ranting on about James Brooke, the white rajah, against whom he had decided to direct his particular ire. Robert did not like Woods very much. He preferred *The Free Press* over the verbosity of Woods's *The Straits Times*, but he tried to maintain cordial relations with everyone in Singapore. And, of course, here in the Lodge, the temple of brotherly love, everyone kept strict control of their tongues.

The Master of the Lodge finally made his entrance, bedecked in his regalia of office, his sash and apron, which brought the conversations to an end. He called on the Wardens as to those present in the south, west and east, then called the deacon to see the door tyled. The Tyler guarded the door throughout the meeting of the lodge. The Tyler and other officers of the lodge recited their duties, and the Master called on the brethren to assemble around the altar. The men gathered, going down on one knee and holding hands. They bowed their heads as the Master recited the verses of the psalm. Then he too came forward to join the circle, and they lifted and lowered their hands six times. This represented, Robert knew, the sign of astonishment of the Queen of Sheba on first viewing Solomon's Temple. At first Robert had thought all this terribly queer, but he was used to it now. Of course his wounded arm precluded any Sheba-like raising and lowering on this occasion, and this was understood.

The assembled men returned to their places and the Master took his seat on the throne. "Brethren, attend to the signs," he said. When the assembly had performed the signs of the various degrees of the lodge, the Master began the Charge of the Opening.

"The ways of virtue are beautiful. Knowledge is attained by degrees. Wisdom dwells with contemplations: we must seek her. Let us then, Brethren, apply ourselves with becoming zeal to the practice of the excellent principles inculcated by our Order. Let us ever remember that the great objects of our association are the restraint of improper desires and passions ..."

Robert ceased to listen. He knew it by heart anyway, but these last words seemed to be cast at him. It was as if a light shone down into the dark recesses of his heart and read what lay there. His improper desires and passions for Shilah, the woman he had possessed and should have kept. His love for Teresa had not been love; he saw it now. He had been hasty in marrying her. She had had other suitors, and he had been afraid to lose her then—and she wanted him so very much, he knew. She had been suitable. He dwelt momentarily on the word. "Suitable", a suitable wife from a respected family.

Robert shook his head. That wasn't fair. He had been happy with Teresa. Until ... the Master was still intoning. He was head auctioneer at one of the firms on Commercial Square and loved all this pompous ritual, the oath-taking, the signing, the almost boyish secrecy. But at least, Robert thought, he wasn't carrying on with ...

With what? he caught himself quickly. Shilah wasn't a "with". She was lovely, sweet-natured and loving, filled with intense passion still for him. She had demanded nothing of him, merely his presence in her life, in Amber's. He had come to enjoy the quiet, pleasant time they spent together with Amber. She never blamed him, not a word of reproach passed her lips. Even after ... he remembered that awful time. She had been found in a pool of blood, unconscious but still breathing. Amber had been two years old. He had been married only a week. A miscarriage, Dr Little had pronounced. Shilah had been pregnant when he got married, for he had continued to sleep with her even during his engagement.

Robert had had the decency then to be mortified. She had lost a great deal of blood. Later Dr Little had confided to him that he suspected an intervention. Future children might be difficult. Probably just as well, he had said, if Robert planned ... he did not say any more, but it was clear what he was thinking. Cheeky blighter, Robert had thought, and told him to mind his own business.

In good time, Shilah had recovered. She had seemed to get over it. She had survived. All had seemed well, and Teresa knew of this old liaison and the child. Robert had ceased to visit Shilah, and since it was over, his wife had accepted it, with reasonably good grace.

But then he had gone to see her in the pretty house on Queen Street that he had purchased for her and Amber. He had climbed the stairs. The house had seemed empty. He could hear the sounds of Amber playing in the garden with her amah. He had turned to join them outside when there had been a noise from the big front bedroom. It was Shilah, singing. Her melodious and husky voice he had always found attractive.

He had gone to the door and seen her. She was dressed only in a sarong, fresh from a bath, and the folds clung to her figure. Her long black hair was down to her waist, gleaming and wet, her fine brown skin damp. He had not seen her like this for years. She turned and saw him, her black eyes, in this unguarded moment, full of soft longing. The same look in her eyes as the night when, a virginal fifteen-year-old, she had come to him in his bed at the police house on the seaside.

His vows, his good intentions, disappeared and he had locked the door behind him and gone to her.

Robert sat musing on this when he realised that the opening charge was ending.

"Let us act with dignity becoming the high moral character of our venerable institution."

He shook himself from his reverie. Dignity and high moral character. Yes, well, at the moment he wasn't a fine example of these virtues, he knew, but he could do nothing about any of it. He had found a renewed love for Shilah which was far more powerful than when he was younger. This feeling had depth, the depth of young love remembered and rewrought. She had been his first woman and he her only man. They were both gripped by this rediscovery. She had told him he must not worry. She wanted nothing from him but this moment, this love. She would never interfere with his life with Teresa, would never expect more than this. She had been to hell, she told him as she lay in his arms, and it was not a good place. He need not fear, she would never go there again. And he pulled her to him and kissed her and looked in her eyes and knew it was the truth. She was stronger than she had ever been, and he found this strength irresistible and inflaming. What Teresa would do if ever she found out, he did not know.

The meeting was called to order and open for business. He fell back firmly into his role as policeman. More than his own welfare depended on him. The state of law and order in Singapore was in tatters, and this was far more serious than any personal concerns.

The first order of the meeting was the subscription for the two new hospitals on Pearl's Hill. The European Seamen's Hospital was finished and the Chinese Paupers' Hospital was almost complete. Acknowledgement was made of Tan Tock Seng whose generous donations had made the building possible, of the services of Hoo Ah Kay, known as Whampoa, as Treasurer and to Seah Eu Chin, who kept the wards supplied with food. The government supplied medicines and medical attendance.

Activities to raise money for the Poor Fund were discussed. Robert rose and explained that a list of fees had been drawn up which he would apply: fees for the numerous processions in the town, for example. The members nodded their heads. Fees for carrying fowling pieces on sporting expeditions, he continued. This met with a few frowns but no dissenters. Robert went on until his list had run out.

"I should mention finally that my sister, Mrs Charlotte Manouk, has also offered the sum of $1,000 per year to be divided between the two hospitals. She has invited other philanthropic members of the Chamber of Commerce to match it."

A murmur went round the hall, and some members clapped. Others remained stoically silent. Charlotte's offer was generous, for she knew this matter was close to Robert's heart. But they both knew that the idea of a low-born woman having such wealth was one which sat uneasily with many of the older merchants. Robert did not care, however. This matter was too important.

"I remind my brothers of the three great principles of Freemasonry: brotherly love, relief and truth. Our fellow creatures who suffer demand from us human affection and charitable relief. I urge you to contribute generously to the Poor Fund." Robert sat down.

Chinese labourers were pouring into Singapore at the rate of ten thousand per year. Many went out to Rhio or into the Malay Peninsula, but many stayed working in the countryside on the island. Inevitably they fell on hard times, and the sight of these poor men in failing health, exposed to the vicissitudes of the climate, becoming quite helpless, was one which neither Robert nor many of his policemen could bear. A mere scratch could, through neglect, become suppurating ulcers, and then these men became street mendicants. The sight had become commonplace in Chinatown and a public nuisance.

That the Chinese secret societies drew their thieving membership from this community made little difference to their abject misery. Every one of his European policemen on their rounds carried a subscription paper for the Chinese hospital and, to their credit, the Chinese merchants rarely refused.

The proposed lighthouse at Pedra Branca was the next order of business. Mr Thomson's plans and estimates had been agreed upon. It was to be a monument to the late and great hydrographer, James

Horsburgh, and the lodge had been requested to officiate at the laying of the foundation stone. The matter was quickly dealt with.

Billy now raised the final piece of business: the continued disorder in the town caused by the Chinese secret societies. There was little the lodge could do, but Robert had been asked to talk about a group which all Freemasons found a fascinating subject. He was glad to do it. With his arm useless, it had allowed him to delve into what had been written about them and he needed to understand them if he was to try to break their power.

"At one time, I believe, many Masons took these societies as a kind of Chinese Freemasonry. Through the work of Dr William Milne, we know much more than in the past about the Three Unities Society, what he has termed the Triads. We know, for example, that the Chinese secret societies are characterised by pretensions to antiquity, that mutual assistance is their professed object and that they hold ceremonies of initiation and oath taking, much like ourselves. Milne has likened the three 'elder brothers' in the Triads to our own order of apprentices, fellow-craftsmen, and masters."

Robert took a long drink of water, warming to his subject.

"Milne freely admitted that he had not been able to obtain information on the Triad laws, discipline and internal management, for they are as secret as our own. However, he is adamant that ..." Robert looked down at his paper and read, "the society has degenerated from mere mutual assistance to theft, robbery, the overthrow of regular government and an aim at political power. Triad members are now exhorted to defend each other against attacks from police officers, to hide each other's crimes and to assist detected members to make their escape from the hands of justice."

Robert looked up. "Recently an action was tried in the court at the instance of a respectable Chinese merchant named Ang Ah. He had been attacked by the peons of the current opium farmers in Singapore for illegal dealings. He was saved by the swift actions of our brother, Mr Frommurzee Sorabjee, who was passing. It transpires that this attack was instigated because this Ang Ah had recently become the renter of an opium farm lately established in Johor by the Temenggong. The Chinese settlers in Johor increase daily, and the

Singapore revenue farmers are feeling the pinch. I have heard that the decrease in the sale of opium and spirits amounts to $100 a day. The immigration of the gambier and pepper planters has been gathering pace. Within the last six months, fifty-two more plantations have been established along the rivers of Johor. This exodus will only increase as the land on Singapore becomes exhausted. The Temenggong is actively encouraging this move, and this government has no option but to support him."

Robert was tiring, his arm was hurting. He had already decided to excuse himself from the dinner which terminated every lodge meeting. "There is a war going on, the depth of which we little understand. I would remind all brethren to be vigilant and to report to me any information that may come into their possession," he concluded.

He sat down and wiped his face. After the Master closed the meeting, Robert left quickly and allowed Charlotte's driver to take him home. She had placed one of her carriages at his disposal whilst he could not ride, and he was glad of it tonight. He smiled. It took some getting used to, this wealthy sister, but he was glad she was here, loving, supporting, faithfully at his side no matter what he chose to do.

He and Charlotte, always so complicit. Nothing had ever changed between them. Since childhood, since the loss of their parents, they had always taken care of each other first. It was not always no questions asked, but few judgments were made. What was the point of such judgments? Their lives, like those of their parents, they viewed as precarious.

22

Noan was entertaining friends. Lilin could hear them all laughing downstairs. Noan had turned into their mother, the little toad. Tea and betel and *cherki* parties.

Lilin was terribly bored. It was raining heavily. It had been raining all last night and all day today. It was impossible to go out; the streets and the river were awash. She could have joined Noan's little party, but these women were so dull and stupid she couldn't bear it. They gossiped about other acquaintances, who had done what, prattle, prattle, their children this and that. Whose husband had got what. New jewellery and sarongs. When she went to the landing she could hear them clearly, gathered around the marble-topped table. One woman's husband had taken a second wife. She had been annoyed at first but now was glad. Her child-bearing days were over. Six was enough, two of them sons. And this second wife would be at her service, particularly after her husband had tired of her, she exulted. At this, there was a ripple of laughter.

Lilin smiled. She had discovered through Noan that Ah Teo had taken his own second wife, a daughter of some merchant from Malacca. Lilin didn't care. They would not live here. Ah Teo had been adamant that this second wife and his first should not be under the same roof. Truth be told, he feared what Lilin might do to her or their prospective children.

The second wife was pregnant. Ah Teo, Lilin suspected, would like to divorce her, but that was impossible, for she lived in her family's house and could not be put out, and he had been poor when he married her and was now much enriched. On both counts, divorce was impossible.

Lilin knew she had become superfluous in this family. A first son had died, appalling bad luck on the family. She had produced no other children, let alone boys. She caused havoc in the family and was unfilial to her parents. If Noan had a son, he would become the most important person in the family after her father and Zhen. If Ah Teo's second wife had sons, she would assume a powerful role in the family, favoured by Ah Teo and probably Zhen. That favour would further marginalise Lilin. Lilin no longer knew what to do about this situation. Bearing a son was now impossible.

Lilin rose and went to her bag, taking out the tobacco pouch. As she formed the cigarette, she realised that, at bottom, she did not care. She heard the voices downstairs raised in departure. She went to the window which gave onto the street. The rain had stopped, finally, and she threw the shutters wide, letting the cool, damp air into the house. She watched the women depart, putting up their rose and green flowered oiled-paper umbrellas, darting out of the gate and quickly along the street like swarms of butterflies.

The activities of the street began again immediately. Men emerged from the shelters of the five-foot ways, like insects from beneath leaves, took up their baggages, bundles, cooking pots and baskets and began to hawk their wares. A bullock cart, which had been sheltering against a wall, emerged and trundled its water barrels down the street. The energy of the town, quelled by the dinning and drenching rain, arose again as the street steamed quietly and fat drops dripped from the eaves.

She went downstairs. Noan was in the family hall, washed fresh by the rain from the air well. Her belly had swelled to a ball; she was seven months pregnant.

She was sewing. Baby garments, Lilin could see, for her new child. Lilin sat in a chair by the pond, and Noan glanced up at her before going back to her sewing.

"I have seen her, elder sister," Lilin said softly.

Noan's needle stopped momentarily then started again.

"Every Monday morning at nine o'clock she takes her son to the big school on the sea front. She comes by the bridge where the big banyan tree stands. Afterwards she goes to meet your husband."

Noan said nothing. Lilin had no idea if this was true, or even if Zhen had seen the white woman since she had heard them talking at the pond. But she had discovered who the woman was by simply asking Ah Soon, Qian's son. He had been happy to tell her about his friend Ah Rex and the white lady who came sometimes to visit his father. Lilin had found out from Gaston who she was. Mah Nuk is what he called her. She lived in a huge house on North Bridge Road and was incredibly rich. She was a widow and had two sons.

So Lilin had gone to look at this house and had been overwhelmed with awe and envy. She had never before imagined such wealth in the hands of a woman. A white woman with no husband, she was free, she had vast wealth and she had Zhen. Lilin hated her with every fibre of her being.

Though she would have liked to linger and watch the house, she had not dared to dawdle along the streets. Despite her boldness, Lilin was scared of the European town. Outside of Gaston's hotel, everything felt alien over here. It was hushed and spacious, the huge mansions barely visible through a screen of dense foliage and trees. Quiet, serene and frightening—not like the Chinese town, cheek by jowl, jostling, noisy, crowded.

Then, as she had turned away, her parasol raised against the sun, a carriage had come down the driveway and stopped at the gates. Lilin had moved into the shadow of a tree. She'd had a clear view of the open vehicle as a man ran to open the gates. The woman carried a parasol like herself, but not of oiled paper. It was made of a soft white cloth, cotton, she guessed. Its rim was trimmed with a deep line of exquisite white lace which fluttered in the small breeze. She was wearing a small bonnet of fine white cotton, trimmed with the same lace, over her jet black hair. Her dress was pearl grey and white with short, gathered sleeves and a high neck. She sat like a princess in her carriage. Lilin could see her skin, lovely and fair, her complexion flawless, her profile perfection. Then the carriage went forward and swept out of the drive onto North Bridge Road in the direction of the bridge.

Since then, she had set a young servant boy the task of watching this woman. He had reported that every Monday morning at the same time she went with one boy to the big school on the sea front. She left the boy there and stayed inside for some time, then went out again, and after that he did not know what she did.

"Would you not like to see the woman your husband loves to misery? The one he longs to be with, would give everything to be with?" Lilin whispered.

Noan rose, taking up her sewing, and walked from the room.

That night Zhen came to the house. Noan made him some of his favourite dishes, *kangkung belachan*, *hong bak*—braised pork in black soy sauce, black noodles and *ki ah kuei*, a steamed rice cake. These she served with Fukian-style preserved vegetables and pickled radish. She had sought Hokkien cooks to teach her these dishes in order to please him, for the spices of her own Nonya cuisine was not always to his taste. Noan loved to cook for him.

Ah Teo enjoyed these dishes too. He did not now always eat at this house, for his second wife was living in a house he had bought on Mosque Street. Tonight, though, he had come to the Market Street house, for he enjoyed his sister-in-law's cooking better than any other's. She had learned, for the pleasure of her husband, to combine the dishes of her local cuisine with Hokkien cooking, and he recognised in this a subtle art. He liked his sister-in-law very much. Sometimes he wished, very quietly to himself, that she had been his wife. He knew he could have found a profound happiness with this lovely, graceful and kind woman. She lacked Lilin's external beauty, but inside her, all was beauty and grace, and he saw it.

He resented Lilin even more for depriving him of the pleasant table and company of Noan and her small daughters. He was a family man, above all. One wife, a loving wife, would have been enough for him. His misfortune was that he had not been given Noan. And Noan liked Ah Teo, understood his torments at the hands of her sister; she was pleased to serve him these dishes he enjoyed in the company of her husband. Ah Teo could see how much Noan loved Zhen and envied him, for he was sure that Zhen did not value it as he should. He saw how pregnant Noan was becoming. His own second wife was just starting to show.

These thoughts had occupied him for some time, when suddenly he rose. Zhen looked up, surprised, finishing his dish. Ah Teo nodded at Zhen and left the room, returning almost immediately with a small bamboo box. He put it on the table. "Ask your wife to come. I have a small gift," he announced.

Zhen looked at Ah Teo in surprise.

"Brother, ask your wife to come," Ah Teo insisted.

Zhen shrugged and called Noan, and when she came into the room, Ah Teo opened the box. Inside was a small cake. "It is made from a powder called chocolate," he informed her. "The English like to drink this chocolate, but it is also used in sweet things. Perhaps you would like it, to thank you for your cooking, for cooking our food."

Zhen looked astonished. Thanking Noan for cooking? That was her job. What had got into the man?

Noan stood waiting for Zhen to give his permission. Zhen shrugged and waved his hand. Ah Teo came forward and took the cake from the box. "It is sweet, like nothing else. Second wife likes it a great deal. Will you taste it?" he invited her.

Noan looked at Ah Teo. His Baba Malay was almost amusing, but she recognised the effort and smiled. She looked at Zhen, always attentive to his wishes. He was finishing his meal. He loved her food, but it was Ah Teo who had brought her a gift, thanked her. Of course thanks from a husband, no one could expect that, but hers might pay a little attention. Insidiously, Lilin's words entered her mind. The white woman was his loved one. He thought of nothing but her.

Noan cut a small piece from the cake and nibbled it nervously. It was sweet and smooth, unlike anything she had ever tasted in her life. She put it into her mouth and looked at Ah Teo. It was a heavenly taste. Her eyes opened wide, and he smiled.

"Brother, do you wish to try?" Ah Teo asked Zhen.

Zhen put down his chopsticks, took some tea and rinsed his mouth. "What? No." He rose and left the room without a backward glance.

Noan watched him leave, a sudden dull resentment entering her veins. It was a feeling she had never experienced before. She was pregnant with his child and had spent hours in the kitchen to make this feast for him, a feast which had demanded study, devotion and care. Momentarily she disliked him. She thanked Ah Teo graciously, and he was happy to see her pleased.

Everything that had happened so far this evening had brought her to a sudden decision. She wanted to see this white woman that Lilin told her about. It became, in an instant, imperative.

Two days later, Noan screwed up her courage. She had never in all her life crossed from the Chinese town where she had been born to the European town. It was, by foot, a small journey, but in every other respect it was immense. Thirty steps, that was all it took. Thirty steps to pass from one side of the river to the other, but it felt like a thousand *li*. She had no idea what to expect, but she knew she had to go.

She dressed carefully and modestly in a long *baju* and a sarong of sombre colour. Her *baju* was closed with the three simple brooches of the *kerosang*, and she had chosen her plainest set. She put on her plainest slippers, too, the most comfortable, for her belly was heavy and her legs often hurt her. She left the house on Market Street at eight o'clock. Lilin was asleep still. The maids had charge of her children. Zhen had not come back last night, and this, more than anything, had propelled her from her bed and out onto the street.

She put up her oiled-paper umbrella covered with the subtle and exquisite colours of myriad painted butterflies. It was her favourite, given to her by Zhen from a shipment from China. The butterfly symbolised love, the undying bonds of young love, the love she felt for her husband. It was not for shade, for the day was not yet hot, but for a sort of protection, a shield from men's eyes.

She walked to the riverside and hesitated. Tentatively she put her foot, for the first time, onto the bridge. A feeling of intense excitement caused her to stop, take hold of the parapet. She walked slowly to the middle of the bridge. The view opened out. She looked up and down the river, up to the English governor's house on the hill. It was an entirely new view on this town about which, she realised, she knew so little.

She looked back too, at the Chinese town, along Boat Quay for the first time. She could see the little wooden bridge which crossed the stream at Circular Road and further along her father's and her husband's godown. A stream of Chinese men, carrying baskets, was crossing the bridge. Intent on their tasks, eyes down, most ignored her completely. They were making for the marketplace, she could see, their loads strung bouncing from poles across their shoulders. She only vaguely understood that the fruit and vegetables were grown over here, somewhere on this side of the river. Usually she went to the market early to get the best vegetables, and it occurred to her that she had never before thought about where they came from.

Buoyed by this small discovery, she walked to the other side of the river. She hesitated a moment, touching her toe to the earth as if the land on this side of the bridge might not allow her to pass. Then she smiled at her own timidity and took a step off the bridge onto the road of the European town. She walked slowly down, alongside the wall of the Chinese compound, which accompanied her somewhat reassuringly to the street which led back to the river, in front of the ship builder and the English building. She thought for a moment but did not like the look of this street. In front of her lay the open field where, she knew, her father came sometimes, for one of his concubines lived on this side of the river somewhere.

She decided the safest way was to walk along the road in front of the big houses. The one on the corner was a big hotel, she knew. But now it was quiet. All the houses were quiet, only some Malay and Indian gardeners moved amongst the bushes, and she was shielded from view by the tall shrubberies. Nothing was moving on the plain, and she looked over its expanse to the prettiness of the sea beyond. She had never really looked at the sea. At Telok Ayer, from the market, it was pretty, the view, out to the fishing stakes on the bay, but here it was wide, a huge world spreading away to the furthest horizon. It was the first time she had seen the ships of the English and the other strange craft which seemed to fill the blue bay. Her world, she realised suddenly, was so small, so constricted. Her whole life was Market Street.

She had arrived at the big English temple and felt afraid. She could see the tree and the bridge in the distance, the place where this woman came in her carriage at nine o'clock. Nobody seemed to be paying the slightest attention to Noan, though she felt terribly exposed. She moved quickly past the temple averting her eyes. It was said that sacrifices had been made when this was built; she had heard stories about them burying the heads of young children in the foundations.

She turned into the road which led along the edge of the freshwater stream. The wind was brisk and cooling. She could see children playing from the boats which were anchored in the bay— children like her own, but not like hers: naked children, jumping into the water.

She began to feel tired. She rarely walked so far or so quickly. Her belly felt heavy, and she needed to sit down. She was very glad to arrive at the big shady banyan tree. Some native men ran off when they saw her, and for the first time she felt the strangest sensation. She was not afraid of these men, though they were odd to her. They were more fearful of her.

Her fatigue had overcome her fear, and she sat down on the low wooden bench, her back to the tree, looking out to the sea. Her head was beating. It did that often now. And her limbs felt heavy. She waited, breathing slowly. When she felt rested, she turned and looked over the little bridge which crossed the freshwater stream, towards the big building which she knew from Lilin was a school.

She felt safe in the shade of this big tree. Her headache had receded slightly, but she felt it gripping her eyes. She closed them and leaned back against the tree, into the arms of the buttressed roots. She must have dozed, for when she opened her eyes next she was looking into those of a turbaned Indian man. She started and let out a cry. She tried to leap to her feet but felt suddenly a great weakness.

"What is it? Is she all right?" Noan heard the voice speaking English. She knew it was English, for Zhen spoke it sometimes in her presence. But she could understand nothing.

"A Chinese woman, memsahib. She looks pregnant and unwell."

Charlotte got down from her carriage, and Alex too leapt off lightly. Noan roused herself enough to sit. Charlotte came up to her syce.

"Can you speak Chinese, Ravi?" she said to her syce.

"No, memsahib," he replied.

Alex came forward quickly. "I can, Mother."

"Yes, yes. Of course, darling. Ask her if she is feeling very sick," Charlotte urged.

Alex went up to Noan and stood in front of her, bowed quickly and put forward this question in Hokkien. Noan opened her eyes wide, understanding almost nothing of what the boy had said. She was too overcome, looking at him.

This was the boy of the white woman, the woman Zhen loved. She took her eyes off his handsome face and looked up, almost fearfully, into Charlotte's eyes.

Her eyes were blue, so strange. She had never seen blue eyes—never. In any other moment, she would have been afraid of these blue eyes, light, like the eyes of a ghost, but Noan read there a look of intense concern.

And the woman was so beautiful, her pale skin and pink lips framed by jet-black hair. Her eyes were round, large, limpid and not, Noan thought, like her own, narrow and dark. She was dressed in a robe of peach-coloured muslin, her figure like a willow, the way Chinese men liked their women, she knew from the picture books.

Her eyes returned to the boy, and she understood instantly that this was Zhen's son. This boy was her husband's son. She saw it in the line of his jaw, the way his face was made. She saw it somewhere in his eyes which looked like Lian's. All this had taken but a second.

Alex realised immediately his mistake. She wasn't Hokkien of course. The women who spoke Hokkien to him and tousled his hair hung around the doors of the houses in Amoy Street and Chinchew Street and didn't dress like this.

"I think she is Nonya," he said looking at his mother. "She speaks Baba Malay. I know only a little from Ah Soon and some of the children in the town."

Charlotte turned to Ravi. "Get some water from the carriage, quickly. A cup for the lady."

Ravi left, and she addressed Alex. "Ask her if she is all right, Zan, please, if you can."

Alex nodded. He knew her language was mostly Malay and,

struggling, he said, "Sick, you, please?"

Noan looked at him and a feeling of tenderness swept over her. He was a handsome, clever and kind boy. Just the kind of boy she wanted for Zhen. She said, "Not well, a little weak. Can you take me home, please?"

Alex was so pleased she understood him, and he smiled broadly. He had understood only a few words: "not well, home."

He turned to his mother. "She is not well. She wants to go home."

A moment later Ravi arrived with a cup of water, and Noan took it, nodding her head in thanks. It was cold, and she drank it all, grateful. Charlotte came forward and took the cup from her hand. Noan was surprised at this gesture. Charlotte handed the cup to Ravi and then sat on the bench at Noan's side.

"Alex, she is so very pregnant, poor thing. What can she be doing here? Tell her I will take her home in my carriage. Where does she live?"

Alex addressed Noan again. "Your house where? Mother take you."

Noan looked into Charlotte's eyes and read there a great kindness. The white woman was concerned for herself, another woman, a woman in distress. Noan knew this instinctively, as all women know and recognise the marks of genuine goodness towards each other. It was a deeply feminine feeling which neither language nor culture could blur. She was pregnant, and this other women, who was a mother, wanted to be of help to her. Noan smiled shyly. "Thank you. The temple on *lau la keng khau*."

Alex smiled too. He knew this was Philip Street, what the Hokkiens called "the mouth of the grandfather temple", for the old Teochew Wak Hai Cheng Bio temple. He and Ah Soon had been countless times inside this temple, offering joss paper to the powerful deity, Teh Kong, the Dark Lord of the North, who they both worshipped for his fierceness.

Alex loved visiting this temple and inhaling the heady scent of the spiral joss which hung from lines over the courtyard. Alex knew his father and mother did not go to these temples. Occasionally he went with his uncle to the church and remembered the faith of his father, but what did it have to compare to the wonder of the Chinese or Indian temples, with their colourful and powerful array of gods, their magic rituals, their odours and sights?

He relayed the information the Nonya had given to his mother, and Ravi came and waited by Noan's side to help her to her feet. Charlotte too put out her hand to help her, and Noan forgot all fear of these foreign people and put her hand in Charlotte's and her arm in Ravi's and allowed them to guide her to the carriage. Alex picked up Noan's umbrella, opened it and handed it to her, to shelter her from the sun.

When everyone was installed, Charlotte too put up her parasol. It was a lovely thing, this umbrella, Noan thought irrelevantly, white cotton lace floating in the air. Charlotte actually at that very moment was thinking the same thing about the delicate bamboo and paper umbrella adorned with butterflies, most delicately and beautifully painted.

Ravi began to pull the horses quickly away from the tree. He crossed over the freshwater stream and into the yard of the school. Alex leaned forward and kissed his mother on her cheek and smiled, leaping down from the carriage. He bowed towards Noan respectfully. "Please be well," he said and with a wave ran off into the building. Noan watched him go.

Ravi turned the carriage and returned over the bridge and along the road by the beachside. Noan was feeling much better. The water had refreshed her, and the air blowing around them from the sea was reviving. The novelty of riding in this carriage was intense. She had ridden in carriages of course. Her mother had one and her father. She used one to go to River Valley Road. It was not that which was novel. It was this sensation of riding with a woman of such a different world, the world, she understood, vaguely, of the people who ruled Singapore. She had never given this any thought before this moment, but now it struck her. This woman was outside everything she understood, yet they shared one thing, one intense and very personal thing. The most unlikely thing: they both loved the same man. And they both had children by this man. All his children, but not equally so. Noan had daughters, but this woman had his son.

When the carriage stopped before the temple, Noan got down. Charlotte smiled at her, and Noan bowed her head in thanks. Charlotte understood. They could not speak to each other, but she understood.

Charlotte spoke to Ravi and the carriage moved away. Noan turned and retraced her steps to Market Street. She knew now that what Lilin said was true. Zhen could not help but love this woman. And she had given him a son. Nothing she, Noan, could do would change anything. She was nothing, meant nothing to him.

She went inside the ornate hinged double doors of the house, climbed slowly upstairs to her room and closed the door.

23

Charlotte was standing in the light of a high flame, shadows flitting around her like spirits. He gazed at her, his eyes drinking her in. The glassy waters of the bay reflected the half moon, the glints of stars and the myriad lanterns strung along the beachside. The hill by the Temenggong's village was called Bukit Chermin—Mirror Hill— and the name seemed chosen by gods as he gazed at these reflections.

He recalled a poem he had read, the first verse only; the rest he could not remember:

"The red gleam o'er the mountains
Goes wavering from sight,
And the quiet moon enhances
The loveliness of night."

A vast feast was laid out on tables spread throughout the village. This was the feast of Hari Raya. Zhen knew of it, but this was the first time he had attended such a festivity. He understood little of this faith of the Malays other than that they fasted for a month and then held this large festival to celebrate its end. His own invitation had come because of the business he was conducting with the Temenggong: the purchase of opium and arrack farming rights in Johor. These different customs and faiths, which he had discovered in Singapore, felt entirely natural. Each people kept to its customs and enjoyed their celebration.

The English government discouraged some festivals, he knew, like the Hindu ceremony of *Pooja*. This ceremony attracted vast crowds to the plain at Serangoon to watch the men swing from high poles with hooks attached into the skin of their backs. He himself had gone and found it fascinating: the noise of the drums and conches, the dusty heat and the men flying around the pole, seemingly unhurt by the deep hooks. It was, he understood, a form of penance. But the British did not like it, and it had recently been forbidden. Other than that, by and large, the government interfered little. At the Chinese New Year, gambling, usually frowned upon officially, was openly allowed for a month—not, however, without disapproval in the English newspapers, which he always read.

He was joined now by his two companions, part of the syndicate. They examined the groaning tables of food. Zhen liked these Malay dishes. Over time he had grown to like many of the different dishes which were hawked daily round the town. Many were familiar, resembling the food on the table of his wife's family. He took up some saffron rice and the bamboo skewers of chicken with the spicy peanut sauce. These he particularly enjoyed, especially when he was drinking in the town.

They joined other Chinese merchants at a table on the foreshore, but Zhen kept a discreet eye on Charlotte. He had suspected she would be here. He felt the urgent need to speak to her, but not yet.

Governor Butterworth and his wife were standing in the company of the Temenggong and his son. Charlotte and Robert went up to greet them. Charlotte thought that Ibrahim looked magnificent. His costume was of fine black silk with gold thread, the high collar embroidered with writhing forms in gold. His headdress was more elaborate than usual: gold and black raised in a high curve and studded with diamonds. At his waist was a belt with a large oval buckle of heavy gold work and one large diamond. In addition to his own bejewelled kris, he wore the ceremonial sword which Governor Bonham had presented to him in recognition of his role in reducing piracy in the Straits.

His first son, Abu Bakar, was dressed in similar if less ornate fashion and stood at his side. Charlotte had been introduced to his principal wife when she arrived, but his women kept to the palace. Everywhere the children ran about in the most colourful costumes like so many brightly feathered birds, the village women serving food and bringing new plates to the tables. Ibrahim moved on, greeting his guests. Each time he moved, a *gamelan* struck up loudly and a drum began beating.

Charlotte greeted Jeannette Butterworth. Robert returned to Teresa and several of his companions. The noise was intense, with the gongs of the *gamelan* beating, the sounds of children playing, the din of conversation on every side. Finally the governor motioned to his wife and bowed to Charlotte. Jeannette pressed Charlotte's hand and turned to greet the group of Arab merchants who had arrived. Charlotte, momentarily, was at a loss and turned to see where Robert might be. She gazed over the crowd and began to make her way towards the large party of Europeans gathered in the verandah of one of the houses. As she moved off, she felt a hand take her arm. She turned swiftly and looked into the eyes of Charles Maitland.

"Charles, how nice to see you. I thought you had departed for Sarawak." She smiled, very glad to see him. Her annoyance with him had lasted a few days and then she had forgotten it. After all, he owed her nothing. She hardly knew the man.

"Charlotte, I am sorry. I feel I owe you some explanation."

"Why, not at all," she began. She thought he looked truly fine in his red uniform with the sash and sword. It was the first time, she reflected, that she had seen him in neither casual dress nor women's garments, and it suited him very well. Men, she thought, should always wear a uniform.

Charles took her by the hand and turned, seeking a quiet place. He had thought and thought about their last meeting. He was anxious he should not leave with her angry at him. He had made a mess of some magnetic calculations and had to start again. He moved her away from the food, away from the houses, down to a quiet place under the palms on the beachside. Boats were coming from the islands, pulling up on the beach and at the short jetty, but the noise was greatly lessened here.

"Please allow me to talk to you. My journey is delayed until after the visit of Lord Dalhousie. My brother Henry is accompanying the party."

Charlotte nodded. She knew of this imminent and much-anticipated visit by the Governor General of India, the first ever made to Singapore. The government and the merchants were in a state of heightened excitement, for they hoped this visit might herald a new interest in the prosperity of the settlement which would be expressed in much-needed public funds and the cessation of Singapore as a penal colony.

Robert, sceptical, was unconvinced. Dalhousie was on a sea voyage for his health, he had pointed out to the Chamber of Commerce, and would be barely more aware of Singapore after his visit of two days than he was before. However, the merchants were determined to put on a show. Charles's brother Henry was the Foreign Secretary to the Government of India, and naturally Charles would stay to meet him.

"I see," said Charlotte, guarded, when he had explained this to her.

"Immediately following Dalhousie's departure, I shall leave on the *Isis*, with Captain Mundy, who is voyaging through the archipelago."

"I see," Charlotte said. Really the man was infuriating.

"Please, let me say this. I must depart, but I would like, would be most grateful, if you would allow me to write to you."

Charlotte looked at him and read an intensity in his eyes. As she was about to speak, a sudden clamour rose from the bay. A party of English soldiers in their red uniforms had arrived in their longboat and recognised Charles. "Charles, you old dog! Good to see you. Join us!" they all yelled.

Charles moved between them and Charlotte and put up his hand in greeting. He knew his companions would be down to get him within a minute of two, and he did not want to expose Charlotte to the lewd talk of the soldier's mess. It was the most unfortunate timing.

He turned to her. "They will be here in an instant. I must go. Please, Kitt? I cannot bear to part with you not knowing if I shall see you again."

"Yes, yes, go with your companions. Of course you may write to me." She put her hand on his arm. "Of course we shall see each other again. Perhaps I shall come to Sarawak."

Charles smiled. "Yes, yes, do. Come to Sarawak." He glanced quickly as he heard the bustle of the men clambering onto the jetty.

"Come?" he said, his eyes glittering.

Charlotte nodded, and he put her hand swiftly to his lips. "I shall write every day," he said and left her quickly, racing along the water's edge. He was anxious she should not be compromised.

Charlotte watched him go, striding athletically, gallantly, his concern for her evident. She felt a small, irrational happiness. That he liked her was no longer in any doubt.

She turned and looked out over the bay, bathed in moonlight and reflected flame, waiting a moment for Charles and his friends to join the throng. Her thoughts were filled with him and with the promise of this future correspondence, close and intimate.

Zhen had watched as this man took her to the water's edge. Watched as they had stood close together, watched as he put her hand to his lips. The blood in his veins had grown warm. He felt a sudden and disastrous impulse to beat this man and clenched his fists, willing a calm. He watched as the man's friends called him away, and then she had turned and gazed out over the water. Something in her attitude told him she was thinking of the red-coated English soldier. He murmured a few words to his companions and strode away. They paid no attention, and he made his way quickly down to the beachside.

When she turned he was there, and she let out a gasp of surprise.

"Zhen," she said, and he saw a small flash of fear and knit his brows. Why should she fear him?

"Xia Lou, do not be anxious. I surprised you. I am sorry."

Charlotte stared at him. She had not given any thought to his presence at this gathering, but it made sense. He had business arrangements with the Temenggong.

"Yes, I did not expect ..." she trailed off, unable to think what to say to him. She had a momentary thought that they had become strangers. After all they had shared, all the passion and the misery. She shook her head slightly.

He saw it, and his heart felt a great coldness. Did she no longer love him? The thought made him tremble inside, and he spoke too harshly. "Who was that man?"

Charlotte squared her shoulders and opened her fan. "I beg your pardon?" she said, raising her eyebrows. But the feeling of strangeness had fled in an instant. Even after four years, it was as if they had spoken just an hour ago.

Zhen knew that when accompanied by this facial expression the English phrase meant something like "mind your own business". He and Qian enjoyed playing games with the way the Europeans used their faces to express meaning. Zhen's face remained impassive. "The man, who is he?"

Charlotte took a few steps along the beach, meaning to go around him. She felt her face grow warm—with anger, with embarrassment too. But he stepped in front of her.

"Zhen, stop this. Let me pass. We shall be seen." Charlotte now feared a great scene before all the gathered dignitaries of Singapore.

"Yes. Then tell me who he is?"

She sighed and moved, now not towards the crowd but into the shadow of the overhanging palm trees.

"He is a friend, that is all. I have friends, Zhen, you know." She looked up but could not see his eyes, it was too dark. He had moved next to her into the shadows. "English women are not like Chinese women. We may have gentlemen friends. And, and, it is you who ..."

He looked down at her. He had moved close, overwhelming her with his presence. She could not continue. She wanted to remind him of his ultimatum, but it seemed pointless, trivial. In the dark she could only sense him, but it was as if she was dispossessed of her own body, as if he owned it, drew it into his, absorbing her into his shadow. She knew at that second that if he touched her, she would give in, melt into his will. Charles flew out of her mind and Zhen came crashing in. Even as she wanted him to pull her into his body, she felt a deep desperation to get away from him.

"Please, I have to go," she said shakily.

Zhen heard the irresolution in her voice. He knew he had only to put out his hand. But suddenly he, too, began to have doubts.

To begin again—all the anguish. She was trying to make a new life without him. This thought robbed him of air, and he turned and walked swiftly away from her.

Charlotte watched him go, shocked at the suddenness of his departure. She leaned against the trunk of the palm. What she had wanted only a second before, she now regretted and she put out her hand towards his parting back.

"Zhen, oh God," she whispered. Two minutes in his presence, and she was reduced to quivering indecision.

When she had regained her composure she went slowly back to the village and sat down next to Teresa. The Chinese party had disappeared.

24

Robert sent for Charlotte when the labour pains began. Teresa's last days had been difficult. The heat was intense, and she had been forced to bathe frequently and lie under the punkah. But at least she had carried this baby to term. The first child had died *in utero*, and Teresa had taken a long time to recover.

Robert and Charlotte were sitting on his verandah. The evening was cool, with a good sea breeze, and she was glad for Teresa. Dr Little was here, and Teresa's mother and sisters. That things were proceeding well was the last they had heard, and now they could only wait. Robert's arm had healed, and Dr Oxley had removed the gutta-percha cast. Robert was rubbing it now and flexing his hand.

"How is the arm, Robbie?"

Robert looked at his sister. "Aye, grand. A little stiff, but that will go. It's nice to be on horseback again." He rose and went to the sideboard and poured them both a tot of whisky. She no longer drank it often, and it seared her throat.

"Oooh, Rob," she spluttered. "Got out of the habit."

He tossed his down and smiled. "Grandmother would have been ashamed of you."

She laughed and remembered.

"I got a letter from Aunt Jeanne on the last packet. I forgot to tell you. She has sent you some nice warm socks she has knitted."

Robert smiled. With every letter came a package. Sometimes biscuits, grown mouldy over the voyage, usually knitted goods. It was clear that no matter how often they reminded her, she thought Singapore as cold as Scotland.

"She is talking of coming here, Robbie. Now that the voyage is less arduous, you know. Waghorn's route has made the voyage very short. Jeanne's letter was dated a mere forty-one days ago. It is miraculous. The voyage on the Mediterranean is comfortable, and the voyage overland in Egypt has become quite interesting. The Peninsula and Oriental Company accommodations seem adequate, although one does hear complaints. Could she do it, do you think?"

"How old is she, Kitt?" As soon as he spoke, they both realised this question had never before entered their heads.

"Fifty, perhaps, something like that. She seems never to be ill. I think she would be all right."

Robert nodded. They both sat silently for a moment, remembering their childhood time together. Jeanne had been their support, the one who loved them in the face of their disapproving grandmother. She had lost her fiancé in the last months of the war with Napoleon and had never married. They had been the children she never had.

"It would be wonderful to see her," Robert said quietly, and Charlotte nodded. They had never known their grandfather. When their grandmother had died, the house and grounds had passed to Robert as the first boy of the eldest son, their father. Jeanne lived there, and Charlotte supported her with a generous pension. This last was something Tigran had insisted on when she married him, and she had always loved him for it.

"I miss Tigran," she said suddenly, voicing her train of thought.

Robbie looked at her. "Yes," he said quietly. "He was a wonderful fellow." He was horrified to see Charlotte's face crumple and tears begin to roll down her cheeks. He rose and went to her, sitting next to her and putting an arm around her. She put her face into his shoulder.

"I want him back, Rob. He understood everything. Why did he have to die?" She began to sob, and he held her tight. He could find no words of comfort. It was simply unfair. Tigran had loved his sister, and they had had a good marriage, good children.

"It's hard, Rob. To start again. It wearies me."

She sat up, handkerchief to her eyes; she took a deep breath. "I have been writing to Charles Maitland. He is in Sarawak."

Robbie returned to his chair. "Charles? Really? Well he is a very decent man. After all that ridiculous hullabaloo over Dalhousie's visit, I'm not surprised he took off. Salutes, dinners, the Chinese and Indian merchants dressed to the nines, cute children's dances, what a carry-on. Naturally the visit served no purpose whatsoever. However, we do now have a ghastly obelisk on the sacred place his noble footsteps fell. Poor Johnny Thomson got the job of building the damn thing."

"Rob, pay attention. I'm not talking of Dalhousie, for heaven's sake." Charlotte smacked his hand.

"Sorry, Kitt. Charles. Yes. Does he have intentions?"

"I don't know, Rob. Yes, perhaps. You know I am rather sick of being a widow."

Robert nodded.

"But I have feelings still, you know." She stopped, and Robert frowned, for he guessed what might be coming.

"Feelings for Zhen?" he asked.

She looked up sharply and then down again.

"Not difficult for me to guess."

Charlotte wiped her eyes and sipped some whisky. The letters from Charles were filled with warmth, with news of his studies and travels, of Sarawak which he described so well. Filled with affection too, for her, she could feel it, though he was careful to profess nothing. He had asked, again, for her to come to Sarawak, and a letter from James Brooke had arrived, pressing his invitation. It was most flattering. But in the back of her mind lay Zhen. Those minutes on the shore of Telok Belangah had unsettled her. The old feelings, buried, had resurfaced so quickly. The simple proximity to him had been enough. What was the use, though? They could never be married, never lead a normal life.

"I have renewed my life with Shilah," Robert announced.

Charlotte's head shot up, and she looked at him. He was gazing at her. "God help me. I am in love with Shilah, and my wife is having my baby upstairs."

They stared at each other.

"Both as bad as each other, it appears," Robert laughed, but she felt the anguish under the surface.

"First loves," Charlotte said softly.

"So, you are not the only one, sister," Robert said. "That's what I mean. I understand."

Charlotte nodded and they smiled at each other.

At that instant there was a flurry of activity and the front door burst open. Teresa's sister appeared on the verandah. "A boy," she proclaimed joyfully. "And mother doing well."

Robert and Charlotte rose and went inside the house.

25

Charlotte was waiting for Alex. School was almost over. She needed to talk to him. She had made a decision. It was time to go away. She needed to put a space between herself and Zhen. Charles had written that he was waiting for her. That was enough. She would go. But she would not take the children. Alex and Adam would stay here. Life, she had understood, was hazardous in Sarawak. Uprisings were common. It was not a place for children. She felt little fear for herself, however. Pirates were a nuisance, Charles had warned her, but Captain Elliott had fitted the ship with extra cannon. Pirates rarely attacked really big, well-armed ships. They had plenty of booty from smaller, less well-defended vessels. The captain had sailed from Batavia for this voyage carrying a cargo of Japan wares and island goods: diamonds, gold dust from Pontianak, rattans and hardwoods. These had been placed on commission, and now her brig awaited only her.

For trade in Sarawak, the ship would carry opium, cloth, iron wares, ship's chandlery, furniture, guns and gunpowder to the Rajah's new town. And for Charles and the other Europeans, medicines, bibles, books, newspapers and magazines, wine, beer, cheeses—things from home which she intended as gifts. Charles had written of their isolation, the need for familiar objects. A request for sheet music had come from Harriette McDougall, the wife of the newly arrived Anglican pastor, and Charlotte had scoured the town and had a vast amount copied. She had added a new upright piano, and tobacco and brandy as gifts for the Rajah.

Charlotte had also purchased a magic lantern. Alexander and

Adam loved the magic lantern show, in particular the Rat Swallower which featured a sleeping man whose mouth opened and closed as the projectionist made snoring sounds. The image of a rat would then move across the man's sleeping body, and jump into his mouth as he snored. She had also purchased the life of Jesus, the stories of Mother Goose and other children's stories, pictures of Christmas, ships, archers and animals, pictures of horseback riding and cowboys from the Wild West of America, all beautifully painted. Everybody loved the magic lantern.

She saw Alex as he left the classroom, as usual next to Ah Soon. Their friendship was very close, somewhat to the detriment of Ah Soon's English as they usually prattled in Hokkien. The difference in their sizes was almost comical. Ah Soon was such a skinny stick next to Alex. It didn't matter, though. Both boys played together, and Charlotte knew Ah Soon was wiry and strong. She waved as they looked up, and they both came racing towards her down the corridor.

Ah Soon arrived first. He was very fast, and Alex punched him lightly on the arm. Charlotte shook the hand that Ah Soon proffered as he had been taught, and curtsied to him. Alex laughed and kissed his mother. She took both boys by the hand, and together they went out into the park of the institution and walked towards North Bridge Road. Today Ah Soon was coming to her house to spend time with Alex in the garden and to read together the new books which had arrived with the mail: *Robinson Crusoe*, *Gulliver's Travels* and a new book of stories she had heard about by the Grimm brothers. *Robinson Crusoe* was their favourite at the moment.

The sight of these two heads together always moved her heart. One was dark-haired, tousled, his locks tumbling over his face; the other was half-shaved, the queue neatly plaited down his back reaching only as far as his neck. She could not quite ever quit herself of the idea that Alex was a half-Chinese boy. In any other house, in any other life, his head would be as Ah Soon's, and his father would be by her side.

Then she shook this idea from her mind. It was ridiculous. The idea that Alex could be a Chinese boy. They sat poring over the words, Alex sometimes trying to translate into Hokkien for Ah Soon, both laughing together. This sight, as she sat in the shade of the trees, was a moment of pure pleasure. When Amber came with Shilah, the boys made room and began to tell her the story, for Amber could not yet read well. She was learning her letters. When the boys tired of the book, they got up and ran about playing hide and go seek. Alex always hid with Amber when Ah Soon was the seeker, and Charlotte and Shilah knew they had great affection for one another. Adam was sleeping, but when he woke, he too would join the children.

Then the games changed to *porok*, the object of which was to kick a coconut shell towards another to strike it off its mark; or to *main china buta*, "blind chinaman", which Charlotte knew as blindman's bluff.

When she called the children for tea, they came, tumbling over each other to the table set aside for them, and began to talk quietly amongst themselves, eating the biscuits and cakes that the cook had made. Charlotte was always amused to see how much Ah Soon liked these English dishes. His favourite was, unaccountably, cabinet pudding with treacle, and she always ensured Cook made one when Ah Soon was coming. Adam and Alex both liked sweet sago with nutmeg and cinnamon, and Amber liked anything Alex ate.

Charlotte poured tea for Shilah. She gave her another book which had arrived in the shipment. It was the *Tales of Mother Goose*, the book by Perrault, which she herself had read in French in her grandfather's library. As Shilah looked through the stories, smiling, for they were as new to her as they were to her daughter, Charlotte wondered whether she should mention what Robert had said.

When Shilah put the book down, she looked over at Charlotte. "Robert's boy is doing well? And Teresa?"

Charlotte looked Shilah directly in the eyes. "Robert hasn't told you, Shilah? It has been over a week."

Shilah looked away, towards the children. "Ah, I see. Robert has mentioned that ..." She stopped and looked back at Charlotte. "Do you mind so very much, Charlotte? I hope it cannot cause harm. I do not wish that to be so."

Charlotte put her hand out to Shilah's. "No, no, of course I do not mind. It is not, truly, my affair. Robert's little boy is doing very well, and Teresa is now somewhat restored. She is staying with her mother in River Valley Road for a while, but I think you know that."

Shilah's cheeks became slightly rose, and Charlotte was sorry for her words.

"They plan to call him Andrew, after our father. Such an abundance of A's in the family, really. Amber, Andrew, Adam and Alexander. I shall insist that if there is another we move on to the B's."

She smiled, and Shilah looked up and laughed lightly. "Thank you, Charlotte," she said.

"Oh, Shilah. My only concern is if Teresa should learn of it. That you should love Robert so much—this is not my concern. I love him very well myself."

Shilah nodded. Charlotte suddenly felt sorry for Shilah. She had been loyal and faithful to Robert. None of this was her fault.

"Robert is a fool, really. Why on earth didn't he just marry you when he had the opportunity? It is entirely ridiculous."

"Please. Please don't be hard on Robert. He was young, his position new and I was a child of criminals, half Indian, not at all suitable to be the wife of an English servant of Her Majesty. I understood all that quite early."

Charlotte sighed. "*Nasi sudah menjadi bubur*," she said. Shilah nodded. There was no going back. The rice had become porridge; it could not become rice again.

In the evening Charlotte went up the stairs to the children's bedroom. Adam was asleep already, and she kissed him on the forehead. His *babu* was in the garden, Charlotte knew. She had recently become promised to a young Bugis man, and they were permitted to meet, with a chaperone, from time to time. The marriage would take place in some three months' time, well after her return from Sarawak.

This was the subject that Charlotte now wanted to raise with Alex. He was sitting in his bed, reading the *Robinson Crusoe* book by the light of the lamp. He looked up as she sat by him, and he closed the book, yawning. His mother's arrival usually meant it was time to turn out the light. His *babu* would come soon and sleep by the side of his bed. This was a subject Alex wished to raise with his mother.

"Alex, darling," Charlotte said, putting his book on the side table.

"Mother, may I ask you something?"

"Why, yes. What is it?" Charlotte said surprised.

"Mother, must I have the *babu* here every night? I am nine years old."

Charlotte smiled. "Mmm, well, let me see. You are nine. It is true that you probably do not need a *babu* at night. But what of Adam? He is just seven. He still needs his *babu*, doesn't he?"

Alex reflected a moment. "Yes," he said hesitantly, evidently searching for a way around this problem.

"Zan, you know that Adam's *babu* will be married in a few months. Then she will not be living here all the time. She will be living with her husband in Kampong Bugis."

Zan nodded. He knew the man who was going to marry the *babu*. He was the son of one of the village chiefs. "Will she still look after Adam?" he asked.

"Well, Adam is still young, so yes, she will come in the daytime to care for him, but perhaps we can talk to Adam and see if you can both do without a *babu* at night. Will that be all right?"

Alex smiled broadly and put his arms around his mother. "Yes, that would be fine, Mother. I shall see to Adam at night. I can read to him. I will make sure he is all right, not frightened. I know the lullabies. I can sing to him."

Charlotte held him tight and kissed his neck, overwhelmed with love for him. "Then we shall speak to Adam tomorrow," she said. "I'm sure he will be agreeable if you are planning to be such a lovely brother."

Alex nodded against her shoulder. "And we can make a room next door for your *babu* in case Adam needs anything. Would that be a good idea?" she asked. Alex nodded again.

She released him and put her hand on his face. "Darling, you are such a treasure to me. Since your father left us, you have been such a brave young man. Thank you."

Alex was pleased and leant forward and kissed his mother on the cheek. "My father was a great man, wasn't he Mother?"

"Yes, a great and good man who loved you and Adam a great deal."

Alex looked suddenly very sad. "I can hardly remember him." Tears sprang to his eyes. Charlotte touched his cheek, then took her locket and opened it, showing him the small picture of Tigran. As she gazed at it, she too felt tears well. She talked to her son of Tigran for a while, reminding him of what they used to do together, of Tigran's gentle nature. Then she took the locket from her neck and put it into Alex's hand. "Keep it for now, to remind you a little." Alex nodded and gripped the locket. Charlotte brushed away her tears and sighed.

"Alex," Charlotte began again, pushing the hair from his forehead. "I am planning a little trip."

Alex nodded and waited.

"I am going to Sarawak in the *Queen* to visit some friends there."

"Visit friends. Are you visiting the Rajah, Mama? Oh, may I come?"

"Well, Alex, I think that this time I need you to stay here. I need you to take care of Adam, of course, for who else is there better to do that? And there will be tests at the school after I get back. You need to pay attention to your books, of course."

Alex looked crestfallen, but his triumph with the *babu* had softened the blow, and she was now very grateful he had raised the issue. He nodded.

"Next time?" he began.

"Oh yes, next time, definitely. When you are both a little older and we can explore together. Adam is too young just yet, isn't he?"

Alex nodded more strongly now. Of course, it was Adam; he was much too young. "Very well, Mother. Will you write to me?"

Charlotte smiled. "Every day. I shall bring back a present for you both."

Alex almost jumped out of bed. "A monkey, Mama? Could we have a pet monkey?"

Charlotte sighed. "I shall see. If all the reports from Malik, and Robert, and Aunt Teresa, and Aunt Shilah and ..." Alex put a finger to her lips smiling. "... are good ones," She mock-frowned.

He laughed. Then he threw himself back onto the bed, and she pulled up the cover.

"I shall be very good, Mama, don't worry."

Charlotte kissed him and turned down the light. She went to the study and made a list of instructions for Malik and Tarun. Shilah had agreed to move into the house with Amber whilst she was away, and Charlotte had made sure Malik knew that in her absence Shilah was the mistress. Malik could be something of a snob, and, despite all his kind and quiet efficiency he was somewhat set in his ways. Still, Amber was Robert's child, and Shilah, he knew, was a respected visitor. There would be no problem.

As for Tarun, she had simply told him not to visit the Chinese town. Alex had studies to complete. His Malay needed improvement. They should spend time in Kampong Glam or even at the Bugis village. She had ordered a kite to be made for him. It was a Malay kite, a *wau bulan*, a moon kite, covered in a vine-and-leaf pattern, with a humming bow at its head. He would receive it after she left. Tarun would teach him to fly it down by the beach near the Sultan's compound. The Malay boys played there.

She put down her pen and poured a glass of Madeira from the crystal decanter. The children, she was certain, would do very well without her for a while. Adam had many friends who came to play, and he adored Amber. He would be thrilled to be living in the same house with her. They would all play with Tarun's boys and the other little children on her compound. Alex would be busy. She planned to be away for two months, no more. She had asked Isabel da Silva to come with her, for Isabel, too, she thought, needed a change of scene. Another prospective marriage had come to nothing when the poor fellow had died.

She looked at the wine in her glass, the ruby darkness of it captured in the flickering light of the lamp. Her thoughts went to Zhen. She drank down the wine and took up her pen and began to write to Charles Maitland.

26

"Na Mo Kuan Shi Yin Pu Sa,
Na Mo Kuan Shi Yin Pu Sa,
Na Mo Kuan Shi Yin Pu Sa."

Noan's head was bowed before the many-armed statue of the goddess Kuan Yin as she joined the throng chanting the mantra.

"Na Mo Kuan Shi Yin Pu Sa."
"Refuge in the bodhisattva who hears the cries of the world."

This chant, with the priests and the women around her, gave Noan great peace and comfort. Kuan Yin was the compassionate one, filled with benevolence. This mantra brought Kuan Yin instantly to your side, and the thought filled Noan with light and calm. She raised her eyes to the goddess, her thousand arms embracing the world, encompassing her and her children in goodness and mercy. She loved this goddess above all.

The child in her belly moved suddenly, causing a pain to shoot round her hip. She put her hand to it and waited, head down, for the pain to pass. Her neighbour, noticing, stopped chanting and put out her hand to Noan, who gripped it. The women here were always a great comfort to her. They all understood suffering, and Noan found the greatest relief with them in prayer.

The chant slowed and then, finally, with the beating of the silvery bell, stopped. Noan rose with the other women and lit a bundle of incense sticks, waving the fragrant smoke around the goddess, thanking her. She put the sticks into the censer and bowed one last time. The other women departed, but Noan stayed. She needed to offer one more prayer. She lit some incense sticks and moved the smoke around her and before the goddess.

"*Na Mo Kuan Shi Yin Pu Sa.* Compassionate One. Bless my children, bless the one who is to be born and bless my husband's son."

As she uttered the words she felt a presence at her side and turned. Her sister stood close by and was looking at Noan in amazement.

"Bless your husband's son? What son? What are you talking about, Noan?"

Noan recoiled, astounded to see Lilin here in the temple. "You. What are you doing here?"

Lilin looked at her sister shrewdly. She had come to the temple knowing Noan would be here. Lilin wanted to talk to her sister about this white woman. She knew Noan had been out. A servant had tattled that she had seen her arrive in Philip Street in a white woman's carriage. This was news indeed, and Lilin wanted to know more.

She had waited as the temple was filled with chanting and the striking of bells. She used to come here often, but now she almost never set foot inside a temple, except occasionally to light incense on the anniversary of her son's death. She liked the perfumes and sounds of the temple, though. It was pleasant, she found, to be there, and she had taken a place at the back of the courtyard listening to the mantra, inhaling the scent of the incense, waiting. Now she was very glad she had.

"Well, sister, I am here to help you home. You look so tired. Come take my arm."

Noan was tired, but she could not make out what Lilin was talking about. Come here to help her? This was unbelievable. But Lilin took up her cloth bag and took her sister by the arm. They bowed to the priest in the large front courtyard and stepped up over the log, into the street.

Lilin put her oiled-paper umbrella up, over their heads, and they made their way along Telok Ayer Street to the market. At a fruit stall, Lilin stopped. There were some benches, and Noan sat, tired.

Lilin paid the Malay stall keeper to prepare two coconuts, and they watched as he took out his large *parang* and, with the deftness of experience, opened the top in one slice. They both drank through the bamboo straw.

Noan smiled at Lilin. They hadn't done this for years. As children they had played here on the bayside. Their amah always had a coin to buy them each a coconut. Lilin looked up and smiled at her sister. She too remembered that time long ago. How different things had been then. They had been close, played and laughed together easily. Even after they had been secluded they had found enjoyment in each other's company.

It was Noan's marriage that had changed everything. She had gotten Zhen, and from that moment Lilin could find no contentment, no forgiveness that she, the lovely one, had not received this gift. Her reward for her beauty, her devotion to her family, her hard work at embroidery and cooking, had been nothing more than Ah Teo and a dead child. That thought surfaced now, and she finished her coconut noisily.

"Well, sister, what is all this about a son? I know you have been to see the *ang mo* woman?"

Noan too finished her drink. The stall man took the coconuts, cut them swiftly in two, tied them into a banana leaf and handed them back. At home the maids would scrape and dry the flesh or make the milk to use in cooking. The husks were used as simple bowls and ladles or fuel for the stove.

Lilin waited, sensing her sister's reluctance. "Well, you might as well tell me," she prodded. "You have told Kuan Yin. I have heard you, and now I shall not give up until you have told me."

Noan knew this was true, and suddenly she wanted to unburden herself. Lilin had seen this woman too, knew more than she. What difference did it make?

"I will tell you what I know, but first tell me about her, the *ang mo*."

Lilin smiled. "I know she is a widow of a *belanda* in Jawa who has a lot of money. She is very rich and has a large house. Her brother is the chief of the police. She has two children. She's a lucky creature isn't she? Luckier than us. I should like very much to be a widow and have lots of money."

Noan looked at Lilin sharply, but Lilin merely shrugged. "No use pretending. I am, in any case, to all intents and purposes a widow. Ah Teo has his new wife and a child on the way. Not that I care."

Noan rose. She wanted to go home, to lie down. Her legs felt heavy, and her headache had started again. Lilin rose too, seeing her sister's distress. She was slightly alarmed. Noan had not been well with this pregnancy, and despite everything she held against her sister, Lilin had, by moments, felt sorry for her.

"Come. Hold my arm. Let's go home," she offered.

Noan took Lilin's arm, glad of the support and glad of the umbrella.

"The boy, the boy with the white woman, he is my husband's son," she said, her voice low and tired.

Lilin gripped her sister's arm. "Can you be sure?"

"Yes, if you saw him you would know. He is like Zhen and has something of Lian's eyes, too."

As they turned into Market Street, Noan stumbled slightly and Lilin held her. She could hear Noan's breath, which had become a wheeze. "We are almost home. Look, a few more steps," Lilin urged.

Lilin was relieved to arrive home. As they crossed the threshold she called for servants, and they helped Noan upstairs to the bedroom. "Thank you, younger sister," Noan called as she left.

Lilin looked at her sister departing. What on earth did Noan feel about the secret she had just revealed? It was difficult to tell. Perhaps they would talk about it later, when Noan felt better. But more importantly, Lilin thought, what do I think about this?

Zhen had a son. Lilin settled her umbrella into a porcelain stand and began slowly to climb the stairs. Zhen had a son. She arrived at the landing and started to walk towards her room. Suddenly she heard a laugh. It was Lian, she knew immediately, for she was close to this child. She went to the nursery and saw the children playing. Lian was six years old. Lilin contemplated this child. Zhen's child. Zhen's child and half-sister of his son by the white woman.

Lilin turned from the door. They were brother and sister, of

183

course they were. Did Zhen know? She was not sure, but something told her that he did not. Brother and sister. Well, if they were to come together, what would their offspring be? The idea appeared fully grown inside her head. Here was a way to destroy both Zhen and his white whore.

Lilin put her hand to her mouth. Incest. Her heart had started beating hard. Here was the way to ruin them, destroy their love for each other.

She smiled. At last, a reason to be living. She had only to plan and wait.

27

Captain Elliott had made the *Queen* ready and stood awaiting her instructions. They had been commended to join the Honourable Company's war steamer *Auckland* in convoy with Sir James's new gunboat *Rajah*, launched at Singapore only a few days ago and now made ready for Sarawak. Her sleek swiftness and her long brass guns were destined for active service in the suppression of piracy in the seas of Borneo and Sulu, but Captain Elliott was of the opinion that her four horsepower engine was insufficient for the intended purpose.

Nonetheless they were joined in convoy and set out together along the Straits of Singapore heading due east to Borneo. The *Queen* soon outstripped her companions, for the wind was high and the sails carried her far ahead. The going was thick and rough with driving rain, and the voyage uncomfortable. For three days there was no relief until, when the wind died down, they finally came in sight of land. The call went up, and Charlotte came on deck with Isabel.

Isabel had never before in her life left Singapore, never set foot aboard a seagoing vessel. Her excitement and girlish boisterousness at the departure had quickly evaporated, and she had spent the entire voyage extremely seasick and confined to her cabin. She looked pale and wan and, through lack of appetite, had lost a good deal of weight. Charlotte had given her crystallised ginger to nibble, and the cook supplied hot ginger drinks. Ginger had long been known as a restorative for seasickness, and she had relied on her own supply during her voyage from England. It had proven efficacious for Isabel in stopping the nausea, but her appetite had yet to return.

Captain Elliott had slowed their rate to allow the other ships to catch them and now ordered sail lowered in order for the *Auckland* and the *Rajah* to come ahead. In the waters which ran about the coastal inlets and numerous rivers of this island, piracy and danger abounded. In convoy then, they began their approach along the northern coast of Borneo. Thunder and lightning, rain and a heaving swell made the voyage disagreeable until the distinctive peak of Mount Santubong signalled the twin entrances to the Sarawak River.

At dusk they rounded the Santubong peninsula and moved into the sheltered waters of the bay before the Morotabas entry to the river. For the first time the ship glided smoothly, and Isabel let out a cry of relief as tears sprang to her eyes. Charlotte put her arms about her friend's shoulders, and Isabel was finally able to give a small smile.

"From here, surely our journey will be filled with sights we have never seen before," Charlotte said, hoping to reassure the poor girl.

The *Auckland* dropped anchor near the *Queen*. For the journey upriver they would all board the *Rajah* under the guidance of Mr Richards, the pilot. When the *Queen's* cargo had been ferried upriver, she would load with antimony, the chief mineral of Sarawak and for which, Charlotte had learned, the country was in fact named. The Rajah paid for his cargoes in kind, and antimony was his main source of income.

The *Queen* would return to Singapore with this cargo and spend several weeks in dock for repairs and cleaning. After two years, every ship in the tropics, no matter how well cared for, became infested with rats and cockroaches and needed to be thoroughly smoked with pitch, sulphur or mercury and cleansed of these vermin. The hull needed careening too, to clean it of barnacles and weeds and repair the wood which was under constant attack by shipworms that ate it to pieces. Following this, she would take a sea run carrying iron goods, cloth and opium to Benjamarsin for diamonds and gold, make a stop in Batavia to pick up a cargo of tea, coffee, sago and teak wood for Singapore. In Singapore she would load with guns and ammunition, cloth and other stores for the Rajah on the run back to Sarawak to pick up her owner.

The night in the sheltered bay proved thankfully uneventful, and with the dawn came a return to fine weather. The early morning mist clung to the trees and mountains, sweeping and swirling along the river carrying an indefinable scent, half sweet, half fetid. Charlotte shivered. The air was cold, everything covered in a sheen of dew. The mountain of Santubong rose, green and luxuriantly wooded, to a great height, dwarfing them. At its foot lay a vast expanse of fine sand strewn randomly with enormous brown boulders, as if giants had suddenly been disturbed at a game of bowls.

The shore was lined with groves of *rhu*, the casuarina trees which, Charlotte knew, the natives called "talking trees" for the sound of the breeze rustling through their lacy branches and feathery leaves. They looked so delicate it seemed a wind could blow them away in a puff of green smoke. In the distance a village lay, Lilliputian brown huts dotting the beach, canoes tethered to the shore, the women and children barely discernible from this distance, the mist swirling like a diaphanous silken ribbon around the green cliffs and crevasses of the mountain and drifting in silence around the trees and along the water like a vaporous breath.

It was very different to Singapore and Java. The jungles and rolling hills of Singapore, the great mountains and plains of Java were touchable, approachable, arable, but here, Charlotte recognised, was true wilderness. Impenetrable, but for the river banks and coastal villages. Impenetrable and merciless to man. Only animals and insects could reign over this wild land of Borneo. She felt a quickening of her pulse, a true excitement at this newness, at the potential for danger.

As the *Rajah* entered the wide mouth of the river, the turquoise blue of the sea changed gradually to a swirl of greens and browns, the one running through the other as if coloured dyestuffs had been poured about them. They sailed on these marbled waters until they left the coast behind and the jungle walls enveloped them. Now the river was completely brown, dark and smooth and slow, lined with low mangroves, plumed *nipa* and leafy *nibong* palms flying into the sky.

It was long and sinuous, the Sarawak River, Captain Elliot had told them, twenty-four miles from the mouth to Kuching, At each bend of the river the little black faces of monkeys greeted them, hanging from branches, chattering and flying from branch to branch, as if angry at this intrusion into their domain. Villages of palm-leaf houses hugged each wide reach, and women and naked children came to the steps to stare at the ship. Fishermen stopped casting their nets and waved and called. Logs of wood suddenly became crocodiles that flopped into the water or eyed them from the muddy banks. Chinamen in small, swift, narrow canoes loaded with fish guided their boats like Venetian gondoliers along the dark waters, making for the market at Kuching.

In a land where the only possible mode of travel was by water, boats of all sorts often filled the river, from the small sampan, scooped from a tree trunk, so narrow as to seem insufficient to contain its numerous passengers, to the large, sheltered houseboats propelled by old men sitting cross-legged, dressed in dirty white cotton drawers and jaunty conical hats. Yet sometimes the river was lonely as a tomb, only the engine of the boat echoing in an eerie and silent world.

Isabel, whose countenance had improved greatly, sat quietly on deck with Charlotte. Neither could find any words to speak of this long, slow journey into they knew not what. An unpalatable breakfast of hard biscuits, melting tinned butter, boiled eggs and dark Chinese tea was not tempting, and both women sat contemplating the riverside as Mr Richards, Captain Elliott and the other men made short work of the meal.

Clearly they would both have to make some adjustments in diet in this far-flung paradise. Some kinds of tinned food had only recently found popularity. The containers were thick and difficult to open. Charlotte did not care for them at all, the more so as she knew that the tin can and the process of preserving food had been invented for Napoleon's troops. It was difficult, even dangerous to open them, requiring a sharp knife or some blunt instrument, and injuries were commonplace. And the tinned foods were expensive. Charlotte recognised the value for the army and navy forces and, even here in isolated Sarawak, she knew that tinned meat, cheese and butter were amongst the supplies for the Rajah, but she did not care for such food herself.

At last, after two and a half hours, as the sun climbed into the sky, a final turn in the river revealed the fort on a low hill covered in cropped grass: a long white building with cannon at the port-holes, manned by a contingent of Malay soldiers. A single cannon shot rang out, and they realised the town had been advised of their arrival. They continued past the fort and into the tiny town, and Mr Richards called for the anchor to be dropped just before the Rajah's residence which was clearly visible on a raised knoll on the right-hand side of the river. It was a large, double-storey wooden residence with a deep verandah and a thatched roof.

Charlotte could see a small contingent of Europeans waiting on the landing place, bristling with yellow flags and parasols carried by the native guards, the famous Dyaks, of which she had been told many tales. The staff carried the Rajah's flag, a red and purple cross on yellow. The river was wide here, and town was open to their gaze.

Opposite the Rajah's compound stood a square wooden building, with lattice work covering its upper parts. A red Chinese temple and a number of thatched huts and low houses led away from the shore towards a rising hill. Atop it stood a large Tudor-style English house. Such a sight in the midst of the wilds of Borneo ought to have surprised, but, Charlotte thought, perhaps she had lived too long in the East that such a sight did not seem in the least out of place. It was, she knew from Mr Richards' narrative, the home of an English Reverend, Francis McDougall, and his wife Harriette, and why should they not choose Tudor?

The thought suddenly seemed comical and made her smile. How mad a place it must be, this little English kingdom in the midst of headhunting tribes, sea pirates and bewildering vastness!

I must suspend judgement, Charlotte thought, until I know something more of the place. Mr Richards had told her of the great benefits of Great Britain's enlightened civilisation which Sir James Brooke wished to visit on the poor Dyaks of the interior. But against the piratical sea Dyaks, who terrorised the peaceful coastal villages, he would join forces with the British Navy for the purposes of punishment and, if possible, extermination. Mr Richards was so enthusiastic and ready in his praise of the Rajah that Isabel had become almost overexcited and Charlotte had settled them all down by asking the steward for a cup of tea.

Now they could see a low barge approaching, conducted by bare-chested Malay and Dyak men, their paddles painted in the colours of Sarawak, red, yellow and black. Within minutes the barge had arrived at the side of the *Rajah* and two soldiers had climbed aboard, together with Charles Maitland.

He came forward with both hands extended and took hers. Charlotte smiled her happiness at seeing him.

"Welcome, Kitt and Miss Isabel, Captain Elliott."

Charles helped the two ladies down into the barge for the short journey to the river's edge. A drum began a rhythmic beating, and several of the native men on shore began a dance, stamping their feet and shaking their long spears. As the visitors stepped from the barge the drum rose to a crescendo and the men set up a long and piercing call, then suddenly fell silent.

Charlotte was introduced to John Brooke Johnson, the Rajah's nephew and heir, a pleasant-looking man in the uniform of a midshipman. The Rajah was awaiting them in the Lodge, as his residence was known. Isabel clung to Charlotte's hand, eyeing warily the guard of honour, some twenty half-dressed and fierce-looking Dyak men, with long feathers adorning their headdresses and arm bands. Intricate black tattoos covered the length of their arms and backs. They wore beads and bangles in profusion and waistcloths of red, yellow and white. These, Charles explained, belonged to the Sarawak Rangers, the Rajah's force of Malay and Dyak warriors.

They made their way up the sloping path to the Lodge, and Charlotte could not repress a tingle of excitement. To meet Rajah Brooke here in his kingdom surrounded by these fearsome men, some with bones in their ears and noses; this was a most extraordinary event that one did not meet with every day. Charlotte felt Isabel's excitement in the squeeze of her hand.

The Rajah was in audience in the main hall of the Lodge. He was sitting surrounded by the local chieftains. As the party climbed onto the verandah, the Rajah rose and came forward, the men seated on the floor parting to let him pass.

"Charlotte and Isabel, welcome, welcome."

Isabel seemed so in awe of James Brooke that she stood stock still. Charlotte dropped into a curtsy and pulled Isabel's hand. Isabel dropped almost to her haunches. Both women lowered their eyes until James let out a long peal of delighted laughter.

"No need for such formality, my dears," he said, chuckling. "We are quite informal here."

James took up Charlotte's hand and kissed it gallantly and then took Isabel by the hand and pulled her up. He turned and made his way back to his seat, and Charlotte and Isabel were accompanied by John Brooke and Charles to their jungle accommodations.

28

The Lodge stood in large grounds. The overwhelming scent of blooms floated on the air, and Charlotte noticed very large bowls of green and golden flower petals along the edge of the verandah. They were the blossoms of the *kenang* and the *champak*, flowering trees which grew near the house.

Within the grounds stood four or five other houses, similar to The Lodge, of double height, surrounded on all sides by long verandahs. The day was pleasantly cool and overcast. Charlotte and Isabel were shown to a house standing to one side of the Lodge on the banks of a stream which wound its way down the hillside and into the river. A small bridge led over this stream to other houses. The Lodge was home to Arthur Crookshank, the Rajah's first minister, and his wife, Bertha, to the Rajah's nephew and to Harold Grant, James Brooke's private secretary, whom the Rajah always addressed, rather disconcertingly, as Hoddy Doddy. Spenser St. John, his brother James, Charles and a group of other men shared a second house.

Bertha Crookshank was indisposed, Charlotte was told. She was pregnant and had contracted a fever. She was currently being cared for by Dr Treacher, although the principal doctor for the town was Frank McDougall. Charlotte felt very sorry for Bertha Crookshank. The prospect of being pregnant and unwell in this jungle town was not to be envied.

Charlotte called to Captain Elliott, who was waiting for her to be settled before taking up his own billet with the St. John brothers. "Bring the chest of medicines directly to the Rajah, please, James. If we can be of service to Mrs Crookshank, it would be a mercy."

The medicine chest was aboard the *Rajah*, and James Elliott turned immediately to carry out her orders. She had brought a large supply of quinine for the swamp fever, also quantities of laudanum, Godfrey's cordial, tincture of opium, a mixture for coughs. Dr Oxley had prepared the chest with other items, bandages, dressings and poultices for boils. Fortunately, Charlotte had been vaccinated against smallpox in Singapore when the government had ordered mandatory vaccinations of the entire population.

Charlotte considered herself extremely fortunate not to have contracted malaria during all the years she had lived in these islands. Almost everyone had malaria from one time or another. Charles, she knew, had contracted it in Batavia and, he told her, he had bouts from time to time. It was simply matter of fact. Everyone was indisposed sooner or later. Charlotte really had quite a morbid fear of it and listened to Captain Elliott on the matter. He advised, whilst in these jungle places, to stay indoors at dusk, for it appeared that was when the miasma was most dangerous and prevalent.

Isabel and Charlotte were shown their rooms. They were large and comfortable, the wood floors polished to a high gleam. It was a pleasant space. Charlotte's room had a wooden four-poster bed, a wardrobe and a chest of drawers, a small table and chair. A net stood over the bed, and shuttered doors led to the verandah. Two young Malay girls stood shyly by the door. They had been sent to take care of the two white women. Charlotte's maid, who had supervised the arrival of the luggage, now took these girls in hand, bustling and pointing to clothes, giving orders, sending them hither and thither for this and that. Charlotte could see she was thoroughly enjoying herself. She left them to their business and went out onto the verandah.

As she gazed out over the small stream which bubbled down to the slow-moving river, she detected, suddenly a whiff of perfume. She smiled. One of the greatest charms of the jungle was these mysterious and exquisite scents which came suddenly from unseen flowers hiding in the heart of the forest and nestling under great leaves on river banks.

Isabel, who had quite recovered her spirits, came noisily along the verandah. "Isn't it exciting, Charlotte? Did you see the headhunters?

I thought I should die, really. Oh, and Captain Maitland is so dashing, and the young John Brooke, isn't he marvellous? I can't wait to cross the river, can you, to visit with Mrs McDougall. I met her in Singapore, and she is such a wonderful woman, bringing the word of the Lord to the natives. Don't you think that is marvellous of her? And her husband, such a saint."

Isabel prattled on, and Charlotte took no notice. She was not sure what she thought of this place at all. Charles Maitland had left her until the evening, and Charlotte now wondered what on earth people got up to in this kingdom of the white Rajah.

Just as this thought passed through her mind, she was informed that the Rajah's butler, Talip, was here and sought to speak to her. Charlotte thought she would very much like to meet a Sarawakian butler, and she and Isabel went downstairs to the lower verandah.

Talip was a Sarawakian Malay; he was an unusually tall, good-looking young man with dark, intelligent eyes, a thick black moustache and an abundant head of curly black hair forming a fringe under his elaborate head-kerchief. Charlotte could see he was something of a dandy. He was extremely neat, his spotless snow-white jacket covering the folds of his yellow and black sarong and narrow white trousers. His feet, however, were bare.

As the ladies approached he bowed solemnly and handed Charlotte a note. It was from Harriette McDougall, an invitation for Charlotte and Isabel to dine at her residence tomorrow evening.

In Malay, Charlotte said, "Thank you, Talip. If you bring some paper I shall respond immediately."

Talip smiled, a charming grin which showed his slightly blackened teeth. "*Puan* speaks Malay well."

Charlotte smiled and nodded.

"Would the *puan-puan* like tea or some fruit?" Talip asked.

"Oh, yes, I'm suddenly starving, it's almost lunchtime," Isabel said to Charlotte in English. "What are we to do about lunch, Charlotte?" Isabel could understand Malay very well, but her grasp of spoken Malay was poor. At home she spoke only English or Portuguese.

Charlotte nodded at Talip. "Thank you, some lunch perhaps.

Rice and curry, some tea and fruit would be nice."

She and Isabel sat in the rattan chairs on the verandah. Talip bowed quickly and moved inside the house, calling for refreshments and paper.

When the tea tray had been laid and served and Charlotte had finished writing to Harriette, she handed the letter to Talip, who had been standing, waiting quietly, in the corner of the verandah. He took it but did not move off immediately, and Charlotte felt a small hesitation.

"Is there something else Talip?" she asked

Talip coughed very slightly, putting his hand to his mouth. "Since *Puan* speaks Malay, would *Puan* like to meet some Sarawak ladies? I know they are most curious about you. I can bring them in the afternoon for tea. They like tea," he added, almost as an afterthought, "and cakes. The Rajah's cook will make cakes."

"Ooh, cakes, yes please, Charlotte, let's meet the Sarawak ladies." Isabel spoke from behind a mouthful of papaya. Her appetite had returned with a vengeance.

Charlotte nodded, the time was fixed, the curry and rice arrived and Talip departed to his tasks.

The afternoon went remarkably quickly. A cool bath and a sleep restored both the women, and when Charlotte went down to the hall, she found it had been prepared for the tea party. Gold brocade cushions had been spread about the polished floor, with, against a wall, two sets of two cushions, evidently for herself and Isabel. A long low table stood to one side, covered by a white cloth on which lay bowls of pineapples, mangoes and mangosteens. Two large red lacquer boxes divided the fruit bowls; they were filled with exquisite, sweet Malay colourful cakes, made from rice flour and a vast array of different spices and ingredients. China cups and saucers were awaiting the teapot. Charlotte was impressed by Talip's silent efficiency.

Talip himself appeared as if by magic. "*Puan* must wait upstairs until all the ladies have arrived, please. *Puan* must be late. You are a special guest of the Rajah, and the ladies must await you. It is good manners."

Charlotte smiled and shrugged. She went to her bedroom and

called her maid to fix her hair. A sound, like the rustling leaves of the bamboo, began to be heard from the garden, and she rose and peeped over the verandah. It was the silken draperies of her guests flitting about. She dressed in light blue and white organza, with earrings of indigo blue lapis lazuli.

Finally Talip arrived, and she and Isabel were permitted to descend. Charlotte had not expected so many ladies; she had thought there would be three or four at the most, but here, seated on the gold cushions, clothed in silk brocades and gauzy veils of rose, lime, blue and lilac, were some twenty women. Charlotte was reminded somewhat of an animated bed of brightly coloured flowers. At her arrival, Talip signalled the women to rise, and they did so in unison, their silk skirts rustling like a summer breeze through leaves.

Two ladies came forward, the wives of the principal Malay chiefs and, placing a hand under both Charlotte's and Isabel's elbows, ushered them to their places, one cushion higher than themselves. Charlotte could not repress a small smile at this exquisite etiquette. It was most charmingly done, however, and the ladies were lovely, young, with dark hair, fine skin and long eyelashes.

Large jugs of lukewarm coffee appeared, laced, Charlotte knew, with lashings of sugar, for the Malays liked their coffee like syrup. Politeness meant she could not decline, and Isabel, who was accustomed to it, drank hers down with gusto. It took some time to serve everyone, and in the meantime no one spoke to her or Isabel at all. They stared at the two foreigners, though, inspecting every garment and jewel, and chattered quietly and gravely amongst themselves. Finally the coffee was served and the gossip was silenced by Talip, who took centre stage in the middle of the room.

"*Makan! la ... Minum! la ... Jangan malu!*"

Thus exhorted to eat and drink without shame, the women rose and helped themselves. Talip placed plates of cakes for Charlotte and Isabel on the floor in front of them. As Isabel was about to tuck in, Charlotte put her hand on her friend's arm and looked at her severely. Not only was it bad manners to begin before anyone else, Charlotte was determined Isabel should not gain the weight she had lost. She was looking better than she had in months. The maid had stitched in her dresses, her skin was looking fresh, and she had a vitality that had been lacking. To be overweight in the tropics was burdensome, dangerous and exhausting. Isabel looked momentarily annoyed but submitted and smiled at Charlotte.

Finally everyone was seated again, and Charlotte stood up and spoke to her guests.

"*Datus, Daiangs*, thank you for visiting us today. We are very happy to be in Sarawak and amongst ladies of such distinction and beauty."

This pretty speech broke the ice, and the women all moved forward around the English women's feet and began asking them questions. Charlotte laughed, and Isabel struggled gallantly with her Malay. The betel and *sireh* sets were brought out for her guests, and the afternoon was a success. Her lapis lazuli earrings had disappeared, a gift to the head *Datu*, in exchange for her own made of silver, glass beads and mother-of-pearl. Charlotte was glad she had not chosen to wear diamonds.

Later, in her room, resting before dinner, Charlotte wondered at the extraordinary richness of the garments and ornaments the ladies were wearing. She had been led to believe that Sarawak was a primitive place, but the materials made here were as fine as any she had ever seen.

As evening approached, Charlotte's maid set out the sandalwood incense to burn on the verandah outside her room and Isabel's. This incense, Charlotte had found in Batavia, was efficacious at keeping insects at bay, and she went nowhere without it.

Dinner was a boisterous affair. After an all-female afternoon, the evening was to be all male. Charlotte realised immediately that she and Isabel would be the only women present. She was glad to have Charles by her side, for the large dining room was overrun with men of various ages and various nationalities. Several of the native princes were present, as were a group of young Dyak boys. The oldest man by twenty years was the Rajah, and during dinner he kept up a constant stream of conversation, telling stories of his arrival in Sarawak and the encounters with pirates, constantly calling out words in Dyak to the group of young boys.

He was an amusing companion, and the young men hung on his every word. Charlotte was reminded of the informality of a mess hall. The men, after the initial introductions, seemed hardly to notice the presence of the women, though Charlotte's looks attracted attention and several paid some flattering attention to Isabel. As the cherry brandy passed around, the party grew increasingly more boisterous.

Charlotte was amazed to see that the boys jumped all over the Rajah as he sat on the long sofa after dinner. Hoddy Doddy was practically seated on his knee, and the Rajah kept a loose arm around the boy's waist. The Dyak boys hung around his legs, stroking him from time to time. No one seemed to think anything particular in this attitude, although Charlotte sensed that Spenser St. John was not entirely approving.

Then the sound of the piano began, and Charlotte turned to see Isabel seated before the instrument. It was not unexpected because all the da Silva children were musical in one way or another.

Charlotte was glad. Isabel had a lovely singing voice and played the piano very well. Her voice rose in a song she knew would please the gathered naval contingent, *The Lass that Loves a Sailor*.

"The moon on the ocean was dimmed by a ripple
Affording a chequered delight;
The gay jolly tars passed a word for the tipple,
And the toast—for 'twas Saturday night:
Some sweetheart or wife he loved as his life
Each drank, and wished he could hail her:
But the standing toast that pleased the most
Was 'The wind that blows,
The Ship that goes,
And the lass that loves a sailor!'"

The Rajah had risen and all the men had gathered around Isabel.

"Some drank 'The Queen', and some her brave ships,
And some 'The Constitution';
Some 'May our foes, and all such rips,

Yield to English resolution!'
That fate might bless some Poll or Bess,
And that they soon might hail her:
But the standing toast that pleased the most
Was 'The wind that blows,
The Ship that goes,
And the lass that loves a sailor!'"

Everyone was clapping and dancing to the lively tune. Charles invited Charlotte for a jig, which she smilingly agreed to dance.

"Some drank 'The Prince', and some 'Our Land',
This glorious land of freedom!
Some that our tars may never stand
For heroes brave to lead them!
That she who's in distress may find,
Such friends as ne'er will fail her.
But the standing toast that pleased the most
Was 'The wind that blows,
The ship that goes,
And the lass that loves a sailor!
The wind that blows,
The ship that goes,
And the lass that loves a sailor!'"

All the men joined in for the refrain of the final verse, they raised the roof, stamping their feet and clapping wildly. When she played the final note, Isabel rose and bowed and every man there applauded her. Her eyes were bright, her skin ablush, and she had never looked finer, Charlotte thought.

Calls immediately went up for her to play it again, and she obliged, this time every refrain sung with gusto by the men led by Rajah Brooke. By the time she had played ten songs twice over, and her finale, *Rule Britannia*, she was finally released, the most popular woman in Sarawak, to a refreshment, and the Rajah called for the Malay band.

To Charlotte's consternation, James Brooke jumped to his feet and came up to her and, without a word, swung her into his arms and set off in a gavotte up and down the living room. James St. John had gathered up Isabel and was doing likewise. All the young men swung into action. Each gathered up a Dyak boy or one of the Malay princes or each other and, arms around each other, began whooping and galloping up and down the floor.

Charlotte was glad to be rescued, finally, by Charles, and the Rajah turned his attention to Hoddy Doddy, who he swept into his arms and began whirling around the floor. Thinking it best to make her escape, she took Charles's arm and called to Isabel who, rather reluctantly, relinquished the arms of Henry Steele, a pleasant-looking young man who was the Rajah's court interpreter. She made her way unsteadily to Charlotte's side.

"Good heavens, is it always like that, Charles?" Charlotte said, fanning herself.

Charles laughed. "No, no. James is very gay tonight. It is the presence of guests and, quite obviously, the presence of Miss Isabel and her singing." He bowed to Isabel, and she smiled gaily.

"Usually we dine together, of course, for we have no other companions but each other, after all."

Isabel, yawning, wished them a goodnight and kissed Charlotte lightly on the cheek. Charles and Charlotte sat outside her room on the verandah.

Soon curiosity got the better of Charlotte. "Charles, the Rajah seems partial to young men, wouldn't you say?"

Charles looked at Charlotte and smiled. "Young men, young women. The Rajah is friendly with everyone. Hoddy Doddy is his favourite certainly."

"Well, yes, I can see that." Charlotte did not know how to pursue the matter further and decided to let it drop for now. She was tired in any case. It had been a long day.

She rose, and Charles rose with her. They stood a moment in silence. Charlotte could not make out what Charles intended, and as the silence lengthened she smiled.

"Goodnight, Charles, until tomorrow."

"Yes, yes, Kitt, goodnight." He bowed over her hand and turned and quickly left the verandah.

Charlotte sighed and locked the shutters. Really this place was something of an enigma, more like a schoolboy's camp than a kingdom. A place where women, white women certainly, were out of place. Even Charles seemed infected.

29

The yellow moon was full. It formed a golden backdrop to the high branches of the trees, which lay at the water's edge. The river flowed in a dark trail to the kampong, which was bathed in the gleam of light. The sound of water, gurgling, running, falling, dripping, pounding, moved by oars; this sound was all pervasive in Sarawak but tonight it was muted. The air was tinged with wood smoke from the villages on either side of the river. Roofed boats moved in silhouette lazily along the water. Only at sunset did the river change its dully brown aspect. Then the setting sun covered its dun surface with tints of gold and lavender. In the distance the long shadow of Mount Matang lay against the sky, floating, in a stream of rose and purple. The heavy perfume of champak lay on the still night air.

Charles was facing this river scene when Charlotte came up behind him.

"It is very charming," she murmured.

Charles turned and looked at her. She was half in shadow and light. "Yes," he said. "Most charming." He smiled, and she did too, lowering her eyes. When she raised them again, she found his had not wavered. His eyes were on her face, but he did not move. Charlotte put her hand to his face, and he took it and put it to his lips, but still he made no move.

"Charles ..." she began, and then, as if the sound of her voice had awakened him, she felt his hands encircle her waist. He held her like this, searching her face. Charlotte put both her arms around his neck, willing him, waiting. He sighed suddenly and dropped his face to hers. Their lips touched. Charlotte closed her eyes and tightened her grip on his neck.

She ran her hand under his shirt, down onto the skin of his back, pulling herself into him. In an instant he withdrew his lips from hers and released her, so quickly she felt a shock. One moment they were crushed tight against each other; the next they were apart. She staggered slightly and put out her hand against the tree.

He had stepped backwards, and she stared at him, uncomprehending, trying to see his face in the darkness.

"Charles?" she asked, unable to see into his eyes.

"I—" he began and stopped. She waited, unmoving. "I think that perhaps this is a mistake. I'm sorry Kitt. I had no right."

"No right?" Charlotte interrupted him. "I give you the right. I don't understand, Charles. One moment so willing, the next so cold."

There was a silence.

"Yes, I owe you an explanation," he said finally.

He held out his hand and she took it. "Walk with me to the riverside," he said.

They turned and followed the gently sloping path down to the edge of the river. At the bamboo fence there were some wooden benches, and he led her to one. They sat, and he released her hand.

"I was engaged to be married when I was a younger man." He looked down. "I was rather madly in love with her, I'm afraid. My temperament is unfortunate. I have a tendency to fly headlong into these things."

Charlotte looked at him. Headlong? Good heavens, Charles! she thought but she said nothing.

"I was twenty years of age and had asked for her hand before I had truly fixed my purpose in life. This was a great mistake. When I decided on a life of science and more particularly a life in the service of the East India Company, she, to my complete surprise, was adamantly against it. My brothers had joined, of course, so it seemed entirely natural to me. But she was so young, I suppose. Only seventeen. The thought of quitting her family, England, it was too much."

Charles turned and looked at Charlotte. "You see, I had no idea what to do. I hesitated, vacillated. I became totally unable to make a decision. I was given a leave of absence from the university. It was all hopeless. I forgot what I wanted, for I thought I only wanted her. Her family was quite strict. There was no formal agreement, but they led me to understand that when she was fully nineteen years of age, such a prospect might ... Two years! It seemed interminable."

He rose and began to walk along the bank, pacing. She could detect, even now, after so long, the agitation of that time.

"I fell into ways of which I am now not proud. I neglected my studies, barely dragged myself to my degree. I could meet her only rarely, she was so protected. Then, it seemed, this terrible waiting time would be over.

"Her birthday was only a month or so away. We began to make plans for the wedding. I was offered a position teaching at the university in London. Not a choice I would ordinarily have even considered. Then I received a letter. She was to be married to another, a baronet. All the cruelty, this forced waiting, had been for nothing. I was not permitted to see her, speak to her."

He sat down on the bench again. Charlotte's thoughts in a tiny flash went, for the first time in a very long time, to Lieutenant Mallory and the *Madras*. Had he felt like this, shattered, destroyed, unable to love again for years? She hoped not, but she had not thought men could be so struck. Now the evidence that it could be so was before her eyes.

"Well, it was a terrible time. I kept on hoping, of course, like a lovesick fool, writing letters, each more desperate, each more pointless. When I read of her marriage I immediately joined the East India Company, enlisted in the Madras Engineers and, fortunately, was asked to join the Magnetic Survey. It was the saving of my life."

He turned and took her hand. "So you see, Kitt, I have rather a hard time allowing myself to ..." He stopped.

"Yes, Charles, I see." She gripped his hand. "But do you love her still? After so long? Nine years."

"No, no, doubtless not. But it froze my heart. Can you understand?"

Charlotte nodded and put her hand on his chest. "And can no

one thaw it, this frozen heart?"

He smiled and covered her hand with his. "I think you know the answer to that. You see, I felt so quickly for you what I had felt for her, and it was heady, unbelievable, but terrifying."

"Fortunately, however, I am not seventeen or promised to a baronet."

"No," Charles smiled. "But I cannot rush headlong like I did before, even after nine years."

Charlotte pulled her hand from his and wrapped her shawl around her shoulders. She was beginning to feel rather annoyed. "Very well, Charles." She rose, and he stood too. She turned.

"No, no, Kitt, please don't be angry. By my calculations we have known each other truly only three months."

Calculations, she thought, degrees of magnetic attraction, mathematical equations. He was infuriating. She made to move off.

He darted around her, stopping her, and put his hands on her shoulders, then took her chin in one hand very gently.

"While we are here, I would like to court you. Would that be so terrible?"

Charlotte looked at him. "Oh, Charles, I am not a girl. I am a woman. I have been a widow for many years." She hesitated, realising the blatant meaning of her words.

Charles dropped his hand.

"Do you love me, Charlotte?" The question was sudden and unexpected. She could not immediately find an answer. Her body responded to him in a way that spoke of passion, but did she love him? She tried not to let the image of Zhen enter her mind, but there he was.

She shook her head. "I don't know, Charles. Yes, you're right. My feelings for you are, well, shall I say it? Not honourable."

Charles laughed, and she laughed too.

"I have quite dishonourable feelings for you, too, make no mistake. So perhaps we could find out if there is something more profound? Something on which we could build a life together? And make these feelings honourable?"

Charlotte put her arm through his. "Yes, that would be nice. But occasionally, since we are no longer foolish young things, may we, from time to time, kiss?"

Charles stopped and faced her. He put her arms around his neck and took her waist in his hands. "Do you imagine that I do not want to kiss you every moment I am awake? Do you imagine I do not have the strongest desire for you?"

Before she could answer, he pulled her against him and put his lips to hers, enclosing her in his arms, kissing her. His lips were rather tight against hers. She sensed that Charles had not kissed very many women, that he was somewhat inexperienced, even nervous.

It was not an arousing kiss. She felt her own lips trying to open, to welcome his to hers in a soft way, but he did not respond. But she did feel his latent power, felt the strength of his arms around her. The wondrous power of a man's arms, at once arousing, consoling and protective, the feel of her slender body tight against his chest overwhelming. Submission. She knew then she wanted to submit to him, not in everything, but in this intimate way she wanted to be ruled by him, tenderly, passionately. She sighed as he released her finally. She knew that she was vastly more experienced than him. It was a strange and tender realisation.

"That is how I feel about you. I would like to be sure you and I want this for a very long time. Can we do that?"

Charlotte smiled. She would teach him, slowly, the ways of love, as Zhen had taught her. She chased that image quickly from her mind, for another displaced it: that of a wedding, she in a wedding dress with him at her side. She looked at him. He was a man she would like to be married to, support in his work, even perhaps give children to, share a life with. He was a man of substance, an English man with whom she had so much in common. These other, more intimate, pleasures would surely come.

She slipped her arm through his. "Yes, Charles," she said, and he looked down at her with a smile.

30

Charlotte and Isabel took their places in the canoe to cross the river. Two Dyak men, part of the Rajah's Rangers, were to row them to the other side and accompany them to the house of Frank and Harriette McDougall. Isabel, fresh faced and refreshed, chattered gaily. The proximity of two young, copper-skinned, muscled and half-clad men seemed not, now, to have any effect on her. She had confided to Charlotte at breakfast that she had never enjoyed anything so much as the previous evening. Being the centre of attention in a place starved of white female companionship clearly suited her, and Charlotte understood. Here, away from her extensive family and the pressures of her mother, Isabel shone. Her natural, kindly and exuberant nature had free rein.

The river was filled with activity of all kinds. Fishermen were casting nets on the shores of the stilt villages. Canoes were constantly passing across the river carrying passengers, for this was the sole means of transport from one side to the other. The *Rajah* was anchored further upriver, near *Julia*, one of Rajah Brooke's gunboats. A constant debris of logs and leaves floated by, carried by the rains down to the sea, and the ferrymen dodged them with consummate ease.

They set foot ashore near the Chinese market and spent a few minutes examining the wares, under the stares of the inhabitants. Then, accompanied on either side by their Dyak warriors, they made their way up the slope. It was a moment Charlotte hoped she might be able to describe to Robert and Aunt Jeanne.

Charlotte liked Harriette McDougall immediately. She was a

slight woman, perhaps thirty years of age, with narrow lips and a slightly sallow complexion. She was pregnant, but that did not seem to stop her exhibiting the most lively energy, and she welcomed her guests with open arms, kissing Charlotte on her cheek and enfolding Isabel into her arms.

"Wonderful, wonderful, to have some English visitors, and not men. Men are all very well, but I tire of them sometimes. Do come and sit in the verandah."

Tea was poured. Harriette told Charlotte of the Rajah's great library at the Lodge. He was a great reader. They discussed the latest books and found a common affection for *Wuthering Heights* and *The Count of Monte Cristo*. She invited Charlotte and Isabel to visit the grounds of the church, which was still only half built. The children were at school in a hut next door, little abandoned half-caste children gathered in to the church, and they sang a hymn, somewhat out of tune and lyrically uncertain but with all the charm of the young. A long hut which served as a hospital ran along the wall on the river side.

Charlotte learned that Harriette's husband, the Reverend, was somewhere she did not catch, ministering to the natives, for he was a preacher but also a doctor. Really, Charlotte thought, what a marvel they all are. What is this faith that drives them to these extraordinary and dangerous exertions?

As they left the school, Harriette called to a man in the act of sawing large planks of wood. "Tomas Stahl," Harriette said, "our indispensable carpenter. He built our house, you know, and now builds the church. Bless him."

Tomas stopped working and came forward. He was a great bear of a man, some thirty years old, powerfully built, his tanned, muscular arms bare, the golden hairs of his chest bursting from his shirt. His head was a shock of red-gold. He was striking in every way and must have struck a kind of awe, Charlotte imagined, in the imagination of the tiny, wiry Dyak men.

He stood shyly and silently as introductions were made, then with a nod, departed back to his work.

"Tomas is German. He was a ship's carpenter, but after the ship foundered, fortunately with all aboard safe, he landed up here. He is rather godless, but we should not know what to do without him."

Charlotte could not help but notice that Isabel's gaze lingered on him long after Harriette had turned back to her house.

The view from Harriette's house, high on the hill, was splendid. It swept down over the town and along the river to the backdrop of the mountains which surrounded Kuching. Around the house was a garden of great beauty. A deep hedge of scented gardenia ran around three sides. Great bushes of the hibiscus, scarlet and buff, glowed in the sun. Charlotte relaxed as Harriette talked about her garden.

"The hibiscus are called shoe-flowers, for they are used instead of blacking to polish shoes. The pink one-hundred-leaved rose blossom all the year round. The golden allamander are a great temptation to the cows if they stray into the garden. The plumbago is one of the few pale blue flowers which like the blazing heat."

Lunch was a surprise that only the English in the Orient could produce: shepherd's pie with curried minced pork and plantain, followed by mango custard. With promises of renewed meetings, Charlotte and Isabel returned to the Rajah's compound. They parted, as the blistering heat of the afternoon began its reign on the day, to the cool of their quarters.

At six o'clock the sun had fallen below the mountains, its rays casting a halo of orange and pink around the peaks. A sleep and a bath had restored them, and the cool of the evening made life bearable. A servant came to accompany them to dinner, and arm in arm, Isabel and Charlotte climbed up to the verandah of the Lodge.

As Charlotte entered the drawing room, her eyes were instantly drawn to two men engaged in conversation with the Rajah. To her absolute amazement she realised that one of them was a man she loathed more than any other. It was Captain Palmer, the man who had tried to violate her so long ago in Java.

She stopped so quickly and dropped her arm from Isabel's so abruptly that Isabel looked at her with alarm. Palmer turned his grey eyes onto Charlotte, and she was thrown into confusion. She sought Charles, but he was nowhere to be seen.

Before she could move, James Brooke saw her and came forward with both hands held out to her. "Charlotte, my dear. You are radiant as usual. The air of Sarawak clearly agrees with you."

Charlotte smiled as best she could, and fortunately the Rajah's attentions immediately turned to Isabel. "Miss Isabel, will you play again for us tonight?"

Isabel laughed, delighted at these attentions and curtsied to the Rajah. Captain Palmer and his companion came towards them, and James turned.

"Ah, Helms, Palmer. Ladies, allow me to introduce Ludwig Helms, my managing agent, and Captain Joseph Palmer. Gentlemen, this is Mrs Charlotte Manouk and Miss Isabel da Silva."

Both men bowed, and Isabel bobbed a curtsey but Charlotte did not move.

"Delighted, ladies," Palmer said, keeping his eyes on Charlotte. "And what an unexpected pleasure to meet you again Mrs Manouk." He smiled.

"Do you two know each other?" the Rajah said and laughed. "Capital, capital, we shall all be a merry band. Come on, Helms."

He took up Isabel's arm and wrapped it in his own, turning with her and leading her to the piano. Helms trotted after them.

"Well, well, Charlotte Manouk. This is extraordinary. Still as beautiful as ever." Palmer moved next to Charlotte and bent his head towards hers. She moved away and took out her fan.

"Captain Palmer, this is not a delightful meeting. Leave me alone or I shall not hesitate to tell the Rajah and all his acquaintance what a cad you are."

Palmer smiled slightly, his arrogance and assurance undimmed.

"Do not underestimate me, sir." Charlotte added, "I can easily have the ear of the Rajah, and he would be sorry to lose my patronage."

Palmer's face changed. Gone was the smile, gone the pretence at charm. His eyes narrowed and he bared his teeth. Charlotte paled slightly but was determined to hold her ground. Palmer was about to speak when suddenly Charles came up and took her arm.

"Charlotte, shall we go in?" Charles moved forward, nodding at Palmer.

"What is it, Kitt? You look pale," he remarked as they moved away.

They made their way to the chairs in a corner of the room. Isabel began to play, a folk tune of some sort, and the midshipmen began to gather around her.

Charles's attention was still on Charlotte, his eyes full of concern. Charlotte hesitated, uncertain how much to reveal. After some moments she said, "I met Captain Palmer in Batavia. He is a man who has a reputation for keeping women, slave women, you understand."

Charles frowned. Slavery was a vicious and unacceptable practice certainly.

"Captain Palmer is not an honourable man and is not to be trusted around women, you understand. I tell you this to put you on your guard and to make sure he goes nowhere near Isabel."

Charles nodded and rose, taking Charlotte's hand. The gong sounded, and Isabel stopped playing.

Talip appeared, dressed in impeccable white, his brown and gold batik sarong around his hips. "Dinner, Tuan Rajah."

"Dinner," James shouted and gathered Isabel onto one arm and Hoddy Doddy on the other and set off for the dining room.

"Kitt, don't worry. I will not leave your side, or Isabel's, until the fellow has gone," Charles whispered.

Charlotte smiled into his eyes. Charles stood by her, the strength of his body, the might of his sword, at her service. He had never been more attractive, and she rather wished that they were alone.

To her relief, Palmer kept to himself throughout the meal. He was seated with two of his shipmates, and after dinner they all took their leave.

Charlotte was so glad she agreed to several dances with the midshipmen and Ludwig Helms, a convivial and cultured man. Charles and several of the young men accompanied Isabel and herself back to their lodgings and Charles came to her door.

"Safe, dear Kitt. Helms is MacEwen & Co.'s agent here for the Rajah. He trades through them. Apparently Helms engaged Palmer's ship to bring him here, and Palmer is seeking to go into business with MacEwen & Co., or some such thing. The Rajah is intent on wresting control of the antimony mines from the Chinese syndicate. I'm afraid I understand little of this sort of thing. I've set a guard to keep watch on the ship. St. John tells me Palmer and Helms will go upriver to see the mines at Bau tomorrow. They will be away for days, rest assured."

"Thank you, Charles, I am assured."

They stood together before her door, and a small silence filled the verandah. Somewhere in the forest a night bird called. The silence lengthened into awkwardness, and Charlotte turned and put her hand on the handle of the door.

"A trip, Kitt. Would you like to come with me? See something of the country?"

He had blurted it out, and Charlotte turned to face him. A chance to be alone with him, far away from everyone else. As if this bizarre outpost on a headhunter's river were not far away enough. She sighed. Perhaps he needed this to declare the feelings he seemed to be having trouble acknowledging.

"Yes, Charles, I should like that."

She saw the flash of his smile in the darkness. He took up her hand and kissed it, then turned on his heel and left.

Charlotte shook her head and locked her door. Really, Charles Maitland, you are hard work, she thought.

31

Lilin waited while the servant arranged the food into the porcelain containers and wrapped them ready to carry. She was taking lunch to Ah Teo and Zhen today. Noan was in bed, and Lilin had supervised the cooking. She had even made her own personal favourite dish, *assam laksa*, a spiced mackerel soup with thick noodles. She knew both men liked this dish, and just knowing she was cooking for Zhen gave her pleasure. Despite everything, she could not help herself. She hated him and she loved him, the two emotions so closely entwined she could not separate them.

She took her favourite *kamcheng* pot out from the cupboard. It was a deep turquoise, covered in a profusion of yellow, lime and pink symbols of longing. The symbols of beauty, wealth and status: the king of the birds, the phoenix, with its rainbow of trailing tail feathers and the luscious king of flowers, the rose-pink peony. Hovering above the peony were two bright-winged butterflies for conjugal bliss, the joys of summer, the spirits of the forefathers, a long life. Also, she knew, the butterflies near the peony meant the romantic desire of a man for a woman. She touched the two butterflies with her finger. A ring of magpies, the bird of joy, ran around the rim. The cloud-shaped *ruyi*, "as you wish" symbol of one's heart's desire, adorned the lid and the *fu*, the protective lion dog of the boodha, was its handle.

She ladled the soup into the dish with infinite tenderness. The cooks had looked in astonishment, for the sight of Lilin handling food in the kitchen was one they had never seen. When the dishes were ready, Lilin sent for Lian.

Lian was dressed in pink silk pyjamas covered in white flowers.

Her hair was plaited and arranged under a rose-and-pale-lime hat with small beaded tassels that swung around her face. Lilin had made this little hat and covered it with butterflies and peonies. Lian looked lovely, as Lilin had intended. Lian came up to her aunt with a smile, and Lilin bent and kissed her cheek. Then she took her hand, and they went out through the elaborate carved swinging doors of the house and onto the street.

The walk from Market Street to the riverside was short, but Lilin sent the servant ahead with the dishes. She and Lian wandered slowly along, and the heads of several women turned. The sight of Lilin with her niece was one which was rare on the streets, but they had heard that her sister was unwell. It was good to see her taking care of the family. There had been gossip about her for a long time, for she did not come to temple or attend the usual round of social functions. There had been malicious talk of her carrying on with white men, but no one could say for sure, and no word of this had reached her mother's ears. The husband had taken a second wife, when his first was still young and fair. Well! But then she had lost a child, and no pregnancies since. It was quite understandable. Bad luck for her to be barren, a pall on the family. They nodded as they passed, and Lilin nodded back, unsmiling.

Lilin had chosen this day and this hour to come to the quayside. She knew that the white whore had left Singapore in her ship weeks ago. She had set spies to tell her if Ah Soon or the English boy came to the river, but for a long time there was no news. She began to be worried, for she did not know how else to show Lian to this Ah Rex, as she now knew he was called. This was merely the first step in her plan. She wanted Ah Rex to see Lian, and she wanted Zhen to see Ah Rex and Lian together. Finally, today, the boy had told her that the English boy was at the river with the Malay cockle-shell boys and with his Chinese friend.

Lian skipped ahead of her, and they emerged onto the riverside. Lian knew the way to her father's godown and turned, following the servant. Lilin followed, keeping her eyes on the boats.

Then she saw him. He stood out, a European child in the crowd of Chinese, Malay and Indian coolies. Next to him she saw Ah Soon,

Qian's son. She knew he was Zhen's friend and that there was talk of Lian being betrothed to Ah Soon. Not from the men, of course, but the servants heard everything.

The boys were practising guiding the cockle-shell boats with the Malay boys, all laughing together. The servant disappeared into the godown further along the quayside to deliver the food. Lian was about to follow him, and Lilin called to her. She came skipping back, and Lian took her hand and gazed at this boy, this Ah Rex who was Zhen's son.

He was very handsome, well built, his long hair swinging around his face as he manouevred the boats. He was skilful, she could see. He was concentrating on his task of bringing the boat to shore, but suddenly he struck one of the *tongkangs*, and the boatman shouted at him and threw out a string of curses. Alex looked up and answered him in kind. Everyone burst out laughing. Alex laughed too. He did it purposely.

Then he felt eyes on him. Ah Soon was busy tying up the cockle-shell boat and trying not to get wet, and Tarun was helping him. He looked away from his friend and up towards the quayside. A woman was standing there. She was a Nonya, he knew by her clothes, a pretty woman, and next to her, holding her hand, was a pretty girl.

When his eyes met hers, he was somewhat surprised to feel a recognition, as if they knew each other. But he did not know this girl at all; they had never met. Then the woman bent and said something to the girl, and the child waved her hand at him. He smiled and waved back, and then she, too, smiled. It was a smile of radiance so brilliant that he was struck. Then he turned as Ah Soon came to his side and looked at the woman and the girl.

"That is Lian. I know her. My father and her father are great friends. That is her auntie."

They both started to make their way through the boats and up the quayside. It was time to go home. Tarun had moved off to chat with the Indian boatmen. They had been allowed to cross the river. Alex had come to Ah Soon's house for lunch with him and his father. Alex liked Ah Soon's house, so different to his own, and he liked Ah Soon's mother, who always made delicious dishes for them to eat in the quiet, shady courtyard with chopsticks, which Alex had now mastered. Afterwards they had begged to be allowed to go into the town.

Since his mother had left, he had not been to the Chinese town, and he missed it. He enjoyed the kite flying of, course, and being on the river at the Bugis kampong, but now he wanted to go over the river. Qian did not mind, for he knew that Tarun would take care of them both, and he had business himself over there with Min and later at the graveside of his father-in-law.

The festival of Cheng Beng was almost here, and he was going to the cemetery on the hill. In the tropics, plant life took over a gravesite quickly, and he wanted to see how many men would be needed to clear it, repaint the headstones and do whatever else was required. On the day itself he would come with his wife and sons, with food and drink, paper money, candles and incense. He would give money and make offerings at the temple which stood on the hillside for prayers to be said throughout the year. His father-in-law had paid for this temple, and Qian continued to be its benefactor. He wanted to show the boys how to be good, filial sons, to pay their respects to their grandfather and grandmother who were watching over them in the afterlife.

Both boys climbed up onto the quay now. Lilin moved forward, holding Lian's hand. She knew Ah Soon, who stopped and bowed to her. The English boy, too bowed, like a Chinese boy. Lilin was fascinated with him. She could see immediately that he was Zhen's son, could see exactly what Noan had seen.

Lian stood looking at them quietly. Then Lilin jumped slightly. Zhen had appeared at her shoulder. He had seen his sister-in-law with his daughter, and so little did he trust her that he had left off his work and come to the edge of the river. Now he picked his daughter up into his arms, and she smiled and turned into him and leant her head into his shoulder. Lilin took a step away, and the two boys did not move.

Zhen then recognised Ah Rex and Ah Soon, who bowed to him. He spoke to them in Hokkien, "Where is your dad, Ah Soon?"

"At the cemetery," Ah Soon said very quietly. Zhen was his father's friend, but always rather overawed him.

"Yes, yes, of course. Cheng Beng is in a few days." Preparations were under way for the Tan family gathering at the gravesite of Tan's mother and father, who were buried on the hill. The coffins Zhen had ordered for Tan and his wife had arrived. They were in the godown being prepared with tung oil. Zhen knew that this filial act was one which gave pleasure to his father-in-law. He had ordered ironwood, the hardest wood he could find.

As he was thinking of this, he contemplated Alex. Lilin watched him from beneath her lids. How could he not see? she thought. Men were entirely blind. He had said nothing to her, had not even acknowledged her presence. She knew he was testing her. She did not mind. She would be obedient, like these men wanted. It meant nothing, this outward show. She kept her eyes down. She toyed with the idea of telling him but dismissed it. Not yet. Much later, when it would be disastrous, that was the time.

Zhen was thinking very hard. This boy was Xia Lou's son. She was far away, he had learned from Qian. This was not pleasing news. Now here was her son, and such a good boy. He cast about for a way to engage him, to seek an avenue for them to meet again. "Can you play *wei qi*, Ah Soon?" Zhen asked.

Ah Soon shook his head and slipped a glance at Alex. Alex, head down as decorum decreed, smiled slightly. *Wei qi* was a game for old men. Zhen realised his mistake. This was very hard. He had no idea how to engage this boy.

Lilin moved slightly, and Zhen glanced at her but said nothing.

"May I speak, brother-in-law?" Lilin asked very low, her eyes down.

Zhen remained unmoving for a moment then nodded curtly.

"Crickets," she said. Ah Soon looked up quickly, then down again, and Alex looked at Ah Soon, frowning.

"Fighting crickets," Lilin added and both boys now looked at her.

Zhen saw it, the flash of interest in the boys' eyes. He had kept crickets too, when he was a boy. There were crickets in the market here in Singapore, but he had not thought about them before.

Zhen put Lian down and motioned to Lilin to take care of her, dismissing her. Lilin smiled very slightly.

"Shall I buy some crickets for you, good fighting crickets?" Zhen asked the two boys. They both looked up now and smiled.

"Yes please, uncle", they both said in unison, and Zhen nodded.

Tarun had noticed the conversation and approached the group. He was not afraid of the big Chinese man. His duty was to Iskandar and his friend. Zhen saw him out of the corner of his eye, knew that he would drag the boys away. Quickly he said, "Ah Soon, tell your father I will bring them to your house. Ah Rex, you will come too."

Alex and Ah Soon bowed to Zhen. He turned, taking his daughter by her hand. Lilin followed behind.

Alex watched them depart. He thought this man was magnificent. His stature, his looks, his deep calm, made him stand out from everyone on the quayside. He was happy, very suddenly, that he would meet him again. When Tarun came up, Alex took Ah Soon's hand, and laughing, they skipped over the bridge. They were chattering excitedly in Hokkien, talking of crickets and cricket fights, and Tarun could not understand. He remembered what Iskandar's mother had said about going to the Chinese town. She was quite right. All this Chinese chatter was utterly annoying. He would not allow Iskandar to come again.

32

The two crickets faced each other, their antennae waving. Qian and Zhen stood behind their respective boys and their champions. The two selected had been fed and nurtured for a week, given ground worms, mosquitos and ground nuts. Zhen had investigated the medical needs of the cricket and discovered ginseng and other potions which would enhance their strength.

The boys had discovered a lively passion for these creatures. Zhen had looked for the black-faced crickets which were said to be the finest fighters in China, but they were not available in Singapore. If he wanted them, he would have to place an order. It was expensive and would take a long time. So he had bought these two, and was glad he had.

The black-faced crickets, he had been told, would fight to the death, biting off legs, gouging each other with their powerful jaws until nothing remained. It was too much for young boys to watch. The two crickets he had bought showed a certain aggression, but one always backed down after about a minute, with little damage done.

Alex and Ah Soon loved their crickets and kept them in little bamboo cages with small dishes for water and food. Alex's was called Jinling—Golden Bell—and Ah Soon's was Zhuling—Bamboo Bell. Alex smuggled his home and kept it in his cage by his bed. Adam liked him too, and both boys played with Jinling, tickling him with a grass blade to make him sing and bringing him treats of honey.

Jinling and Zhuling, urged by the boys' prodding, began to fight, hopping forward and retreating. Zhen had discovered from the man who sold the crickets in the market that a fighting cricket should mate with two or three females before a fight, as it increased his aggression and his strength. He was not sure how he was to introduce this aspect of cricket life to the boys and rather thought he would not bother. These two cowardly crickets would serve their purpose.

Jinling took a big hop forward, and Zhuling retreated, then suddenly moved forward, biting and waving his antlers. A small tussle ensued; then Jinling retreated and the match was over. The crickets were put inside their cages and given their dinner, and the boys ran off. Zhen and Qian sat in the courtyard.

"What do you think you are doing?" Qian looked at his friend, who said nothing.

"Every other day for a week, you come here to watch two pathetic crickets put on a display of bravery which would shame a girl. Why?" Qian asked. He knew the answer, but he was not sure if Zhen did. He could not tell him his thoughts on the matter of Ah Rex. He was Charlotte's son.

"I like to spend time with the boys, you know. Ah Soon is a good boy."

Qian nodded. "Yes but I don't think it is Ah Soon you come to see, eh?"

Zhen looked over at his friend. "Perhaps not entirely. Ah Rex is an interesting boy, don't you think?"

"I think he is her child. I think he is Xia Lou Mah Nuk's child, and that is enough."

"Well, what is wrong? I like him, and I think he likes me. He speaks our language to a degree which is remarkable. He is a remarkable boy."

Qian shook his head. "He is her son, and if she finds out, she will not be pleased, I think. You take advantage of her absence."

Zhen rose. "Her absence, yes. Doing what? With whom?"

Qian stood too. "Is that it? Is Ah Rex only a means to her?"

Zhen glared at Qian. "No. Yes ... I don't know."

He began to pace the courtyard, then stopped. "No, I like this boy very much, that is all." The he turned and left the courtyard, and Qian sat down. He felt a shiver of premonition.

The day was fine, and filled with gusting wind. Alex had brought his Malay kite to show Ah Soon, and they had walked through the Chinese town and up onto the winding path to the top of Mount Wallich. Ah Soon had a Chinese kite, a red and gold dragon with a long, long, tail, and both boys were keen to show off their skills. Zhen walked behind them. It was strange to be climbing this hill, the one on which he had stood watching her ship depart, on which he had hurled his misery into the wind. The hill had no memory of his pain; it stood as a sentinel, unchanged by the feet which passed about it.

From the top, the view extended down to the town and the bay, out along the river, into the harbour and out, far into the hazy sea where the islands lay. Ah Soon and Alex looked at this view, an aspect of Singapore they had never seen before, pointing out the ships and the temples, trying to find their homes. Then they forgot it in the excitement of raising their kites. Alex was first; he had more practice, and without a thought he launched his kite. On this high hill, the wind was fierce, and it caught instantly. But it was so strong that Zhen had to run to him and hold him, for the kite would have pulled him off his feet. Zhen felt his heart pound at the thought of injury to Xia Lou's son. He put Alex to one side and got the kite under control, releasing more line, then tied the line off to a tree branch.

"The wind is too high here for you. I will set Ah Soon's kite up, and we shall watch."

Zhen launched Ah Soon's dragon kite and paid out the line until both kites were high, then tied it off. They watched as the kites soared and swooped in the high wind, pulling the lines, making them dip and turn.

They sat on a large flat rock and shared the rice rolls which Ah Soon's mother had made them.

"School tests soon," Ah Soon said to Alex in English.

"Mmm, yes, I've been studying. I shall do far better than you."

Ah Soon punched Alex on the arm, but both boys smiled.

"Is your mother coming home for your Christmas?" Ah Soon asked, then stuffed a second rice roll in his mouth.

Zhen sat perfectly still.

"Yes, thank heaven. I miss her. She has written to me to say she will come back in a few weeks. And she promises she has bought a present for my birthday as well."

Ah Soon nodded. Ah Rex was older than him by one month by the English calender, but by the Chinese reckoning it was entirely different.

"I shall be eleven years old, you know, when you are merely ten," Ah Soon said.

Both boys grinned. This Chinese way of calculating birthdays was a source of amusement to them both, for Ah Soon proclaimed seniority. The Chinese believed that the newborn child was one year old at birth and this gave Ah Soon a considerable advantage over his friend.

"When is your birthday, Ah Rex?" Zhen asked in Hokkien.

Alex swallowed his food and answered respectfully. Somehow, in some strange way, he always felt immensely respectful when he spoke Chinese, much more than when he spoke English.

"May—*si geh*—sir."

Zhen frowned. Ah Rex was born in May, and he would be ten years old. That meant he was born in 1841 by the English reckoning.

The boys rose and began to explore the hill. Zhen sat, thinking.

Xia Lou had left Singapore at the end of the tenth English month, October. She had married her husband in early December. Zhen had made love to Xia Lou for the last time all those years ago in ... He looked up. She had been pregnant when she left! Pregnant when she married her husband. He stared at Ah Rex chasing Ah Soon.

Ah Rex was his child!

Now he could see it all, written in the face of this boy. He was astounded he had not noticed it before. The boy's height and strength were so clearly his own. He stood up but felt so shaken by this discovery, he immediately sat down again.

He was glad they were playing, racing around the trees, for his mind was in utter turmoil. Then he felt a feeling of joy suffusing his chest. A feeling of joy, of parenthood to this son by the woman he loved better than any other on the face of the earth. This boy, this child of this woman, was his son. They had made this boy in the heat of love. He kept saying it over and over, silently imprinting it on his mind. The close affection he felt for Ah Rex was the natural love of a father for a son.

Xia Lou, Xia Lou. He said her name again and again. How I love you, you who have borne my son. Zhen watched him running, the beauty of his son's strong body now so very dear, so very clear. He wanted to speak to Xia Lou, desperately wanted her to return. Suddenly, he remembered, and a feeling of deep concern filled him. She was not here; she was with another. They could take this boy from him.

Zhen rose, agitated, and stared out over the vast distance of blue, hazy sea. Where are you? he thought.

33

At that moment, Charlotte was in a boat propelled by four fierce Dyak warriors, travelling upriver into the heart of the Sarawak jungle. At her side was Charles. Their party was completed by Kassim, Charles's young Dyak servant boy, and Inchi, their half-Malay, half-Dyak guide.

When Charlotte had told Isabel of her proposed absence for three days, she had expected Isabel to pout. Quite to the contrary, Isabel was happy for her to depart. She would stay with Harriette and help in the school and the hospital, she said. Harriette was delighted to have Isabel's pleasant and musical company and the arrangements were quickly made. To Charlotte's relief, Palmer and his party had departed Kuching three days before headed for the lands of Bau, where the gold and antimony mines lay.

What had begun as a pleasant outing on the river rapidly became oppressive as the river narrowed and the jungle held them, bereft of air, between its impenetrable green walls. Charlotte wondered for the tenth time that morning why she had agreed to this journey. Charles had promised her a voyage of discovery, but at that moment, fanning herself to no avail, Charlotte simply felt limp and irritated.

In two hours they arrived at Ledah Tanah, where the river divided, and Charles explained the importance of the place to the history of Sarawak. It was the very place where James Brooke had helped put down a native rebellion against the forces of the district governor of the Sultan of Brunei, who claimed suzerainty over all the lands of North Borneo. Its success had given James the territory of Sarawak to rule as his kingdom.

Charlotte looked around at the walls of green and the sluggish brown water. Whatever exploits had taken place were invisible. The heat beat at her like a fire, and she found no interest in his narrative.

They landed at a place where the jungle had been removed. A house on stilts stood here, a simple place where river wanderers might stay the night, and Kassim brought water to drink and fruit to eat. Charlotte pulled at her clothes. They were ridiculous. She never wore stays, a garment of torture she had ignored absolutely ever since living in Java, but she was wearing one petticoat too many. She longed for a simple sarong and a cool blouse. She went inside the house and took off her petticoat and her camisole. Wearing only a blouse and skirt, she felt ready to continue the journey.

Within fifteen minutes the boat turned towards shore. There was a government bungalow, Charles explained, just a short climb up the hill. He began organising food and stores. The river here was pretty with *nibong* and mountain fig, and joined by numerous streams and creeks which ran fast over a broad expanse of shallow shingle. This promised relief, and, without a further thought, Charlotte stepped out of the boat and went to it, throwing off her shoes and sitting down, fully clothed. It was a sensation she remembered from Java, from the river which ran through Brieswijk, her estate, and she lay back, eyes closed, allowing the water to run over her body, extinguishing the flames of the day.

It was Kassim's nervous laughter which alerted Charles, and he turned and saw her. Her clothes, drenched with water, were attached to her skin, and every outline of her body was delineated.

Charles ordered Kassim on up to the bungalow. Fortunately Inchi and the Dyaks had gone ahead. He went to her. Her breasts and nipples lay open to his gaze under a veil of wet, translucent cotton.

"Charlotte, for heaven's sake. You are making a spectacle of yourself," he said, his voice tense with anger. He looked away. Charlotte opened her eyes and sat up. She saw his face and looked down. She rose and pulled the wet clothes from her body.

"I had not realised. I was so hot," she said, but she was not happy with Charles's reaction. No need for such a display of offended manhood, she thought.

Charles removed his jacket and held it out to her, his eyes averted. She put it around her shoulders and walked away from him, now thoroughly annoyed. Why on earth had he brought her to this God-forsaken place? Kuching was bad enough.

When they reached the bungalow Kassim was busy cleaning the floor with water and shaking the mats. At least the structure was well made, with fine net screens on the windows and around the verandah. It was used by visitors of a scientific mind, scouring the region for the local flora and fauna, and for the Rajah's guests seeking adventure on the dark rivers of his kingdom.

Whilst the men prepared the bungalow and the fire, Charlotte watched two of the Dyak boatmen head down to one of the creeks with woven baskets on their backs. This creek was barred from bank to bank with bamboo palisades. Standing in the creek, the men began pounding the root of a plant on a log which lay above the water, crushing its juices and allowing them to drain into the creek. Charlotte could not make out what they were doing.

When Charles came up, she asked him.

"The bamboo barrier forces the bigger fish to gather. In a minute they'll all rise to the surface, stupefied. They are beating the root of the tuba plant, which intoxicates the fish."

Charlotte stood and looked down, and sure enough dozens of fish were zig-zagging around in the water before floating to the surface. The men took their baskets and scooped up the fish, filling them in seconds.

"Is it harmful, Charles?" Charlotte said, turning.

He smiled. "Only to the fish."

The bungalow was finally clean. There were two rooms. One had been prepared for her, with a thick woven sleeping mat and a grass pillow. The second room was for Charles. Kassim and Inchi would sleep on the verandah. The Dyak boatmen left a basket of fish and set off to the other side of the hill, where they had friends and relatives. They would return in one day.

Despite the netting, Charlotte lit sandalwood incense and lemon oil all around the verandah and in the rooms. Her clothes had dried on her, and as dusk began to fall, the heat went out of the day. Cool now, Charlotte, forgave Charles and began to enjoy this extraordinary experience. To find oneself utterly out of the civilised world, entirely surrounded by nature, this was a humbling thing. The hand of man had merely brushed the land here, and it was terrifying and majestic at the same time.

Charles poured a small glass of whisky for them both, and they sat watching Kassim and Inchi prepare the food. The sun was setting; an orange glow cast a halo over the forest, and a host of butterflies began flitting along the river.

Charlotte had not seen jungle cooking and watched with interest as Inchi took several banana leaves and poured rice grains onto them, then folded them into tubes. He packed the rice-filled tubes into four fat bamboo containers and filled each with water and set them upright onto the fire. The fire had been alight since they arrived and was very hot.

Next Inchi moved some hot stones into a hole, wrapped the fish in banana leaves, put them on top and covered them with a thin layer of earth. He served them on big green banana leaves, and their fingers were their utensils. It was simple, but hunger made it delicious.

After dinner, Inchi brought out his nose flute and entertained them most pleasantly for half an hour with its sweet and eerie sounds. He and Kassim were charming companions. She said good night to Charles, and as she retired to bed, Charlotte thought that all in all it had been a most exciting day of new discoveries. She was looking forward to a day spent alone with Charles exploring the streams, for he had told her there were diamonds to be found in these waters. She fell immediately into a deep sleep.

34

After a breakfast of tea, mangosteens and creamy custard apples, Charles led Charlotte off on foot up one of the streams. Within ten minutes the trees had fallen away, and limestone cliffs rose on either side of a small canyon. The walls of the canyon were covered in stone shapes of shells, leaves and small reptiles. Charlotte ran her hand over them, astounded, and turned to Charles.

"What carvings are these?" she asked.

Charles went up to her. "Not carvings but fossils."

Charlotte frowned. "What?"

"Petrified remains of things from a past age which we do not understand yet," Charles explained. He took Charlotte's hand and led her to the middle of the stream, where large stones lay in vast profusion.

"They are called *batu tikus*–rat stones," Charles said. A sweep of skeletal stone bones wound across the stream bed. "A man called Cuvier has hypothesised that they are the fossils of creatures destroyed in a great catastrophe." He shrugged. "We do not know."

Charles showed her deep holes nearby in the river bed. "Diamond diggings, abandoned," he said. They both searched in the pebbly sediment for a while, and Charles found one small yellow stone, and they laughed with pleasure. They stopped searching and drank some water and let their feet linger in the cool stream. Then they turned and retraced their steps.

As they rounded the bend and came into sight of the bungalow, they both noticed a second boat tied alongside their own with a Dyak boatman lolling in it, waiting.

"We have a visitor, it seems," Charles said, frowning, a note of displeasure in his voice.

As they climbed the hill, Charlotte looked up and into the eyes of the man she had hoped never to see again. Captain Palmer was standing looking down at her, his face impassive. She stopped abruptly and gasped. Charles looked at her and then followed her gaze. He frowned, then took her hand firmly in his, and together they stepped onto the verandah.

Palmer noticed the clasped hands, and his mouth twitched. It was impossible for Charlotte to express how much she loathed this man, and she was glad to stand just behind Charles as he greeted Palmer.

"Captain, I thought you were in Bau at the mines."

Palmer extended his hand, and Charles was forced, out of gentlemanly politeness, to drop Charlotte's and extend his own. Palmer touched his hat and looked at Charlotte.

"At Ledah Tanah I heard you were staying here. I thought I would pay my respects. I am very pleased to see you again, Mrs Manouk."

Charlotte made no pretence at politeness. She went into the bungalow and shut the door of her room. She was in a state of violent agitation. Just the presence of this man filled her with unease. She could hear them talking, Palmer and Charles, but she would not go out there. Inchi brought some hot tea, and she stayed in her room. Finally after half an hour, there was a knock on her door and she rose.

"He has gone," Charles said. He saw Charlotte was trembling, and he took her in his arms.

"It's all right. He and Helms were returning to Kuching. Helms went on ahead because he has business with Sir James."

"What is Palmer doing? Is he going back to Kuching also?"

Charlotte moved out of Charles's arms and walked to the verandah. She looked right and left, down and along the river, but Palmer's boat was gone. She sighed and sat down.

"Inchi" Charles called. "Bring some lunch."

As Inchi began to lay some dishes on the table, Charles took Charlotte's hand.

"Palmer left a companion and the other three Dyak boatmen at

Ledah Tanah to come here. They will overnight there and return to Kuching in the morning. There is nothing to worry about." Charles was trying to reassure her, but Charlotte did not feel reassured. Just the fact that Palmer was in the district, barely fifteen minutes away by boat, knowing where they were, made her feel agitated. She barely ate.

"Charles, could we go back this afternoon?"

"What is it you fear, Kitt?"

"You don't know him, Charles. He is a vicious and unprincipled man. In Batavia he was known for his cruelty to his slave women, whom he kept in abundance, though it was illegal and immoral to do so."

Charlotte looked at Charles. "He ... he ..."

"What, Kitt, what is it?"

Charlotte was reluctant to tell Charles about the incident in Java when Palmer had lured her into a lonely old Christian cemetery where he knew her Mohammedan guards would not follow. He had assaulted her and would have done worse if she had not been saved by the presence of mind of her guards, who were following outside the walls.

She could not tell him this. Charles was filled with honour. He might feel obliged to act, to challenge Palmer, and Charlotte knew Palmer would not fight fairly. And she would not tell him for another reason as well: after the incident of the wet clothes today at the river, of which Charles had so obviously disapproved, she worried that Charles might think she had somehow behaved in such a way as to incite Palmer's attack. After all, Charles had not been there—he could not know.

"I dislike him, Charles. He is a beast and capable of anything," she said at last.

Charles smiled and touched her hand. "We have no boatmen, and Kassim has gone to the Dyak village as well for the evening. They will all come back tomorrow morning. I will put Inchi on guard tonight. He will be vigilant. I'm sure there is nothing to worry about here in the Rajah's lands."

Charlotte looked around. They were alone here with only Inchi to stand guard? She could not believe it.

"Charles, you must have Inchi with you inside tonight and bar the door and windows. Promise."

Charles frowned. Charlotte was truly worried. Doubtless her dislike of this man and a feeling of isolation in the wilds of the jungle had played with her sensibilities. It was only to be understood. He thought she was overwrought, but he felt so tenderly for her, he rose, and took her into his arms.

"Don't worry, yes, I promise," he murmured against her hair. For the first time he felt like her protector, the husband he might be to her.

He took her chin and turned her face to his. He brushed his lips against hers, and she took his face in her hands and guided his mouth to hers, her lips slightly open. As they touched, he felt a great rush of passion, the feel of her lips so soft, her tongue gently against his lips. He tightened his arms around her, the inflaming image of her body in the river filling his mind, the cloth wet and clinging to her every curve, and she responded, deepening the kiss.

"Kitt," he said, when they parted.

Charlotte wanted so much more than this kiss. She felt it in the deep pulsations of her body. The awful weeds of widowhood were like chains. But she knew he would be shocked if she took him by the hand and into the bedroom and showed him what married love with her could be. She had felt the power of his response to her, and it was enough, for now. She and Charles were on the brink of something quite wonderful.

She let Palmer go out of her mind. Charles was right. Whatever had passed before, even Palmer was not so demented as to attack the guests of the Rajah for no reason, in his own land.

35

Charlotte woke to a noise. She rubbed her eyes. The room was pitch dark; the candle she had left burning had gone out. She had made sure Charles threw the latch over the wooden louvered shutters of the two small windows and the door. It left the rooms airless and hot, but she had gone to sleep reassured that both Charles and Inchi were nearby. For the first time in her life she had put her Javanese kris under her pillow.

The noise that had awakened her sounded like rats, a muffled scratching. Charlotte had a horror of rats and sat bolt upright. She felt for the candle and then stopped. There was a cry, a human cry, suddenly cut off. She rose from the bed and went to the door which joined the two rooms. A flickering light glowed faintly through the small cracks in the wooden planks. She was about to open the door when she heard another muffled groan and the sound of a whispered, hissing voice. She stood frozen. The voice was Palmer's, she was certain.

She looked around, panicked. The only exit was by the window, which stood ten feet above the ground. What was happening next door? Anxiety for Charles made her tremble, but then the noises stopped, and she moved slowly away from the door. She ran to her pillow and took the kris, then back to the door, terrified, her body flattened against the wall. She felt her heart beating out of her chest; her breath came in gasps which she tried to silence.

Nothing happened. The night was filled with the noises of frogs croaking, but no sound came from the next room. Charlotte tried to calm herself, breathing deeply, stopping the feeling of utter panic which was overwhelming her.

Suddenly the door burst open and knocked against her as Palmer entered the room. She screamed. The blow from the door momentarily stunned her, and the knife skidded away across the floor. Palmer grabbed her arm, drew back his hand and struck her so hard she flew across the room.

"How delightful to meet you again, Mrs Manouk, under such romantic circumstances. I think we have a little unfinished business."

Charlotte tried desperately to think. She felt her face on fire from his blow, but somehow, pain had heightened her senses. She could see the two men, next door, in the lamplight. They both looked dead, unmoving. She felt tears start to overwhelm her, then bit them back. She had to survive, and there was no place for tears here.

He stood looking down at her. She knew he would want to gloat, to terrify her before he did what he had come to do. Rape and murder, she was certain of that.

If he had come and thrown himself on her that minute he would have succeeded, but he did not. There was a sound, a moan from the other room, and Charlotte realised that one of the men was alive. Palmer realised as well; he turned to look and walked over to one of the bodies. Charlotte saw her opportunity: she groped around her and in a moment, felt a flood of relief. She gripped the knife and rose. Palmer was kneeling next to Charles, she could see, his own knife raised to strike a final blow. Palmer was going to finish him before turning his attention to her. She knew by the indifferent turn of his back to her that he was certain of her cowering fear, that he believed her to be waiting like one of his slave women, unable to act, to defend herself against his violence and filth. She felt a surge of fury, like a wave, rise inside her chest. She ran into the room and plunged her dagger into Palmer's neck, striking him again and again.

Palmer dropped to the floor. He twisted around to look at her, his eyes open wide with surprise. Blood was pouring from his wounds, but he lunged at her and fell heavily on his back to the floor as she moved away. Charles was bleeding, and Inchi looked dead. Palmer was still alive, breathing, she could see, blood coursing from his wounds, eyes closed. He could not live, but she needed to be sure.

A great coldness entered her, and she saw very clearly that she had to finish him.

She approached Palmer's body, her knife raised. Palmer opened his eyes and looked at her, accusing and vicious. He shot out a hand and took hold of her ankle. She fell to her knees, her body half fallen onto his and screamed in shock. He took hold of her hair with a grasp of iron. An explosion of murderous fury took hold of her and she plunged the kris into his heart, over and over again, until his hand fell limp from her head and she scrambled away from him.

She was covered in blood, her breath short and rasping, and she could do nothing but sit and look at Palmer in the yellow half-glow of the lamp. Time stood still, and she sat frozen, the flickering lamplight illuminating this scene of horror. Then Charles moved and groaned, and she woke from the nightmare and went to him.

He was injured in the shoulder and chest, his blood pooled around him. Charlotte took a sheet from the bed and wound it round him, stemming his wounds. She went to Inchi and touched him, but he was dead. She looked at Palmer's body with the iciness of hate.

And suddenly she hated this place too. She wanted to be gone. She wanted no judicial enquiry, no pointless British justice in a place where only the rule of the jungle applied. No scandal and accusations of murder. It would all be done with here, this night.

She put a cloth under Charles's head and gave him some water. He had stopped bleeding but lapsed into unconsciousness. His breathing seemed easy, though. She could not get him out of here tonight. The men would come tomorrow at dawn and take them down the river.

She would tell them of an attack. A man had attacked them all in the darkness. She had resisted and taken a blow, but she had struck him with her knife. He had fled and fallen from the verandah down the hill. She had barred the broken door and he had not returned. She had no desire for a doctor to look at the wounds on Palmer's body which spoke of her frenzy. How could they know what had transpired here tonight?

She looked at Palmer. He was not breathing, but still she had a horrible feeling that suddenly he would open his eyes and grab her hands; she stood away from him, watching his chest. After five minutes she knew he was dead. Reason entered her mind, her emotions subsided, yet she did not wish to go near him.

She took a digging stick which Inchi used and poked Palmer, first on the arm, then on the chest and head. He did not move. She found the courage to do what had to be done. With the digging stick she levered him towards the door. There, she had no choice but to take his legs and pull him through the door onto the verandah. She pulled him to the edge, shaking and panting with the effort, and pushed him off the verandah. His body crashed down the steps, rolling down the hill on the dry ground, and she heard a splash. She caught her breath and followed.

At the water's edge she pushed him into the river and watched as his body floated away on the swift current. On the voyage from Kuching, their constant and silent companions had been crocodiles. Charlotte was certain Palmer's body would never be found.

She went back into the house to await the morning. As she latched the door, a peal of thunder cracked over the bungalow, and a driving rain began.

36

On the return to Kuching Charlotte said not one word. She sat with Charles's head on her lap and Inchi's young body at her feet.

The Dyak boatmen and Kassim had arrived as dawn broke, and she had burst out of the bungalow and fallen onto the verandah with relief. Palmer had gotten into the bungalow by the simple expedient of inserting his knife between the shutters and flicking up the bar. Charles had not locked it down.

Kassim let out a great howl when he saw her and when he saw the blood-filled room. He and Inchi had been friends, and he flew to the side of the dead man and began to cry. The Dyak men, used to blood, had talked quickly amongst themselves and taken charge of the situation.

Within half an hour they were all in the boat.

Charlotte's eyes never stopped searching the water for signs of Palmer's body, but the river was swollen and churning from the night's rains, muddy and filled with branches and debris. The boatmen were incredibly skilled, riding the rapid currents and avoiding the dangers on its surface with consummate ease and courage.

The current carried them swiftly down river, and as they entered Kuching, she breathed a sigh of relief. One of the boatmen called to a Ranger at the landing place, and he set off, running fast up the slope to the Lodge.

Within minutes James Brooke, Mr Crookshank and the other men had arrived and carried Charles to the house. Dr Treacher came, and Charlotte left Charles in his care. The Rajah led her to the sitting room, and suddenly tea arrived and everything returned to normal.

Only then could she allow the tension to drain from her body. She burst into tears.

Harriette and Isabel were sent for, and she had never been happier to see two women more in her life. Her face was swollen and bruised from Palmer's blow, and Harriette sent for a paste made from the leaves of the hibiscus plant to salve it.

Thereafter began a great telling of the story. Mr Crookshank made notes but said nothing. They had all been sleeping, she said, she in one room, Charles and Inchi in the other. She woke to a noise, and the attack was underway. She had taken her dagger and opened the door. There was a low candle burning. The man had his back to her and was about to kill Charles. She had stabbed the man with her kris in the neck and back. He had flung a blow which caught her face, then had fled. She could not say who it was, but it was a white man.

Crookshank began to press her for more details. Did she know Captain Palmer was missing? Could it have been him? If so, what possible reason could he have?

Charlotte began to weep again. Palmer had visited them briefly and gone away, she said. She did not know why Palmer should do such a thing or even if it was him. She'd had not one moment of sleep since the attack. Her distress was obvious to all, and in the face of it, Harriette and Isabel both rose in unison and frowned at Crookshank. She had been incredibly brave, they told him warningly. Now it was time to let her rest.

Finally Charlotte went to her room and lay down. Though she had thought the haunting spectre of the violence might prevent her from rest, within a moment the deepest exhaustion filled her, and she slept.

She woke hours later as the sun was setting. Isabel was sitting by her bedside.

"Oh, Kitt. Are you all right?" she said. She rose and kissed Charlotte's hand.

Charlotte nodded. "Could I have some tea, Isabel, do you think?"

Isabel called the maid and ordered some tea and some fresh water.

"Charles?" Charlotte asked.

"Well enough, well enough. Don't worry. His wounds were not fatal. A wound to the shoulder and the chest, but Dr Treacher says he should recover."

Charlotte rested her head back on the pillow. Thank heaven, Charles was all right.

"You saved his life, Kitt. Everyone is talking about how brave you were. It must have been terrifying."

Charlotte put her hand on Isabel's. "I shall tell you all, but not now, dear Isabel. What of Palmer?"

"No one knows. It must have been him, but he has disappeared. Mr Crookshank has made enquiries of his ship, but he is not there, nor anywhere as we can see. It is most queer, for no one can understand why he should attack Charles and you."

The tea came, and Charlotte drank cup after cup. Her thirst seemed unquenchable. Finally she let her head drop back on the pillow and went to sleep again.

In short order the bungalow was examined, the natives questioned, an inquiry held. Charles confirmed the attacker was Palmer. But for Charlotte, he attested, he should certainly be dead. Her courage was beyond all belief. Palmer had disappeared. From his ship, witnesses attested to his vicious and violent nature. He could be volatile and unpredictable. Certainly he was capable of such an attack.

Thus, the matter was concluded judicially, but gossip and talk went on for weeks. It was the most thrilling and exciting thing to have happened in Kuching, and the small English and Malay communities relinquished the subject with reluctance. Charlotte was obliged to repeat the events so often that they had ceased to be horrific and began to feel merely like a *conte de fée*. From time to time, native sightings of Palmer were reported. He had assumed the life of a dreaded ghost. Gradually the town settled down.

Charles recovered enough to walk in the grounds of the Lodge. He and Charlotte spent hours talking about the attack. He was filled with remorse at not believing her. His dismay and her own lingering concern for him caused her to reveal more than she might have otherwise, and Charlotte told him of the assault in Java. How sorry she was not to have trusted him with this information, for it might have saved his injuries. That Palmer had returned to harm her, Charles no longer doubted. Charlotte had no remorse at killing him. She was glad his dead body had been consumed by crocodiles and glad Charles did not know.

One evening as they sat in the semi-darkness of the garden, he turned to her. "Kitt, we have survived something terrible. To do so changes a man. I think I have been annoyingly timid." He took her hand.

"Marry me, my darling Charlotte. I love you most deeply and tenderly. I cannot imagine life without you."

Charlotte took Charles's hand and put it to her lips. "Finally, Charles Maitland. I thought you would never ask."

Charles smiled, his joy glowing in his eyes. "I shall write to my brother tonight. It is a mere formality, but I must announce our prospective marriage to him and, indeed, to the Company."

"Oh, Charles, it'll take months!" Charlotte dropped his hand.

Charles took her waist in his good arm and pulled her tightly against him. "It will take three months, the time for letters to come and go. We shall be married in four. I shall have a ring made here, with Sarawak diamonds, by the clever Chinese jeweller in the bazaar, and we shall announce our engagement in one week. I shall be much recovered, and the Rajah will give a dinner. I shall see to it."

"Kiss me," he said, and she smiled and put her lips against his. He made them soft, and she put her arms around his neck and fell into the kiss. He was a changed man, the restraint and reserve gone, as if this almost deathly experience had fundamentally altered him.

"Nothing will stop this marriage, Charlotte, nothing," he said, when they had kissed. "I've never wanted anything more in my life. I know that now."

"In Batavia, then, Charles. We shall be married at Brieswijk by the English bishop. You're right. Three months will be nothing. And you will see the estate. I will make the arrangements."

Charles smiled. "Whatever you desire. You see? We need three months. I shall be fully recovered and ready for my conjugal duties to Mrs Maitland. Very ready indeed."

She laughed, delighted, full of love for him. Three months, yes. Time for her boys to get used to this idea of a new father. She would take Alexander and Adam back to Batavia, and they would see the place they were born. The wedding would be as lavish as hers had been to Tigran. They would honeymoon in the hills, at her mountain home in Buitenzorg. She could hardly wait.

37

"Oh, Kitt, it's lovely," Isabel squealed, holding her hand with the ring of three translucent, pale yellow diamonds.

Charlotte hugged her friend. The announcement of the engagement had galvanised the town. The community was small, and English and Malay alike had turned out to celebrate.

"I hear that you have some news yourself, Isabel," coaxed Charlotte.

Isabel flushed and looked towards Tomas, in conversation with Dr Treacher. She looks so well, thought Charlotte. This place, away from her overbearing mother, the centre of such adoring attentions, this has been good for her. And apparently Tomas Stahl had been even better. Harriette had confided that Tomas was smitten, and Isabel was beside herself with love for him. It was a delightful match, and one of which her mother would most certainly disapprove.

"Yes," Isabel said. "I am sorry you are leaving so soon. We plan to marry in one month, the time for my mother to get used to the idea that I am to marry a carpenter, and perhaps come here." She looked wistful.

"I am useful here, Kitt, can you understand? I love Tomas so very much, of course, but I can also do some good."

Charlotte nodded. Isabel would be happy here. She was carrying Isabel's letter to her mother and father back with her on the *Queen*. Captain Elliott was here at the grand dinner which the Rajah had prepared for the occasion. The *Queen* was waiting for her.

Now that their plans had been made, Charlotte longed to go home to Singapore and see Alexander and Adam. Letters had been few, for ships called rarely at Kuching. She felt this awful isolation. She would miss Charles terribly, but soon, very soon, they would be together. She had so much to prepare, so many letters to write. And Charles would come to Singapore in two months, his duties done in Kuching. After their marriage, he planned to return to London to address the Society. They and the children would stop in India to stay with his brother, then all go together and see England and tour Europe. The future lay bright before them all, and she was impatient to begin.

Harriette and Frank came up, and she embraced them warmly. What good friends, what stalwart people, stout-hearted and genuine. She loved them both very well. Frank was a doctor and had taken over the care of Charles, for Dr Treacher was always busy elsewhere. And Harriette had given Charlotte a little orphan monkey which had been brought to her, as a gift for Charlotte's boys.

She looked at them all. They were all so very good and brave here in this strange outpost. She was sorry to leave them, but not sorry to depart Sarawak. What had seemed, from the distance of Singapore, something rather inspired, brave and romantic, now seemed merely folly: the hot-headed dream of a man not quite grown up and his schoolboy companions.

As for the missionaries, though she loved them well, Charlotte could never quite grasp what drove Harriette and Frank to such extraordinary exertions and dangers and realised that perhaps she never would.

38

Charlotte watched the boys in the garden. The young monkey she had brought back was their constant companion. He was a delightful creature who cheekily roamed the house and garden at will, eating the fruit from the trees. He seemed to understand that he was safe only in the confines of this home and never strayed. The boys loved him, and called him "Rajah Brooke".

Alexander's examinations at the Institution had gone quite well. He had excelled in Hokkien and Malay but had done less well in English, which was somewhat worrying.

Today was the day the dhobi wallah came to attend to the washing. Tarun's wife, Jun, was gathering the sheets and covers from the beds. The delicate laundry of the household she and her sister attended to, but the bed sheets and coverlets were given to the dhobi, and Charlotte insisted on boiling. This was carried out not down on the Rochor River but on her premises. This was a practice she had learned from Batavia, and it was strictly supervised. Bugs and infestations of all kinds could result from unclean bedding. Every six months all the mattresses were burned and replaced.

From Zhen's love of cleanliness and from life in Batavia, Charlotte had seen the benefits of soap and water. The Mohammedans were particularly clean in Java, washing frequently, especially before attending mosque. In Scotland bathing was discouraged as harmful and even degenerate. Tigran, and his sister Takouhi, however, bathed frequently, enjoying the relaxing and perfumed waters. In the tropics, bathing was a physical necessity, and Charlotte simply ignored the Church's restrictions on such matters, as, indeed, she did on all such other regulations.

Charlotte was finishing a letter to Charles. She smiled. She felt in a girlish whirl of happiness. She had given serious consideration to the marriage settlement. She would settle a large sum on Charles immediately but would retain control of most of her fortune and the guardianship of her children. She had not fully discussed this with Charles, but that could wait until he returned and they officially announced their engagement here in Singapore. This was when she intended to tell Alex and Adam about Charles and their forthcoming marriage.

A sudden scream disturbed these thoughts, and Charlotte rose and went onto the landing. Jun was standing in the doorway to Alex and Adam's bedroom, her hand covering her mouth. She looked at Charlotte as she came along the landing. The sheets had fallen from her arms and lay in profusion about her feet.

Charlotte was somewhat worried. Sometimes a snake found its way into the house, usually downstairs. There had been a cobra in the kitchen once that had caused a fearful fuss. But occasionally other small creatures found their way upstairs. "What on earth is the matter?" she asked. Jun pointed mutely, and Charlotte approached the room with some apprehension. She peered around the door but could see nothing. She frowned.

Jun had gathered up the sheets and passed them to her sister. Both women were still standing staring into the room. Then, in the silence she heard a pretty sound, a chirpy cheery song.

The two Malay women stared at each other and then smiled. Charlotte looked at them.

"Sorry *puan*. My sister was frightened. I forgot to tell her about Master Iskandar's cricket. Sorry, *puan*, sorry."

They gathered up the sheets and went down the stairs. Charlotte followed the sound. Bending, she looked under his bed and there, in a small bamboo cage, she found the small culprit.

She pulled out the cage and looked at the cricket, which was still singing gaily. She examined the cage. It was beautifully made, and inside were small bowls of food and water. She shook her head and smiled. So Alex had found a cricket somewhere. Perhaps Tarun had purchased it for him. She put the cage on the bedside table and went back to her letter.

At dinner that night the boys were full of the simian Rajah Brooke and his antics. At night he was left outside in the garden. Charlotte had spoken seriously to the boys and told them she would not abide a cage. If Rajah Brooke stayed, then so be it. If he ran off into the jungle, then that was how it was meant to be. Charlotte knew, for now, the monkey was tame and happy, but as he grew he might seek the companionship of his own kind. Still, he must be free. The boys had reluctantly agreed.

"Alex, I see you have found another little pet. Your cricket half terrified the maid today."

Alex, in the middle of a mouthful of curry and rice, suddenly swallowed noisily and began to cough. Charlotte looked up at him. She knew her son. Something was amiss; she felt it instantly. Alexander had his face down into his plate, his serviette in front of his mouth. He took a drink of water and said nothing.

"He is called Jinling, Mama." Adam spoke up smiling cheerfully. Alex shot him a glance, but Adam did not see. "Ah Soon has one too; he is called Zhuling. I should like one too, Mama, when I am older. Alex says I am too young, but may I, Mama, when I am older?"

Charlotte looked at Adam and smiled. "Well, we shall see. What pretty names."

Adam took another spoonful of curry and nodded seriously.

"And where did you find Jinling and Zhuling?"

Adam waited for his brother to answer, but when the silence continued a little he spoke up. "From Ah Soon's father and his friend. They meet to have fighting matches. Alex told me."

Alex said nothing but shot a glance of annoyance at his brother. This time Adam saw it and fell quiet. He put down his spoon and stopped eating, and his face crumpled a little. He had said something wrong, he knew, but he wasn't sure what. He loved Alex and always wanted his approval.

Charlotte watched her sons. Seeing that Adam was suddenly upset, she changed the subject. "Well, well, never mind. There is fruit trifle for sweet. And after, shall we play pick-up-sticks or build a house of cards?

Adam looked up and smiled and picked up his spoon. Alex seemed to relax, and Charlotte decided to say nothing more. She knew now who had given Alex the cricket. It was Qian and Zhen. Zhen and Qian had been spending time with the boys whilst she was away. She would question Tarun tomorrow. She began to tell the boys about the Dyak warrior men and how they went on pirate raids to gather heads, and immediately the boys perked up and the matter was forgotten.

Afterwards, Charlotte thought about this matter for several days. Tarun had confirmed that the boys had gone once or twice into the Chinese town after they visited Ah Soon's house. Charlotte could not blame Tarun. She had agreed that Alex could play with Ah Soon, and she realised that this cricket business had taken place at Qian's home.

She sent a pleasant note to Qian: she understood the boys had fighting crickets. From now on she would like Ah Soon and Alex to meet at her house to enjoy this activity. If he was agreeable, they could meet every Friday after school, and she promised that they would only speak English. She had several English books for Ah Soon and his little brother.

A day or so later, when Qian received the note, he understood instantly. Xia Lou knew about Zhen's involvement with Ah Rex. She was trying to stop it without upsetting the children. He would have to speak to Zhen.

When Alex learned that he would not longer go to Ah Soon's house for the cricket fights, his angry reaction was instant and totally unexpected. Alexander was a boy who was usually in command of himself. Charlotte had never really seen his temper since he had outgrown babyhood.

"It is not the same here. You don't understand," he announced.

Alex was containing his annoyance with effort, Charlotte could see. She waited to hear him out.

"It is not the same, Mother. It is a Chinese thing, not an English thing. Ah Soon's cricket fights on his side with his father and my cricket fights for me and Uncle Zhen."

246

Charlotte's heart gave a jump, and she sat down and motioned him to sit also, opposite her. "Well, I see. I did not understand that. Perhaps you can explain it to me, Zan. Uncle Zhen?"

Charlotte's eyes grew quite narrow, but Alexander did not see. He calmed down in the face of his mother's words.

"Uncle Zhen, yes. He is a friend of Ah Soon's father. He teaches me things, Chinese things. I like him so much. He tells me about China. We speak Hokkien together and he ... well he shows me ... Oh, I don't know. I wish my father was here."

Charlotte felt her heart go out to him. He sought a father. He missed Tigran, as she missed Tigran.

Instinctively, had they found each other, these two, who were father and son? She put out her hand to Alex, and he took it, drawing close to his mother.

"I'm sorry, Mama. Uncle Zhen says that a man must control his mind. He would not like this. I got angry. It is not acceptable. I am sorry."

"I see. Well, all right Alex. If it is important to you, you can continue to have the cricket fights at Ah Soon's house."

Alex came into his mother's arms. She held him tight against her. She loved him so much, it was overwhelming. Soon she would have to speak of Charles and her marriage, but not yet.

Now, though, she must speak to Zhen. He had entered into her son's mind, somehow. It was time to confront him. Her marriage, her son, these were her own life. This had nothing more to do with him. She wrote to Qian and asked him to arrange a meeting with Zhen. As she sent this note out from her home, she was suddenly filled with a feeling of dread. But why? What had she to fear? She was in control of her life, of her fortune, of her children. Wasn't she?

39

The meeting had been arranged at Qian's home. Charlotte fixed her hat in the mirror. Her hand was shaking, and she chided herself. She had changed her dress twice. It was ridiculous. She had settled finally for a wheat-coloured silk. The boys were both at Shilah's house, visiting with their Uncle Robert. Charlotte did not even begin to question anything about Robert's family arrangements. Teresa was still at her parents' home at River Valley Road with Andrew. The new baby was fractious and difficult, and Teresa wanted her family around her.

She removed her hat. It looked English and silly. She did not especially like hats. She left her head bare, her hair arranged in a chignon. Unconsciously, she knew, she was preparing herself for him. She went downstairs quickly, not wishing to think of anything, and took up her parasol and left the house. She wanted to walk, it was not far. A pleasant walk in the late afternoon breeze.

Despite herself, she always ran her fingers along the low fence of her friend Takouhi's house, feeling her friend's presence in the wood. She crossed Coleman Street and, as always, she remembered George Coleman with love and smiled. She arrived on the corner of High Street and North Bridge Road, the corner where Qian's Chinese home dominated the street.

It was as if the years had fled. She felt those first impressions as her feet trod the streets. With each step towards him the years fell away. She felt eighteen again, her age at their first meeting. She had not set foot again in the nutmeg garden on Bukit Larangan since she had left. She did not even know if it was still there. It did not matter.

When she arrived at Qian's door, she was dangerously aware of Zhen's power and her own vulnerability. But her son's life was what was of concern here. His life and future—this alone—was the business before her now.

Upon her knock, the door swung open and a servant bowed. Qian came to greet her.

"Is he here, Qian?" she asked, and he nodded. He could feel the waves of anxiety from her. Nothing had changed. The atmosphere was heavy with their emotions.

"He is here. Do not worry. I am close by."

Charlotte put her hand on Qian's arm. He was a good friend. He bowed to her and led her to the courtyard with the green porcelain table and chairs and the gnarled old tree. He opened the double wooden doors, and Charlotte went inside. The light was muted, spilling into the courtyard. Zhen was seated at the table. He did not rise as she entered but merely looked up at her.

His eyes were hooded, expressionless. She knew him well enough to know how well he hid his feelings. He raised his hand and indicated the chair opposite him. Charlotte felt her temper rise. She was not his chattel to order about. She did not move, but her heart was pounding. She shook her head a little, annoyed at herself. Why did she let him have this effect on her, as if he owned her?

Zhen picked up the small teapot and poured golden tea into the Chinese cups decorated with peonies and butterflies of turquoise and rose.

"Once you liked drinking tea with me," he said, and her heart missed a beat.

She knew what he was doing. Peonies and butterflies symbolised married bliss. He had married her that evening long ago with a ceremony of tea. He was reminding her of the many times when he had made her tea, before making love, after making love. Tea was connected inextricably to love of him.

She had to sit. She almost feared more that he would rise and come and stand next to her. So she sat, the table between them. The teacups remained untouched.

Zhen put his hands together on the table. He had elegant hands, the nails perfectly groomed, strong hands but with a delicate lightness.

Charlotte stopped looking at his hands. That was enough. "You are spending a great deal of time with my son and making him presents. Why?" she demanded.

"Because he is my son too."

Charlotte gasped and opened her eyes wide, looking directly into his for the first time. He gazed at her, willing her to deny it. Her eyes had such depth, like the still waters of a lake, filled with changing colours. He felt his body's reaction to her, the need to fall into the depth of her eyes. Every impulse told him to rise and take her into his arms, kiss her until she lost her will, but he stopped this feverish thought and waited.

Charlotte tore her eyes away from his. She took up the tea and drank. Her throat felt parched. Slowly she put down her cup and said, "Why do you say such an extraordinary thing?"

"Because it is true. Because I know the dates. Because he looks like me."

Charlotte had no answer.

Zhen softened his tone. "He is our son, Xia Lou. Made by our passion, and I love him."

Charlotte looked up. "Oh, Zhen," she said. She wanted desperately to go to him and fall into his arms and tell him, "Yes, yes." She'd cried a million tears when Alex had been born, desperate for him to know this child was his child. Now she was terrified, not knowing what he meant to do.

She took a deep breath. "Very well. Yes, he is your son. But he can never know."

Charlotte looked into Zhen's eyes. "He can never know, you understand," she said fiercely. "It would destroy him."

Zhen rose, and Charlotte gasped. He stood looking down at her. "Destroy him? To know his own father?"

Charlotte stood too, defensive. "Tigran is his father. A great Dutch merchant is his father. Not a Chinese merchant, a Dutch one. It is everything to Alex. He remembers Tigran. He has two aunts, half sisters and half brothers in Batavia. Adam shares his blood. He is the heir to a great fortune and a great name. That is what he knows."

"He is half Chinese," Zhen said, anger rising in his voice.

"He is not! He is English. An English boy who speaks Chinese. God help me, I wanted him to speak Chinese. Because, because ..."

Charlotte stopped. "Because he is your son, too," she whispered.

Zhen took two steps. Before she could move, he took her waist in his hands and lifted her into the air, holding her above him. She looked down at him. It was as if the years flew away. They were eighteen again, in the nutmeg orchard.

"A son, thank you, *xiao baobei*, my little treasure."

She took his face in her hands, and he lowered her face towards his, taking her waist in one arm and pulling her into his body. Their lips were almost touching, but he did not move, waiting for her to close the tiny gap.

If she did it, Charlotte knew, she would be utterly lost and so would Alex. Her mind flew to Charles. She pulled away, pushing against his shoulders, and he lowered her to the ground.

"I am engaged to be married," she said, and his hands fell away from her instantly and he took a step back. She tried not to think about the trembling his touch had brought upon her. She had to end this meeting as quickly as possible.

"You cannot tell Alex, for it would crush him. At the moment, I think, he loves you. You are his uncle. Maybe in some way he feels a kind of connection to you. I don't know, and I'm sure he doesn't know either. If you want to see him, spend time with him, I will agree, but you can never tell him."

Zhen's usually well-controlled mind was in turmoil. She was going to marry? The soldier, the one at the bay.

"Marry?" he said, and Charlotte realised he had not heard what she had been saying.

"Yes," she said and told him a colossal lie. "We will stay in Singapore. You will see Alex, spend time with him, but he can never know. If you want to see him, he can never know, or I will take him away."

Zhen turned away from her and went back to the table. He sat and picked up the teacup. He did not want to look at her. She was planning to marry the English soldier, to lock herself away from him irrevocably, and, at the merest whim, she would have the power to take his son away. The joy of a moment before was extinguished utterly, and for the first time he felt a cold dislike of her.

He rose and threw the cup across the courtyard with such force it smashed into a thousand pieces. Charlotte gave a cry. He looked directly into her eyes.

"As you wish," he said coldly and raised his hand in imperious dismissal.

Charlotte felt her heart crumple. The shattered cup told her everything. What had been between them was broken. She had not known what to expect, but this frightening, icy acquiescence was filled with pain.

She turned, close to tears, and went through the doors. She knew he would never want to meet her again, and the feeling was like dropping into a deep dark well.

40

Noan was lying in her bed. The maid had left. Her hair was brushed, and she was in her nightdress. It was of soft, white muslin. The room was cool. It had rained, and the windows to the air well stood open, a fresh breeze blowing the curtains. The pregnancy was almost at an end, she could feel it. The baby was low; it would not be long now. She was glad. This child had tired her out. It would be good to be rid of this weight at her belly. She knew the midwife had moved into the house, downstairs, readying for the birth. Someone had told her.

She did not stir. She felt as if she could not move her body at all. But her mind was working. She was unwell; she knew it. She opened her eyes. Sometimes her vision became blurred, which frightened her, but now it seemed all right. Her face was too red, her ankles had become very puffed, and she had gained so much weight, much more than with her last pregnancies. She remembered looking at herself in the mirror and thinking, I am only twenty-three, but I look so old.

She thought about what Lilin had told her. Her sister, she knew, had meant to hurt her, but somehow she could find no hatred for her. Lilin was the most suffering girl, deeply and desperately unhappy. Noan could not quite understand why, but she knew it had to do with love. It had always had to do with love. She did not love her husband; perhaps she had loved another, who could say? Lilin's life was so chaotic. Fortune seemed at first to have smiled on Lilin, giving her beauty, intelligence and liveliness. Noan had sometimes envied her as a child, for she was not the lovely one, she knew, though her father had loved her so well.

Her father had been unwell. She wanted to give him this child, and she longed for it to be a boy. She knew it would be a balm for his heart: a grandson, finally, to carry on the family, carry out the rites.

No, not the pretty one, but she had received a gift, an unexpected gift. She had been married to Zhen. He had given her joy and pain—no more, she supposed, than most women experienced. She loved him utterly. She stared deeply into her mind and read there this love of him which sustained her. He did not love her like that, she knew. He loved the woman, the white woman who had given him a son.

Lilin's words reverberated in her brain. Noan could be sure that when this birth was over he would not come to her again. She had better expect to see very little of him in the house and almost certainly never again in her bed. Their father was ill. He had passed his businesses to Zhen. Zhen was the head of the house now, and nothing would stop him doing exactly as he wished. He would take this woman, this white whore, as his concubine.

Lilin had spat these words out, the spittle of venom landing on the table which separated them. Noan had become accustomed to Lilin's attacks, her constant ravings about Zhen. But this time, something felt true. He had a son by this white woman. Noan had not given him a son. She could not be sure, despite the birth predictions, that this child was not another girl. Her fear, her greatest fear, was real. A concubine. Another woman had given Zhen a son. Once a man took a concubine, he never came to his wife again. Suddenly everything had come crashing down for her, like a house that had been lashed by storms and resisted as long as it could. Finally the tempest had arrived, and there was nothing to hold up the crumbling foundations.

She had collapsed. Lilin had sprung up and around the table, supported her sister, afraid, suddenly, horrified at her words. The maids had come and carried Noan to her bed. The midwife had been sent for and her mother had rushed back to town.

The herbalist came and gave her acupuncture and herbal drinks. The maids bathed her and kept her clean. Her mother cried softly at her bedside, but she could not do anything about it. She saw it but could not respond. When she was awake it was as if she was asleep and dreaming.

Zhen came and sat at her side, took her hand, but it seemed as if she could not see him. Against objections he sent for the English doctor, Dr Little. His examination, difficult and cursory, in the presence of her suspicious and hostile mother, nevertheless established her state of health. She seemed well, though the swelling in her legs was not a good sign. Her breathing, however, was unconstricted, her pulse a little fast perhaps, but the baby was alive. He estimated labour onset within a few days.

If the maid raised her and offered her food, she ate, she drank water. But otherwise there was almost no reaction. She seemed, he reported to Zhen, well ... stupefied.

Zhen did not understand. Dr Little explained, there were cases when a patient responded to nothing—febrile negativism, it had been called. No one was sure what caused it, but cases of shock, a terrible experience perhaps. This science was in its infancy. Was there anything like that?

Zhen had shaken his head. He did not know what was happening.

Then, unexpectedly, Lilin had asked to speak to him.

Zhen hesitated. He viewed Lilin with constant and unremitting suspicion. Her actions towards him were always inappropriate and alarming. Her stubborn and shameful actions to her husband were beyond anything. Her attitude to her parents was unfilial. She was the cause of constant concern and worry to everyone. If Zhen could truly say he hated anyone, it would be Lilin. In China, Ah Teo, with such a wife, would have been justified in selling her or returning her. No one would have blamed him. But here in Singapore, to whom could she be sold or returned? She had never left her own family.

Though suspicious of her motives, he agreed and met her in the courtyard. Lilin looked different; that was what he first noticed. She wore no paint on her face, her skin was washed and clean. She was dressed conservatively, in a long *baju* and sarong. Her hair was neatly arranged. This transformation was extraordinary, but Zhen believed nothing.

She sat across the porcelain table from him and lowered her eyes. Modesty, he thought, and looked at her more sharply.

"Thank you, brother, for meeting me. I wish to speak about

Noan." She did not raise her eyes. He remained silent.

"Your wife thinks that you will leave her after the birth of this child."

Zhen said nothing, waiting, knowing now that she was responsible, yet again, for catastrophe in this house. He wanted to rise and take her and break her neck, but he sat impassively, waiting.

Lilin realised that Zhen was not deceived by her changed appearance and became slightly afraid. She decided that honesty with a touch of emotion would be the best course of action.

"I was jealous of Noan," she confessed. "I said things I should not have said. She is pregnant, and I was jealous. I have lost a boy, a son."

Zhen did not react. Lilin kept her eyes resolutely down.

"Please forgive me. Speak to Noan. Reassure her. In return I will stop my wild ways. I will be obedient, return to the family—help take care of the children."

Lilin looked up suddenly and saw Zhen's eyes on her. She felt a thrill, the old thrill, the old and never-ending desire for him. But she lowered her eyes again quickly. "Please help her. I beg you. Please forgive me."

Lilin spoke in Baba Malay. Zhen's proficiency in this language was much better. He understood most of what she said. But he did not trust her. He narrowed his eyes, thinking. He could do little to bring this woman under control. Confinement had not worked. She had made the lives of her relatives, her husband and her parents' miserable. But if she calmed down, if somehow she felt contrite. He was not convinced, but what alternative was there? And she had admitted her evil towards his wife. Now he could try to help Noan.

Zhen realised, with a sudden clarity, that he loved Noan. Not like Xia Lou, of course, that was impossible. But in a deep way, Noan was his wife, the woman who made his life comfortable, who strove to please him, to cook the food he liked and make him at home in this house where he had been a stranger. She had given him three children whom he loved, and now a fourth was waiting to come. Waiting to come, and Noan unresponsive. The thought was chilling, and he rose. Noan needed him, needed to wake from this horrible place, give birth to their child.

He stood looking at Lilin. She did not move, her face looking resolutely at the floor. His presence was always a powerful excitement. She sensed him, standing, looking down at her, and wanted to fall at his feet, then kiss them, crawl up his body, wind her arms around him, feel his skin on her skin. But she sat, trembling inside, waiting.

"You will obey your husband. You will obey your father. You will obey me. You will go to your room now and stay there until I tell you to come."

Lilin nodded her head. How predictable was his response. Everyone would be delighted at her obedience. These men—that's all they understood. Tacit obedience. Her mistake, she now realised, was open rebellion. The appearance of obedience was all they required. Why had she not understood this years ago? She was bored with it, this constant struggle against them, bored with Gaston, whose wife had decided to return, bored with that life.

Zhen would help Noan, and the thought gave her great relief. For the first time in her life, Lilin wanted something for someone other than herself. Whatever revenge she wreaked on Zhen, she did not want anything terrible to happen to Noan. She understood this now, quite suddenly. She felt regret.

She let her head droop unconsciously, in an expression of sadness. Zhen saw it and felt the honesty of the movement. He looked at her for a moment and then moved away, towards the bedroom.

Lilin rose, watching him climb the stairs, his body lithe and supple. The emotion of a moment before evaporated. But her resolution remained. She went to the nursery where Lian was sleeping and bent her head and kissed her pretty pink cheeks.

Zhen closed the door quietly behind him. This bedroom was where they had been married. He looked at Noan, lying silently on the bed. He had tried to be a good man to her. Perhaps he had not been the man she wanted. Zhen knew well how Noan felt about him, but his heart had always lain elsewhere.

He went up to the bed and took off his jacket. He lay behind Noan and took her into his arms, cradling her. Though she was unresponsive, he began to kiss her neck and shoulders, touching her gently with his hands. She was swollen, not only her belly but her feet and ankles. He felt a great compassion for her.

"Noan, Noan, soon we will have another child."

He kissed her gently, nuzzling her neck. She felt him move next to her, but still it was as if she was dreaming him.

"You bring me joy. Boy or girl, it will bring me joy. And we shall make more children, many more." Zhen caressed her belly.

"Lilin is cruel. An unhappy, cruel woman. Do not believe what she says."

Noan lay still, unresponsive. It was as if she could not hear.

Zhen turned her to face him. Her face was red, bloated. He knew there was something terribly wrong. He put his hand on her belly and felt the movement of the child.

"Tomorrow I will bring herbs for you to drink. But you must wake up." He took her face in his hands. Her poor, bloated face. "Wake up, Noan."

He remembered that Xia Lou loved it when he kissed and nibbled her lips, as if she was sweet sugar that he could not resist. He touched his lips to Noan's and began to kiss and bite gently, the lower lip, the corner of her mouth, taking her lips in his softly, sucking and nibbling. He put his hands in her hair and held her.

Noan realised, suddenly, that she was not dreaming. She opened her eyes and looked into his, and awoke from that long trance. He smiled at her and continued kissing her until she raised her arm and put it around his neck.

"You," she said hoarsely, keeping her lips on his, "you will not go to the ..."

She stopped, confused. Zhen continued to hold her hair with his hand, firmly, keeping her head near his, kissing her lips and cheeks.

"Ssshh," he murmured. "Nothing will change for us. You are my wife. I am a man of the Tao, Noan. Your joy is my strength."

The reverie dissipated like clouds in the wind. Zhen did not lie. She pulled his lips to hers, crushing his lips to hers and he held her tight, kissing her. Noan sighed, touching his face.

"My head, it hurts so much. Husband, I ..."

Without warning she fell back, and her eyes closed. At the same time, her waters broke and Zhen felt the sudden wetting of the bed. He rose, horribly alarmed, and went to the door, calling the maid. Within a few minutes the midwife had arrived, and he was bowed out of the room and the door closed.

Nothing was ever told to him of that terrible night. The midwife never spoke of finding Noan in a swoon, her contractions started. Nothing could revive her. For an hour they tended her, bathing her body, the midwife feeling the contractions. And then, without warning, Noan had convulsed, her body shaking violently. Her head had jerked up, and her breath rattled in her throat, and then she had simply stopped breathing.

The midwife's apprentices were thrown into a panic, whimpering, their eyes wide with fear. Evil spirits had entered her body, surely. They trembled and moved away from the bed. But the midwife had seen it all before. The awful bloating was a symptom of something very wrong. She had seen many women in this state, and few survived. It was too common to be a cause even of horror any more. The mother was dead. Now only the child could be saved, and by saving the child, they would save the mother too, from a life of eternal damnation.

The midwife had sworn severely at her helpers. She ordered one to immediately inform Noan's mother and send for the undertaker and priests. She took out her instruments and made a long cut in the abdomen and released the child. Within seconds the baby let out a lusty scream. The midwife slipped a necklace of red woven cords and a dragon pendant of red jade over the baby's head. This would ensure that the soul of the child would attach itself to the necklace and not to the cord, which she quickly cut. The birth was over. The child was born, and the mother was dead. The child was bundled up and removed instantly from the scene of death.

The midwife sewed up the body, chanting incantations, keeping the spirit at bay. Everyone knew that the newly dead were confused and would search instinctively for a living body to enter. One of her helpers banged a gong. Spirits disliked loud noises more than anything. The two others, intoning incantations, quickly cleaned up the blood, dressed the corpse and moved her to another room. Noan lay on a mat, a yellow cloth covering her face, her body covered in red cloth, with silver bank notes to ease her passage. Spirit money was burning in urns on either side of her. Two priests entered the room, sprinkling realgar wine about the floor, lighting incense, pasting paper cuts of Zhong Qui, the dispeller of demons, on the door lintels and windows, surrounding the body with red candles. Soon the undertaker would come and the body would be ritually washed and prepared for the coffin.

The priests began banging a small gong and shaking the bells, intoning the Sutra of the Bloody Pond. A cockerel was brought in and its throat cut swiftly; the blood flowing onto the floor, helping to rescue Noan from this *xue hu yu*—court of the bloody pond— the destination of women who died in childbirth.

Noan's mother stood looking down at the dead body of her child. Her beloved first child. She did not care that she should not touch the body, which was impure and full of the pollution of death. She knelt and took Noan's hand from under the cloth. Tears sprang to her old eyes. She had loved this little firstborn, her obedient child who prayed for her parents, her husband and her children. But, thank the gods, Noan had given birth to a son. Now her soul would not be trapped in the bloody pond. The midwife had known of the gravity of this birth, had made sure the child was born quickly. She was grateful to this woman. Now Noan would not return as a Jiang Shi, a vampire, her soul wandering the earth. In three years when her bones were disinterred, there would be a ritual—the breaking of the bloody bowl—and the son would drink red liquid, symbolising his mother's blood. He would free his mother from this hell, and she would be reborn.

Noan's mother tied the amulet containing the Sutra of the Bloody Pond and the Lotus Sutra to her daughter's wrist and put her cheek onto the cold hand and cried for joy at this blessing. Then she rose and returned to her husband and her son-in-law.

Baba Tan and Zhen were in the sitting room. They had both known since the girl had been sent out, for all the family was present in the house. Tan had not moved since hearing this, the sounds of the gongs reverberating faintly from above. His daughter was dead. A grandson had been announced, but this joy was suddenly eclipsed.

His health was waning; he could feel it. A few short years ago he had felt like a young man again with the nubile young concubine. He was only forty-three years old now, but a bout of fever had laid him low, and he had not fully recovered. The death of Lilin's son had affected him in strange ways. He had never shown his grief at the death of that baby boy. It was forbidden to show the slightest emotion at the passing of a very young child. If a child died it was *yao shou*—deprived of longevity. To die so young meant an infection, an evil spirit. But somehow, he had mourned him quietly, inside. Now, Noan, his favourite child. He sank into the chair and said nothing.

Zhen, too, was sitting in a chair, his head lowered. He could hear the servants moving with quiet efficiency, covering the mirrors, any glass, with red paper. The gods on the altars were covered in red cloth. The rituals of death were swift, for time was of the essence, before the miasmic pollution of mortality could take effect.

Not Noan, he thought. Sweet Noan. He felt turned to stone. His philosophy should accept her death as a natural movement, her soul passing into the infinite, the birth of his son a completion of a circle. Master Zhuang said that death and life are destined; heaven lies in the constancy of morning and evening. But at this moment he could not find comfort in that idea.

Noan's mother looked at these two men, the most important in her life. Her husband: she had tried to honour him as was her obligation. She had given him children, not sons, of course. Not sons, but daughters, and her first daughter had married well. Her son-in-law was truly a son, for he would carry out the rites for them when they died.

She saw her husband had lost strength. He had sought a new woman to confirm his virility, his continuing power as he aged. What creatures were men. They had few burdens. They had no need to find strength to cope with the vicissitudes of life. Women carried these burdens for them. In life and after death, women kept the spirit of the family alive. A thought, never before contemplated, entered her head. In strange ways, men, who were supposed to be the heart of the family, actually meant very little. They made children, they brought money, but in every other important way they were irrelevant. Men could not find the strength in death, for they had not the fortitude to give life. The women carried both burdens. Her husband could not cope with this, but she must.

She went up to Zhen and bowed before him. "Please go to buy water from the river," she said quietly.

Zhen looked up. He did not understand. His knowledge of funerary rites was very poor.

"Sorry, honoured mother," he said. "I do not understand."

"Water," she said. "You go to the river, to the spring, and gather two buckets of water. A servant will go with you."

She held out her hand. In it were two coins. "Pay the river god for the water."

Zhen took the coins and stared at them.

"One bucket is for you to wash your son. His first bath must be by his father."

Noan's mother swallowed and stopped briefly, checking her emotion. "The other bucket is to cleanse your wife."

Zhen looked up. Noan's mother had known this man for six years. The small revelation which had struck her a moment before she put to one side. Zhen was an exemplary son-in-law, had become a son, for he had taken their name. He was a man who acted with circumspection, wisdom and good sense. He was beloved by her husband, she knew, and treated her with every respect. He had been a good husband to Noan, given her children, now a son, which had saved her, which redeemed her soul. In all that time she had never seen him betray the slightest emotion. But her heart softened now as she saw tears come to his eyes.

Zhen rose quickly, holding the coins in his fist and left the room. Zhen did not go to the river, though. He went to the spring, one of the small springs which ran at the base of Bukit Larangan. This water was at its purest here, emerging untouched from the earth. He knelt before the spring bubbling between two rocks. He cupped his hands and took the water into them, watching it move over them in an unceasing stream, over the coins which lay there. He cast the coins into the lower stream and watched them tumble away, then put the water to his mouth and drank, running his hands over his face. There was no sense in this death of Noan. It was as random as her birth.

"*Life follows upon death. Death is the beginning of life. A simple transformation from being to non-being, from Yang to Yin.*" The words of Master Zhuang echoed in his mind. He wiped obstruction away. He watched a water drop glint in the sunlight and fall slowly from his hand. Noan had reentered the great river. She was not locked in some ghastly hell, as he knew her mother believed. She was free, soaring like the wind over the treetops, flying with the water over rocks. His son had been born. "*Life follows upon death.*"

He called the servant to bring the pails, filled them and turned back to the house.

41

Noan was gone, buried on the hill near her grandparents.

The men had gathered to consider the family arrangements. Zhen had three girls and his baby son, Kai.

The boy and two of the girls would be raised at River Valley with Tan's own young children, supervised by their grandmother. Lian, Zhen's second daughter, would be given to Lilin. She had no child, and her behaviour had improved so much it was deemed suitable for her to take this child for her own. Zhen had little say in this matter. Baba Tan, having lost his eldest daughter, was adamant that his second must have the dutiful affection of a child.

Ah Teo made no objection. He was happy to be rid of Lilin. His second wife had given him a son and was pregnant with another child. Lilin was given a residence, a new house on South Bridge Road. Zhen had made it clear he would not share a house with her. The Market Street house was put up for rent and quickly taken by a Spanish merchant for his wife and growing family. Zhen moved into his shophouse on Circular Road, glad to be done with the painful memories of the mansion.

Zhen felt deeply mistrustful of Lilin. But his children must be cared for, and Lilin had proved contrite, and Zhen knew that Lilin cared for Lian in a way she did not for any of his other children.

Zhen knew what lay ahead. Endless proposals by the matchmaker for suitable brides. Even Baba Tan would not be immune to her blandishments. Zhen was young and very eligible. There were scores of young daughters of Chinese merchants scattered throughout the whole of the South Seas for whom he was a most desirable match.

Merchants who could add great wealth and influence to the Tan house.

Lilin's anguish at her sister's death rapidly dissipated. She entered her new home, her hand in Lian's. She smiled. From today her whole life would be dedicated to one thing. To raise Lian to distrust men, to groom her beauty to entrap just one man, Zhen's son Ah Rex, and to destroy Zhen and his English bitch.

Ah Rex was soon to be ten years old, and Lian was just eight. Today, with Lian under her power, she would start to tell the little girl stories about boys, how one special one was waiting for her and begin to plant the seeds of mistrust for all but Ah Rex.

She would begin the dedicated task of teaching Lian English. For this she had to consult Zhen. She had already engaged the services of a Eurasian clerk and planned to pay him well for his abilities, but she dared not do it without Zhen's approval. To get this she had to plant the seed in his friend Qian's head. Only this way, if Zhen thought it came from Qian, would it have any hope of success.

She approached Qian at his godown. Lian was missing her sisters, so she was spending a day or two at River Valley. She had cried for several days, but Lilin had cuddled her and played with her, and together they had walked along the bayside at Telok Ayer, and she had bought Lian a pretty hair pin and told her she was Auntie's special girl.

Gradually, Lilin knew, Lian would grow to love this undivided attention. And Lilin liked it too. It was good to spend time with her pretty little girl who turned heads when they walked together. Instead of sharp gossip, now Lilin reaped praise.

Qian received Lilin coolly. He knew her reputation, knew of all the havoc she had caused the Tan household.

"I should like English lessons for Lian," she said to Qian, adopting a tone of modest petition. Lian was promised to Ah Soon. Would it not be well for his son's future wife to have some knowledge, to assist him in his life? Ignorant women made ignorant children. Qian's own wife, it was well known, was clever and shrewd. Many went to her for advice. She was a credit to Qian's reputation. Lian could be such a credit to Ah Soon. Would Qian consider it and speak to Lian's father?

Despite himself, Qian was pleased at her words, for there was truth in them. Swan Neo was clever, and Qian's household was one of efficient and tolerant harmony. Despite, or perhaps because of, the unusual nature of his domestic arrangements, he admired Swan Neo and was glad she was at his side.

He told Lian he would broach the subject with Zhen, and several days later, Lilin had her answer: Zhen did not object. She smiled. Whilst they imagined Lian was destined for Ah Soon and she was respectfully obedient, they would grant her any reasonable wish.

Now she had merely to think how to get Ah Rex's trust and bring these two children together.

42

Charlotte spent the next weeks planning her wedding. She had written letters to Scotland and Batavia. She tried desperately not to think of Zhen and their dreadful parting. When she felt optimistic she thought it just as well that they might never meet again.

When she felt lonely, she felt despondent.

Charles, she thought, it is time for us to marry and to leave this town. Only then will I begin to forget.

In the meantime Charlotte had kept her word. Alex and Ah Soon were permitted to play games with crickets with Uncle Qian and Uncle Zhen. She allowed Alex to spend time in Baba Tan's godown with Zhen, helping with the merchant business. She knew Alex liked to be by the quay. Tarun had taken Adam with him once or twice, but her younger son's Chinese was not fluent, and Adam had quickly tired of these trips. He much preferred his English school friends, English games and Malay companions, to the rough and tumble of the riverside.

But Alex loved it and loved his Uncle Zhen. For Alex, Zhen always had time, to show him the godown and how it worked, to take him upriver to the sago factories, to fly kites on the hill, to tell him of his own childhood growing up in China, to fill him with legends and tales of his homeland.

The days went by in a monotonous regularity of heat and rain. Charlotte had received a letter from Aunt Jeanne, announcing her departure from Scotland and her great joy at Charlotte's remarriage. Charlotte had arranged everything through an agent in Aberdeen. Both she and Robert agreed it was time for their aunt to come and see them and their children. Charlotte was looking forward to spoiling her, showing her Singapore and her great estates in Java.

She was sitting in the garden, attempting to determine where Jeanne might be now. The Peninsular and Oriental Steam Navigation company would carry Jeanne from London via Gibraltar to Alexandria. Thence the passengers travelled Mr Waghorn's route down the Nile from Cairo to Luxor to view the ruins, then across the desert by camel train to the Red Sea port of Quesir. From there a ship went to Pointe de Galle in Ceylon.

The final part of Jeanne's journey was on the *Lady Mary Wood*, which carried mail and passengers from Ceylon to Singapore and Hong Kong. How much this journey had changed since her own, a mere ten years ago! It was nothing short of wondrous. What had been long, dangerous and fearful was now short, enjoyable and romantic.

She looked up as Robert walked quietly over to her table and sat down. "Robbie," Charlotte said, surprised to see him.

Robert said nothing, and Charlotte frowned. She rose and went to him, kissing his forehead, pushing away a stray lock of his hair. Robert put his arm around her waist and pulled her into him, holding her. Charlotte knew something was very wrong.

"Teresa knows," he said simply, his voice muffled against her dress.

Charlotte stroked his hair and was silent a moment, thinking of her words.

"It was inevitable, Rob. People talk. Women talk. The da Silva women are numerous, and all watch each other's business. It was only a matter of time."

Robert released her. "Teresa asked me straight out. She said I must choose. She was planning to come back to Beach Road next week with Andrew, but she told me she would not bother if I was going to continue with what she called a "disgusting affair".

Charlotte regained her seat opposite her brother. "I see. What do you intend to do?"

"I don't know. Apparently it has come by some mischievous means to the ears not only of Teresa but of Butterpot, and he has called me to make an account. I am to present myself after his return from Prince of Wales Island next week."

Charlotte nodded calmly, but she was alarmed. Robert had recently been appointed as Superintendent of Police for Singapore. After a year of the increasing and freakish eccentricities of a Mr Hammond, appointed by the Indian government to this post as well as that of Police Magistrate, his doings, reported widely in *The Free Press*, had caught up with him and, following an outcry, Hammond had been recalled. Robert had finally received long-overdue justice.

Now though, if the Governor was calling Robert to account it was very serious. If Butterworth considered Robert's behavior immoral and harmful to his office, Robert could lose his hard-won position and status in Singapore.

"Rob," she began, unsure what advice to offer. She had not fully formulated her thoughts when Malik came into the garden and stood by her side and she looked up. "What is it, Malik?" she said irritated at the interruption.

"Reverend Moule is here to see you, Memsahib," Malik said with the utmost dignity.

Charlotte frowned, looking to Robert. He shrugged. Reverend Moule was pastor of St. Andrew's Cathedral. Charlotte met him from time to time at dinners and church functions, but he had never called on her.

"Doubtless he wants a contribution of some sort," she said as Malik disappeared to fetch the prelate.

Moments later Henry Moule appeared on the lawn, trailed by Malik. Robert rose to greet him. The two men had cordial if distant relations, Moule could be long-winded and pompous.

Today Henry looked immensely pleased at seeing Robert and shook his hand vigorously. "I'm so very glad you are here, Robert. So very glad." He mopped his brow with a large handkerchief, then bowed over Charlotte's hand. She motioned him to sit and asked Malik for refreshments.

"Reverend, to what do I owe the pleasure of this unusual visit?"

"Forgive me, ma'am, for not calling on you before. You are not a frequent visitor to the church, and I do not like to impose. On occasion it has given offence."

Moule might have continued in this vein for some time, but a thought seemed to cut him short. "Mrs Manouk, I come to you today as the bearer of sad news. Please prepare yourself."

Charlotte half-smiled. Prepare herself indeed! Was the church fund in grave need? Was God not in his heaven and all not right with the world?

"Ma'am, I have received a communication from Mrs Harriette MacDougall in Sarawak. She did not feel able to write to you directly and has asked me to convey the contents of her letter."

Charlotte was growing annoyed. Harriette could not write to her directly, when they corresponded regularly? What nonsense was this?

"Well," she said, "go on."

"Mrs Manouk, Harriette has asked me to convey her deepest sadness at the death of your fiancé, Charles Maitland. God bless his eternal soul."

Charlotte rose as if pulled from her chair by a mighty force. She looked down at Henry Moule, her face filled with alarmed misapprehension. She could not have heard right. "What?" she said, shaking her head.

Robert rose quickly and came to her side.

Henry rose too. He threw a beseeching look at Robert, who took his sister's waist in his arm.

"Mrs Manouk, Charles died one week ago. He seemed well recovered from the wounds of his attacker, with only the occasional lapses, but succumbed to a sudden and violent fever. Reverend MacDougall strove with all his skill to save him, but he died on Monday last."

Moule took a letter from his pocket and put it on the table. "Harriette has sent this letter. Charles's last words were for you. Please accept my deepest condolences, and if I may offer you any spiritual comfort, the church is always open to you."

Henry bowed deeply and departed quickly. Charlotte stood looking at his receding back, then shook her head, standing silently. Robert dared say nothing. He held her and when, suddenly, her legs failed, he helped her sit in the chair.

Charlotte tried to understand this. Charles was dead? Charles, her Charles, the man she was going to marry. The man she was ready to love to the end of her days. This man, was it? There must be some mistake.

Robert waited. He drew his chair near Charlotte's in alarm. Her face showed not the slightest expression.

"Kitt," he said softly.

Charlotte turned her face to Robert's, and she put her hand on his cheek.

"I'm very tired," she said.

"Yes, Kitt, let's go inside. It's late, time for bed."

Robert felt his throat thicken with grief for her. He put Harriette's letter in his pocket and helped his sister into the house. Malik was waiting inside the door, anxious. Robert whispered quickly to him, and Malik went to seek Charlotte's maids.

Robert waited whilst the maids changed her clothes and helped her to the bed. She fell instantly into a deep sleep. It was the shock, Robert knew, and sent a message to Shilah. He sent a boy for Dr Oxley and then a message to the police house saying he would not be back today.

When Shilah arrived, Robert took her into the living room and closed the door. He took her silently into his arms and kissed her. Shilah responded, winding her arms around his neck. She loved Robert with every part of her body and soul. She knew that his wife had found out about them. She could do nothing but wait for Robert to decide what to do. But it made her afraid, and she kissed him with terrible desire, an awful thought that this might be their last kiss. Why else had he asked her, so unexpectedly, to come to him here?

When he released her, she felt tears waiting behind her eyes. Robert could see them and took her hand. "Shilah, my love, my decision is made. I'll not leave you again. Come what may."

Shilah took Robert's hand and put it to her lips. She felt relief flood her body, but alarm too.

"But the Governor. Your position? And what of Andrew?"

Robert raised his hand in dismissal of these thoughts. "I have other interests. I will not be ruled by the damned East India Company. Whatever Teresa says, Andrew is my son, I shall see plenty of him.

Leave this for now. At this moment, we are here not for us but for Charlotte."

Shilah listened with mounting distress as Robert told her of Charles's death. The fact of Charlotte's engagement to him had not been universally known. Charlotte had planned to tell her children and make a grand announcement when Charles returned to Singapore; he had been due in two weeks time. But Robert had known, for Charlotte had confided her growing affection for this man, her impatience at his return. And so Shilah had known also.

Now, filled with grief for her beloved friend, Shilah went immediately to Charlotte's bedside.

43

Robert was at the police office contemplating his meeting with Butterworth at three o'clock that afternoon when John Hale, one of his constables, burst into the room.

"Come quick, sir. Argument in the Chinese town which is getting out of hand."

Hale was sweating and breathless. It was evident he had run from Chinatown. He was not a man given to exaggeration, and Robert rose and took up his rifle and signalled to two peons to come with him.

"Need more men, sir," Hale said as they left the precincts of the Court House and headed towards Thomson's Bridge.

Robert swiftly ordered one of the peons to get a contingent together as quickly as possible and wait for him at the bridge. He needed to see what was going on.

As they strode over the bridge, Hale filled Robert in. "Around midday a dispute began between two Chinese over a catty of rice. Apparently one is a Hokkien man and the other from Macau, and the argument got out of hand. When I was called from the Telok Ayer station, the quarrel had come to blows and the two men had been joined by their countrymen on either side."

Robert was alarmed. These disputes between rival factions of the Chinese community had been simmering for a long time. As he, John and the peon approached Amoy Street, the noise of ferment could be clearly heard. Robert was appalled. Several hundred men were attacking each other with staves, stones and knives along the length of the street. The lower shops were shut, but from the upper floors, men were hurling bricks, sticks and furniture down on the men below. Dead and wounded men were lying in profusion, and blood spattered the street. More men were arriving at every minute, and the fight was being carried with the ferocity of hate to the surrounding streets. Shops had been plundered and destroyed.

"There must be five hundred men here. We can do nothing. This is a gang war. We need military force."

Robert and Hale withdrew to the bridge. "I am going to see Butterworth," Robert told Hale. "Stay here and keep me informed."

Robert raced back to the Court House. Butterworth was in session in the Magistrate's Court, so Robert sent in a note and waited. There was no reply. Clearly Butterworth had not grasped the seriousness of the situation.

It was not long before John Hale had sent a peon with news. The riots had spread all over Chinatown from Telok Ayer Street to Circular Road. Pillage and murder was rife. Robert knew he could wait no longer. He rose and opened the door of the sessions court.

The Colonel was expounding on a point of law and glared at Robert.

Robert hardly cared. He strode to the bench and confronted Butterworth. "Sir, your order for military action in the Chinese town is urgently required. The place is amuck with murder and plunder."

Butterworth was red with anger, Robert could see. "How dare you break in, sir. I am in session," Butterworth said furiously.

"With respect, Governor, the Chinese town is about to go up in flames, and you will soon have Chinese thugs beating down this very door."

Butterworth rose. He signalled to his clerk to suspend the session and, without a word to Robert, left the court. Outside the Court House, he called for his horse, a white mare, upon which he pranced at every occasion around the *padang*. As he mounted he turned to Robert.

"This is gross dereliction of duty, Mr Macleod. What with this and the other moral question, I think your days as Superintendent of Police are done."

"Sir, do not go down to the town. It is too dangerous. Be warned."

Butterworth snorted his disdain and urged his horse forward. Robert and the peon stepped away as Butterworth trotted up High Street with all the ease of a man on military parade.

"The man's an idiot," Robert hissed, as Mr Church, the Resident Councillor, came to his side. Together they followed Butterworth's horse. As they turned into Hill Street, Church let out a cry, for there was Butterworth, surrounded by a mob of angry Chinese men at the junction of Hill Street and River Valley Road. They were screaming and pelting him with rocks and mud. Butterworth was turning his mare round and round, panicked, the mud on his face obscuring his vision. In a moment he would fall, Robert was certain, and be trampled.

The Chinese had no quarrel with the European town, but the Governor had foolishly got into the riot, and things had become so heated that the men hardly knew what they were doing or who they were attacking.

Robert ran forward, his rifle to the ready, and fired a shot over the crowd. The peon, his stick raised, advanced with Robert. The men began to scatter back to the bridge, but further they would not go. Fighting was raging on the other side. Robert took the mare's reins and quickly led Butterworth back down the street and turned the corner.

"Are you hurt, William?" he said as Butterworth got off the mare.

Butterworth wiped the mud from his eyes and glared at Robert.

"Shut up," he hissed and turned to Church. "Get the army. Send word to Cameron to send in the troops." He thrust the reins of his horse at the peon and strode back to the Court House. Robert watched him depart, Church on his heels.

Within half an hour, Robert saw the troops marching in a body into the town. He gathered his contingent of policemen and crossed the bridge. As soon as the troops appeared, the fighting stopped and the men ran off down the side streets, only to begin again as they passed.

Attempting to bar their passage was pointless, and Robert called on the captain of the troops to split them up and send them in different directions. This request was met with cold indifference.

Soon the Governor, cleaned up, appeared with Mr Church and several of the magistrates and passed along the streets where the rioting had been greatest. The sight of armed troops and the gathered European contingent, by degrees, produced an air of quietness, and the streets became calm. As the evening began to fall, the disturbances seemed over.

Eventually Robert joined the Governor and the captain of the troops. "That's put an end to that," Butterworth said and the captain nodded.

"Yes, sir. The sight of the red coats and your esteemed authority has brought the situation under control," the captain said, saluting Butterworth.

Robert raised an eyebrow and looked at the Governor, who only an hour or two ago had been covered in mud. "For now," he said.

Butterworth turned to Robert, glaring. "What do you mean?"

"I mean, sir, that this calm is only temporary. The Chinese do not like to fight in the dark, but there are forces at work which make me certain that the morning will bring a renewal of violence."

"Rot," the captain said, and Butterworth smiled. "The Governor has judged the situation very well. There'll be no more nonsense now, sir, I'm sure." He saluted Butterworth again.

"Yes, quite. Thank you, Captain, your gallantry will not be forgotten this day. Dismiss the troops back to barracks."

The captain saluted again, and Robert sighed. "I would strongly advise troops staying overnight, Governor," he said.

"Alarmist nonsense, Superintendent. The matter is under control. You may post your men if you like, but the troops will go. I will judge the situation in the morning."

He eyed Robert. "I do not forget that we have business to be discussed." Butterworth raised his hand in dismissal and set off back to the riverside, flanked by the magistrates.

Hale came up to Robert and the two men looked at each other. Hale shook his head. "John, set a guard," Robert said, "keep vigilant. At dawn tell me what is going on."

Hale nodded, and Robert went home to Beach Road.

44

Robert rose before dawn. He had passed a fretful night. It was hot, and sleep had been difficult.

He went downstairs, roused one of his peons and sent him to the Telok Ayer station for a report. As soon as he was dressed he rode to Charlotte's house.

Malik was already on duty. The man was a paragon. No change, he reported. The memsahib had woken and drunk some tea. Dr Little had come by and prescribed a sleeping potion.

Robert climbed the stairs and opened Charlotte's bedroom door. The room was dark and stuffy. He went to the window and opened it. He looked at his sister. She was asleep, curled like a child, and his heart went to her.

He took up the potion on her table. Madragore and opium. He frowned. Charlotte had spoken to him of her addiction in Batavia and warned him of his own prolonged use of it for his injury. He would not have her at risk of such a dangerous habit again. He took the bottle and put it in his pocket.

He left the house and rode swiftly to the police station. Light was just beginning to appear as he arrived. Hale reported no movement in the night. Bodies had been removed to the dead house in the Chinese hospital grounds at Pearl's Hill. Tan Kim Ching had been consulted, and he was dealing with the situation. Robert nodded. Perhaps Butterworth was right. Perhaps calm had been restored.

Within the hour, this conjecture was proved very wrong, and Robert's initial prediction was justified. At daybreak, pillaging began in a far more organised manner. Wherever a Hokkien store was located within a predominantly Teochow area, the shop was looted, set alight and the shopkeeper either beaten or murdered. Upon reports of the renewed violence, Robert gathered his entire force and went from place to place, breaking up the gangs and removing the wounded and dead to the hospital.

Within an hour it was obvious his force was too small. Three of his men, including John Hale, had been beaten and had retired, bloody, to the European hospital.

Butterworth reluctantly responded to the new crisis, and Colonel Cameron himself headed the Madras sepoys and a corps of navy marines landed from H.M.S. *Sybille*, *Lily* and *Rapid*. The sight of such a large occupying force brought calm to the streets, and the fighting continued only in desultory attacks on passers-by.

To forestall further problems, Robert sent word to all the European merchants to attend a meeting at noon at the Police House. When John Thomson arrived at the head of a large group of sympathetic government officers, Robert's spirits were buoyed, and together they set off to wait upon Butterworth.

Butterworth was dressed in military uniform festooned with his medals and insignia. Robert and John exchanged glances.

"Sir," Robert began.

Butterworth held up his hand and looked at them with a jaundiced eye. "Gentlemen, I thank you for your visit and understand your anxieties. Every exertion is now being made to put an end to these disorders. I have taken charge and, with the assistance of the Senior Naval Officer, we have no doubt that peace will soon be restored."

"Colonel, with respect," Robert said, "I think you are underestimating the gravity of the situation."

Butterworth threw haughty glance at Robert. "So you say, Superintendent, so you say. I shall be happy to have your written report. However we must differ on this matter. It is not serious, and I shall handle it."

"Sir, may I ask at least that you take the precaution of swearing in the civilians as special constables, in case their services are urgently needed in defence of their homes and property, and, even the town itself?"

Butterworth stared at Robert as if the idea was quite ridiculous. He smiled slightly and threw a complicit glance at Mr Church, who lowered his eyes.

"It is entirely unnecessary. However," he said, his voice filled with condescension, "if you men insist and if it will allay your fears, then, naturally I shall do so."

"Thank you, Colonel. Noon at the Police House, sir." Robert turned and left the room, filled with fury. "The man is a fool. He has no idea what he is up against and refuses to listen," he said to John.

"You've done what you can, Rob."

The swearing-in took place with seventy of the Europeans stepping forward. These were invested with the authority to arrest, detain, bear and use arms. As he headed back over the river, Robert sent his two European policemen and several peons to round up the Chinese merchants and bring them to the Reading Rooms on Commercial Square. All the shops and the godowns were ordered to be closed.

When the Chinese merchants arrived, they shuffled amongst themselves. Mr Church, as Resident Councillor, exhorted them to use their influence to restore order. Robert was unconvinced that this plea would do any good. The Chinese merchants would have little stomach for this.

He spotted Zhen and went up to him. "What do you know of this business? Your *kongsi* has the power to stop it, certainly."

Zhen shook his head. This rioting had sprung up out of nowhere. But he was not surprised. The age-old hatreds of the two factions had been brewing for some time. Now, though, the rival *kongsi* were organised, taking advantage by bringing more men in from the countryside.

He considered what to tell Robert. "Things that have been brewing for some time have come to a head. I do not believe the Europeans are in any danger. This is between the Chinese. I can do nothing to stop it."

Robert looked Zhen in the eyes. He was sure Zhen was speaking the truth. Robert also guessed that Zhen knew more than he had said, but he was being honest: the matter was not in his hands.

"Believe me," Zhen said. "This is kind of blood-letting. We can do little but wait for it to pass. But it is serious. Be vigilant over the next few days."

The merchants departed. Robert saw they had no power to deal with this situation, and he knew Zhen's words were true. In hopes of discouraging disorder, Robert called for a curfew, and all business ceased. With the restoration of peace, Butterworth sent word that troops should go back to the barracks at nightfall and await orders. Robert sent a written protest, explaining that sources had told him of what would transpire. The protest was ignored.

The next day was Sunday. Robert called all the special constables together at the Reading Rooms and addressed them. "I know there will be trouble tomorrow. I believe the rioters will expect the Europeans to observe Sunday and not come into town at all. With the troops gone, I firmly believe they will take advantage of this and bring reinforcements into town."

He looked over the faces of of his fellows, old and young, merchants and traders, not soldiers or policemen. "My men are done in with the last two days and nights. I need every one of you to be on duty in the streets at four o'clock," he said. "Five groups of eighteen men, fully armed. I will head one, Henry Cluff, the Deputy Superintendent, another, Mr Hale a third and two Magistrates will lead the other two. The Governor will not be convinced of the seriousness of the situation. It is up to us."

"We're with you Robert," called John Thomson, and the others answered.

Robert smiled. "Thank you, men. Now go home and get as much rest as possible. We will meet here again at three o'clock."

Robert posted a small contingent of his men throughout the town as the troops pulled out at seven o'clock. The streets were calm. Before the storm, he thought, but was glad to go home and fall fast asleep.

The night passed without incident. At daybreak every man had reported for duty. They alone had the entire charge of the town.

At first, as day broke, few Chinese ventured onto the streets, but reports came to Robert that in Circular Road, the upper part of

Market Street, Telok Ayer and other places, houses were crammed to bursting with men, and there was a raging ferment indoors. Robert knew that it was only the sight of his patrols that was preventing this ferment from sweeping out onto the street and the whole town going up in flames.

A little before six o'clock, a gang of men attempted to plunder a house at the corner of Circular Road and South Bridge Road, but Hale's patrol dispersed the mob. Robert's patrol met with knives and swords on Philip Street; two other patrols broke up violent riots on Market Street and within two hours had taken fifty rioters into custody. Two of the merchants were wounded.

Robert joined John Thomson and eight other men with the two wounded merchants, along with the captured rioters, and marched them, covered in blood, to the steps of the Court House and called on the Governor and the authorities to take charge. "Now, sir, will you not see sense?"

Butterworth stood, appalled at the sight of the town's European merchants, bloodied, beaten but angry, with fifty wild Chinese in tow. For the first time, the full extent of the very real danger to this community hit home, and, finally, he acted All the Chinese boats on the river, which were swarming with men, were corralled into the centre and patrolled by the cutters of the naval men-of-war in the harbour.

Marines and sepoys descended on the town to relieve the tired special constables. The rioters took to their heels and headed out of town and into the countryside. Reports of violence rapidly came in between the warring factions. The police station at Rochor was attacked and six men killed.

By Monday all the violence was in the country districts, particularly Paya Lebah and Geylang. The special constables joined Robert and Cluff in rebuffing mob attacks on the stations and bringing in refugees.

On Tuesday, houses in Tanglin were burned and hundreds of men on Bukit Timah Road were turned back by the special constables and two of Robert's policemen. A pitched battle took place near Cluny. Murders of villagers at Siglap and Serangoon were reported, with dozens killed. A mob of hundreds of men near the police station at the fifth milestone on Thomson Road was turned back after vicious fighting which left scores dead.

On Wednesday, Butterworth issued a proclamation calling for calm, warning of the intervention of the military and ordering all junks in the harbour to anchor in position.

Finally the disorder was so widespread that the steamer *Hooghly* was despatched with sepoys and Malay special constables to land at intervals around the entire island. From information received, Colonel Cameron destroyed a Chinese jungle stockade of arms, plunder, rice, opium and arrack at Bedok. A further proclamation was sent around town warning the populace of dire consequences if the violence continued and reminding them that this was not their country to do as they wished.

By Thursday the town at least was quiet, and businesses opened. But the countryside continued under fire and sword for seven more days, leaving plantations in ruins, houses and orchards destroyed, roads dug up and villages burned. There was uneasiness in Malacca which, fortunately, came to nothing, and in Johor there was some trouble with the disruption of rice supplies from Singapore, and trade was suspended.

The lock-up and the gaol were crammed with over five hundred prisoners. Acts of unspeakable excess were reported and arrests made from the rural areas, where no rein was put on the hatred of, as the Grand Jury heard, "people who lived in a state of semi-barbarism with little or no idea of what law and order is and where one faction had, by a preponderance of numbers, great power over the other." At the end of the sessions, six men were sentenced to death and executed, sixty-four were sentenced to hard labour and eight were transported.

When it was all over and the town had settled down to its repairs, Robert called to see Butterworth. Robert knew very well that the Governor was in a difficult position. He had acted so tardily it had caused the riots to get fully out of hand. The island had been pillaged and his authority diminished. Without the civilian population's forethought and courage, the town would have been burned to the ground. Questions had been asked in India. Robert's report had been unstinting in its exposition of the facts.

Robert stood before Butterworth's desk and waited. His report was open in front of the Governor.

Butterworth tapped the paper. "Have you sent this to anyone else, Superintendent?"

"No, sir. But if you think it useful I would be happy to send it directly to the government in India."

Butterworth looked at him sharply. "That won't be necessary, Mr Macleod."

"No, sir. For the present I will leave it to your discretion."

There was a silence.

"Is there any other matter you wish to raise with me, Governor Butterworth?"

The Governor steepled his hands. Robert waited. Butterworth was thinking hard, but there seemed no way out of this particular conundrum. The Governor looked up, directly at Robert.

"No, Superintendent. Carry on."

Robert smiled and bowed slightly. "Thank you, sir."

45

Jeanne had hardly changed. She was older to be sure, grey streaks in her curly black hair. She had remained as slim as a girl, though, and nothing could hide her beautiful eyes. She had been a great beauty, and Robert and Charlotte knew she had had many suitors. But she had refused them until they came no more. Young, her memories of her dead fiancé had refused to relinquish their hold on her heart, and when she'd felt those ties loosen, it had been too late.

By then Robert and his sister had come to Aberdeen, and Jeanne had loved them like her own children. Charlotte and Robert had made some mathematical calculations and decided she was around fifty-six years old. Robert could not quite believe it, for though her skin bore the signs of long walks in the Scottish winds, she was lithe and bonny.

As she stepped onto the quayside, she saw him and smiled. It was the smile of the mother she had been to those two orphaned waifs, sad and afraid. He felt his heart lurch with love for her.

Robert put his arms around her, and tears welled. So long, so many years had passed, and he had forgotten how much they owed to her, for without her they would surely have perished from misery.

"Aunt, Aunt, I am so glad you are here safe."

Jeanne held Robert very tightly, the emotion of seeing him again quite overwhelming. He was so handsome, so much a man, but she remembered him still as a boy. They had been a gift to her, these two. When she had lost her father, her fiancé, then her beloved brother, she had also almost lost her faith. But then He who had closed a door had opened a window and given her the care and love of these children.

She drew herself under control, a habit of a lifetime. "Robbie, my boy. It is good to see you."

Robert released her, and they smiled at each other. He wiped his eyes. It did not do for the police chief to stand around in open displays of emotion, and he took her hand.

As she settled into the carriage and began to look around, Robert spoke. "Aunt, something terrible has happened since you left Scotland."

Jeanne looked at Robert and listened. By the time they arrived at Charlotte's house, Jeanne understood. The memory of her own tragedy, of learning of Edward's death had, with time, naturally faded, but it had never quite gone away. She had felt like dying too, for life had seemed at that time to hold little meaning. Neither Jeanne nor her mother were given to melodrama, so of course no such expressions took place, and Jeanne had borne it alone, weeping soundlessly at night, only to put on the face of the day every morning.

At the house, Jeanne went immediately to Charlotte's room. Charlotte was sleeping, and Jeanne stood looking down at this precious child. She was so lovely, still. Too thin, but that was the grief. And it was three o'clock in the afternoon. This would not do. She bent and kissed Charlotte's damp forehead. The room was hot. Actually, the whole town was hot and very uncomfortable. She had said nothing to Robert, but the heat was oppressive. She now felt rather foolish for sending knitted socks on every packet.

Jeanne went downstairs and told Robert to get the servants to make some tea. She was going to wake Charlotte. It was time to set the household onto a proper routine. Routine might not heal Charlotte, but in times of misery, routine was the net without which, Jeanne was certain, they would all be swept to sea.

"I will go to my room Robbie, and change, for it is most fearsomely humid. Is a bath possible?"

Robert smiled. His aunt was here, and she would know what to do.

Light flooding the room roused Charlotte from sleep. She blinked, putting her arm across her face.

"My lovely Kitt, wake up. Here is a nice cup of tea."

Charlotte opened her eyes. She recognised the voice of her aunt. She was sitting on the side of the bed, and Charlotte looked up into her face. It was unbelievable.

She sat and threw herself into Jeanne's arms. "Oh, Aunt Jeanne, oh. You. Here."

She burst into tears, and Jeanne held her and rocked her until they subsided. It was like the first morning Charlotte had woken, a little girl in a strange, cold place. Jeanne had waited by her bedside, knowing she would be afraid. She wanted the first face Charlotte saw to be hers, the face of a loving friend.

Within days Jeanne had completely taken charge of the house. Malik adored her precise, Scottish nature and attention to detail. She roused Charlotte early each morning and, with Alex and Adam in tow, had Ravi take them on a ride around the *padang* or occasionally out onto the roads of the island, which had returned to relative safety.

Charlotte had spoken of Charles only once. She had finally found the courage to read the letter Harriette had written and the last letter from Charles. He had known he was dying only at the very last, and it was brief, the merest words of love for her, but in his shaking hand. She cried until she was exhausted and turned to Jeanne for comfort.

"I can offer little comfort, my wee bairn," Jeanne said. "It is a platitude, but time does help. We go from hour to hour, then day to day."

"I feel I am lost," Charlotte said. "Everything I do is terribly trivial and pointless."

"You have your children, Kitt. Alex is terribly worried about you, and Adam is missing you. It is time to pretend."

Charlotte looked at her aunt, a frown furrowing her brow.

"Pretend?"

"Aye, yes. Pretend. To get us through this, we must put on an act. At first the act is difficult and we fall in and out of it, but gradually, each day, it becomes natural until finally the act is not an act any more. It has become true. We go on with our lives, and the pain of memory intrudes only occasionally. You should know this better than I, for you have lost more than Charles. You have lost a husband with whom you have shared the desires of the flesh."

Charlotte stared at Jeanne.

"Do not be so shocked, Kitt. Do you think I am a dried-up old prune who does not think of such things? When I lost my Edward I was like you. I thought that life was the most silly thing. What on earth was its purpose? I thought like that much too long, my bairn. Remember Charles and his goodness, be angry at his death so young, but do not allow this loss to drag you to a terrible place."

Charlotte contemplated Jeanne. That she knew exactly how she felt there could be no possible denial. She felt a sudden great strength. Jeanne had lost all her youth to grief. This was her warning.

She rose and went to her aunt, sitting next to her, and Jeanne put her arms around her. "Today we shall go to church and remember Tigran and Charles and Edward and all those we love. Your mother and father, my dearest brother. Why, even your grandmother, eh?"

Charlotte smiled.

"Then, we shall rise and thank the Lord for his comfort, and stride out like good Christian soldiers into the fray once more. For there is nothing else to do."

46

"Do you think it is wise?" Qian glanced at Zhen as Ah Rex disappeared up the stairs of the brothel.

"It is time. He is thirteen years old. Min will be careful. The girl is experienced. She knows what to do."

Qian looked doubtful. "His mother does not know."

Zhen frowned.

"No," he said, annoyed. "This is man's business. I am his father. In this I know best."

Qian shrugged slightly, but he was not entirely convinced. Ah Soon was almost the same age as Ah Rex, and Qian was not sure he was ready for such an encounter. But Ah Soon and Ah Rex were two different boys. Ah Rex was every inch Zhen's son: bold, adventurous and brave.

"Still, not to tell Xia Lou. It is unwise." Zhen made a motion of dismissal with his hand.

"Ah Rex will not speak of it to her. I have told him for weeks now that he must learn about 'rain and clouds'. He understands that this is between men."

Zhen looked at his friend. "Ah Soon, too, you must decide. My daughter is promised to him, and I have hopes that he will not be so useless as his father."

Qian smiled. "In good time. Once Ah Rex tells him, I am certain he will want to know too."

Qian poured some tea for Zhen. They would wait for Ah Rex to come out, for they both knew he would be filled with excitement and need a guiding hand.

"What of the Cholon rice merchant's daughter? Baba Tan is keen for you to remarry, is he not?"

A fleeting look of sadness touched Zhen's face. "He's unwell, Qian. I care for him very much. It is a great sadness."

Qian nodded. Zhen and his father-in-law were as close as any blood could make them. Zhen was the son Tan had wanted, and Zhen loved him as well as his own father, now dead for two years.

"But I have no intention of marrying a thirteen-year-old girl for the sake of a share in the rice trade. What on earth would I do with her?" Zhen laughed.

"Sire more children," Qian said. "It is expected of a young, virile and rich merchant to make as many sons as possible."

Zhen said nothing. Since the death of Noan, he had been besieged by matchmakers representing countless eligible families. He had remained steadfastly aloof. Fortunately, Zhen's son, Kai, was healthy. He had no desire for another wife.

"He died, you know, the man she was to marry," Qian said, looking at Zhen.

"Yes, I know. Ah Rex was very worried for his mother for a long time. But she is better. Her aunt came."

"Yes, so I have heard."

Zhen contemplated his teacup. Xia Lou had shown great grief for this man. He had not thought of it whilst the island was in uproar and after, for a long time, he had been busy. But Ah Rex's concerns had been clear. His mother was in mourning. When he thought of this, he felt a coldness inside. For a long time he had not cared, wished her miserable and grieving, wished her punished for deserting him.

"Have you seen her?" he said to Qian.

"Once only. She was walking with her aunt in the market. She was thin, too thin."

Zhen frowned but said nothing.

"She and her aunt help at the school for Chinese girls at North Bridge Road. The Miss Eva goes too, sometimes. Do you remember her at the church school we went to?"

Zhen looked at Qian. Remember? Of course he remembered. Everything of that time was as vivid as yesterday. It was there he had found Xia Lou, fallen in love with her. But he said nothing. There was nothing to say. Now that the danger of losing Ah Rex had faded, his anger had faded, but those early memories remained undimmed.

47

"I cannot approve of his actions."

Jeanne was adamant. Robert's living arrangements were a cause of concern. His wife was living with his son in her mother's house whilst Robert consorted with a ... Jeanne could not find the words. When Robert was with her, she said nothing but her disapproval was clear.

Charlotte had tried to explain about the long association of Shilah and Robert, point out the mistake Robert had made, but Jeanne would have nothing of it. Amber, of course, she welcomed into her heart as Robert's child, but she would not countenance meeting Shilah.

Charlotte was finally able to think of something other than her grief for Charles. When she began to pay attention to the household again, she discovered that Alex spent every day with Zhen. They had grown as close as the father and son they were. Both Charlotte's sons adored their great aunt, but Adam, in particular, loved to spend time with her. She talked to him of Scotland and his Scottish grandfather, and for the first time, Charlotte realised that she would have to send them back. Adam wanted to go. It would be of benefit to their education. And, she recognised, it would separate Alex from Zhen and the intensity of their relationship.

Jeanne was a popular addition to the European community. She was often invited to dinners and functions of all kinds and was a favourite with Jeannette Butterworth. It was several months before Charlotte realised from her acquaintance that Jeanne was also receiving the special attentions of Martin Macallister, a merchant from Aberdeen.

"Aunt," Charlotte said one evening after dinner. They were playing piquet. "Do you not think Mr Macallister is a fine-looking man?"

Jeanne stopped looking at her cards and stared at Charlotte, who smiled to see her aunt actually blush.

"What on earth do you mean?" Jeanne asked, slightly flustered.

"Mr Macallister. All the ladies say he has a very fine figure and excellent hair."

"Hair," said Jeanne. "What do I give a fig about a man's hair? Are you quite well, Charlotte?"

"Now, Jeanne. I believe Mr Macallister thinks that you are a very fine woman."

Jeanne threw down her cards. "Really, Kitt. What do you mean?"

"I believe it is time for a dinner party. Shall we make a guest list?"

She smiled at her aunt, and Jeanne gave up her small pretence. Charlotte took up her pen and pulled forward the piquet pad.

"First of all, I think, Mr Macallister."

They both laughed.

48

Lian's twelfth birthday was approaching and Lilin was having a celebration. It was Lian's animal year, and it was full of luck.

When Charlotte received the ornate red and gold invitation for Alex she frowned. Did he know this girl? Actually, she realised that for the past year she did not fully understand her son at all. He had changed very much. He was quiet, withdrawn. He rarely talked to her and only addressed the most polite but cursory sentences to Jeanne or Robert.

He continued to study hard at the Institution, and his teachers were pleased with him. His exceptional Chinese abilities were noted with amazement. He spent a great deal of time in the Chinese town, but he always returned home at the appointed hour. He no longer played games with his brother or Amber when she came. He had become something of a stranger, and Charlotte guiltily wondered if her own grieving had marked him in some way, for she had never truly explained about Charles.

She realised, suddenly, that she needed to speak to Zhen, that in fact Zhen currently knew her son better than she did. It had been a very long time, and the estrangement between them remained. She knew he had lost his wife in childbirth and that he had a son. Perhaps this celebration for his daughter would be the time to renew a conversation about Alex. Charlotte intended to send her sons to Scotland within the year, and she felt, with some trepidation, that she owed it to Zhen to tell him.

The party for Lian was held at Baba Tan's mansion on River Valley

Road. A great many carriages were pulled up in the drive of the house, and Charlotte realised that this was quite a large function. As she walked in with Alex and Adam, she saw Baba Tan and was shocked. He looked very ill, older than his years. She was sure he was not yet fifty.

She went up to him and curtsied very low. Tan smiled at her. He held out his hand, and she rose and went to his side. He looked so thin. She felt tears starting behind her eyes. Alex and Adam bowed to Tan, and he waved at them.

"Baba Tan, it is so good to see you again."

"Mrs Mah Nuk, thank you for coming today."

He spoke very quietly. A woman laid her hand on his shoulder and whispered. This, Charlotte thought, was his second daughter. Zhen's wife had been the first daughter. Zhen had not remarried, and she had wondered about that many times.

She said goodbye to Baba Tan and watched as he was wheeled away into the verandah.

"He is dying."

She turned, recognising his voice.

"I did not know he was so ill," Charlotte replied, looking into his eyes. It had been a very long time since they had been so close together.

Zhen nodded. "A few months, perhaps."

Alex was standing next to Zhen, looking at him with something like adoration. Adam was bored, shifting his feet from side to side.

"I am sorry. I know you care for him," Charlotte said.

Zhen bowed to her formally, then turned to the boys. "The other children are in the garden. Shall we go?" Zhen looked at Charlotte.

"Yes, to the garden. Off you go, boys."

They both ran off. Drums and gongs could be heard in the distance.

"Zhen ..."

But before she could say another word, three ladies of her acquaintance came up and urged her to join them on the verandah. "Isn't it extraordinary?" they all said. "A Chinese birthday party. There is a dragon in the garden. Come and see, Charlotte."

Zhen bowed slightly and left.

The house and garden were festooned with red silk banners, and a long gold and red dragon was prancing around the children at the bottom of the garden, preceded by drums and gongs.

Charlotte paid her respects to a group of old Straits Chinese ladies seated together at a large, marble-topped table on the verandah. They all waved their fans and showed their black teeth in smiles of welcome. The garden was filled with tables, and clearly every child in the European and Chinese communities over the age of eight had been invited.

A magician entertained the children on one side of the garden and a group of jugglers and tumblers on the other. It was a most entrancing and lively scene, with the vivid decorations and flags, the Chinese children in their clothes of blue, gold and red and the array of entertainers dressed in every colour under the sun. On every table on the lawn stood a basket of twelve red eggs.

Charlotte saw Ah Soon playing with Alex and Adam. She was disappointed that Zhen had disappeared but very glad that her heart had been up to the task of meeting him again and remained quite steady.

Charlotte listened with half an ear to the ladies prattling on, nodding from time to time and fanning herself. When refreshments were served, she looked around for the boys. Adam was frolicking with his friends from school. Alex was not to be seen, but she did not worry. Alex could take care of himself. He was doubtless with Ah Soon and their school friends.

She joined the other ladies in their discussions. The Temmengong was to hold a fancy dress ball in the Assembly Rooms to raise funds for the new Sailors' Home. This last was close to Charlotte's heart, for the Sailors' Home was to be at No. 3 Coleman Street, the home of her long-dead, beloved friend George Coleman.

Alex was inside the house with Ah Soon and a group of other Chinese boys. Each boy was hanging on Alex's every word, for he was describing his experiences in the brothel in Amoy Street. The boys didn't notice the woman at the door. Lilin could not understand them, but she could see that Alex was the leader. He was strong, tall, handsome. She knew that he had been introduced to the ladies at the Heaven's Gate brothel.

She smiled and walked into the room. The boys all fell silent.

"Alex, come with me please," she said in English.

Alex rose and bowed instinctively to this lady. She was Lian's aunt; he could not disobey.

The other boys ran off, and he followed Lilin down the corridor and into a sitting room.

Lian rose as Lilin entered and smiled shyly at Alex. He was thunderstruck.

He had first seen Lian when she was seven years old. She was pretty then, but not prettier than other little Chinese girls in the town. He had forgotten her, of course. Since then, he had met her many times on the quay with her aunt or in the godown with her nurse. She had begun to speak English, and that was quite unusual. He had noticed her prettiness but thought no more of it.

Now, though, with the experiences of the last year, this tremendous discovery of what women could mean, what pleasures they brought, he looked at her with very different eyes—the eyes of an almost-man. He knew only Chinese women, and here was a girl beyond his dreams.

His eyes met Lian's. There was something, a recognition. She was lovely but it was more than that. He felt a connection to her as strong as a cord, a visceral pull.

"Lian, greet our guest."

Lian rose obediently and came forward, close to Alex, bowing to him. She wore a long white *baju* over her flowered sarong. He smelled jasmine in her jet-black hair.

"Hello, Ah Rex," she said softly, her accent sweet and lilting

Lilin took Lian's hand and held it, caressingly, moving her long fingers gently over Lian's soft skin. Alex could not take his eyes off her hand. Lian stood, head bowed, submissive, beautiful, the bud of her ear, the curve of her perfect cheek mesmerising. Lilin smiled slightly and, taking up Alex's hand, put Lian's in it, covering it with hers.

"Shake hands, Lian, it is the Western way."

Alex stood unmoving, the feel of her hand in his, cool and soft, arousing and tender at the same time. Her lashes lay on her perfect cheeks. The atmosphere in the room was suddenly charged with sexuality. He felt his arousal, an unbidden act of blood. He knew if they had been alone he would have kissed her, and not gently, and the thought, suddenly, was outrageous. She was, by European reckoning, only eleven years old and the daughter of his favourite man. He dropped her hand and took a step back, bowing to her and her aunt respectfully.

Lian moved forward and took up his hand again, pulling him towards the door.

"Come and break a red egg for my birthday," she said in almost perfect English. "You must be first."

Her sarong moved gently around her ankles, whisper soft. Her hair fell like black silk down her back. Her almond eyes gazed on him with infinite softness. He followed her as if in a trance. Lilin smiled and went with them out into the garden.

Alex was silent in the carriage ride home. Charlotte glanced at him and frowned. He seemed to be sick. She had seen him mooning around the garden, watching Lian. Was he old enough, really, to have thoughts of girls? He was fourteen, would be fifteen in a few months. Perhaps she should speak to him. The thought horrified her. She felt totally unequal to the task, which was a father's affair. Perhaps Robert.

Then her mind flew to Zhen. Had he spoken of this? Could he? He was the only man Alex really trusted. She sighed. It was so difficult.

Alex sat staring at the horses' tails twitching. His mind was filled with confusion. He had never seen anyone like her. Lian, Lian. Her name was a poem. He wanted her, that was the only thought which found a place in his brain. But how? Betrothal to him was the only way to stop a marriage to some other man. But to marry a Straits Chinese girl? They only married amongst themselves. Her father, no matter how much they liked each other, would not agree, and his mother would have a fit. The feel of her cool, soft skin on his suddenly filled his mind, and he became instantly aroused but, just as quickly, brought himself under control, the way Auntie Min had shown him at the brothel. A lack of control, she had taught him, made a man a fool and made sex a misery for a woman. She had taught him a lot, but he knew he had a great deal more to learn. He was desperate to meet Lian again. But he knew that after the twelfth birthday all Straits girls were confined to their homes until they were married. The thought was torture and misery, and frustration overwhelmed him.

49

Zhen spoke severely, and Alex jumped.

"What?" he said, staring at the boy.

They were playing *wei qi*, a game Alex had grown to love, especially with Uncle Zhen.

Alex bowed his head. "I asked who Lian is to marry."

Zhen had been looking at the board. He had given Ah Rex a head start and was beginning to regret it. The boy learned fast.

"That is none of your business," Zhen said firmly.

Alex felt chastened. Zhen rarely spoke harshly to him.

They played in silence for some minutes. Alex could wait no longer. It was stronger than himself. "I ask, Uncle, for is it possible for Lian to marry a white boy?"

Zhen stared at Alex. He did not like the way this conversation was going.

"Why are you asking these questions, Ah Rex?"

The boy hesitated, and Zhen knew almost exactly what he was thinking.

"I am almost a man, Uncle. My mind has turned to such matters."

Zhen smiled. Almost a man, indeed. A year or so of interesting sexual education, and the boy thought himself a man.

"You are not a man. You need more education, clearly, or you would know this."

"Yes, Uncle," Alex said. A silence ensued whilst they played.

"But Lian is promised, is she?" Alex ventured again.

Zhen stopped playing and looked at Alex. "Lian is promised to Ah Soon. She will marry him when she is sixteen years old."

Alex said nothing. Then he threw down his pieces with a clatter and stood. "I must go home." He bowed respectfully to Zhen, turned and left.

Zhen was stunned. It was obvious that Alex was considering himself as a husband for Lian. What on earth had happened? This was very alarming. Zhen understood Ah Rex well, how he thought and felt. His son would not have spoken of this unless he was serious.

Alex almost ran back to North Bridge Road. He was furious. Lian, his Lian, promised to Ah Soon. It was ridiculous. Over the past weeks he had written her letters. Her English was good. Her aunt had no objection. She allowed him to bring letters to her house. Once, against every expectation, he had even been permitted to sit with Lian in the courtyard under the watchful eye of her aunt. They had spoken of many things. She was like a beautiful piece of jade, but she was clever, too, and knew of English things.

She had not said so, but it was clear that she cared for him. Her eyes peeping over the moving fan told him. Her letters spoke of her preparations for marriage, learning embroidery and cooking, learning how to be an obedient wife. He was jealous, and now he was angry.

Alex watched his mother prepare for the fancy dress ball. She looked beautiful, so much better than she had for a long time. Alex, with his heightened sensibility, had realised that his mother had loved the man who had died, the man, Charles, in Sarawak. Uncle Robert had spoken of this man's death but said no more.

He looked with loving eyes on his mother. He had been moody and difficult, he knew. He longed to bring himself under control, but thoughts of Lian occupied his mind from morning to night.

Charlotte finished her toilette. She had chosen to go as Cleopatra, in gold and black muslin, and the maid was putting the finishing touches to the Egyptian headdress and necklace which Jeanne had brought from her journey. Jeanne had chosen an allegorical theme and was dressed as "Spring", with a garland of flowers in her hair and a gown of flower-printed organza. Charlotte knew Jeanne had never enjoyed herself more. Singapore offered an infinite variety of amusements amongst its European population, and this chance to meet a Prince of Pirates and the representatives of the Celestial Kingdom was too exciting.

Charlotte picked up her fan, decorated for the occasion with rather fanciful attempts at Egyptian figures. She went out on the landing, and Alex came up to her and bowed charmingly.

"The Queen of Egypt. Your majesty."

Charlotte smiled, delighted. He was so rarely of good humour lately, and she was grateful he was now. She kissed him. Adam was spending the evening with a group of young boys at the house of the Reverend Dickinson, the new vicar of St. Andrew's Cathedral. Adam went to church with Jeanne every Sunday and even during the week. He enjoyed it, and Charlotte felt unable to discourage him, despite her own feelings. The two boys had grown apart; their interests were so divergent.

"Will you be all right, Alex, all alone?" Charlotte asked as Jeanne came out onto the landing.

Alex smiled and kissed his mother's hand. "Perfectly. Have a wonderful evening, mother, Aunt Jeanne."

As their carriage turned out of the grounds, he went to his room. He had told Malik he would be studying, then would go to bed. He was not to be disturbed. At the first chance, he ran quickly down the stairs, out of the house and through the garden to the back gate. Lian's aunt had said he could come this evening to talk to Lian for one hour. One hour! His heart was light as air.

50

The ball was a great success. The Temenggong came as one of his illustrious ancestors, whose more ancient dress seemed exactly the same as his usual one. Several Chinese merchants were dressed in various sorts of costumes from Chinese opera. The Governor and Jeannette Butterworth came as Sir Stamford and Lady Sophia Raffles, to general applause. Robert came alone as a rather bad imitation of Napoleon.

She saw Zhen. He was dressed in the military costume of a Chinese general. It suited him. He bowed to her but did not approach.

As the speeches were made and the champagne flowed, the band struck up, and couples came together in dance. A Staffordshire milkmaid was in the arms of a Chinese emperor, and a Bugis pirate took to the floor with Lady Godiva.

When John Thomson came up to ask her hand for a dance, Charlotte pleaded the heat and they both sought the freshness of the garden. John had not dressed up other than to wear a rather daring red cravat. She and John were the greatest companions. They both loved to sail and often went together to the surrounding islands. Jeanne was fond of John, and he came frequently to dine and play cards. Charlotte accompanied him on his sketching excursions throughout the island.

Ordinarily they were completely at ease with each other, but this evening Charlotte detected something uneasy in John's attitude. He had been working under great strain in terrible conditions finishing the lighthouse on Pedra Branca, a tribute to his patience, fortitude and engineering skill.

The last thing she had expected was his proposal. When they sat at one of the seats which dotted the garden, he had immediately fallen on one knee, and the words fell so quickly from his lips that she hardly had time to think. He was sweating, shy and filled with anxiety, she saw.

She fanned herself. "John, you have taken me entirely by surprise," she said. "I thank you, truly, but you must allow me some time to reflect."

He looked embarrassed, and she softened her voice. "Will you do that, John, allow me some time?"

John rose and took her hand, kissing it. "Of course, dear Kitt. I shall await your answer. But please, do not make me wait too long."

He turned and left, anxious to be gone. This question: marriage. Again she was faced with a choice. John was a loving and wonderful man. That he would make a devoted and adoring husband was evident. That she felt nothing more than friendship for him was also not in question. Only her surprise and a desire not to hurt him had stayed her response. She would tell him tomorrow that such a marriage was impossible.

She retreated further into the side garden of the Assembly Rooms. The night was warm, but here a pleasant breeze wafted from the river and played gently in the trees.

"Xia Lou."

She turned, knowing who it was. She was glad he had come.

"Zhen," she said.

"I must speak to you of Ah Rex."

Charlotte smiled. "Yes. Alex has been a difficult boy lately."

"Yes," Zhen said and moved towards her. She retreated a step, without thinking.

He stopped and gazed at her. She looked so well. Her health had returned. The costume she was wearing was enticing, her white bosom covered in a strange necklace. Her hair under the gold and turquoise headdress flowed over her shoulders, black as night.

"What is this dress?" he asked, his train of thought diverted.

Charlotte smiled. He was clearly perplexed.

"Much like yours," she said. "A strange copy of ancient things half-imagined. The Queen of a country called Egypt which ruled the world thousands of years ago."

Zhen frowned. "E-jipt," he said. "And you are the beautiful Queen."

"And you a handsome and valiant general of China."

They both smiled, and their eyes met in a long moment of quiet tenderness.

Zhen broke the silence. "Ah Rex is talking of marrying my daughter, Lian."

Charlotte stared at him. "What?" she said finally.

"He believes he is in love with Lian. He has talked to me of this."

Charlotte frowned. "My son, Alex, has talked to you of marrying your daughter?"

"Our son, Xia Lou. It is child's talk, but he thinks he loves her. I think we must tell him that Lian is his sister. This is dangerous."

Charlotte said nothing.

"Well?" he said.

"No," she said and looked up at him.

"Zhen, listen. I am going to send Alex and Adam to Scotland. I have spoken of this to my aunt, and she agrees that this is the right thing to do. They will leave within a month."

Zhen reflected on her words. Ah Rex was an English boy, no matter how well he spoke Chinese. Perhaps this was the right thing to do. He would receive a good education. And this would surely put an end to these thoughts of Lian.

"How long?" he asked.

"Three years," she said. "Until after his seventeenth birthday. Then he will come back to learn the family business. In Batavia," she said.

Zhen dropped his head. His sadness was so palpable, she rose and went to him, forgetting everything else. Zhen loved Alex, and Alex was his son.

She put out her hand to his arm and he took it in his. "Xia Lou, I will agree. Ah Rex is a passionate boy. I have ..." Zhen hesitated. He could not tell her everything.

"I have talked to him of these matters," he said.

Charlotte nodded. She suspected as much. He was a good father.

"I am glad. He needs a guiding hand. I am quite incapable of the task." She smiled at him in gratitude and felt the old yearning. Sense and passion, the perfect complement for a marriage. But all so impossible.

Zhen too felt the pull to her. He had to agree to this departure. It was wise. But he feared, suddenly, that she might go too.

"You will stay, Xia Lou? You will not go."

"I ..." she said "... don't know."

"You must stay." He had increased his grip on her hand. She let out a small cry, and he released her.

"Are you not tired of this?" he said, his voice low.

She felt the same old sensations. As if they had merely interrupted a conversation which took place not many years ago but yesterday. "I am tired of many things, Zhen. I am tired of being a widow."

She hesitated. "I have received a proposal of marriage."

To her surprise Zhen merely sighed. "I, too, am chased morning to night, to marry young girls, take wives, two or three. What can I do with them?"

She laughed. He had said this with an air of studious annoyance.

"Yes, two or three wives is rather a lot. We are permitted only one husband, thank goodness."

He smiled. He knew she was joking. He missed her, longed for her.

"Marry me," he said suddenly.

She stared at him, struck momentarily dumb.

"What, Zhen? What do you mean?"

"Marry me. We are married by all the natural laws. But is clear that I must marry you by your English laws." He took a step closer to her.

"I will become a Christian and we will marry in your church. Lots of Chinese become Christians. Then I can have only one wife. You."

Charlotte felt the power of his will. He would do it. She had only to say yes, and he would set the wheels in motion. He was true to his word.

Charlotte took him by the hand and led him to a seat. She was desperately trying to think. The thought of marrying him was thrilling, the first, best wish of her heart. She would have him every day and every night, companion, friend, lover. But the thought was hedged with fear. They would be considered bizarre and disgusting by some. Not, perhaps, by those she cared about. But the fear was not for herself. It was for her sons. What would be their future if their mother took this step?

She thought of life in Batavia. The Dutch men married their native women and their offspring went to Holland and married into the great families. The English lords took their half-breed daughters from India, married them to members of the aristocracy and put their sons in Eton. Alexander and Adam were the sons of a great colonial family. They would have wealth, education and breeding. They would make their way, perhaps. But what of their marriages, and what of Robert? His sister the wife of a Chinese man. It would ruin him, bring shame on her children and his. She shook her head slightly.

But she loved him for it. She gave up all pretence. It was the most tremendous relief, and she put his hand to her lips, thanking him. He moved closer to her, putting his arms around her, and with a deep sigh she rested her head against his chest.

"Oh, Zhen. We cannot decide now. It is too big."

She felt him nod, his head on hers.

"Sunday," she said. The boys were going with Robert and some other men to hunt birds out at Bukit Timah. She would ask him to keep them for two days. Amber would be delighted, and Shilah would not mind.

A group of merry revellers burst into the garden, singing. Zhen rose and stepped away from her.

"Sunday," he said.

51

They met by the shipyards on Beach Road. She had borrowed Robert's little boat, *Sea Gypsy*. He had sent his pony trap to take her there and given her the seaside cottage at beautiful Katong.

The tide was up; it was six o'clock, and they would have daylight for the trip to Katong. She had made this voyage so many times it was easy; she could have done it at night. It took only about half an hour. They would arrive at sunset. This was what she wanted: to watch the sun go down over the beach at Katong with him. She was wearing her sailing clothes—loose trousers, a shirt, leather sandals, a hat to restrain her hair. She knew she looked like a boy dressed like this. He would never have seen her like this, and the thought excited her. The driver put the boxes in the boat, provisions for the two days and two nights they would be together. She paced a little, impatient for him.

She recognised him by his size only. He too was dressed differently, in a plain Malay *baju* and trousers, loose shoes, his queue wound round his head underneath a hat. She smiled as he looked around. He was nervous, she realised. Nervous about meeting her? That was not possible. Nervous about the sea? Yes, she knew he did not like boats.

She went up behind him and put her hand quietly into his. He turned and looked down at her and forgot his nervousness at the odd sight of her, dressed like that, standing close to him. They looked like a couple of coolies, and he smiled slightly at this thought.

They got into the boat, and two young Malay boys pushed them off. She raised the sail and caught the land wind immediately. Within a moment they were away from shore heading for Tanjong

Rhu. Zhen held on to the sides grimly. This was not enjoyable. But as he saw how sure she was, how quickly she handled the sail, how smoothly the little boat skimmed across the calm sea, he relaxed and found her more than admirable. She was brave and clever, quick and lovely. Arousing, too, out of the ordinary way, in these boyish clothes. Charlotte saw him watching her, no longer nervous of the water. She smiled, a slow smile of complicity, and he looked at her, impassive as always. She knew, though, the depths of his emotions and took off her hat, letting her long black hair blow in the wind. He did not move, but she felt the intensity of his gaze like heat. Sometimes he frightened her with this gaze, and now, feeling uncomfortable, she put her hat back on her head, containing her hair.

When they rounded the cape, they followed the coast. The sailing was easy; the sun was sinking slowly behind them; the wind was warm as breath on their skin. He looked around. He had not seen the coast of this island since the day he had arrived, years before, and he could not remember it like this. It was a rainbow, the intense turquoise of the sea, shot now with purple and pink, the white sand turning pale orange as the sun sank, the coconut palms leaning out to sea, the green jungle beyond, and then the high red cliffs hovering above, made vibrant by the sun, filled with small, high streams flowing out of the earth where deep clefts formed in the rocks. He watched the day begin to fade, fire into water, golden light into purple dusk. This time was when the earth was most in balance: sunrise and sunset—when the brightness of Yang and the dark night of Yin mingled most sweetly, transforming each into the other.

She pointed to the shore, and he turned his head and saw a wooden cottage on stilts hiding back amongst the coconut palms. Charlotte turned the boat towards shore and lowered the sail as the boat slid silently onto the sand. Zhen leapt into the water, glad the journey was over. He pulled it higher up the sand as a small wave picked it up and beached it. He looked at Charlotte, making the boat safe, throwing out the rope to him.

"Wait," he said. "Wait, do not leave the boat. I want to carry you."

She watched him, and an old poem sang in her head from long

ago, a Malay *pantun* she had learned when she first met him and when she had first come to this place.

> "Last night, about the moon I dreamt
> And tumbling nuts of coco palm
> Last night with you in dreams I spent
> And pillowed lay upon your arm"

Now it was true. Charlotte felt the thrill. It was always there, even after all the time that had rolled between them—the profound thrill of waiting for his arms. He tied the boat firmly to a coconut palm. Then he took off his hat and let his queue fall. She knew he was proud of his queue. They preened themselves, these Chinese men, like cats, and loved the queues which fell, some, to their ankles. His fell almost to his knees, and he took prodigious care of it. He sometimes carried the faintest scent of some exotic pomade he used on it. He had shaved his head freshly too, she could see. What she had first thought of as odd, this half-naked head and long tail, she now found exquisitely beautiful, perfectly suited to his smooth Chinese face, revealing the high bone structure, his black almond eyes, his full lips.

He took off his coat and dropped it in the sand grass. He stood in the glow of the sun, a golden god, half-naked like the idols were in the East. The tattooed god on his chest emphasised his muscled torso, the flatness of his abdomen, the narrowness of his waist. She smiled. He always knew how well he looked, but it was not vanity, or perhaps it was a little, but, more, it was to excite her, to entice her, and it did. She sat on the edge of the boat, and she put out her arms to him and he lifted her into his, wanting to feel her in them, hold her tight against him, remind her of his strength, his youthful power. She dropped her head against his shoulder, buried her face into the silky skin of his neck. Love and desire for him flooded her. How could she ever have wanted another? She took his queue in her hand, his head in her arms, kissing his neck, his cheek. He walked up the beach to the house and waited with her in his arms, savouring her, allowing his skin to remember the way it was for them, feeling the response of his body to her lips.

He dropped her feet in the sand by the steps of the house, and they stood a moment, watching the sun fall into the embrace of the sea. Then they kicked off their sandals. There was a water jar with a ladle, and he threw water over their sandy feet. The dying sun cast a dull, ruby glow inside the house. The wind from the sea was brisk, and the verandah was cool. Mosquitos should not be a cause for anxiety, Robert had told her. Too much wind. Nevertheless the old Malay keeper had lit the sandalwood incense which wafted on the breeze.

Charlotte followed him, her hand in his, their fingers entwined. He gripped her firmly, not wanting to let go, she knew, feeling the emotion in this grip of their hands. She knew he loved her with every part of his being the way she loved him. The way their hands felt together told her this without any words. There were rarely words.

She had come to understand that the Chinese, like the English, simply did not speak such things. He showed her in the poetry he sent her, in the touch of his hand, in his constancy. Once she had said, "I love you", in his language and he had looked quizzical and said, "I love you" back to her, but it was a gesture, she felt, to please her, as if the words meant nothing. The depth was in the unsaid. What had he told her about Taoism? The Tao that can be spoken is not the true Tao. It was mysterious and incomprehensible to her, but she saw it a little in this non-voicing of their feelings. "The love that can be voiced is not the true love."

She gripped his hand a little tighter, and a feeling of weakness flowed, a looseness in her limbs, as if love for him robbed her of energy, permitting a laying-down of her whole being into his hands. Was this the essence of love, this giving-up of one's self utterly into the hands of another? How much trust there was in this act! Yet she could do it with him, and he with her. There would be no hurry tonight; it would go very slowly, she knew. He would make it slow, waiting, savouring. It was his art, this slowness, his gift to her and himself.

Even as she thought this, she felt the beat of her blood, the sexual longing beginning, the pressing need. Her mind wanted this slowness, but suddenly her body did not. It had been too long. The desires this man had awakened in her she had half-buried for the years of her widowhood, but now, with him here, they flooded her. As they reached the verandah, she ran her hand down his queue, touched his back and he turned. She pulled herself into him, winding her arms around his neck, pressing her breasts against his chest. He dropped his lips to her neck, kissing her, small kisses, the length of her shoulder, into her neck, under her ear. She dropped one hand, down, between his legs, feeling for him, wanting to feel this hardness. She groaned, and he stayed her hand, holding it there, not allowing her to move it as he knew she wanted to. He felt her urgency.

He made a decision. She was unprotected, the oil of neem in the boat. He would bring her to orgasm safely and then she would relax. He released the cord and let his pants slither down to the floor. He let her touch him now. He felt her deep arousal in the drooping of her body against him, the weakening of her grip on his neck. He took her waist in his arm, supporting her, and put his hand against her, gripping her, and she moaned a deep moan and began to tremble so much he knew he needed to do this quickly. He picked her up and took her inside the house, through the netting to the bed, pulling off the trousers and throwing them to one side. She took his hand and put it between her thighs, eyes closed, willing him.

She was so ready that the moment his fingers slid inside her she burst, drenching his hand, arching her back and coming again. Even that was not enough, and he knew she was in an unstoppable place; it was out of her control. It was inflaming, and he felt the throb deep inside his own body, overtaking his mind. Every other thought left him but the imperative to be with her. She exploded again as he slid into her, hot liquid gushing from her, her hips grinding against him. He took her body in his arm, pulling her into him, his lips on her throat and mouth, her legs gripping him. Wave on wave came from her. They both moved now, almost unconscious of each other, lost in physical need. Despite all his experience, he knew he would not hold on, her desires too great, his love for her too great, the feel of her against him too great, and as he had that dim thought, he flooded into her, roaring, black as night, head filled with stars, lost to everything but this moment of ecstatic oblivion. He raised his head and drew a great breath of air into his lungs, breaking the surface from the depths, craving air.

Even as the light returned to his brain, he felt her spasm again and heard her fevered moans, his name on her lips. She had waited for him too long. They had both waited such a very long time. He continued to move, his hardness returning almost instantly through this unstoppable desire for her, waiting for her to be sated, and when he felt her tenseness subside, her legs relax round his waist, he withdrew and began to rub her, moving his fingers lightly, bringing her down, kissing her lips softly until she responded, pulling his head to hers, sinking into his kiss. The final orgasm was light, a ripple, a sigh, and he knew it was over.

He pulled her tight against him, moulding his body to hers, wrapping his legs around her. Nothing felt like this. Only she made him feel this way.

He thought it had only been a moment but when he opened his eyes again, the red-gold light had gone and a faint rose hue was beginning to filter through the shutters. She lay against him, entwined in his arms; they had slept all night just like this. He couldn't believe it. A small panic rose in his chest. They had slept all night. They had wasted this time together. But he did not let her go. He had wanted to take all night, make love to her all night. Now it was almost morning. He looked down at her face, beautiful, resting against his chest, her hair falling wildly around her cheeks and shoulders, and saw the look of pure peace, of quiet repose, and realised that this had been right. The pure spontaneous release of the Tao, the coming together, the letting go.

He closed his eyes and went to sleep. When next he opened them, she was not in his arms. She was on the verandah, talking to the Malay woman from the kampong. He lay, waiting for her, cool in the strong, salty morning breeze which came through the shutters standing ajar and through the open door. Xia Lou, Xia Lou; it was like the soft swishing of the waves on the shore. He knew how to say her hard English name, this "Charlotte", but he did not like it and never used it. He heard the gulls wheeling and calling and then the sound of her feet softly on the creaky wooden planks. He pretended to be asleep, waiting for her to approach, his eyes closed, the anticipation of it suffusing him with pleasure. He knew she had stopped at the bedside, gazing at him. Her long black hair hung tangled around her ivory shoulders, over the slope of her breasts. Her lips were parted, her white teeth showing slightly, her eyes like an evening sky, languid. He did not have to open his eyes to know the look in hers; he had dreamed her too often. He lazily opened his hand, and she realised and laughed. She moved onto the bed, into his arms, better than a dream.

"The old woman is here. She is making breakfast. Coffee and tea, fried fish and rice, coconuts, papaya and mangoes." She caressed his cheek and kissed his ear, softly, whispering. "She will leave it in the kitchen. She will be gone in fifteen minutes."

She saw him smile, eyes closed, the faintest smile, a mere turning-up of the corner of his mouth, and snuggled against him, her arm across his waist, holding his queue in her hand, his hand in her hair. They had one day and one more night. Last night had released all the tension coiled deeply inside her for years. Now they could go slowly.

Time flies, wasn't that what was said? *"Time's winged chariot hurrying near."* She forgot the words exactly. But it wasn't like that. It was as if time slowed. Every moment, every gesture, slowed down so that she could record it clearly on her mind. Not all of it, just tiny moments, captured. The drip of the mango juice from his lips, kissing those lips covered in the juice, unable to stop herself rising from the table and going to him, he taking her on his lap and covering them both with sweetness, releasing her sarong, dripping mango on her breasts, moving his lips over her, down her body. And later, all the stickiness from the fruit, from their own juices, rinsed away in the sea. Sleeping then together, in the hammock, under the coconut palms.

Walking, there was a walk, along the beach, but she could not remember much of that, only holding his hand. They bathed in the freshwater stream which fell from a high, steep cleft in the hill, a clear and cooling waterfall, washing each other free of salt and sand, kissing, unable to stop kissing, as water tumbled around them.

Then, suddenly, it was night and they made a fire on the shore. The Malay couple came with fat, freshly caught fish and rice, spiced crabs, pickled vegetables, *sambal*, water and lemon oil to burn. They all sat for a while and talked as the fish cooked on the fire, inhaling this delicious aroma, she translating for Zhen from time to time, her Malay better than his, the sparks of the fire cracking, shooting small red fireworks into the dark night air.

She was not sure what this Malay couple thought of them, a white woman and a Chinese man. They made no sign that it was even unusual, but she knew the Malay nature a little, its quiet grace, its circumspection. The old woman had smiled, her teeth gapped and brown, her mouth red with the betel chewing. We grew up here, she said, pointing at the old man, wiry and fit-looking, but with a bent back and blind in one eye. Charlotte knew Robert had engaged them to care for the cottage for they were too old for anything else.

We grew up and married here, she said. So long ago we married. Long before the white men came. When the island was ours. Her mother and father were *orang suku laut*—sea tribe people. She had been married to this man at thirteen, when he was fourteen. He was from the land people at Kampong Siglap. They had ten children and too many grandchildren to count. Young then, old now, she said and looked at the old man, and they both laughed.

Before they moved off down the beach, the old woman said,

*"Asam di gunung, garam di laut,
bertemu dalam satu belangah."*
"Spice of the mountain, salt of the sea,
meet in one cooking pot."

Charlotte understood. It was a kind thing to say and she knew the old woman at least sympathised with them, with their youth, their love. She saluted her, both hands raised to her forehead. Zhen too had understood and came and curled her into his arms to watch the embers die, swirling in the sea breeze.

That night was surprising in many ways. In her wish to please him, she asked him to tell her how. There were many things that, for love and fear of losing her, he did not dare raise with Xia Lou, but now, he saw her sensuality was completely open, and he showed her the ways of love learned from the old pillow books.

It was a night of revelation, a deeper discovery of each other after so many years of knowing each other, sometime humorous, for she occasionally found his Chinese application to the task and air of seriousness amusing, and he was infected by her lightness and laughed too, and the sea wind blew across their skin.

When they arrived back at the beach at Kampong Glam, she did not know what to say to him. As she tied up, he got out of the boat and waited for her. They had kissed goodbye before they left, a lingering kiss, soft and deep. She was enclosed in his arms, the sure hardness of him, protective, loving, soon to be lost, and she had trembled. She had felt him trembling too. It was so unusual that she had pulled him to her, hard, trying to get inside him and make it go away.

Then she had sailed the boat with his arms around her, neither able to abandon the other for the few moments left to them. He had forgotten any fear, his trust in her complete, and enclosed her waist in his arm, holding her tight against him as she raised the sail, so tight she had to protest, but loving his hold on her, winding her arm behind her, round his neck pulling him close. The whole journey he kept his arm around her waist, his hand on hers on the tiller, his lips on her neck as the sun rose slowly behind them. They sat quietly together, cheek to cheek, skimming over the rose-hued waves. They had agreed not to meet again, not for a while. It was too dangerous.

They gazed a moment at each other, and then he turned and walked away quickly up Sultan Road, leaving her to go to Robert's house, which stood on the corner of Middle Road and Beach Road. It was not far. She did not care who saw her dressed this way, alone. She sailed often—let them think what they wished.

She changed in the bedroom there, which Robert kept for her and the children. Shilah was not here. She had timed her arrival knowing that Shilah was teaching at Miss Grant's school. She knew very well that Shilah would not have made the slightest comment— Shilah herself had endured much. Still, Charlotte was not yet ready to share this. Her Chinese lover. A lover she now knew, that she could not ever give up, for their bodies and souls fitted together.

She fixed her hair in the mirror and put a little colour to her lips and saw him reflected back in the eye of her mind. She knew she had to make a decision.

She left, putting up her parasol, and walked slowly back to her home on North Bridge Road.

52

The next month was full of drama. Jeanne received a proposal of marriage from Martin Macallister and after due consideration refused him. When Alex had heard of the voyage to Scotland, he had retreated into silence. Adam was delighted and could not wait to go. And Charlotte found she was pregnant.

She stood before the mirror, her hand on her waist. Inside lay Zhen's child, another child of his. But this one she could not, would not, hide from him or the world.

Jeanne was standing at the window of the bedroom, gazing down at the street. Charlotte knocked lightly, and her aunt turned and smiled. She wiped her brow with her handkerchief. Charlotte knew that Jeanne suffered from the heat.

"Aunt, will you not regret your decision?" Charlotte asked.

Jeanne held out her hands to her niece and smiled broadly. "Nay, lass. The whole matter was rather outlandish, I'm sure you agree. And what could be the purpose of such a union? No children of course at our age, and him bound to live in Asia. I confess I find it too hot, my dearest child. I could not abide it. The attachment is not deep. We shall both survive it."

Jeanne put her head to one side and raised her eyebrows slightly. "It was flattering though, I must confess. I had forgotten how giddy a man's attentions can make us."

Charlotte laughed.

"I shall miss you, but I shall be glad to entrust Alexander and Adam to you. They shall be no trouble."

"Nay, nay, of course. No trouble. Your wee lads are angels, aye they are. You've given me a great gift, a great trust. To see them both safely back to Scotland and in college, that's a joy. They remind me of Robbie when he was a lad."

Jeanne stood up and went to her drawer and began removing some garments, laying them on the bed. The maid was to pack her trunk later in the afternoon.

"I love you both, you know it, aye? You and Robbie, like my own."

Charlotte went to Jeanne and put her arms around her aunt's shoulders, resting her cheek against hers.

"We are your own, Jeanne. Without you we should have perished. Oh, not bodily perhaps, but in every other way that matters. You were the rock we clung to, and you never let us go, not once." Charlotte felt tears rise and hugged her aunt to her.

Jeanne released Charlotte slowly. "Aye, aye, there. We shall be very fine. 'Tis a pity you'll not come with us, but never mind. Alex has already told me exactly how he is to take care of me and Adam during the voyage. We shall have the protection of Frank and Harriette McDougall, who are returning home for leave. They shall be excellent companions. And I have to confess, my sweet Charlotte, I shall not miss this heat."

Charlotte wiped her eyes. She smiled, but somewhat ruefully. She had lied to her aunt. There was no reasonable reason why she should not go with them all back to Scotland. No reasonable reason, only the exigency of this pregnancy and its secrecy, her own desire not to leave Zhen. She was very glad that the McDougalls would accompany Jeanne and the children. Harriette was the most excellent of women and a loving mother, and Frank the bravest and most chivalrous of men.

Jeanne could see Charlotte was affected and touched her niece's arm reassuringly. "The boys shall be great companions. We shall see the pyramids together and ride a camel and travel like the pashas of Egypt in the luxury you've paid for. Are you sure you can afford it, Charlotte?"

Charlotte laughed a long peal of delight. "Afford it? Oh Aunt, that is quite enough. Have you not understood that I am the richest woman in the Indies?"

"So you say, so you say. But first-class berths on the steamers cost a pretty penny, eh? And private carriages and accommodations for everyone."

Charlotte put her arm through her aunt's and led her towards the door. "Come and have some lunch."

At lunch, Alex contemplated this new situation. He must go to Scotland. He saw the reason of it. He wanted to go to college. He wanted to become a man, able to fend for himself and care for a family. In a way, he wanted to see the world. The great world outside Singapore. And Lian would not be married until she was sixteen. She would be free when he returned to claim her, no longer a boy.

He had spoken to Lian and her aunt. Lilin had not been pleased, but she had encouraged them to write to each other. When he returned, he would claim her.

Lilin had left them alone. He had taken Lian's young, sweet body in his arms and held her, and she had put her arms around his neck and put her cheek on his, and they had not moved, imprinting this memory in their minds. Then he had kissed the palm of her hand and promised to return to claim her. He had brushed the tears from her lovely cheeks and put his lips to hers. A chaste kiss, but filled with promise. A kiss he could dream about for three years.

53

"Well, sister, so we shall both be a disgrace, the scandalous Macleods of Singapore." Robert smiled at Charlotte, and she laughed.

"So it would appear. But happy, Robbie, at least."

Robert nodded. Charlotte had told him of her pregnancy and her decision. She poured Robert more tea. They were in the garden of her house, under the deep shade of the tembusu tree. They were waiting for Zhen. Charlotte was determined, now that her decision was made, that Robert, at least, must acknowledge Zhen. Neither she nor Robert could mix socially when they were with Shilah or Zhen; they were very much in the same boat. But they could all be with each other, enjoy each other.

"I like him, Kitt, you know. Always have. He is a good fellow, his dealings with the *kongsi* notwithstanding."

Charlotte put down her cup. There was one more thing Robbie must know, and she steeled herself to tell him.

"Robbie?" she began and hesitated.

Robert looked at his sister. Her lip was trembling slightly, and he frowned.

"What, Kitt? What is it? Are you unwell?"

Charlotte smiled and took his hand. "No, no," she reassured him. "I have something difficult to tell you."

Robert laughed and ran his hand through his sandy hair. "Something more difficult than the fact that you are pregnant by a Chinese man and plan to live with him openly before the eyes of his community and ours? What on earth could be more difficult than that?"

"Alex," Charlotte said quickly. "Alex is Zhen's son."

Robert stared at her. There was a silence. Robert frowned.

"What?" he said at length. "How?"

Charlotte opened her mouth to speak, but Robert had leapt to his feet.

"What?" he repeated. "Alex is Zhen's son—what on earth? You were pregnant when you left, before you married Tigran?"

Charlotte nodded.

"Sit down, Robert, for heaven's sake and let me explain."

Robert did not sit down. He began pacing back and forth. Charlotte sighed.

"Tigran knew. There was no deception. He accepted Alex as his own son. Alex knows nothing. For him, Tigran is his father. But he is close to Zhen. They have spent a great deal of time together. Zhen has also accepted that Alex cannot know of this. It would serve no purpose now. He is an English boy—"

Charlotte stopped speaking as Robert sat down abruptly and interrupted her.

"Zhen knows?"

"Yes," Charlotte said. "He knows, but as I was trying to say, what he can accept for Alex he will not accept for this child." Charlotte put her hand to the small bulge at her waist.

"This child he wishes to acknowledge, boy or girl. This child he wishes to raise together with me."

Robert was silent.

"Do you understand, Robbie? That is why I must be with him, let him be the father of this baby. Let him be my husband. Yes, 'husband'; it is not too strong a word. He considers us married by the Chinese rites."

Robert took a drink of tea.

"I should have seen it. Now you say it, it seems obvious. Alex looks like him. But what of his children with his wife? Good lord, the man has children by two women!"

Charlotte smiled.

"Yes, yes, I know. And so, Robert, do you."

Robert looked at her and made a *moue*.

"Yes, I suppose that's true. Sounds appalling when it's someone else, but rather more acceptable when it's oneself."

Charlotte laughed.

"But what kind of life can this child have with an English mother and a Chinese father?"

Charlotte looked down at her waist.

"I have no idea. We are in uncharted waters, it is true. We can only love this baby and wait and see."

Charlotte leaned forward and took Robert's hand. "Can't we, Robbie? We can all love this baby, no matter what?"

Robbie smiled and patted her hand.

"Yes, Kitt. We can love them all. After all, we too were disgraceful little half-bloods to our own grandmother. Jeanne did not care, and we turned out quite well."

He grinned at Charlotte who nodded. Then she sat upright, practical suddenly.

"Zhen knows we shall raise this child with both an English and a Chinese education. He wants the child to have the advantages of a European upbringing, and he will teach it about its Chinese culture. Zhen is a Taoist, Robbie, they are quite different. This baby is a natural extension of Zhen's love for me: that is how he sees it. He is a sensible and loving man. A man I can talk to. We have discussed this at length, I assure you."

Robert listened, and when she had finished he said, "Well then, the devil take the hindmost. What shall be, shall be."

Malik appeared suddenly, waiting. Charlotte looked up.

"A gentleman, memsahib, to see you. A Chinese gentleman."

Oh dear, Charlotte thought. Robbie and even the whole town might accept what she was going to do, but she was certain Malik would never like it. His tone of voice said it in volumes. She would nip this in the bud immediately.

"That gentleman will be spending a lot of time here, Malik. In fact that gentleman will become like the master here. Please adjust your attitude and show him in."

Malik looked scandalised but bowed.

"Yes, madam." He turned quickly.

Charlotte sighed and looked at Robert. "Trouble already, eh?"

Robert shrugged.

"He's missing Jeanne. He adored her. Get used to it, Kitt. The servants are the worst. Little snobs some of 'em. And, you're a woman. What I do, well, no matter what, I am a man. Other men accept it more easily. Many of them are in similar situations here, you know. Not so openly admitted, but nevertheless. Men think of me as a policeman first. What I do in my own home is not of much interest to them. Butterworth more or less admitted it. I have been officially called to account, and so long as Teresa does not make a scandal and I don't introduce Shilah to polite society—at least his—then least said ..."

Charlotte bit her lip. She knew what Robbie was saying was true. As a woman, her open life with a Chinese man would be disgusting to all. Her wealth might shield her somewhat, but she would have to get used to this attitude. The little life inside her was not going to go away. Still, a shadow of doubt and fear crept into her mind.

Then she looked up as Zhen came into the garden. He was dressed in a black silk Chinese gown and trousers over his high-soled Chinese shoes. Handsome, straight, powerful. As her eyes met his, she sighed and rose. There was no going back. This man was part of her spirit. He would not fail her, and she must not fail him. Robert stood too and went to greet him.

Zhen bowed to Charlotte and shook Robert's hand. They sat down and Charlotte, smiling at Zhen, called for Chinese tea.

54

Zhen took Charlotte by the hand and helped her from the carriage. They had followed the road to Tanjong Pagar and up into the hills of Telok Belangah, the seven hills of what the Malays called the Telok Belangah *mukim*. The one they were climbing now was Bukit Jagoh—Champion's Hill. She had smiled when he told her of this place he had bought. Her champion, for that he was. He had bought it many years before, when she had left for the second time. She had not realised how much he had wanted her, planned for a life together. It made her feel secure, this knowledge of his constancy.

Now he pulled the carriage to a halt on the fringe of the tree line. The path wound away to the right. They walked, hand in hand, until it fell away into a grassy knoll, Zhen stopped. Charlotte could not believe her eyes. A white mansion stood on the top of the knoll. A mansion with a high porte-cochere, and a lacy parapet above. They drew close, and Zhen looked at her. She felt his tension. He had waited years for this, she now realised. He had been building this house all the time they were apart.

She turned and put her hand to his face. "How long?"

"Finished two years ago. Waiting for you."

She moved into his arms and pulled his face to hers, brushing her lips along his. He smiled and pulled her close, kissing her. She felt his body relax as his arms tightened around her.

They walked into the house. It was unfurnished, waiting for her hand. The lobby had a vast chandelier at its centre. It looked like the entrance to Tir Uaidhne, Takouhi's house, and Charlotte realised that he wanted to offer her this house the way George Coleman had built a mansion for the woman he loved. She squeezed Zhen's hand, thanking him. They walked on through the lobby, between the double arms of the staircase towards French doors. Zhen went ahead quickly and threw them open wide.

Charlotte stepped out onto the wide covered verandah and gasped. Before her, down beyond the green lawn, beyond the parapet which edged the hill, out there lay the ocean, the sparkling, glinting blue of the Straits of Singapore, all the shapes of the islands lying in the haze along the horizon. A ship, like a toy, scudded over the sea, far away. It was breathtaking. They walked down to the parapet. To either side of them lay the great sweep of the ocean and the land curving away into the distance, rising and falling in gentle and undulating wooded hills and valleys.

The hills of Singapore, their retreat and their home. A refuge, Charlotte thought fleetingly, then moved into Zhen's arms, wrapping them around her like a cloak of protection. He put his lips against her neck and his hands to the swollen belly where his child lay. A flood of happiness swept through her. There would be doubts and fears, troubles perhaps, in the future, but here, at this moment, she knew there was no other way. He was her fate and her destiny.

The Straits Quartet

by Dawn Farnham

Singapore's most passionate series of historical romance

Drawing on real-life historical personalities from 19th-century Singapore, author Dawn Farnham brings to life the heady atmosphere of Old Singapore where piracy, crime, triads and tigers are commonplace. This intense and passionate romance follows the struggle of two lovers: Charlotte Macleod, sister of Singapore's Head of Police, and Zhen, triad member and once the lowliest of coolies who attempts to beat the odds to become a wealthy Chinese merchant.

Opium, murder, incest, suicide, passion and love ... an intoxicating combination in the sin city of the south seas.

| THE RED THREAD | THE SHALLOW SEAS | THE HILLS OF SINGAPORE | THE ENGLISH CONCUBINE |

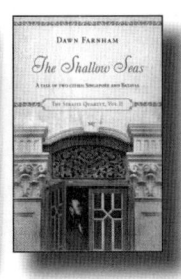

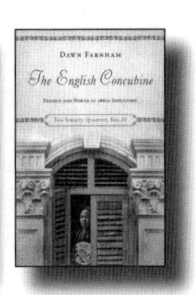

A Crowd of Twisted Things

by Dawn Farnham

In December 1950, the worst riots Singapore had ever seen shut down the town for days, killing 18 people and wounding 173. Racial and religious tension had been simmering for months over the custody battle for wartime waif Maria Hertogh between her Malay-Muslim foster mother and her Dutch-Catholic biological parents.

In May 1950, Eurasian Annie Collins, following this case and filled with hope, returns to Singapore seeking her own lost baby. As the time bomb ticks and Annie unravels the threads of her quest into increasingly dangerous territory, she finds strange recollections intruding, ones that have nothing to do with her own memories of her wartime experiences: disturbing visions and dreams which force her to doubt not just her past life, but her whole idea of who she truly is and even to question the search itself.

Twisted memories, twisted minds, twisted lives, twisted beliefs, the twists of fate and their tangled consequences.

A Crowd of Twisted Things is at once a lament for the loss and damage of war, an unravelling mystery and a journey into suppressed memory and the nature of self-delusion.